The Legend
of
Tyoga Weathersby

By

H.L Grandin

Best Regards
H.L Grandin
2012

The Legend of Tyoga Weathersby

For information call: 304-285-8205
or Email: acorn.book.services@comcast.net

Designed by Acorn Book Services

Publication Managed by Acorn Book Services
www.acornbookservices.com
info@acornbookservices.com'304-285-8205

Back Cover Photo by MAG

ISBN-10: 0985726725
ISBN-13: 978-0-9857267-2-0

Printed in the United States of America

Dedicated To:

My precious wife, Mary Ann,
who provided endless encouragement and unwavering support.
Without her belief in me, Tyoga Weathersby would never have come to life.
She gave me the gift of many quiet hours,
and endured the aloneness without complaint.
She fills my heart with The Promise every single day.

With Special Thanks To:

My cousin Paul who has filled my life with adventure
and daring-do — even when there was none to be had.
Without his companionship, this book would never have been written.

My dear friends, Maria and Bob, whose encouragement
and confidence gave me the heart to continue even when I was certain
that I had nothing more to give.

My editor, and friend, Lauren,
who gave me the courage to leave paragraphs behind,
guided me through the arduous editorial process
and is responsible for bringing
The Legend of Tyoga Weathersby
to you—the reader.

The one released.

Table of Contents

H.L. Grandin

Cast of Characters

THE WEATHERSBY FAMILY

Tyoga Weathersby .... The Legend
Joshia and Rebecca Weathersby .... Tyoga's Grandparents
Thomas and Emma Weathersby .... Tyoga's parents

THE ANI-UNWIYA CHEROKEE

The Wolf Clan of Tuckareegee

Tes Qua Ta Wa .... Tyoga's Lifelong Friend and Companion
Sunlei Awi .... Tyoga's Love and Tes Qua's Sister
Prairie Day ....Chief Silver Cloud's Daughter
Nine Moons & True Moon .... Sunlei Awi & Tes Qua's parents
Chief Silver Cloud & Wind Song............ Prairie Day's Parents

Mountain Creek Clan

Walks Alone & Night Sky ....Sunlei and Tes Qua's cousins
Grey Owl .... Cherokee brave who marries Winged Woman,
daughter of the Chief of the South Fork Shawnee
Their children are Yellow Robe's grandchildren

The Chickamaugua Cherokee

Lone Bear & Blossoms in Spring .... Sunlei's Aunt and Uncle

THE SHAWNEE

The South Fork Clan

Chief Yellow Robe .... Chief of the South Fork Shawnee
Seven Arrows .... Chief Yellow Robe's son
Winged Woman .... Chief Yellow Robe's daughter

The Mattaponi

Chief Blue Coat .... Chief of the Mattaponi in New Kent

TWIN OAKS

Trinity Jane O'Doule ... White woman raised by the Powhatan
Three-Toe Brister .... Tyoga's Right Hand and
Twin Oaks overseer

THE BRITISH

Governor Edward Nott .... Governor of Virginia Colonies
Henry Carry .... The Governor's Aide de Camp

Preface

It is hard to believe that *The Legend of Tyoga Weathersby* has taken an entire lifetime to write—but it's true. Well, not an entire lifetime, but I have spent a good portion of my nearly sixty years on earth as an observer, a quiet listener, a voracious learner, a student of early American history and a lover of the miracles of the natural world—those spectacularly displayed for all to observe and admire, and those as ethereal as the 'feel' of the deep woods at sunset.

My cousin, Paul, and I grew up hiking the Appalachian Trail. Many of the scenes described in the book are places I have been, traveled through, and experienced first hand. We spent many nights camping under the stars, and several unforgettable evenings on the top of Old Mount Rag. The trail to the summit, and even the configuration of the rocks at the peak, described in the book are depicted exactly as they appear to this day.

The top of Old Mount Rag is unchanged from how it would have appeared to Tyoga in the 1700s. He would have undoubtedly taken a seat on the "top-rock" and gazed off into the horizon just as I have done. I am certain that his heart would have soared at the majesty of the Appalachian Mountains, and that he would have wondered about the world beyond—just as I have done.

Paul and I even had to abandon a summit campsite and run blindly off of the mountain top in a hurricane-force storm, just as Tyoga and Sunlei are forced to do. We also endured a rainy night at the confluence of the Rapidan and Rappahanock Rivers. Thankfully, we fared better than Tyoga and Tes Qua.

My wife, Mary Ann, and I have spent many hours walking the cobblestone streets of Williamsburg, the dusty trails to the tri-corner fort at Jamestown, and the haunting overgrown fields surrounding Wolstenholmes Towne in my native Virginia.

I remember standing speechless at the hastily dug graves of the victims of the massacre of 1622. Vividly, the scene came alive in my mind. I could hear the war cries of the Powhatans as they attacked the unsuspecting colonists. The visceral terror of the stunned settlers when their trusted Native American brothers rose up and slaughtered them with their own farm tools came alive in my heart. Hundreds of men, women, and children were killed on that day. Standing next to the shallow graves on the very ground that soaked up the teardrops of those left behind is an experience that I will never forget.

But this story is more than a recounting of the adventures of Tyoga Weathersby as his life is forever transformed by the deep spiritual connection forged between himself and the magnificent leader of the Runion wolf pack. It is a story of young lovers who connect on the rarified plane reserved for those who have been blessed with the discovery of the "other." The solitary soul that completes us in ways that allow us to fulfill our promise and be all that we can be. The love of a lifetime, that never repeats.

Almost everyone has had to part with someone they have loved. But few have experienced the wretchedness of releasing "the one," not because it was the easy thing to do, but because it was the right thing to do—for her. There is no greater expression of love than releasing another so that they may, one day, love again. But the indefinable bonds that meld life force and imprison souls are never truly forsaken. They sentence the condemned to live with a heart forever shackled and a destiny unfulfilled. They punish empty moments with the brutal thoughts of what might have been. Tyoga bestows the ultimate gift to the woman he loves—freedom to find another.

The cultural matrix for the story is the Ani-Unwiya. A shadowy reflection of a real tribe of the Cherokee, the Ani-Yunwiya —but a fictional tribe nevertheless—is my homage to a culture with which I have been intrigued since I was a little boy. I remember enjoying a fascination with all things Native American that, at times, verged on an affinity for the culture strong enough to put the re-incarnation debate to rest.

When we played cowboys and Indians, I was always an Indian warrior. While others vied for the title of "The Lone Ranger" I stood off to the side, secure that I would not have any competition for the role of Tonto.

Growing up along the Potomac River, about two-miles south of George Washington's Mount Vernon estate, provided ample opportunity for me to collect arrow heads, obsidian knife blades, and stone axes from the campsites of Native Americans who lived along the shores of the gently flowing river. I would hold an arrowhead in my hands for hours examining the flake patterns wondering that a hand, just like mine, once held it and examined it in the same way. How long had he worked at fashioning its edges? What did he talk about while he was working? At what did he aim when he let the arrow fly?

I hope that my admiration and respect for the cultures that have called the North American continent 'home' for millennia is evidenced, not only in those passages that document the loving bonds between family members and close friends; but also in those passages in which their behavior may be interpreted by today's standards as inhumanly barbaric.

I caution the reader to judge not too harshly.

The act of ending—or preserving—a life in the context of the Native American cultures, and understanding how their deeply-held beliefs were expressed, even in the manner by which life was ended —or preserved—is today a difficult construct to understand—let alone appreciate. "He died well," means something completely different to us today. Indeed, the act holds little merit in the context of our current reality. That a people so loving and tender to family and friends was capable of extracting spiritual significance in the ritualistic horrors of savage cruelty flies in the face of our modern notions of humanness and magnanimity. Does our lack of understanding, or our inability to place ourselves in like context, negate the honor in their profoundly held beliefs? Not at all. They have a great deal to teach us yet.

As a young man, and even to this day, my fascination with wolves rivals the esteem with which I hold Native American cultures. I spent many hours alone in my backyard, or in the woods along Bucknell Creek, reading everything I could get my hands on about wolves. *White Fang* was, of course, the piece of literature that got me hooked. Time and study led me to appreciate the magnificent creatures chosen by natural selection to somehow transcend the miracles of adaptation.

The wonder is that the animals' a posteriori acceptance of situation and circumstance is reconciled without prejudice or the need for contrived retribution. Their eyes reflect a wisdom that is not learned or experiential, but rather found in the silent molecular code responsible for the fundamentals of being like color, height, and demeanor. They know simply because they don't understand how not to.

To ascribe a "nobleness" to this is a mistake. While their stature and demeanor may reflect those characteristics we most readily associate with nobility, to attribute 'noble-ness' to the species is an anthropomorphism that does the contrivance injustice. Wolves are wise simply because it is the stuff of which they are made.

So are we.

We haven't really lost the ability to "listen," we have just misplaced the ability to understand what we are hearing. We retain nature's gift of 'seeing' beyond what is visible to the naked eye. Unfortunately, we have forgotten how to decipher the vision.

These gifts Wahaya-Wacon reawakens in young Tyoga Weathersby. He is chosen because of who he is. It is the spark of "aliveness" ignited by the wolf that sets him apart. He belongs—but remains an outsider. He is included—but remains alone. He is a leader—but pushes rather than pulls.

In writing *The Legend of Tyoga Weathersby*, I have tried to give the reader a glimpse into the "bridge" culture that existed in the early 1700s. In the days when the Appalachian Mountains were considered the western frontier, there were those incredibly courageous souls who chose to leave the relative comforts of colonial living to brave the wilds in search of land, wealth, and, above all else, the freedom of self-determination. At first, they were a lawless breed of mountain men who blazed the trails, killed or befriended the Native Americans, and lived by their own wiles and ingenuity. The homesteaders followed with their axes and plows, and carved the earth to suit their needs and, for the most part, befriended the Native Americans in order to ensure their own survival.

The children of these homesteaders created a bi-lingual culture that bridged the chasm between two colliding worlds. They were at home in the villages of the Native Americans who accepted the children of their white neighbors as their own. They became increasingly less comfortable in the white world of religious intolerance, societal taboos and ever stringent government authority and control.

Tyoga Weathersby was a child of the frontier. His experience was shared mainly by the white orphans adopted by Native Americans. He ran naked and free through the Appalachians with his Ani-Unwiya brothers and sisters, and spoke Tsalagie with a better command than that of his native language.

Just a word about the Cherokee language, and the way that dialogue is used throughout the book: Tsalagie, the language spoken by the Cherokee Nation is a complex language. There was no way to transmit thought through the written word until Sequoyha invented the Cherokee alphabet in the early 1800s. The translation of the sounds from the Tsalagie to the English alphabet makes pronunciation of the words nearly impossible. How do you say "U-gv?" So, I created a pseudo-Tsalagie. Yep, I pretty much made up the words. Where possible, I based the sentence structure on the Tsalagie dialect, I placed the translation of the words in parenthesis after the Tsalagie in some places. In other places, I have not put any translation because – and this is the really neat thing - whatever English words you wish the Tsalagie to mean will work just fine!

Here's a quick example: There is a scene when Tyoga's nemesis, Seven Arrows, shows up unexpectedly and he asks Tyoga, "So, where is the wolf now?"

Tyoga replies, "He is here Skunulka."

You can make that mean whatever you want it to mean. "He's here, you Jackass," works just fine; as does "He's right here, you slimey bastard,", or … well, you get the point. There will be places where the meaning of the pseudo-Tsalagie isn't as obvious, but the story is constructed so that almost anything you decide the character says will work.

With all of this said, allow me, dear reader, to proclaim with unapologetic bravado, (and this is going to require some capitalization) I MADE THIS STORY UP. Yes, my friends, while some of the story is based upon historical fact, ie. Openchanecanough was the brother of Powhatan and was the Chief of the Powhatan Confederation when he ordered the massacre of 1622. But was he rescued by Tyoga's grandfather? *Naahhhh. Made that up.* The mystic connection between the spirit of the wolf and Tyoga Weathersby's soul is the critical twist that perhaps defines a new genre, for it most certainly is not historical fiction. If the reader is in any way offended by the characterizations or portrayals depicted in this book, here's an idea: stop reading it and donate your copy to the local library. *The Legend of Tyoga Weathersby* is an exciting story, meant to do nothing more than entertain.

It was a joy to write. I hope it is as much fun to read.

The Legend
of
Tyoga Weathersby

Prologue

The Awakening ~ 1688

Riveted by the morning mist that cloaks the Appalachians in the mysteries of time, distance, and space, Tyoga Weathersby stood by his papa's side in the pre-dawn silence atop Carter's Rock. Even at six years of age, his love of all things wild and free drew him to the openness of the mountains, plains, and valleys of the Blue Ridge with a siren's call that simply wouldn't be denied.

His papa, Thomas, understood. He had been the same.

Recognizing at an early age that Tyoga was different, Thomas nurtured his son's adventuresome spirit and allowed him the freedom to range and roam far beyond the means of such a young lad. Untethered by the restrictions placed upon others his age, Tyoga experienced the wild with an intuitive sensing that was known only to those who were open to the awakening. He felt the rhythms of time and perceived the silent cues that filled the ether of the Appalachians with an unsettling welcome and shrouded intrigue.

Carter's Rock was a simple granite outcropping about two-thirds of the way up the Appalachian peak that the Cherokee called Teshtahey. A two-hundred-year-old giant oak tree stood alone just to the southwest of the Rock, and marked the spot where well worn mountain paths converged before disappearing into the bottomless bog of unnamed hollers. The hard-packed trails bore silent witness to the bare feet of stone-age hunter/gatherers, the mocassined soles of Appalachian tribes who called themselves nothing more descriptive than "The People" and, most recently, the boot heels of mountain men, fur trappers and pioneers.

Carrying his son on his back like a papoose, Thomas had been bringing Tyoga to the Rock since he was a newborn. Leaning his cradle board against the giant oak, he would sit in silence with his son at his side for hours on end. As Tyoga grew, they visited the Rock together many times. Usually they would do no more than listen to the wind and watch the eagles soar. Every so often, Thomas would turn to his son and say, "One day, Tyoga, you will know how to listen to the whispers in the wind. The eagles will speak to you and you will know the secrets of the rain. The strength of the wolf will flow through your veins, and the courage of the bear will steel your resolve. Stay true to the beating of your heart. The promise is in you. It will always show you the way. You have only to be awakened to its gifts."

Tyoga heard these words often standing here on Carter's Rock, but he had never understood their meaning. He knew that it was important for him to listen to the words, but he was growing impatient with watching the sun rise on countless mornings and listening to the same endless story about some "promise" that seemed to never come.

Today, the rising of the sun would be like no other.

It was June 21st. The occasion of the summer solstice. The longest day of year. The rising of the sun marked not only the beginning of a new day, but also the passage of time and the dawning of a new cycle of life. For millennia, mankind had marked the perfect balance of darkness and light by celebration and sacrifice.

On this day, the blinding beams of light would bestow a gift that would change Tyoga's life forever. The celebration of the gift would be his to determine. The sacrifice, his to bear.

The outline of the mountain range creasing the east rim of the Shenandoah Valley pierced the darkness as the rising sun pushed its silhouette forward to softly shadow the world awakening before them. With the innocence of childhood that permits inquiry without context, Tyoga broke the silence of the magical moment by asking, "Papa, do you ever hear things?"

The hint of a smile pulled at the corners of his father's lips when he replied, "What do you mean 'hear things', son?"

"I don't rightly know, papa," Tyoga replied. "Sometimes I just hear things."

Thomas knew that his very young son was ill-equipped to explain any further. But it was the sign that he had been waiting for all of Tyoga's life.

"Yes, son. I do hear things." He turned his gaze toward Craggy Gap far off in the distance. "I started hearing things when I was about your age."

He paused as his mind's eye took him back to the scene of a little sandy-haired boy standing next to his father about thirty-five years earlier. The smile changed from pride to resignation because what was about to happen to his son would change his life forever. He turned and looked at his boy for the last time—as he was—an innocent child of six. After the awakening, he would be innocent no more. He would know. With a deep sigh, he let the journey begin.

"More than just hearing, Tyoga, I understand," he finished his reply.

"But, Papa, what do you hear? What is it that you understand?" Tyoga asked.

"I've been waitin' for you to ask boy," he said with a smile. "I reckon you're ready now." He placed his massive hand upon his son's bony shoulder, and looked down into his tiny, freckled face. The awakening would be difficult for his young son to understand, so he tried to find words to prepare him for what was about to be.

"Son, nature ..." he stopped.

Too big, too much.

He held his arm out and waved it slowly over the vista that surrounded them from horizon to horizon and said, "Tyoga, all men used to be able to hear the silent words that nature speaks. Her message helped them understand how all of this works, and where they fit into her plans. But somewhere along the way, most men have lost the gift to listen, hear and understand. But Weathersby men, all the way back to your grandfather Joshia, have been awakened to the promise. We have been given the gift to understand that all of us are one with nature, no

less privileged in her ways than the bear, beaver, fox or squirrel, and …"
He stopped.

Still too much.

He took a deep breath, and simply said, "Ya know how before it rains, the birds quiet down and go to roost in the trees; Hester lies down in her stall; and the rabbits and squirrels hole up?" He looked deep into his son's eyes to see if his words were making any sense. He couldn't tell if he understood, but Tyoga was listening intently. Before he could start again, Tyoga's eyes lit up and he said, "Papa, I know when it's gonna rain, too."

He smiled gently at his son's lively, inquisitive eyes, and said, "I know you do, son. But there is so much more."

Knowing that he could not explain it any better than that, he turned his son to face the east, and said, "It's time. Face the gap. Close yer eyes. An' wait."

"Wait fer what, papa?"

"You'll know. Hush now. Be still. You'll know."

Tyoga closed his eyes and faced Craggy Gap. The sun hadn't risen and the chill of the morning air made him shiver. He stood there on Carter's Rock soldier-straight, frightened at the vulnerability of standing with his back to the woods, eyes closed, guard down; for even at this tender age he was wary of recklessness and the dangers hidden in the shadows of early dawn. His papa's hand resting on his shoulder secured their safety, and quieted the alarms sounding in his head. His slow, deep breathing lulled his spirit into acceptance and serenity.

Slowly—ever so slowly the awakening began.

A pinpoint of light cleaved the divide at Craggy Gap and in an instant exploded into the magnificence of a new day. The first rays of morning light were released like thunderbolts crashing against his freezing cheeks.

His head began to spin wildly as his tiny body was enveloped in the cloak of newness and warmth. The blinding beams of light that herald the sun's perpetual rebirth cocooned his spirit and filled his soul with the harmony of being. He had been called to share in the mystery of oneness with mother earth.

This was his moment.

His spirit broke free of its earthly bonds and soared in weightless oneness with the beams of the rising sun. All that was malevolent in the primal forest was illuminated and cast aglow with the brilliance of the dazzling light. Sounds became sight, scents could be tasted, distance could be felt and time simply dissolved. The ancient mysteries locked deep within the very bowels of Mother Earth—secrets of the natural world understood only in the truth of their being—disclosed themselves to him as unembellished natural law. Secrets revealed only to those who have been granted the wisdom to not only listen—but to hear and understand—were passed on to yet another Weathersby.

He was startled at the revelations, and frightened at the savage rawness of the natural world. He began to open his eyes and turn to speak when he felt the heaviness of his papa's guiding hand. "Keep yer eyes closed. Listen. Listen and hear the promise," he heard his papa's voice as if coming from a great distance away. "Do ya see, Tyoga? Do you understand? Is it tellin' ya? Can ya hear? Are ya listenin', boy?"

Time seemed to stop for young Tyoga. He stood stone still for a long time. He did not want the soaring to stop, but as the sun rose fully over the Gap, he was settling back into himself and permitted to rejoin his world—forever changed.

He did not open his eyes, but furrowed his brow trying to make sense out of what had just happened.

The mysteries revealed made no sense. How could so much beauty mask such horrific brutality? How could majesty and gentleness exist in the midst of such depravity and coarseness? How could the discordant extremes of love and hate, good and evil, right and wrong be permitted to confound the life of man, yet remain completely devoid of context and attribute for the rest of the natural world? Is the chasm between man and beast so profound that reconciliation is impossible, or is the veneer separating the two so thin that the difference does not really exist at all?

The velvet touch of his papa's gentle hand upon his forehead released the worried wrinkles and allowed him once again to hear. He heard his Papa's voice, this time very close to him say, "Tyoga. When you open your eyes it will be as if you are experiencing the world for the very first time. Don't be afraid. From this moment on, you'll be one with the trees and the air and the sun. The eagle will guide you. The raven will settle you. The whisper of the wind will prepare you. You will never know fear again. Your courage will inspire your friends and frighten your enemies.

"But, my son, your journey has only begun. The gift of the promise allows you to hear, but understanding its message will require more. You will be tested by the very power that has awakened you. But beware the victory. For in the spoils lie both a blessing and a curse. The choice you make will set your course for the rest of your life. I hope that you choose mercy. I pray that the price exacted for your kindness is less than the loss of your soul."

Thomas looked down at his young son and noticed the difference. He felt the tears filling his eyes, and looked off into the distance.

Patting his son on the shoulder, he added, "All things happen only as they must. There is no right or wrong in the doing, it is only in the outcome that these things are marked. Be strong, my son. Now open your eyes."

Tyoga opened his eyes and slowly surveyed his surroundings from horizon to horizon.

"Papa, I know."

Part One

1694

The Legend is Born

H.L. Grandin

Chapter 1

Trapped

It was a beautiful autumn day. The mountain sky was deep azure blue. The valley breeze carried the scent of the harvest and the sounds of the forest creatures preparing for the lean winter months ahead. Black bears were gorging themselves on the last of the blueberries and wild huckleberries that grew along the mountain trails. Enormous sunflowers, their gigantic yellow-wreathed heads bowed in acknowledgment of unheard applause, were alive with the cackle of ravens and jays as they feasted upon the bursting seedpod. The beavers were felling ash and elm to reinforce their sturdy dams, and stockpiling succulent birch branches in their underwater pantries. Scouting the hollows of Appalachia, she-wolves searched for a deep burrow in which they and their cubs could survive the brutal forces of the mountaintop winters.

In the late 1600s, the peaks of the Appalachain Mountains and the dark glades of the Shenandoah Valley were still the frontier wilderness. Little was known about the land west of the Mississippi River. The remarkable expedition of Lewis and Clark would not happen until the end of the century. Only the hardiest mountain men braved the unknown dangers of hidden mountain passes.

The pristine land was rich with the gift of life, and bursting with the promise of renewal anchored in the permanence of granite, quartz, and pyrites. The rivers and streams etched the land with serpentine runs of sparkling clarity. Thunderous waterfalls flooded cavernous gorges, and lacey traces carved their delicate patterns on moss-covered canvases of marbled slate. The forests were filled with the majestic canopies of five-hundred-year-old chestnut trees with their enormous boughs rising to the heavens in joyous celebration of the life they nourished and sheltered below. Ancient pines, birch, cedar, elm, maple, walnut and hickory carpeted the undulating landscape for as far as the eye could see.

The ridges of the Appalachains obscured the valleys below like ocean waves hiding their shadowing troughs. The cool air rising from their depths on a leeward ridge was the only hint of their existence. The air was crisp, clean, and clear.

There was no sound. The silence was broken only by the whisper of the wind in the pines, the murmur of cascading mountain streams, and the bark of frolicking squirrels. From floor to canopy, songbirds filled the ancient forests. Perched high above the forest floor, their incessant chatter pronounced judgment upon the happenings below. The plaintive cry of a lone wolf would echo unabated along the mountain's spine and careen off the granite valley wall until absorbed in the depth of primal indifference.

Such was the world known to Tyoga and his Native American brother, Tes Qua Ta Wa.

Tyoga had grown up as a living bridge connecting two disparate cultures. His family had settled in a savage and raw land. He had been given the rare gift of living among the Indians who had accepted him—and the Weathersby family—as members of their tribe.

The rhythm of daily Indian life had so influenced his formative years that he grew restless in the more regimented lifestyle of the Weathersby family home. The European traditions of molding the land to conform to the dictates of plow and hearth were at odds with the man he would ultimately become.

The Indians lived in harmony with the natural world and allowed their lives to be governed by nature's cues. Waking when roused by the warmth of the rising sun, following the game and harvesting only that which they needed to survive, growing from seed those crops nurtured through generations of careful cultivation, and reaping the forest's seasonal bounties of roots, berries, leaves and legumes was their way of life. Young children ran naked and free, embracing their true nature and accepting the gift of entitlement bestowed to the bear and beaver, eagle and elk. Free to stand safely alone among the tall whispering pines while reveling in the wind's embrace and the warmth of the sun on their naked skin, they were a people as sensuously alive and secure as the birds in the sky, the otters in the rivers, and the wolves in the protective embrace of their pack.

Seasoned mountain travelers at the age of twelve, Tyoga and Tes Qua were enjoying the warmth of the autumn day. Leather breached and loin clothed, the two scampered along the multicolored tapestries that were the woodland trails this time of year. Brilliantly colored autumn leaves, soft and spongy beneath their moccasined feet, gave an extra spring to their boundless energy. Discounting the peril, they'd leap from boulder to boulder sure-footed and confident, each trying to outdo the other with distance and danger.

Stopping at favorite outcroppings on their way to the trout pond, they lay their naked backs against the rocks and basked in the glow of the sun's rays. The sun-warmed rocks relaxed their taut young muscles, triggering an instinctive sensual pleasure. Fingers locked behind their heads, the boys gazed up to the heavens for hours. From time to time, they interrupted the silence with interpretations of the cotton ball clouds silently floating upon the updrafts of the mountain breeze.

"Ut se Ty. Kamama."

"Ahh, that don't look like no butterfly. Eet sa tsa-yo-ga."

"Tla. Kla tsa-yo-ga. Kamama."

"Well, it looks more like a bluejay than a butterfly to me."

As was their habit, the two spoke in competing tongues. Tes Qua's English was clean and formal as he had learned the language at a very early age thanks to his constant companionship with the Weathersbys.

Whereas Tes Qua spoke English with the deliberateness of one who had the advantage of seeing the written word, Tyoga had learned the dialect of the Amonsoquath while sitting around the campfires of his Indian brothers' lodges. Tyoga had no written guide in learning Tsalagi. He learned by imitation and mimicry.

What the boys enjoyed even more than interpreting the puffy white clouds passing by was watching the eagles soar high over head on the rising thermal currents of the clear mountain air. Untethered by earthly bonds, the masters of their universe were free of the laws that govern all other creatures. Recognizing no boundaries or limits, accepting no sanctions nor offering any mercy, they were free.

The two boys appeared the picture of carefree indulgence and disinterested serenity as they lay on their backs on the sun-drenched rocks. But years of traveling the backwoods together had taught them to remain alert. Even with eyes closed and hands clasped behind their heads, their ears searched for any sound that was out of place like the misstep of a predator's paw snapping a dry branch, the covey of quail exploding into sudden flight, or the flock of scolding crows suddenly mute—eerily silent. It was a dangerous time in the mountains.

Unexpected meetings between predators and prey were frequent—and final. The field mouse in search of pine seeds and oats instead fattening the breast of a fortunate fox. The trout by the thousands fighting the currents in brisk mountain streams seeking a meal of fingerling fry instead becoming fat on the haunch of a three-hundred-pound bear.

It happened only minutes after the two left the comfort of their mountainside perch and resumed their trek to the trout pond.

Leading the way, Tyoga high jumped downed chestnut and spruce trees that blocked the path, feeling the route, sensing the path more than watching his footsteps. A few steps behind him, Tes Qua matched Ty's deer-like leaps with ease and grace. Traveling along at their usual fast-paced trot, they rounded a bend in the trail and slowed where the path led them downhill along terraced escarpments to the banks of the pond's feeder stream. Where the path reached the water's edge, Tyoga left the trail to hop-scotch along the knarled roots of an old cedar stump on the left and stair-stepped mossy granite slabs that lay like giant dominoes along the bluff to the right of the trail.

Tes Qua stuck to the trail that ended at the water's edge. Planting his left foot, he pivoted along the bank of the stream to follow Ty. He heard the hideous sound seconds before he felt the pain.

Chapter 2

The Raven Will Settle You

Tyoga was ahead and below Tes Qua when he heard the numbing screams.

He couldn't make sense out of the cries. Tes Qua was stoic in pain, steady in crisis, and uncompromising in courage. But the gutteral animal wail he heard coming from Tes Qua was instinctive and beyond such control.

Oblivious to the thorny under brush tearing at his buckskins, he cleared the distance between them with dear-like bounds. He was by Tes Qua's side in an instant. Wrapping his arms around his brother, Tyoga held him tight while his body writhed in pain, his face contorted with confusion and shock.

Unsure of what had happened, from which direction the assault had been launched and from what, or whom, he must brace himself, Tyoga's eyes focused animal-like on the forest that enveloped them. Framed by the wild and frenzied moments that bridge life and death, when instinct and reflex measure the divide, Tyoga assessed his surroundings with the clarity of eye that discerns even the most obscure and clandestine threats. Prepared to give his life in defense of his friend, the images burned into his mind's eye with lightening speed and exquisite detail.

Crouching low he surveyed the underbrush immediately in front of them—nothing—clear.

Whirling around on his mocassined heal, he checked the out-croppings behind and overhead—clear—nothing.

Spinning to his left, he scanned the clump of trees on the knoll on the far side of the stream—clear.

He ducked his head and folded Tes Qua in his arms while focusing his other senses—listening for the "zzsssstt" of arrows slicing the air, or the staccato retort of musket fire and the sulphur stench of acrid smoke. Nothing … nothing.

When the blood splattered his face in rhythmic course, his attention was once again focused on Tes Qua.

Looking down at his writhing companion, Tyoga saw what was left of Tes Qua's lower leg. "To 'hitsu, Tes Qua? To 'hitsu?"

"Tlaosda. Tlaosda."

In their frenzied madness to sate Europeans' hunger for pelts and furs, white trappers set powerful traps that yawned their promise of a cruel, agonizing death. It was unfair in its dismissal of nature's sub-lime balance, untroubled by the savagery of its methodical course, unparalleled in resource, and unchallenged by the wiles of nature's own. Hidden and chummed, their hypnotic allure beckoned the unwary fox, bear, beaver or wolf. At watering hole and scent rub, the savage death would wait. Silent. Cold. Cocked. Lethal. Meting out its wanton brutality with reckless abandon.

Once tripped, the mighty jaws sink razor sharp jagged teeth through flesh and bone. Tendons, cartilage, arteries and veins are cleaved as the teeth course along their gruesome path. Tearing muscle and severing joints—the mutilation so lightening quick—so unexpected—that it takes a heart beat or two for the agony to register.

The fortunate animals mercifully suffer only the misery of swift amputation, sentenced to an abbreviated life minus a limb. The others—after hours of hopeless combat with an unyielding oppressor—recognize the futility of further resistance and accept the inevitability of their final hours.

When the massive jaws of the bear trap clamped down on Tes Qua's left ankle, the tearing of flesh and cracking of bone were muted by the primal scream of searing agony.

Tes Qua was crumpled down in the trail half-squatting in a rapidly growing pool of blood. Sitting on his right foot, his left knee was bent to his chest, his hands groping feebly at the horrible wound as if sending them there would make some sense of the horror and pain.

Cradling his friend in his arms, Tyoga's mind was racing wildly out of control. His eyes were wide with alarm while Tes Qua's blood splattered the trees and the rocks. The trail turned bright red under their feet. His own hands joined Tes Qua's at the wound in search for an answer as the spurting arteries covered his arms, his chest, and his face with the warm lifegiving liquid. *Make it stop!* Tyoga's mind screamed. *How do I make it stop?*

When his brave companion's body grew limp in his arms, he screamed, "Na deya Tes Qua. Don't die. Na deya. I won't let you die." His eyes welled with tears. His own body shook with helplessness and confusion.

AAWWWWKKKKKKKKKKKKK

The shattering cry reverberated off of the canyon walls and sliced through the hushed forest air with the harsh proclamation of unquestioned authority. The gruff, screaming scold of a raven summoned sharply from high overhead. The dissonant cry bounced off of the peaks and bluffs behind and above the boys, and eerily echoed off the canyon walls.

The sound shook Tyoga to his core. As his eyes slowly cleared, he turned to look over his shoulder to the crest of the rise. There, in an ancient chestnut tree, the eyes of a solitary raven were riveted upon him. The bird's marble black eyes glared from their deep-set sockets straight into the heart of Tyoga's quaking frame. He did not survey the scene, judge the circumstance, nor take stock of their peril. He did not weigh meaning, offer resolution, nor suggest course. His gaze fixed upon Tyoga like a black robed headmaster, displeased, but not yet ready to pronounce his vedict. Their eyes locked.

Tyoga remembered the promise. He understood.

"Yo'si' gwu, Tes'a. We're gonna be awrite."

The ball of Tes Qua's left foot was wedged deep and hard against the pan of the massive trap. The ligaments that supported the foot's natural architecture were sinewy white bands slapping at Tes Qua's ankle and calf, wildly searching for the purchase of muscle and bone that moments before had anchored them in place. Blood poured from incised vessels through the jagged gash and painted the stone upon which Tes Qua had come to rest a brilliant crimson.

One jaw of the trap had imbedded its two-inch teeth deep into the marrow of Tes Qua's ankle bone. The white of the joint capsule shone pearl-like through the surrounding pool of blood. The other jaw had snapped through the small bone in Tes Qua's lower leg. The jagged fragment of bone had pierced through the skin on the other side of his mangled limb.

The enormous trap was tethered to the base of an oak tree by a heavy, rusty chain. Thankfully, it wasn't secured to the tree by a lock, but by a long iron pin that served as a clasp laced through several links in the chain.

Tyoga released the clasp and the chain was free of its mooring. Slowly, Tyoga lifted Tes Qua's limp body and began the arduous trek up a steep embankment to a bluff about fifty yards away from the stream. He laid him gently on a flat table of rock that stood alter-like at the far end of the ridge. Stripping off his loin cloth, Tyoga balled it up and placed it under Tes Qua's head.

He raced back down the embankment to the stream, moistened a clutch of maple leaves and brought it to his friend's face. The cool water jolted Tes Qua from the mercy of semi-consciousness, and the agony returned in waves of wretchedness. He instinctively reached for the trap, but Tyoga intercepted the reflex with a gentle grasp. "Ne'ya, ditlihi. Don't touch it."

Calling Tes Qua "ditlihi"(warrior) was the Indian way of strengthening a companion's resolve as they marched into battle, or began a dangerous hunt. With a clearer eye and a more controlled demeanor, Tes Qua hiked himself up onto his elbows.

"What are we going to do, Ty?"

"Let me have a look-see. Stopped bleedin' some." Tyoga bent down close to the trap to inspect the wound more closely. The bleeding had slowed, and the gelatinous ooze was congealing on the surface of the gash.

"First thing, I gotta try ta op'n the trap," he said calmly and quietly. Turning to look Tes Qua in the eye, he added with apologetic resolve, "May hurt some."

Tes Qua closed his eyes and nodded.

Tyoga removed the leather thong securing his Do'tse pouch to his belt. "Here." He handed it to his friend.

Tes Qua put the leather strap in his mouth and bit down hard.

Hopping up onto the alter rock, Tyoga stood facing Tes Qua so that the trap and Tes Qua's broken leg and mangled foot were at his feet. Squatting down, he touched the jaws of the trap. He glanced up at his friend to see if the touch caused additonal pain. Tes Qua didn't flinch.

Unfamiliar with the workings of the bear trap's pan and spring mechanism, he was unsure how to release his friend from the enormous jaws that clung so cruelly to his lower leg. He interlaced the fingers of his left hand between the razor sharp teeth that had snapped the small bone in Tes Qua's leg. He could get a pretty good grip above where the jagged end of the bone protruded through the skin. He cocked his head to the right to survey the other jaw of the trap. That's when he saw the iron long springs on either side of the trap's hinge.

Tes Qua lay back down. His head rolled to one side. His mouth went slack and the leather strap fell to his chest.

"Do'hitsu, Tes'a?" His friend didn't answer.

Better this way. Sleep my brother. Sleep.

Tes Qua's unconsciousness gave Tyoga the opportunity to try whatever he could to release his friend. Placing a foot on each of the long springs, he hoped that his weight would pinch the springs enough to loosen the jaws sufficiently to pull Tes'A's leg free of its grip. The weight of a twelve year old proved to be no match for the trap's long springs.

He placed both his feet on a single spring to concentrate all of his weight on one side of the trap. The long spring surrendered a bit to the new approach. If he could apply equal weight to the long spring on the other side of the trap, he might have a chance to free his friend.

Surveying the area around them, Tyoga saw a granite boulder that appeared to be heavy enough to compress the long spring into submission. It was the perfect size and shape. Rolling it over to the alter rock, he lifted it up and carefully slid its smooth flat surface onto the long spring. The spring collapsed under its formidable weight, but the jaws did not budge as the tremendous force of the remaining long spring was more than sufficient to keep the trap clamped in place.

Snatching a long straight hickory stick from the ground, Tyoga steadied himself and carefully placed his left foot onto the flat iron face of the opposite long spring. Supporting himself with the hickory stick, his right foot left the ground and his entire body weight came to bear on the long spring. Slowly, the jaws began to release their grip.

Muscles straining in his legs, arms, shoulder and back while he supported himself with the hickory stick, he quaked from the force of his effort. He felt the jaws continue to loosen their vice-like grip while the sweat poured from his brow, into his eyes, and dripped off of his nose. When he flung the sweat from his eyes with a shake of his head, he caught a glimpse of a horrible sight.

As the jaws were opening, the teeth imbedded into Tes Qua's ankle were not releasing their hold on the bone. The more Tyoga opened the trap, the more Tes Qua's foot was being torn from his lower leg.

Beholding the gruesome sight, Tyoga realized the odd transformation that had taken place in the macabre device. Designed to entrap, maim and ultimately kill, the trap had become an instrument of a new, merciful purpose acting as a splint, holding foot to leg.

The cruel jagged teeth that ravaged and sliced were now protective and conservatory. The trap hadn't changed, and neither had its purpose, really. But the utility of its charge had been completely revoked.

Tyoga couldn't bear the thought nor the act of re-imprisonment, but with the strength draining from his now numb arms and violently shaking legs, he closed his eyes with the realization that the only course was to relinquish the progress so costly gained. He tightened his grip on the hickory stick while transferring his weight from the spring to his arms, and listened helplessly to the sickening sound as the teeth of the devilish jaws once again sank their teeth deep into his friend's flesh and bone.

When Tes Qua woke up, it was late afternoon.

Tyoga had gone to the pond several hundred yards downstream to retrieve some supplies that they had hidden along the banks from their last fishing trip. There was a black obsidian tomahawk that Tes Qua's uncle had given to him, a steel bladed knife that the boys had taken from the body of a trapper who had frozen to death on the summit of old Mount Rag several years ago, and a water gourd. Tyoga had filled the gourd with fresh water, placed the fishing weirs in the stream, and had built a fire in hopes of attracting some help.

"A'tey a Ho?" *(How are you doing?)* Tyoga asked his friend when he saw him stir.

"Ney da do, Ty." *(Not well.)*

"I know. Hurt much?"

"No," Tes Qua answered. "I can't feel anything."

"Tsadulis tsaldati? I caught some fish."

"Tla. I'm not hungry."

"Thirsty?"

"Hey ya. Esginehvsi." Tes Qua took several long gulps of the cool mountain water from the gourd Tyoga handed to him. "What are we going to do, Ty?"

"Gotta go fer help, Tes'a. Gonna be dark soon. Cain't be here in the dark. Bad spot. Lotta sign."

"Can you make it back before dark, Ty?" Tes Qua looked around their campsite. "It's a pretty long way back to Tuckareegee."

"Maybe. Maybe not. Won't be too long after tho'," Tyoga replied. "An' I'll be back dark or no. Would'a lef sooner, but I couldn't leave ya sleepin'. Best get along now tho'." He pulled the obsidian tomahawk that he had secured in his belt and handed it to Tes Qua.

"Here's the tomahawk, Tes—just in case. Tes'a, yer gonna have ta tend th' fire. Some wood piled up here for ya, but cain't leave the fire go out—or ev'n git low—ya unnerstan?"

Tes Qua opened his eyes and looked at Tyoga for a brief instant. He saw the words that Tyoga did not want to say expressed in his face.

Tyoga gently shook his friend to convey his stern and meaningful message. "Ya cain't leave it go out, Tes'a.—Cain't let it git low ev'n."

He stood, and with several leaps, he was gone from sight.

He hadn't gone twenty paces before they both heard the murderous howl of the first wolf.

Chapter 3

The Primal Decree

Tyoga stopped in his tracks at the haunting fugue. He didn't breathe. He only listened. The birds were still lively overhead. The crows raucously cawed their angry chastisements, and the squirrels scurried through the underbrush.

Restless, he hesitated another instant, cocked his head, and turned back toward the spot he had left Tes Qua. He waited to hear if there would be a response to the wolf's lonely plea. When none came, he relaxed a bit.

"Nothin' ta do 'cept keep goin'. Jest a lone wolf lookin' for some company," he said out loud.

He continued on his mission with more urgency in his pace. He had traveled about twenty minutes when he heard the plaintive wail again. This time the hair on his arms responded to the cry as if its tone had electrified the air with its woeful plea.

The wolf's macabre wail echoed from the canyon wall on the other side of the ridge. The scream pierced the dusk with its primal decree and shrouded the forest with its promise of death. He was close.

Tyoga froze in place, ears piqued toward the ridge, eyes hard, and his senses alive. He heard the rustle of leaves as rabbits disappeared into briar patches. He noticed the nearly imperceptible raindrop crunch of bark as the squirrels scurried up the towering pines. Their tiny needle claws secured them to the trees as if they had been stitched to the trunks. The delicate trill of the songbirds ceased, cut short in mid-measure by the maestro's baton.

Only the crows continued their dissonant scolds.

Tyoga didn't have to wait long to hear the response to the wolf's call. It came from across the valley. One. Two. Three. Distinct cries. Separate at first, and then in concert. All came from the same direction. Each chorus was closer than the last. They were moving fast—directly toward Tyoga.

While searching his surroundings for concealment, Tyoga fought to control the terror that threatened to cloud his thinking. There was little time to hesitate and even less to choose.

He realized instinctively that the pack of wolves converging on the ridge was the Runion pack. This rogue wolf pack filled the bravest hearts with the paralyzing terror understood only by the hunted. These wolves had tasted human flesh. With disregard for the abundance of natural prey, they would with wanton abandon target the lone mountain man's riverside camp or an Indian hunting party on the trail of game.

The ruthless alpha male had wielded his dominion over man and beast since the late 1600s. The Runion family's campsite had been invaded by the pack of murderous killers on the night of May 22, 1678. No one was spared. The half-eaten carcasses of mother, father, and two children were enough to make the blood run cold in even the most hardened mountain men. It was the uneaten body of the two-month-old baby girl who had been disemboweled—seemingly for the shear pleasure of the kill—that had placed the price upon the Commander's head.

When the news of the savage slaughter of the Runion family made its way east to the tiny town of Brunswick, even the hardiest frontiersman stayed clear of the valley.

The Native Americans feared the pack as much as the new settlers. The bounty placed upon the leader of the pack by the white men was too much for the valiant warriors of the tribes of the Chesapeake and Appalachans to resist. Many tried to kill the commander. A fortunate few returned empty handed. Most never returned at all.

Tyoga raced toward a tangle of downed cedar trees and crouched down behind them. Grabbing handfuls of mossy loam, he began rubbing the masking scent over his chest, arms and shoulders. When the pack crashed over the rise and broke into view, Tyoga gasped as if he had plunged into the icy waters of the Susquehanna. He held his breath and dared not move while the cold yellow eyes of the killer clan scanned the ravine and the slopes beyond where Tyoga lay hidden and camoflauged.

The Cherokee shaman had taught him that no living thing can secret itself completely. Hiding is but an illusion designed to deceive the hidden. While the hand is the instrument of shadow and concealment, it is also the betrayer that leads to detection and discovery.

Tucking each hand into the opposite armpit, Tyoga held his elbows close to his sides. While watching the pack drift on the crest of the rise, he pressed his body hard into the protective scent of the rotting earth and stamped his form into the moist dirt blanketing the decaying cedar trunk.

They were magnificent creatures. Their dominant mastery over all that they surveyed filled the air with a coercive sorcery that was at once charismatic and numbing. His brain screamed at him to close his eyes, shut them out, or look away, but he was mesmerized by their beauty and grace. Like balls of iron drawn to the magnetism of their allure, he could not take his eyes off of them.

The wolves rode high on the pads of their saucer-sized paws, hinged to the ends of long legs that seemed fragile and delicate from wrist to knee. Above the knee of the forepaws, fleshy knots of massive muscles attached to barrel chests that housed an enormous heart and lungs. The sinewy sheets that anchored haunch muscles to tendon and bone gave their hindquarters a deceptively sleek appearance.

The power, speed, and stamina generated by the sublime architecture were unrivaled in the natural world.

The wolves seemed to possess the facial dexterity to convey the emotion and sentiment usually reserved for human kind. Joy, trepidation, anticipation, fear, and something akin to the self-awareness expressed in gratified contentment percolated from the tempered masks of the mighty warriors.

A sudden change in posture, the lightening quick rationing of dilated pupil, and the metallic numbness of identity lost signaled a dramatic alteration of the pack's focus and resolve.

Tyoga dare not breathe.

As if mustered by a commander's call, the restless troops circled each other with their snouts pecking at the air in search for the scent of the crier. The pack froze in reverent deference when he appeared in the clearing, a hundred yards away.

The statuesque beasts stared toward, but away from the master with their heads bowed in submissive display while never making eye contact, yet never losing sight of their lord.

He was twenty yards from Tyoga.

He could hear the demon breathe, smell his pungent musk, and discern the low gutteral threat emitting from his huge silver breast. Tyoga didn't move.

With a chirp-like bark the directive was passed. Across time and generations, as distinctively expressed as eye color, gait, height, and scent, the coded communique was understood. With a knowledge requisite upon species and kind, the effect was immediate and palpable. The changes were subtle and nearly imperceptible.

Tyoga felt it happening. He had felt it before. The transformation would change the pack of seemingly carefree romping dogs into a bloodthirsty killing machine. So organized, so focussed, and so lethal that the prey—be it rabbit, buffalo, or deer—was already dead as it quietly grazed.

Their huge heads lowered as their necks retracted ever so slightly into massively muscled shoulders. Their taut bodies elongated as their spines swayed to lower them to the ground. Blood engorged their thickening legs and expanding chests to support the chase. Their pupils dilated. The yellow of their iris ignited into flaming amber-orange.

Horrified, Tyoga understood.

Prey down. Food.

Tes Qua.

The pack was off before the thought was finished.

Tyoga was right behind them.

Chapter 4

The Siege

The sun was setting when Tyoga arrived at the scene.

The remaining glow from the western sky cast a demonic pall upon the forest floor. It was the pivotal time of day when predator became prey, and those that were neither melted into the lengthening shadows to be secreted away until dawn. Details are lost in this shadow-world. The second tier senses of scent and sound become the arbiters separating life and death.

Tes Qua's attempts to keep the fire burning had failed, and the few remaining glowing embers were fast on the threshold of becoming barren ash. Tyoga could make out the silhouette of his friend leaning with his back against a massive chestnut tree. Clutched in Tes Qua's hand was a once flaming pine bough that he brandished in defense against the circling pack of snarling wolves. As if writing his final prayers in the wind, the glowing end of the branch etched random patterns in the air like desperate fireflies signaling for the attention of a disinterested mate. Lying on the ground was the gleaming black blade of the obsidian tomahawk that was just out of his reach.

With fearless abandon, Tyoga leaped from the surrounding bushes to place himself between his friend and the marauding wolves.

His arrival startled the pack and confused the Commander. They had been only moments away from the kill. The intrusion broke the ancient pact between predator and prey, and now their growling bellies would have to endure additional insult.

Tyoga recognized the Commander immediately. His eyes glowed hot amber with the fire of unquestioned dominance and superiority. Their eyes locked in primal embrace.

Unaccustomed to challenge of any sort, the wolf was uneasy with the boldness of this unknown adversary. He trembled with restraint and curled his frothing black lips to reveal two-inch long incisors that had made easy work of buffalo, deer, and bear. Those adversaries, he would have attacked and dispatched without malice or hesitation.

His reluctance to charge Tyoga resonated in the barely audible, yet deeply passionate, roar emanating from the wolf's massive chest. The control of the growl belied the primordial hatred for this smelly white, hairless creature. For reasons not completely understood to the Commander, Tyoga required his deference. The two stared at each other for a long time.

Without warning or sign, the pack eased away, back into the shadows.

"Te da ho mena aiolluimet, Tes'a!!" *(Get the fire goin'!)* There was no response.

"Tes'a!! Tes'a!" Tyoga demanded in a voice just above a whisper.

Turning to catch a glimpse of his friend, he could see that the attack had begun before he had arrived. Tes Qua's chest and arms were covered with bites and nips, each as clean as if inflicted by the slash of an obsidian blade rather than the rapier fangs of the killer wolves. They had played with him for awhile. Assessing his strength as a warrior, they had taunted and teased with half-hearted shows of aggression. One would charge and savagely bite at the flaming pine bough that Tes Qua was using to defend himself, only to retreat to the safety of the pack and fain honor and courage at the coup.

This cruel ritualistic behavior helped the pack determine the necessity for a quick kill. The stronger and more powerful the adversary, the quicker the deed must be done. It was discerned that Tes Qua was a trapped and powerless prey. They had used him for sport and would feast at their leisure.

Tyoga's arrival had changed the dynamic. He was an adversary to be reckoned with—strong, powerful, and driven by an instinct the wolves understood and feared: protection of kind. He stood close to Tes Qua while calling to him at irregular intervals, not only to assess his condition but to reassure himself that he was not alone—though very much alone he was.

Never taking his eyes off the blackness into which the pack had retreated, he placed his foot on the handle of the tomahawk and slid it back to Tes Qua. Slowly, quietly, Tyoga inched his way toward him. Reaching with his hand behind his back he touched his friend's bleeding shoulder. Tes Qua responded with a semi-conscious moan, and then sprang to alertness ready to fight for his life.

"Syla Tesa. Syla. It's me," Tyoga said reassuringly. "Are ya still alive?" he said only half-jokingly.

Before Tes Qua could answer, the pack began to slowly emerge from the cover of darkness.

The more dominant males circled the scene, while the weaker members hovered in the underbrush to await the Commander's assessment of the intruder and the order to attack.

Tyoga's eyes remained riveted on the more aggressive members of the pack as he made his way to the fire pit and kicked at the ashes and coals. A faint glimmer of red appeared deep within the pit. If he could get some dried leaves onto the coals, there was a chance that he could coax the ash to flames. Fire and light would be his greatest weapons.

But he needed time.

When the timid wolves ventured forth from the cover of the shadows to join the more dominant members of the pack, he thought, "Cain't let 'em regroup. Gotta keep 'em scattered."

Whirling the hickory stick that he had used to balance himself while trying to free the trap from Tes Qua's leg high over his head like a battle-ax, and screaming his most horrific war cry, Tyoga charged the confused wolves with unchecked ferosity. Taken by complete surprise, the Commander bolted and charged off into the underbrush with the rest of the pack scattering in disarray.

With precious moments won, Tyoga wasted no time. Dropping his lance to the ground, he grabbed handfuls of pine needles, dried twigs and leaves, and threw them loosely on the bed of hot coals. He dropped to his knees and blew several precious breaths onto the coals. The tips of the pine needles began to glow, and tiny fragile flames licked the dried leaves until they burst into yellow smokey flames. He snatched the dried pine bough from Tes Qua and threw it upon the naissant flames. The dried pine ignited into billowing plumes of light that illuminated the forest floor like a cathedral foyer bathed in the light of votive offerings.

Tyoga could see ten to fifteen wolves circling in the shadows beyond the protective dome of light that momentarily enveloped the camp. The glassy red pupils of the wolves' hollow eyes reflected the firelight—jagged amber orbs dancing in pairs as their majestic heads bobbed and weaved in a primal dance of ritualistic display. Circling restlessly in the silent shadows of the night, their restraint was like a scornful laugh mocking the futility of the combat to come. The dried kindling lasted only a few moments before the blaze dwindled to modest flame and the blackness of the forest descended like a death shroud upon their bleak encampment.

The darkness covered the wolves and Tyoga could see them no more.

He could hear the pack beyond the ring of firelight. They were so close that he could smell their stale breath. They seemed content to wait.

Tyoga took advantage of the time to tend to Tes Qua. The gashes inflicted by the snapping wolves ripped out chunks of flesh as if he had been whipped by a cat o'nine-tails. Tyoga cleaned the dried blood from his friend's arms, chest and neck. Tes Qua revived at the gentle touch of his care and sat up more resolutely against the trunk of the tree.

"You came back, Ty," he said through the painful grimace that contorted his face.

"Yeah. Heard them wolves sound the dinner bell," he replied. "I figured it was you they was aft'r."

"What are we gonna do, Ty?" TesQua asked. "They'll be back. You stole their kill. Especially the big silver back. He'll be back sure 'nuff."

"They'll be back aw'right, Tes," Tyoga agreed. "How are you doin'? How's the leg?"

"Can't feel anything, Ty. Except its starting to ache some above my knee. We gotta get out of here. I won't last much longer in this trap. If we don't get me to Yonevgadoga soon to take care of this—I'm gonna lose my leg like Sessqu'Na did. We gotta get out of here."

"Ain't nobody gonna lose nothin', Tes," Tyoga said with a hint of annoyance in his tone. "Don't talk like 'at. You always go seein' the bad end of things. And don't we always git loose? Don't we git loose? Well, we're gonna get quit of this mess, too. You just hang on. Just hang on."

The rustling in the woods was closer now. But the sound of the wolves' heavy breathing had stopped. Tyoga looked around for anything that would burn. There were plenty of dried leaves and pine needles. Some dead pine limbs overhead were still clinging to the trunks of trees. But there wasn't enough wood to last until dawn and to venture beyond the dim light of the campsite was unthinkable.

"Not much here about to make a fire with, Tes, but we'll manage. I'm gonna move you closer to the fire. You keep it burnin', Tes. Not too big. Jest enough to give me some light. The wolves can see in the dark like its day. They'll have the advantage. So keep it burnin' jest enough for me to see."

Tyoga lifted his friend in his arms and placed him next to the fire pit as the first deafening howl shattered the stillness of the night. The viciousness of the primal scream was overwhelming. When others joined the chorus, the boys clamped their hands over their ears to shut out the sickening dirge. They had to shout to one another to be heard over the din.

"What are they doing, Ty?" Tes Qua shouted.

"I don't know, Tes 'A'!" Tyoga shouted back. "Never heard wolves howl like this so close."

"They're right there, Ty. We could reach out and touch them. Why are they howling?"

This was different from anything Tyoga had ever heard tell. Wolves howl to call to one another from great distances, to locate members of their pack or to help guide them home to their dens. A lone hunter will call to the pack to tell them of his location so that they can join in the hunt and the kill, but never had he heard of wolves howling so close to their prey.

This was a time for stealth and quiet.

His instincts told him that he was an unwilling player in a deadly game. But what were the rules? How was it played? He had to be ready for anything.

"I don't know, Tes Qua!" Tyoga screamed.

The howling stopped as suddenly as it had started. There was a great crashing through the underbrush. They could hear the sound of the wolves' paws penetrating the stillness of the night like the ridge of a screw through a pine board. They dissolved into the blackness.

All was deathly still.

Tyoga's soul was alive with the night. The hair on his arms stood on end. His breathing came in shallow gulps. The mountain has its ways. It whispers in divine subtlety through an ether that permeates the pines and the moss. The alarm is carried on the silent heaviness of the air. The quiet is ponderous, dark, and engulfing. Every living thing, without understanding, acknowledges the intent. But those to whom the promise speaks glow in receipt of the silent cues like a towering pine in a lightening storm.

Tyoga knew. He understood.

"They're coming, Tes. Get ready. They're coming."

Chapter 5

The Battle Begins

Frantically, Tyoga grabbed the old trapper's knife he had retrieved from the trout pond after Tes Qua had been snared by the trap. He found the hickory stick he had used as a lance to rush the pack, and knelt down next to Tes Qua.

"Tes, take off your che'wollas. Quick," he said.

Tes Qua removed the ornamental dear hides he wore above his biceps and threw them to Tyoga. With rapid agile butchering strokes, Tyoga sliced the two-inch thick bands into slender laces a quarter of an inch wide.

"Tay chee n'qua lo'che mien."

He handed the laces to TesQua who wadded them into balls, plopped them into his mouth and began to chew the raw hide. Tyoga filleted the other arm band and popped them into his mouth.

After a few minutes of chewing, the boys' saliva had turned the leather laces into wet, rubbery bands coated with a natural adhesive the consistency of snail slime. Tyoga motioned for Tes Qua to pass the laces he was chewing to him.

"Nay cha."

Flipping the hickory stick, Tyoga handed Tes the fat, rounded end. Placing the bone handle of the old trapper's knife on the end he cradled in his lap, he quickly wound the wet leather lacings around the shaft of the lance and the knife handle. Faster and faster, tighter and tighter, he wound the lacings until he doubled over the end into the final coil.

" Tes 'A, a'loqua heta 'slo day na'"

With a nod of his head, Tes Qua held the wet lashings over the heat of the glowing coals while Tyoga collected more wood and pinecones for fuel. The pitted blade gleamed in the amber glow of the rising heat. As the leather dried, the thongs constricted and the knife melded to the shaft of the hickory pole like it was one.

"Tes Qua, lean back against the rocks and keep the fire burning. Throw anything that'll burn into the pit when you see the flames dyin' down."

Tyoga stood up, put his hand on his hips and surveyed the campsite. Staring off into the darkness he lowered his voice. "Tes Qua, we've got to make 'em think that there are more than two of us here. If we make a lot of noise it may confuse them enough to give us at least a fighting chance. It's all we got. Get ready."

A lone wolf howled from the ridge over the rise across the stream from the boys' prison-camp. There was no immediate answer to the call, only the gentle chirp of crickets and lonely call of night birds as the haunting invitation drifted away to the east. Several minutes passed before a reply resonated from the copse directly behind the two young men. It was a long, beckoning howl. Plaintive, yet resolute. The hair on the boys' arms raised in attentive acknowledgement of the message somehow deeply understood yet bewilderingly elusive. Again, there was no immediate response to the cry. Several minutes passed before a new voice echoed in solilioquy. This cry was in the adjoining valley to the left, past the trout pond and beyond Clingham's Dome.

"They've split up. Why? What are they doing?" Tyoga thought out loud.

"Ty, if they come at us from all directions we're finished."

"I know. But they won't. 'Least ways I don't think that's what they're doin'."

"Well, what are they doing? Why don't they just come and get it over with? Kill us and get it over with," Tes Qua said with a hint of desperation in his voice.

"'Cause it's more 'n that, Tes'A. It's me and the silver back. There's more 'n that, between him and me."

"What are you talking about, Ty. You're talking crazy." Inquisitive folds furrowed Tes Qua's brow. He had grown to understand that Tyoga's understanding of the natural world was experienced in foreign ways. As if to reassure himself that Tyoga's declaration was nothing more than a passing comment, he reiterated, "It's just a killer wolf wants to eat you for supper, that's all, nothing more. What are you talking about?"

Tyoga's response confirmed his fear that he was tuned into a reality beyond that which he was capable of understanding. "Don't know yet, Tes. Can't explain exactly. Somethin' in his eyes when he looked at me. Something he knows that he wants to see if I'm worthy of knowin' too."

"You're crazy, Tyoga! Loco. It's a hungry wolf—wants to eat you s'all."

Tyoga turned and looked hard into Tes Qua's dark eyes.

"No, Tes Qua'," he said with firm conviction. "There's more."

The forest became deathly quiet. Not a sound. No breeze. No movement at all.

"Quiet now," Tyoga whispered. "Here they come."

A magnificent beast appeared beyond the glow of the firelight. Head down. Burning yellow eyes pierced the darkness while looking beyond and through Tyoga. They burned deep into his soul.

He approached slowly, cautiously. He was stalking the boys as if they were unable to see him even though the wolf was completely vulnerable out in the open. As if following the command of hidden generals—there by order not by choice—he slowly picked up his left forepaw and allowed it to hover in mid-air before floating it silently into the dusky loam of the forest floor. He froze for an instant before doing the same with his right. His rear legs and haunches were slightly bent as if approaching a buffalo through the tall prairie grass. Fearful. Tentative. Resolute.

Tyoga clutched his newly fashioned weapon in both hands and prepared to plunge it deep into the wolf's back. He fought the urge to throw the spear at the wolf and stop him in his tracks before he was close enough to pierce with hand-held lunge. He couldn't risk throwing the spear. To miss would mean certain death.

The wolf's approach became more deliberate and determined. Tyoga could see the fleshy ribbon-like black lips framing the deep blood red of his gums and tongue. The three-inch incisors were bared by the demonic snarl. A pasty thick saliva drooled from his mouth and dripped to the ground. The rumble resonating from deep within the cavity of the wolf's barrel chest grew in intensity and pitch.

The stalk was over.

Tyoga had to do something to take control of the impending attack. If he couldn't regulate the ferocity of the charge, perhaps he could control the timing. With a stomp of his foot and a scream like an eagle, he triggered the charge.

The wolf took two lightening quick steps and leaped for Tyoga's throat. Tyoga and Tes Qua responded with horrifying screams when the beast's massive body left the ground. The treacherous jaws were open wide and the wolf's aim was true. Tyoga's throat was but inches away when he stepped backwards, planted the shaft of the spear against the ground, and heard the woosh of air as the knife blade plunged deep into the wolf's heaving chest. Caught at the apex of his six-foot leap, the wolf's one-hundred-and-fifty pounds slithered along the shaft of Tyoga's spear until the blade reappeared through the muscle and flesh of his back. With a pathetic cry, the deed was done. The magnificent hulk lay lifeless at Tyoga's feet. He grasped the handle of the old trapper's knife, its pitted blade dripping red with the blood of the beast. He placed his foot on the warm, lifeless body, and pulled the shaft of the spear free with a forceful tug.

Tyoga and TesQua's eyes met briefly before a second wolf appeared from the shadows. This one was smaller than the first. Quicker. Less tentative. Less fearful. Dispensing with the stalk, the wolf took two bold lunging strides and catapulted himself into the air toward Tyoga's chest. The wolf was fast, but Tyoga was faster. With a lightening quick juke to the left, the wolf missed his mark and flew past Tyoga. Pivoting to his right, and bringing all his weight to bear on the shaft of the spear, he thrust the weapon through the wolf's shoulder blade even before he landed on the ground. Keeping a firm grip on the lance he followed through with all of his body weight until he felt the knife blade pierce the wolf's chest wall and sink into the soft ground.

Before he could remove the lance and turn, the next warriors were creeping from the shadows. This time there were two.

Tyoga faced the beasts with no weapon in hand. Surveying the ground at his feet, he picked up a rock and plucked a partially burning pine bough from the dying fire. The two wolves extended their muscular necks, dropped their heads, and began their menacing approach. They didn't step in tandem, but each silently stepped forward after the other had made its move. This hunting technique broke the prey's concentration by dividing its attention between the two advancing animals. Though no more than a fraction of a second, the diversion was all that a pair of stalking wolves needed to make the kill.

Tyoga backed away while not diverting his gaze from animal to animal, but staring directly between the two advancing wolves. Their pace quickened.

Unexpectedly, the wolves stopped their advance. They raised their heads and cocked their ears while listening to a sound not yet detected by the boys. When the piercing cry of the Commander's howl was audible to Tes Qua and Tyoga, the wolves had already disappeared into the cover of the thick underbrush.

A second howl filled the night air with icy contempt. There was no mistaking the audible signature of unquestioned authority that was the Commander's voice. The order had been given to retreat. Despite the easy prey at hand and the gnawing hunger in their bellies, the pack was subject to his absolute authority. He ruled his domain with the majesty of a conquering warlord. His justice was meted out with cruel indifference. With no deference to sex or age, to challenge his authority was to invite a swift and slashing death by lethal white fangs and savage raw fury. The pack obeyed.

Tyoga looked at Tes Qua. As if in slow motion he bent his knees and whirled around to scan the underbrush. His ears piqued to determine the direction from which the cry had come. He absently dropped the stone from his right hand, and placed the smoking bough back into the fire pit. It burst into flame and light danced off of the huge trunks of the surrounding pines.

"This ain't right, Tes'a. Somethin' ain't right." Tyoga removed the spear from the lifeless body of the beast that had only moments before lusted for the taste of his flesh.

"Why did the other wolves leave, Ty? Why did they up and go?"

"Don't know, Tes'a. Shhhhhhhhhhhh. Somethin' ain't right."

The boys were quiet. In the silence, they could discern the flowing of their blood through their veins, the pounding of their hearts, and the rivulets of sweat soaking their quaking frames.

Tes Qua looked around the campsite. The fire was slowly dying. He looked up at his friend and said in a slow measured, commanding voice, "Tyoga. Run. Leave me here and run away. I'm gonna die anyway. Run, dithili. Save yourself. Run as fast and as far as you can."

"Seysha! Seysha, TesA, Nay ya ho!" Tyoga barked back. "That's exactly what they want me to do. They want us to separate. Alone we don't have a chance. Together we can make a stand." He took a deep breath, stood up tall and strong and said, "We walk out of here together or not at all. That's just the way it is, Tes."

Tyoga could sense that the Commander was near. He was coming for him. He would not sacrifice others of his pack to Tyoga's cunning and speed. He would do the deed himself.

The boys smelled his musky coat before they heard him make a sound. The rustling of the underbrush was his only betrayer.

Tes Qua said in a hushed voice, "Behind you, Ty. He's behind you."

"I know," he responded in a near whisper. "Stay quiet and low. Git as low in the rocks as you can."

Tyoga looked up toward the stars and inhaled the clean night air.

"If he kills me, Tes'a ..."

"I know. I know."

Chapter 6

The Exchange

Glowing amber eyes filled the darkness all around the boys' campsite.

From the south, two of the Commander's foot soldiers paced on the other side of the big rock against which Tes Qua was leaning. The rustling in the underbrush to the north signaled the presence of other members of the pack. The ravine and the feeder stream the boys had been following on their way to the trout pond was in front of them, to the west, and about forty-five feet down a steep rampart. A hundred yards downstream was Blackwater Falls, a 200-foot step in the gorge that had pounded the rocks below for all of time.

Tyoga looked at the lay of the land and knew what was happening. Wolves are pack animals. Not only do they rely upon the safety in numbers for physical protection in times of territorial confrontation with rival packs, but their prowess as a living, thinking hunting machine was so sophisticated that it served as the model after which humankind fashioned their own hunting strategy. The wolves were boxing them in by using the environment as their tool.

Cunningly, the boys had been cut off from any possible retreat.

Like an apparition forged from the vacuous shadows that bridge the light to the dark, the Commander materialized from the darkness. His eyes were filled with a dispassionate resolve that projected an odd separation from the outcome of the impending confrontation and the decisive role he was to play in it. With a weary determination, he advanced toward Tyoga.

Tyoga watched as the Commander's eyes lowered ever so slowly toward the ground. He saw the wolf extend and tighten his huge neck muscles and assume the aggressive stance of a mighty stalker before downing a two-ton buffalo or fending off the slashing antlers of a bull elk. Sure of the outcome of the battle, he didn't slow his pace like the others had before him. There was no need for stealth or hesitation. He would kill the smelly hairless creature before him, not only because he had killed members of his family, but because if he could not, then the legend would go on to proclaim that Tyoga Weathersby was the one.

Tyoga backed away, the ball of his foot touching feather soft upon the pine covered loam. First the left foot. Then the right. He did not take his eyes off of the Commander. He was sure that the others were not invited to this dual.

"A ho ya, Ty."

Tyoga did not reply to Tes Qua's admonition to stop backing away. Although he hadn't heard the words, the message had registered. He slowed his retreat, and prepared to stand his ground. He would live—or die—on this spot. Neither was true.

The Commander slowed his pace. Each massive paw hesitated in mid air before being carefully, thoughtfully placed in advance of the other. Unblinking, his eyes burned with a lustful hatred. The deep reso-nating rumble of contempt echoing from the barrel chest of the beast changed to a more aggressive pitch, shallower, more deliberate, ready to attack. Tyoga sensed that the charge was only seconds away.

He tightened his grip on the shaft of his makeshift spear, planted his left foot against a protruding root, bent slightly at the waist and waited. He was covered in the sweat and dirt and blood of both man and beast. The braids of his long sandy hair had long since fallen into disarray. Wet matted strands clung to his brow and fell about his shoulders and back. His breathing was fast and shallow. He fought to stay focused and calm.

Everything in him told him to run. This was a fight that he could not win. He could run a few hundred yards downstream, leap from the falls, and swim free from this nightmare. How joyous would be the embrace of the cool, dark, mountain water filled with the tannins that gave Black Water Falls its name as it washed the sweat and blood from his tired, aching body. How wonderful it would feel to gulp mouthfuls of cold, sweet mountain water. He could feel the bubbles lifting him to the surface, and see the acrid tan of the water break into the joyous clarity of the crisp night air as he was lifted free ... lifted free ...

The strike was lightening fast. Sensing that Tyoga had lost his concentration, the Commander struck with savagery. He did not leap into the air and aim at Tyoga's throat as he had expected and prepared himself for, but the full force of his charge was focused at Tyoga's knees only inches below the knife blade of the makeshift spear. All two hundred pounds of the beast slammed into the boy, knocking him flat to the ground.

Tes Qua watched in horror as the makeshift spear went flying from Tyoga's hands and into the underbrush beyond the light of the dwindling fire. In the blink of an eye, the wolf pivoted and embedded his fangs deep into Tyoga's right thigh. Before Tyoga had time to realize what had happened, before he even realized that his spear had flown from his hands, the massive beast was dragging him by his thigh toward the fire and Tes Qua.

Flexing his abdominal muscles to keep upright, Tyoga threw his arms behind him to cling to the dirt in order to slow the death drag toward the fire, Tes Qua, and the rest of the pack lurking in the shadows. He felt his fingernails bend to the quick and break while he frantically searched for anything within his grasp that he could use as a weapon. The beast's massive head was within striking distance of his right hand, but he would not relinquish the purchase of soil that was slowing the horrifying cortege to strike at the wolf. Instead, with their eyes locked in an embrace that would not relent, he kicked at the head of the dog with his left foot.

Intent on the kill, the wolf was not making a sound. He was drooling uncontrollably and Tyoga felt his face being slathered with the thick pungent mucous with each kick.

The death drag continued toward the fire and Tes Qua.

Through the din that was most assuredly his dirge, Tyoga began to make out the cries of his companion.

The legend does not say what he was screaming. But when Tes Qua came into view, as if in a dream, Tyoga could see that in his cocked right hand was the glistening blade of the obsidian tomahawk.

"Closer, Ty. Let him drag you closer. Don't stop him. Don't stop him."

Just as Ty relinquished his rake-like grasp of the forest floor, he felt the outline and weight of a jagged granite stone. He secured it in his right hand, and let the procession proceed.

The wolf had taken only three more steps when Tyoga heard the whirl of the spinning tomahawk. As he saw its flight he lifted the stone and pounded it down as hard as he could upon the head of the deadly beast.

The weapons hit simultaneously.

With a chilling, human-like scream of pain, the wolf released his grip on Tyoga's thigh.

The tomahawk had hit the Commander hard in his left haunch. While its flight was true, its edge was not; but the sting of the impact left its mark. The crushing blow to the wolf's head had been even more exacting and the wolf spun twice to nuzzle his thigh and shake the pain from his brow.

"Tes Qua'. The fire. Git the fire goin'. Quick."

"Ty," Tes Qua shouted. "Your leg."

Tyoga looked down at his leg. The fangs had torn flesh and muscle, but the puncture wounds had not incised any major vessels. The wounds were not bleeding badly. "It's okay, Tes. Ain't bad. Tend the fire. Quick. My spear. Can't see the spear, Tes. Did ya see where it went, 'ta?"

"No time, Ty. He's coming again'."

Tyoga did not have the time nor strength to get to his feet. Like a crab scurrying to safety, he shuffled backwards toward the ledge while searching with hands and feet for anything to use as a weapon. When the wolf launched a crazed final charge, his hand felt the handle of the tomahawk. With a powerful swing of the weapon, he stemmed the horrific charge with a cutting blow to the wolf's left foreleg. He heard the sickening thud and muffled crack of bone as the weapon found its mark. With a wimpering scream of indignation, the wolf backed away while limping toward the shadows beyond the fire's glow.

Tyoga got to his feet and now became the aggressor.

He circled around in front of the retreating beast before he had time to melt into the underbrush, and forced him to back away toward the precipice of the drop-off into the gorge. There was no more ground for him to yield without tumbling to his death. Slightly bent at the waist, Tyoga approached the still defiant, snarling wolf. This time, the tomahawk was in his strong right hand.

Still standing on his three good legs, the wolf was looking beyond Tyoga while figuring out a way around his adversary to reach the safety of the pack.

Jockeying for position, Tyoga kept him cornered. When the wolf made his move to run for the cover of the woods and the safety of the pack, Tyoga charged him with the tomahawk raised high above his head. The flecked glass edge of the obsidian blade came down on the wolf's head, crushing him to the ground.

Blood poured from the open gash above his left eye, but still he would not surrender. Staggering to his feet, the wolf tried to clear his head with a mighty shake that sent thick sticky streams of blood and saliva flying through the air.

Tyoga could not believe his eyes when he saw the mighty beast rise from the ground. Exhausted and filled with the anguish of mortal combat, he was certain that he could not sustain another attack.

"Te heya, Ty. Now. Throw it." He heard the voice of his companion as if from afar.

Tyoga grasped the handle of the ax at its base, raised it above his head, and let it fly.

As if in slow motion he watched its spinning course through the air, handle-head, handle-head—once, twice, three times. At the last instant, the wolf juked to the left and over the ledge it flew, handle-head, handle-head.

The wolf was seated at the ledge, his once proud head bloodied and hanging down. He was panting for breath and holding his injured forepaw off of the ground. His eyes met Tyoga's, and the snarl once again curled his murderous lips.

It wasn't over.

Staring hard into the piercing yellow eyes, Tyoga picked up a large jagged granite boulder and held it high above his head. Slowly, steadily he walked toward the ledge. Tyoga straightened his elbows and went up on tip-toe to muster every ounce of strength to leverage into the final blow. He was only inches away from the battered broken body of the majestic king, when suddenly the growling stopped and the Commander lay his bloody head on the earth at the feet of his conqueror.

The fiery passion of combat drained from the yellow brilliance of the vanquished dog's eyes and was replaced by a docile hazel green filled with admiration and promise. As if reckoning with distant voices, he closed his eyes in acceptance and resolve. He opened his eyes again only after he heard the thud of the stone as it was released from Tyoga's grasp and crashed to the ground.

Enveloped by the inky blackness of the night, Tyoga's silhouette was outlined by the glow of the dying fire.

Inches away from the pearly fangs that had lusted for the stain of his blood, Tyoga dropped to his knees and stared deep into the wolf's eyes. He was shocked at the clarity of his own reflection mirrored from the glassy chasm of his eyes.

Rooted in the timeless rhythmic change, metered not in years but in millenia—the serenity spilled from the pools of cocoa brown and morning gold to fill Tyoga's soul. He shivered as waves of sensation electrified his spent body with a curious urgency that he did not recognize but understood. With resigned acceptance, he welcomed its embrace. His blood flowed through his veins with a purpose and strength that had previously been shackled by propriety and convention. He sensed more than felt the transformation that was taking place within.

What he had spent to stay alive was repaid by what had been given. In their primal struggle to defeat and to conquer, both man and wolf had surrendered something to a cause yet unknown. The part of themselves they had given to the test was reborn in a communal exchange.

Both had given. Both had received.

It was as if they had perished together in their struggle to survive, and arisen as something new. They would never be the same.

Tyoga continued staring into the wolf's eyes, and watched as his own reflection silently dissolved away. With a curious sigh, and a blink of his eyes, the wolf released the young man from the embrace of their stare.

It was done.

Tyoga rose to his feet and backed away from the beast. The wolf lifted his head from the ground.

He heard Tes Qua screaming, "What's the matter with you, Ty. Kill him. Kill him or he's gonna kill us both."

"No, Tes 'A. It's over."

He looked down at the wolf lying at his feet.

"He could have called for help. He could have ordered us killed at any moment. But he didn't. And now the choice is mine." Bowing his head to approve the words, he added, "I choose mercy. Life is my gift."

Stopping his retreat, he said, "Ta oh hey, Wahaya." *(Rest, Wolf.)* "Ta oh hey peaose." *(Rest in peace.)*

He turned his back on the wolf and started back toward the fire and his friend.

Like a specter materializing from the darkness, Tes Qua watched him emerge from the shadows of the night. Slowly, his features began to reappear as they were illuminated by the dying flames of fire.

He knelt down by Tes Qua and extended a bloody arm to comfort his friend.

Tes Qua's eyes widened in amazement and fear. He could only gasp the word "Wahaya!" *(The wolf)* before passing out.

Tyoga turned expecting to see the wolf at his back.

Nothing was there. The wolf was gone.

The night was still.

CB ED CR ED

As he melted into the night, the Commander turned a final time to inspect the boys' camp.

He could see by the confidence in Tyoga's gate, the carriage of his shoulders and the cock of his head that the exchange had occurred exactly as it was meant to be.

The wolf shook his head and surveyed the blackness that surrounded him. He sniffed the air and turned back toward the boys.

His reluctance to leave them was born of the bond forged between himself and Tyoga, but there was something more. When it came down to the choice between life and death, the young man had chosen mercy and compassion. While the Commander had tested Tyoga's courage, strength and will to survive; benevolence was the sign for which he had been waiting. The wolf understood that the admirable—and singularly human—trait that made him worthy, was a fatal flaw in the wild.

For the beauty and majesty of nature is always balanced by the raw brutality that dispassionately tips the scale in favor of life or death. There is no justice in the choice. There is no judgment of worthiness, nor distinction between right or wrong. In nature, there are but two possible outcomes, and each is in keeping with nature's plan.

In truth, there is no choice at all.

With a resigned exhale, and a lick to his forepaw, the Commander looked at the campsite on the ridge for a final time. Cutting through the blackness of the night was the penetrating amber glow of Tyoga's piercing stare.

The wolf limped away.

His spirit, he left behind.

Chapter 7

The Journey Home

The night had only begun for young Tyoga.

Kneeling beside Tes Qua, he gently brushed the jet-black sweat-soaked hair from his eyes. He had passed out from the loss of blood and excruciating pain of his badly mangled lower leg.

Without the anesthesia of adrenaline rush supplied by the fight for his life, Tyoga's own battle scars began to make themselves known. The wound to his thigh was worse than he had thought but not nearly as bad as it could have been. His broken nails from the death drag left several of his fingertips bleeding. The ones that had broken off at the nail bed made the slightest movement of his fingers indescribably painful. There was a three-inch gash on his forearm administered by either fang or claw. It wasn't a deep wound, and it had stopped bleeding.

Somehow, he had to get his friend back to the village and to Yonevgadoga (Standing Bear) the medicine man, but to be able to do that, he had to take care of himself first. At the ledge where he had cornered the Commander, he stepped over the precipice and slid down the slope on his backside to the mountain run at the bottom of the ravine. The cool water felt good on his face and stemmed the sting of his wounds and hands. He cleaned the wounds on his thigh and arm, and then submerged his swelling hands in cold rushing water. The rest would have to wait until he got back to the village. He slowly climbed up the ravine's steep incline back to his friend's side.

The bleeding had stopped and the jaws of the killing machine secured Tes Qua's ankle to his lower leg. To remove the device would only cause the blood to start flowing again, and when the trap was released, Tes Qua's foot and ankle were coming off with it. The trap had to stay.

Tyoga weighed his options.

He could not leave Tes Qua alone and go for help himself. His friend would be dead without someone to care for him over the next twelve hours. He had to get Tes Qua out of the mountains and to the care he desperately needed.

It was at least a two hour trip following the most direct route to Tuckareegee over the mountain trails and through the high passes. The terrain was too steep and treacherous for him to carry his friend through the night on his back. Some places along the trail were covered in coarse, loose gravel and one misstep would be the end of both of them.

No, he would have to take the long route through the lowlands following the rivers and streams in the hollows that he knew so well. While the terrain was rough and some portions of the trail were narrow and steep, there were as many places that were wide, smooth and flat. Instead of a two-hour journey, it would be an all night trek.

There was only one thing to do. He would have to carry his friend to safety by making a travois, a sled used by the Indians to drag game from the woods. He set about the task.

Tyoga retrieved the makeshift spear from the underbrush where it flew when the Commander launched his first attack and removed the trapper's knife from the shaft. Then, he cut two eight-foot long birch saplings and trimmed off the side branches. He cut the branches into two-foot lengths that he notched at either end. Removing his leather britches, he slid the long birch poles into each pant leg. At eight-inch intervals, he poked tiny eyelets along each pant leg, through which he could lace the branches to the long poles, which acted as dragging shafts.

Cutting Tes Qua's loincloth into strips of leather for cordage, he secured the stays to the long poles to create a frame sturdy enough to support his weight. Skinning the two dead wolves took only minutes, and their pelts provided a cushioned platform upon which he could rest his friend.

After putting Tes Qua on the sled, Tyoga picked up the ends of the poles, and started the long journey home.

It was a dark clear night. The stars were out and with no cloud cover, the temperature was dropping fast. The new quarter moon provided only enough light for Tyoga to see the trail and the surrounding terrain on either side of the path. He would be able to see well enough to leave the footpath where it became too steep or rocky and drag the travois to one side of the trail.

The first big challenge confronted him before he had taken five steps.

No visible trail led from the escarpment down the steep slope to the stream below. He turned around so that he was facing the travois, and stepped backward off the precipice of the ridge. Holding the poles high above his head to keep the sled level, he inched down the slope until the end of the litter supporting Tes Qua's head eased into the loose soil and rock that covered the slippery slope. Taking baby steps he backed down ever so slowly while praying that the poles at the far end of the litter would hold fast in the loose rocks so that he could control the rate of decent.

About half way down, he lost his footing on a flat piece of slate that slid out from under him like a wet moccasin on a frozen pond. Struggling to steady the litter, he fell to his knees. The sharp granite shards sliced his knees and shins as he slid fifteen feet down the slope while holding the poles of the travois high above his head. The heel of his left foot caught the lip of a small crevasse to stop the slide into the ravine below.

Tes Qua moaned at the jostling, but remain unconscious.

It took Tyoga over an hour to maneuver his friend down from the ridge, which, at the best of times, had been a thirty-second romp for the two of them. When they finally arrived at the stream along which the bear trap had been seated, Tyoga stopped, fell to his knees and took a long cool drink of the fresh mountain water.

Tyoga looked back over his shoulder at his unconscious friend.

Where is the dread and despair? Shouldn't I be fearful that I won't be strong enough to get Tes Qua to safety?

No where could he find those natural human responses. Before the events of that evening, he would have been a frightened white boy alone in the woods, injured, tired, hungry, cold, and engaged in a seemingly futile battle to save the life of his friend. Courage had taken their place.

Like a buffalo in a blizzard, or deer in a lightening storm, he was part of the fabric of nature's course. The realization that whatever should occur will happen and unfold exactly as it is meant to be was an absolute revelation.

The promise had prepared me to anticipate and read nature's signs and subtle cues, but did the wolf somehow teach me their meaning and let me know intuitively what to do when the guideposts were revealed?

A surrendering peace flooded his mind and soul.

He looked to the heavens and saw the stars peaking through the boughs of the willow trees lining the gurgling stream and remembered his papa's words to him after his awakening.

"In all things there are but two outcomes – and each is in keeping with nature's wondrous plan."

He would be successful in getting his friend to the help that he needed—or he would not. In either case, their journey would end exactly as it was meant to be. He did not question whether he had the strength to get Tes Qua home. He did. He no longer questioned his decision to take the valley route. It was the decision that was made. It was right. He would see it through. Or not.

He looked at his friend and quietly spoke his name,. "Tes 'a? Tes 'a? Esginehvis?" *(Are you thirsty?)*

Tes Qua did not answer, and Tyoga did not persist. He needed rest now more than water. Unconscious was the best place for him to be.

He rose from his knees, picked up the travois, and put his back to the task. As he pulled his friend through the night, the rhythmic cadence of his footsteps melded with the sounds of the forest and the ether of the night. Moving beyond fatigue he walked through the darkness. Unwilling to yield to exhaustion's call, he staggered forward.

Forging ahead, he stepped back in time and he thought of her.

ɔ͡ʒ ʃɔ ɔʒ ʒɔ

He could not recall his life without her.

Sunlei Awi (Morning Deer) was Tes Qua Ta Wa's baby sister, and the daughter of Nine Moons and True Moon. Tyoga and Tes Qua were born in 1682, and Sunlei came along about a year and a half later. The three were often entrusted to the care of one of their mothers. Tyoga's mother, Emma, would leave him in the care of True Moon in the Ani-Unwiya village during planting or harvest time; and Tes Qua and Sunlei would stay with the Weathersbys during hunting season. Oftentimes, when True Moon was engaged in a task, the three were left in the care of Tes Qua's aunt, Awigadoga (Standing Deer). In the Native American tradition, the three children gained sustenance often from the same breast.

It was their time together in the Amansoquath village of Tuckareegee that the three grew to cherish the most. In the joy of their nakedness, they ran through the village unfettered by the constraints of the more puritanical mores of the Scotch-Irish traditions practiced by the Weathersby household. They learned about the ways of the forest, and the honored traditions of the Native Americans around their campfires. Romping through the glades and hollows of Appalachia, they were free.

Tyoga remembered that special day at So-hi pool when his relationship with Sunlei was changed forever. He could hear her voice and smell her skin as he trudged on through the blackness of the night.

So-hi (Hickory Nut) was an ancient goblet shaped sinkhole that was filled with mineral rich spring water. The crystal clear aquamarine swimming hole was one of the trio's favorite spots. Although it was visited by many of their friends, its hidden access and the rigors of entry imbued So-hi pool with an air of mystery and pleasure that somehow seemed unique. They never spoke of the pool in the company of others as if the words would betray an unspoken pact. So-hi belonged to them and no one else.

Four Months Earlier

"Come on in, Sunlei," Tyoga and Tes Qua urged a reticent ten-year-old Sunlei from the boulders surrounding the pool. "Tlano Ty—the water's too cold," she responded to their taunts.

"Oh come on. Don't be afraid. It feels good," Tyoga persisted.

"Jump in, Ulv *(sister),*" Tes QuaQua chimed in.

Bending at the waist to put his back into pulling the right stay of the litter over the roots of a giant hickory tree, he saw her beautiful face as it appeared on that day looking down at him from the banks of the pool.

Even at ten years old, the beauty into which Sunlei would blossom was readily apparent.

Her ebony eyes were pools of inky blackness reflecting the world not as it is, but reconfigured by an internal filter with a timbral quality unique in its perspective and joy. The world was reborn as an intuitive truth when strained through that filter. Sunlei would not be persuaded to abandon her reality. With a singular voice, the world mirrored in her eyes accepted the rightness of natural course. It stubbornly—even fiercely—rejected contrivance and scheme. As blackness protectively secrets hidden truths; so too, Sunlei's onyx orbs gave no hint of the private world within. The blackness was lifted only for those she welcomed to join her inside.

The gentle arch of brow that ringed her raven eyes was supported by a prominence of cheek that proudly proclaimed her regal Native American heritage. The chestnut skin of her forehead was covered with the fringed bangs common to young girls of the Amansoquath tribe. The remainder of her thick black hair was worn in braids that reached the small of her back.

The rest of Sunlei's facial features departed from those of her sisters and cousins. Her nose lacked the broad bridge common to her tribe, and was button-like, just slightly turned-up at the end. Her jaw line closely reflected the more slender facial structure of the white man, and her lips lacked some of the broad fullness of others in her tribe.

There had been shadowy talk in the village about an ancestor who had been kidnapped by fur trappers while foraging in the woods who was then sold to the Pontiacs in southern Canada. When the woman was finally reunited with her Uni-Unwiya family, her sandy-haired, three-year-old daughter was accepted into the clan as one of their own. Through the generations, a blue-eyed or light haired Amansoquath served as a reminder of their ancestor's cruel treatment at the hands of the white man. But, in the Indian way, all were accepted as members of the tribe.

In his mind's eye, Tyoga saw her bend over to pick up one of the baby ducklings she found in a nest several yards away from the bank of the pool.

"Look, Ty. Tes 'A, look," she chirped excitedly. "Baby ducks! Come and see!"

"Let 'em be, Sunlei," Tes Qua yelled from the far side of the pool.

At the frenzied cackling of the mother hen, Sunlei hurriedly put the duckling back into the nest, took a step down onto the rocky out-cropping and dove into the blue-green water of the swimming hole.

"Ty, the water's freezing." Sunlei began swimming toward the shore. "I'm getting out!"

"Oh, no, you ain't," Tyoga playfully replied.

Tyoga dove down, grabbed her ankle and pulled her down into the crystal clear turquoise water.

Releasing his grip, he let her swim to the surface, all the while holding a protective hand beneath the soles of her scissor-kicking feet. If she ran out of strength before reaching the surface, he was ready with a helping hand. Her legs were muscular and strong. He watched her legs frantically propel her to the surface. Her bronze skin glistened in the clear cool water as the noonday sun ignited her arching back with flashing amber hues. He gave a gentle shove just as her head broke the water's surface.

He reached out to put his arm around her waist and pull her naked body to his to keep her head above water. Coughing and spitting water at him, her protests about being nearly drowned were met with the laughter borne of a friendship ordained in unquestioned devotion. Tyoga would permit no harm to come to Sunlei as long as he held her in his arms.

More than knowing it, she felt it in his embrace.

Fighting to break from his grasp, Sunlei screamed, "You almost drowned me, Ty!"

"No, Sunlei. To hi ju—you're fine."

Tyoga remembered hearing Tes Qua laughing while tossing stones into the water around them from the bank.

"Ha le wi s ta, Tes Qua!" *(Stop it)* Sunlei screamed at her brother.

He recalled how she suddenly stopped struggling to let him hold her afloat.

Quietly, their eyes met. By the time Sunlei finally looked away, their relationship had been forever changed.

Ꮳ Ꮥ Ꮳ Ꮥ

Tyoga gripped the handles of the litter with such force that he felt the blisters on his hands burst when he recalled the magic of that special moment being shattered by the splash of a large stone hitting the water menacingly close to their heads.

Glancing up at the rocky rim of the pool, Tyoga saw the outline of their tiny tormentor, Seven Arrows. Two years younger than Tyoga and Tes Qua, the eldest son of Chief Yellow Robe of the South Fork Shawnee reveled in antagonizing his older Cherokee peers with impudence that he was certain protected him from reprisal. Careful to never travel alone, he was surrounded by a cadre of obedient pawns who submitted to his orders without question or hesitation. His derisive laughter descended from the banks of the sunken pool to fill the crater with sarcastic disdain.

Tyoga recalled the feeling in the pit of his stomach as their eyes locked in a seething sizzle. His face contorting into a menacing grimace, Seven Arrows bent over to pick up another large stone. Tyoga felt his eyes well with the anger of the recollection.

"Ne yeah ya at alo, descop-te," *(Don't touch that stone)* Tyoga cried out. When he finished the words he looked over to the far side of the pool where Tes Qua had been standing. He was nowhere to be seen.

Ignoring Tyoga's command, Seven Arrows continued with his taunts.

"Sunlei, why are you in the arms of the smelly white dog? You should be with a strong Shawnee brave." He smacked his open palm against his naked chest. "Move away from the white dog and let me see if he can catch this little stone."

At these words Tyoga gently pushed Sunlei toward the shore. At the bank with only two kicks, she lifted herself from the pool.

Tyoga floated on his back and closed his eyes. "Seven Arrows," he said, "throw the stone. Go ahead and throw the stone at me if you dare."

At this challenge, Seven Arrows lifted the heavy stone over his head with both hands. Tyoga did not change his posture but continued floating gently on the surface of the pool.

"But you will not throw the stone," he said. "You will not throw the stone because you are a coward. Look around you, Seven Arrows. You are a coward standing alone."

Seven Arrows's eyes darted all around the pool and then toward the woods behind him. He did not know that his three companions had scurried away at the not-so-gentle urging of Tes Qua Ta Wa, who now prowled the woods behind him.

"So, little coward, what will it be?" Tyoga teased. "Are you brave enough to throw the stone down on me as I float helplessly in the pool? Or will you drop the stone and run after your brave friends?"

Tyoga remembered the look in Seven Arrows's eyes when he dropped the stone to his feet.

Bowing his head, Seven Arrows walked slowly toward the dense underbrush before he paused and turned toward the pool. "You will remember this day, Tyoga Weathersby. What you have begun today can only be ended by me. You will never know when or where."

Tyoga could hear the joyous laughter when Tes Qua and Sunlei jumped in the pool when they thought that Seven Arrows had left them in peace to enjoy the rest of the day. The three frolicked together secure in the special bond of friendship their shared encounter with Seven Arrows served to strengthen.

After a while Tes Qua asked, "Is anyone getting hungry?"

"Yeah. A gi yo si," *(I could eat.)* Tyoga replied.

"I have some berries in my pouch. Let's catch some fish and have lunch," Sunlei said.

"Sure." Tyoga pushed her toward the shore. "Tes Qua, you start the fire. I'll get the fish."

The cool clear water enveloped his body when he propelled himself toward the bottom of the pool where schools of perch darted about like flocks of sparrows. His ears began to ring with the sound of Sunlei's cries when he recalled breaching the surface with two perch wriggling at the end of his makeshift lance.

After throwing his lance to the shore, he jumped out of the water and ran to where Sunlei was kneeling in her brother's arms. Tes Qua looked up at Tyoga with sad, confused eyes while he wrapped his other arm around Sunlei.

Under the stone that Seven Arrows had raised above his head to fling down at Tyoga were the crushed remains of the five baby ducks. Resting next to the nest was the mother hen, her decapitated head nowhere to be seen.

His ears burned with the sound of Seven Arrows's cruel laughter echoing in his head.

∞ ∞ ∞ ∞

The snapping of the cross-stays was violent and sudden. Tyoga planted both heels in the soft earth of the trail, and strained to keep the sled from pitching Tes Qua to the ground. It was the second time that he had fallen to his knees. He steadied himself and slowly lowered the travois to the ground. The sudden jerking awakened Tes Qua.

"E s gi ne hv si." *(I'm thirsty.)* Tes Qua struggled to get the words out of his parched mouth and cracking lips.

"I'll get you some water, Tes. Hold on."

When Tyoga returned from the stream, Tes Qua had passed out again. He lifted his friend's head and gave him a drink of the cool water. Through eyes dulled by fatigue and pain, Tes Qua looked at Tyoga with a stare that focused far away. All he said was, "Da gi y 'we ga." *(I'm tired)* His eyes closed. His body went limp.

Time was growing short.

The repairs to the travois were easy to make, and within minutes Tyoga was once again straining to pull his friend to safety.

It was the middle of the night, when the woods grow cold and dark. Successful predators had eaten and gone to sleep. Those that had not were still on the hunt and desperate for food.

The blisters on Tyoga's hands had burst hours ago, and now they were bleeding. His hands were on fire. His right moccasin was gone. The wound on his thigh had started bleeding again. Somewhere along the trail, the trapper's knife had fallen out from his belt. He was alone, injured, and defenseless.

Still, he marched on.

He lifted his feet in mechanical repetition without feeling them plant and propel him forward. His mind wandered back to those cool autumn nights when he used to huddle close to the fireplace in his family's South Henge cabin to listen to the stories his father would tell him and his brother, Davy, about Grandpa Joshia Weathersby.

Filled with the many hardships his grandfather endured bringing his young family across the ocean to settle in an untamed New World, his stories rooted the Weathersbys to the land, and solidified their longstanding relationship with the Ani-Unwiya. They explained the deeper truth that bound the young boys' lives together. The relationship between their two families had been built upon a foundation rooted in ancestral honor, courage and brotherhood.

Tyoga would honor that tradition—or die trying.

Chapter 8

Rescued

Tyoga awoke to the cackling shrieks of fussy morning crows. Sometime during the night, exhaustion had finally overcome the young man. He didn't remember stopping. He didn't remember placing the sled on a bed of moss, nor curling up along side his bloodied friend and passing out.

Tyoga rubbed the sleep from his eyes and checked on Tes Qua. He was shivering with fever and dripping with sweat. Seeing that he had succumbed to fatigue near a stream, he pulled some clean maple leaves from low lying branches, soaked them in the water, and touched the wet leaves to Tes Qua's dry, cracked lips. He did not awaken to drink.

As soon as he noticed the sudden quiet, Tyoga dropped to his stomach beside his friend. The birds had stopped their morning chatter and the only sound was the rustling of the breeze through the pines. Off in the distance, he heard what he thought was the sound of human voices over the rise. He remained perfectly still.

As the voices grew fainter, the terror that numbed his hands at the realization that someone was headed their way was replaced with the terrifying thought that maybe they weren't. He had to know. With the effort that it takes to move toward the unknown, he gathered himself and began moving quickly and quietly through the underbrush. Staring into the distance toward the voices, he instinctively placed his bare feet on the mossy patches on the north side of the trees to keep from alerting the party to his presence. He would only have seconds to decide whether it was help or harm that was on the other side of the hill.

He listened.

He couldn't hear the voices any more.

As he got to the top of the ridge, he caught a glimpse of four or five men rounding a bend that looped down to the stream on the other side. He could tell by their gait and the confidence with which they moved that they were seasoned warriors, but he was too far away to distinguish the tribe or village of their origin.

Fear of being left alone with his dying friend overwhelmed reason.

Standing on tiptoe on the very crest of the ridge he shouted out as loudly as he could, "O-si-yo!" *(Help!)*

The men stopped.

Jumping up on a hickory stump, he shouted again. This time he heard them crash through the brush as they ran toward him.

Falling to his knees atop the stump, he repeated in a failing voice, "O-si-yo."

He didn't care who they were or from what village or tribe they hailed.

He was spent. His spirit was exhausted.

Sitting back on his haunches, he said again, "O-si-yo."

When the men got to his side, they found Tyoga sitting with his eyes closed, shoulders slumped, head bowed and his raw swoolen hands, palms up, resting on his thighs whispering, "O-si-yo."

Without a word, one of the braves folded the shaking Tyoga in his arms while the others rushed to where Tes Qua lay next to the stream in the gultch below.

He felt a strong thick palm caress his cheek and looked up into the kind gentle face of Yonevgadoga (Standing Bear), the medicine man.

They were saved.

Chapter 9

Recovery

Tes Qua slipped in and out of consciousness for days. The medicine man had cured animal bites and skin rashes; lanced boils and set broken bones. He had treated braves returning from battle by cutting arrowheads from organs and limbs, binding open wounds, treating the fevers that frequently followed infection and illness. Never before had Yo-nev ga-do-ga's skills been so ardently tested.

He administered willow bark and yarrow tea to battle Tes Qua's fever while his body fought the infection from the bear trap wounds and the bites inflicted by the wolves. He managed Tes 'A's pain with a bittersweet herbal tea that acted as a powerful sedative. A salve of hog lard mixed with greenbrier leaves and bark controlled the bleeding.

After several days it became apparent that the mangled ankle and broken leg, which included torn sinews and slashed tendons, were beyond the means of a Native American medicine man. Yonevgadoga knew that he would have to rely upon the white mans' medicine to repair Tes Qua's injured leg. He asked Anigilohi (Hair Hanging Down) to go for Tyoga's mother, Emma.

Tyoga's grandmother, Rebecca Weathersby, was the daughter of Jacob Entwhistle, a reknown physician in Chenowith on Moor in Southern England. Rebecca had grown up watching her father tend to the ill and seriously injured. She brought with her to the New World herbal remedies, bleeding instruments, and the necessities to fight inflection and close wounds with needle and thread—a concept foreign to Native Americans. In her time, she had been known throughout the region for her medical knowledge and skills. Rebecca had been midwife, dentist, herbalist and bone setter for the settlers and tribes that dotted the Appalachians. She had taught her daughter-in-law, Emma, everything that she knew about the healing arts.

Emma was more than willing to come to the Ani-Unwiya village to tend to the injuries of her son's Indian brother. She reattached torn tendons, repaired severed muscles, and stitched torn skin. The wound was dressed with linen binding wrapped around hickory splints to stabilize the damaged joint. The rest was up to Tes Qua and E-do-da *(God)*.

While the worry surrounding Tes Qua's recovery was palpable throughout the village, the talk around the lodge fires in the evening when the elders passed the pipe was of the battle young Tyoga had waged with the leader of the Runion pack. Although Tyoga did not share the events of that night with anyone but Sunlei, Tes Qua told his father and the other elders about the savage encounter. The People spoke in hushed reverent tones about the magic that had infused their white brother's soul. They could see how the spirit-life he now shared with Wahaya-Wacon *(the spirit-wolf, the great-wolf, a descriptor that confers a spritual component to greatness)* had transformed him.

Since the battle on the ridge, Tyoga began to see the world through the eyes of an observer—at once engaged, but oddly apart. He experienced the natural world not in terms of sight and sound, but rather in the context of time, space and dimension. Those around him revealed themselves not in the actions observed by others, but in the subtlety of expression, carriage and gait. Deception betrayed by texture, tone, and scent, honesty revealed by sincerity of eye and crease of brow. People revealed themselves in myriad ways, unknown even unto themselves— and he wondered why others couldn't see.

Days went by while Tes Qua fought for his life. Tyoga and Sunlei never left his side. By day, they tended to his needs and bodily functions. By night, they slept by his side bathed in the warmth of the fire and confident in the gentle ease of lying in each other's arms.

"Ty, et ta yaheh?" *(Are you asleep?)* While Sunlei spoke English well, she and Ty always spoke in Tsalagie when they were by themselves.

Tyoga opened his eyes and saw that Sunlei was snuggled so close to him that her forehead nearly touched his lips. The warmth from her body radiated through the collar of her doeskin tunic, carrying the sweet scent of cinnamon and sandlewood. The fire flickered silently in the center of the lodge and the crickets and tree frogs filled the night air with a reassuring stuccato sizzle.

Tyoga inhaled deeply and replied, "No. I'm awake."

Sunlei wiggled closer to Tyoga and he draped his right arm around her. They breathed in unison for a long while.

Sunlei whispered, "Ty, do you think that my brother be all right?"

He didn't answer right away. He thought back to that night and the horrific battle that both of them had been through. He was amazed that Tes Qua had survived at all. He propped himself up on his left elbow and turned his head toward Tes Qua.

"Tes is strong," Tyoga replied. "You should have seen him fight the wolves, Sunlei. Even with his leg still caught in the trap, he saved my life with a toss of a tomahawk. He's strong and he'll never give up."

While reassured by his words, Sunlei knew Tyoga so well that she was certain that he wasn't saying what was really on his mind. She let it go. He would tell her when he was ready.

"Ty," she began in that halting voice that indicates reticence to continue, "the People say that you defeated the wolf pack because the great spirits willed it to be so. They say that you now have strong medicine and will be a great man someday."

Tyoga got up and threw some cedar onto the fire. The flames sent shadows dancing up the walls of the lodge, and illuminated Sunlei's face in the richness of a pastel amber glow. He sat down cross-legged on the floor in front of the fire and stared into the flames. He remained silent for a long time.

He finally replied. "At first, I thought that we survived that night because it wasn't our time. But now I know that there was something more to it." He paused to choose his words carefully. "Sunlei, I've watched wolves hunt plenty of times. They hunt as a pack. They work together to corner their prey. They stalk together and think the hunt through.

They know where each member of the pack is supposed to be and they kill all at once with every wolf taking part. The Runion pack could have done that to us—but they didn't. The two wolves we killed would have killed us for sure if we hadn't killed them first. But I think that the big one—the leader—sent them in to test us. Two more were coming in to get us—but the big one called them off. Then, he came at me alone."

She joined him by the fire. Standing next to him, she brushed his hair from his eyes, sat down, and leaned her head against his shoulder. The flames danced in the inky blackness of her beautiful dark eyes. She placed her hand on his thigh, when Tyoga began to speak again.

"He never even looked at your brother. He never took his eyes off of me. When I looked into his eyes as he was moving toward me I thought they were filled with hate. I don't think so now. He didn't want to kill me at all. It was like he was testing me."

Sunlei lifted her head from his arm and looked up at him while he continued to stare into the flames. "Testing you? That doesn't make any sense, Ty. He's just a wolf."

"Is he?" Tyoga asked

He stood up and walked over to some sweet basil hanging on the wall. He pinched off a tiny stalk of the dried herb and crushed it in his hand. Bringing his palm to his nose he closed his eyes and inhaled its pungent summertime fragrance. He smiled at the memories it triggered.

He remembered that day on Carter's Rock when he stood with his papa and the secret was revealed in the blinding light of the new dawn. Since that day, that very moment, he had experienced the wonder of the promise in a thousand different ways. The whispers of the dawn, the silence of the sunset and the dizzying array of indulgence introduced in between.

He hadn't really understood how the revelations of the promise would change his life—but the truths revealed to him on that day so long ago were codified in the life and death drama that played out on the plateau that dark and dangerous night. The baptismal journey through the night to save Tes Qua's life while repeatedly falling to his knees only to rise again and carry on, and his Ani Unwiya brother's remarkable recovery all made sense somehow. How could he explain it to Sunlei in a way that she could understand?

Turning toward Sunlei, who lay with her eyes closed, curled up next to the fire on the soft bear hide, he smiled at the changes that had taken place in his childhood playmate. While her physical beauty was apparent to all as adolescence chiseled away the pudginess of child-hood, it was the ethereal beauty of her gentle face that was slowly transforming her into an astonishing young woman. There was a mystic quality of joyous independence that oozed from the depths of her boundless black eyes. She radiated a oneness with the universe that was born in the wisdom of acceptance far beyond her years. She too was part—but separate. She mattered—but sought no recognition. She followed—and led from behind.

That Tyoga and Sunlei were meant to be together was an accepted destiny as incontrovertible as summer following spring and the eagle owning the sky. The friendship they had shared from their earliest years did not need the bridge of puppy love to blossom into commitment and devotion. The connection between them was so strong, that even when separated by the length of a lodge, that they were together was evident to all. Their eyes would lock in an impassioned embrace that silenced the world around them while asserting their oneness in a communion that transcended words. With no regard to distance or time, their spirits were now and forever as one.

When Tyoga sat down next to her, she opened her eyes. He lay back, propped himself up on an elbow and continued, "When he first charged me, Sunlei, he didn't go for my throat like the others. He knocked me to the ground. He grabbed me by my leg when he could have grabbed me by the throat and killed me. When he had me clamped in his jaws, he dragged me toward the fire and Tes'A. The pack was in the same direction. He could have called them in for the kill at any moment, but he didn't."

"Why, Tyoga?" Sunlei asked. "Why do you think he did that?"

"I don't know." He brought the crushed basil in the palm of his hand to his nose.

"I don't understand why."

They both fell silent. The sounds of the night filled the lodge. Sunlei tried to comprehend what Tyoga was trying to tell her. She understood the words, but struggled to make sense of their meaning. She knew that she was lying next to a young man who would one day leave an indelible mark upon his adopted people. She hoped that the lore that would follow him into eternity was one of which she and their children would be proud.

The gifts he had been given would orchestrate the rhythms of his life and one day reconcile the man he was to become and the journey that he was destined to take. The day would come when he would walk alone, and in that aloneness, his path would be different and unique. He recognized that the difference he would have to endure was both the gift and the curse of the promise.

"Tes'A says that you defeated the leader, but you didn't kill him," Sunlei said with her eyes heavy with sleep. "Why did you not kill him when you had the chance? Why did you allow him to live?"

"It wasn't I who allowed him to live. It was he who spared my life."

"I don't understand," Sunlei whispered as she fell asleep with her head on his shoulder.

"Neither do I," he sighed to the flames. "Neither do I."

Chapter 10

South Henge

With Tes Qua on the mend, Tyoga trekked the fifteen minutes south to his family home, South Henge, nestled in a sunny glade about one hundred yards from the banks of Tonkin's Run. With winter coming, he needed to help with harvest chores and prepare the root cellar to store perishable foods over the long winter months.

Tyoga's grandmother, Rebecca, fell in love with the land the moment she had set eyes upon it in the summer of 1623. The son of the Ani-Unwiya elder, Kicking Bear, had shown it to her and her husband, Joshia.

When they stepped to the top of the earthen embankment, or henge, that marked the southern boundary, they stopped dead in their tracks. A lush grassy meadow, knee high with bulbous oat grass, bellflower and coriander spread out before their eyes. The northern border of the property was a riverstone jetty that interrupted the rapidly flowing shallows of Harley's Run like a giant thumb pressing its will upon the river's course. The half-mile arch was thick with cutthroat and brown trout struggling to steady themselves against the pummeling of the fussy flume. The west boundary of the meadow melted into a stand of pine and cedar trees. To the east, the deciduous woodlands of Appalachia flowed up and over a formidable crest before disappearing into an unnamed hollow. The echoes of a never-seen waterfall rose from the blackness of the cavernous gorge.

Tyoga's grandpa, Joshia, had built the one-room log cabin in the glade about four months after the Powhatans had saved the Weathersby family from massacre by secretly guiding them from their homestead along the James River to the safety of the Ani-Unwiya village. When Tyoga's father, Thomas, was about twelve years old, the single room was expanded to three when a kitchen with a giant stone hearth was added to the north side. In 1631, when Thomas married Emma, the original loft was converted to a complete second story to make the Weathersby home one of the largest in the Appalachian frontier.

While Tyoga loved the freedom of the Cherokee way of life, and the warmth of his Indian brother's lodge, South Henge was his home. The knotty pine walls oozed with the scent of holiday pies, Bay Rum, and lye soap. Grandpa Jos' bentwood rocker rested in its nook by the hearth, above which the deer hoof gun rack held the old Weathersby matchlock.

Sitting on an oversized oak stump that had rested alongside the family forge since before he was born, Tyoga was mending the mules' plow harnesss. The Ani-Unwiya were fine tanners and he had picked up the art of leather working by watching the tribe elders make sheaths for their knives and quivers for the arrows of the younger braves.

Tyoga's mother Emma was in the garden digging a crop of potatoes and picking broadleaf chard. The first hard freeze was only weeks away and this would be the final crop for the season.

Tyoga looked up from the harness to see her stretch her back, pick up her basket of harvested vegetables, and walk toward him. He waited until she was by his side.

"Mama, tell me about Davey," Tyoga continued mending the harness he was working on.

Taken aback at his question, Emma hesitated before answering.

More than most, she had noticed the changes in Tyoga since his battle with the Runion wolfpack. She had not said anything because the changes had been so subtle that only a mother would know. She sensed, more than observed, the difference. This uncharacteristic question was more evidence of the change. Tyoga's younger brother, David, had been dead for three years, and never before had he wanted to discuss the circumstances of his untimely death.

"Why, Tyoga," she replied while stretching out her back again. "Why are you asking me about what happened to your brother? You found him lying on the floor with that hideous reptile curled in the crook of his arm."

"You're right about that, Mama," he said in a soft voice, "but I want … I need to know more."

"All right." Rather than recount the entire story, she waited for him to ask his questions.

Placing the harness on the ground by his feet, he looked up at his mother standing by his side. "Why did you let him keep the snake, Mama?"

"Davey loved animals, Tyoga. Not just some animals, but every creature that walked, hopped, slithered, or crawled." She wiped her hands on her apron, and placed them on her hips. "Davey wasn't like you, Tyoga. He didn't know what you know. He didn't understand the way that you understand. When he came walking in that very door," she said while pointing to the front door of the cabin, "holding that half-frozen water moccasin against his chest to keep it warm, there was no turnin' him around." Tears filling her eyes, she gazed off into the blackness of the forest as a smiled creased her lips. "He stayed up all night with that snake. Moving it closer to the fire when he though it was getting cold, and pulling it back when the coals got too hot. He was determined that that snake was going to survive." She choked when the tears began to flow more readily. "I knew better. I should have thrown that snake into the fire and killed it myself. But I didn't. Now I have to live the rest of my life knowing that I could have done something to save …" She stopped speaking and dried her eyes with her apron.

Tyoga picked the harness up off of the ground. Silently, he began working the awl through one of the leather side stays.

Emma picked up her basket, and turned to go into the house.

Before she could take a step, he reached out and gently grabbed her wrist. "Mama, it wasn't your fault, you know."

"Tyoga, water moccasins are dangerous snakes," she replied with a hint of annoyance in her tone. "He was just a child. It's a parent's job to protect and defend their children. I knew better. He didn't. If I had only … My baby boy—your brother—would be alive and with us today."

Tyoga placed the harness at his feet again, and stood up. He stepped in front of his mother so that she was looking into his eyes.

"Ma, there isn't anything that you could have done to change the course of events. I saw you get out grandma's doctorin' tools and watched you cut the X's over the fang marks, and try to suck out the poison even though you knew that it was too late. I even watched you open his arm with the razor when his skin began to split because of the swelling. There wasn't anything more you could have done. Ma, the real point is that water moccasins aren't dangerous. Snakes don't take into account good will or bad intent. They react not by design, but in the only way that they can."

"Ty, Davey never hurt the snake, he took care of it and protected it."

"But, Mama, he did hurt the snake. He harmed it in the worst possible way. He put it in that hog's head, and placed it on the shelf."

When she didn't understand, he continued, "You can't lock nature in a crate or a box, Mama. You can't place it in a barn or behind a fence. You see all of this?" He waved his arm to indicate the acreage that he and his father had plowed and manicured. "This isn't real. This isn't what matters. It doesn't belong to us any more than the trees and the dirt and the rain. In time, it will all be gone—consumed by what really matters."

While she was a bright, educated, inquisitive woman, Emma was a Weathersby by marriage. She couldn't hope to be awakened. She would never know the promise.

Tyoga turned away from his mother and faced the west. It was mid-afternoon, but already the warmth of the sun had been blocked by the peak of Polish'd Mountain. He closed his eyes and opened his heart to the whisper of the promise.

Standing behind her son, Emma noticed, perhaps for the first time, his broad shoulders and well-defined waist. Mature beyond his years, and wise in ways that hadn't been apparent before his encounter with the Runion wolves, he was growing into a fine young man.

She watched as her son's breathing slowed and deepened. She stepped away when she noticed the swelling in his upper arms, and the back-panel of his leather vest tighten across his shoulders. When he turned to face her once again, she raised her right hand to her lips, stepped back and gasped nearly inaudibly.

The gentle hazel swirl of his eyes that she was so used to seeing was gone. The emerald hue that pacified his gaze had been stripped away. In spite of that, she recognized her son beyond the amber hues that had taken the place of his eyes.

"Ma, the truths that you cannot see are hidden from you for a reason. They are concealed from most men, because to know them is to change what was meant to be. Nature is cruel, but not calculating. While we are rarely given second chances, we are constantly given choices. Once the choice is made, there are only two outcomes. We see before us fire and water, the earth that we stand on and the air that we breathe. We place judgements on all of these things, and pretend to understand right from wrong. The reality is that there is nothing in nature that is good nor anything that is evil. It wasn't the choice to care for the snake that cost Davey his life. It was his notion that he should care for it—and that it was the right thing to do. There was no choice to be made. The snake was meant to die, not our Davey. He should have let it be."

Emma took a step toward her son and gently placed her hand upon his shoulder. "Tyoga," she said barely above a whisper, "how do you know these things to be true?"

He did not answer.

"You speak as if there is no right or wrong, and that animals—" She hesitated before continuing her thought. "And even people are meant to live or die. How is it that these are choices? Who would choose to die? Who would choose to take a life?"

Tyoga sat down on the oak stump.

She walked around so that she was facing him, knelt down in front of him, and placed her hand on his knee. She saw that her son's eyes were returning to their hazel swirl. She realized that she had witnessed something that would set Tyoga apart from everyone else. What it meant she could not say.

After a while, Tyoga looked down into his mother's loving eyes and said,. "No, Ma, it's more than that. Sometimes the choice isn't to live or die. It is to kill or be killed."

Together, they watched the shadows grow until darkness filled the glade, and South Henge was consumed by the blackness of a moonless night.

Chapter 11

Of Fearless Stock

When the sun had finally set behind the mountain, Tyoga's mother patted him on his back and walked slowly back to the cabin.

She knew that this was Tyoga's favorite time of the day. The growing shadows draping across the mountains quieted the clamor of the day. A placid calm enveloped the natural world and prepared its creatures ending their day for rest.

But the growing darkness likewise ignited baser instincts for those that would spend the blackest hours in predation.

Tyoga felt the lure of both prey and predator.

It was the hour of the day for reflection.

If Tyoga was not watching the sunset from the outcropping at Carter's Rock, he would be perched in the old bentwood rocker his Grandpa Joshia had made for his wife to sit in while she knitted, crocheted, or spun wool into yarn.

Staring into the flames in the hearth, Tyoga rocked the evening away while lost in his own thoughts. More often than not, he would read by the light of the fire until well after midnight. Including tomes by Shakespeare, Herodatus, Marlowe and Middleton, their home library was substantial by frontier standards. Tyoga had inherited his mother's love of reading and education. He had never attended a formal school, but his mother served as an excellent teacher.

Emma was the daughter of Kenneth Longsworth, an educated man with a successful law practice in Albermarle County, Virginia. A bright girl, she began reading at an early age. Noticing his daughter's acumen with the written word, her father spared no expense on the finest tutors in Virginia and Maryland. Her education became his passion.

In colonial America, young girls were not afforded the same educational opportunities as boys. After all, young men had to earn a living to support a family. However, Mr. Longsworth was so devoted to advancing his daughter's education that he was able to persuade Reverend John Todd, Senior, to accept young Emma as his first female student.

Her command of foreign languages was bettered by no young man in his charge. Her mastery of advanced mathematics was unmatched, and came as a complete surprise to the cognoscente who agreed in the complete inability of the gender to comprehend the abstract as a matter of principle.

Emma's decision to marry Thomas Weathersby not only sent a flood-tide of consternation roaring through Virginia's societe` aristocratique, but wounded her father so deeply that they were never to speak again. Though well educated himself, Thomas Weathersby was considered "that backwoodsman" due to his birth and devotion to the frontier.

A strong willed woman, Emma used her strength to fortify her determination to share her love of learning with her children. Like his mother, Tyoga could read at an early age. While comfortable speaking in the frontier vernacular when traveling the backwoods of Appalachia, proper grammar and erudite employ of the spoken word were valued in the Weathersby home. Sometimes, his father, Thomas, would walk in the front room to join his son in the quiet before the stone fireplace and they wouldn't speak at all.

Other times Tyoga's father would regale him for hours with tales of his youth and the adventures of his own father, Joshia, during his struggle to settle in the New World.

Thomas Weathersby was a gifted storyteller, which was revered and rewarded in the Indian culture. He was always a welcome visitor in Tuckareegee. Fluent in Tsalagie, his Native American brothers loved to listen to him tell a story of daring-do.

That evening, when he heard his father enter the front room, Tyoga turned to ask him, "Papa, will you tell me the story of Grandpa Jo and the Powhatan?"

"Son," his father replied, "you know that story by heart by now. I bet that you could tell me about Grandpa's run in with Openchanecanough better than I can tell it myself."

"I reckon you're right, papa," Tyoga replied. "But I'd like to hear it again just the same."

It would be the first time that he heard the story since doing battle with the Runion wolves. He was certain that the story would have a new and more important meaning to him since the encounter and exchange.

Obviously pleased at his son's request to hear the story again, his father stood up, walked over to the fireplace mantle, and picked up his long-stemmed clay pipe. He sat down on the stone hearth and began.

"Your grandpa Joshia settled along the banks of the James River in Virginia, on a plot of land that was just across a narrow channel from a place called Hog Island. Hog Island was a tiny spit of land in the middle of the river where the settlers allowed their hogs to graze and fatten up, ya see. Anyway, the homestead was about seven or eight miles from the Jamestown settlement, just to the southeast of a land grant called Martin's Hundred.

"Grandpa Jo built a log and earthen cabin in a shallow glade along a fresh water run south of a settlement called Wolstenholme Towne. The site was protected from the wind that constantly blows off of the James by a gentle rise before the shoreline. The north and east were protected by a stand of pine, birch and ashe."

Thomas looked off into the distance as if he were gazing upon the tiny cabin. "Papa was sure proud of that place. I don't recollect it, but when I was a youngun, he and Mama often spoke about how pretty it was." He shook his head as if to free the vision from his sight, and reached for a fiery brand to light his pipe. Several long drags on the stem of his pipe filled the room with the familiar scent of tobacco that made Tyoga feel safe and warm—and innocent once again.

"It started to snow on January 2, 1622," his father continued. "The blizzard raged for ten straight days. When the storm finally passed, an eight-foot snow drift sealed the door to the cabin. It took your grandpa a full day to dig a tunnel through the drift to get to the little feeder stream for water. Another three days passed before he took that very flintlock hangin' over yonder off the wall," he said while pointing to rifle mounted over the fireplace, "kissed your grandma, Rebecca, goodbye and headed out into the freezing winter wilderness in search of game. Two days into his hunt, Grandpa crested a rise and made camp at the base of a giant walnut tree. This was a site that he had used often when searching for game. Ringed by a dense hedgerow of wild rose bushes, it was a perfect site for hunting deer. The shrubs formed a natural windbreak, and, as the sun set, the camp was smothered in the darkness of growing evening shadows. But what your grandpa liked best about the campsite was that not ten yards away was a deer path, just as pretty as you please, meandering down the slope to the east. Downing a ten-point buck took no more effort than kneeling on your bedroll and pullin' the trigger. Yes sir. It was the perfect huntin' camp.

"Well, Grandpa found the ring of stones he had left in place from his fall hunt and he soon had a blazing fire to keep him warm. He wrapped himself in his buffalo robe, removed his elk hide boots, and placed them near to the fire to warm and dry."

His father stopped and chuckled. "All he had to eat was a tough plank of salted sturgeon. I remember him tellin' Mama that it tasted so awful that it puckered his tongue like a chunk of lye soap." He shook his head with a smile on his face. "It was all he had to eat so he made do with what he had, but he never let Mama forget." He laughed out loud and stared into the quiet of the cabin.

His papa's eyes darted around the room as if to see whether anyone else was around. He slid along the hearth to get closer to Tyoga, who was sitting in the rocker. With a suggestion of trepidation in his voice, he continued the story. "Before there was even a sound, your grandpa knew. Alone in the woods at twilight sounds become something more than noise. The darkness provides cover and concealment. The big predators—bear, wolves, mountain lions—have the clear advantage as the time between discovering you're being hunted and an opportunity for you to escape becomes little more than nothin' at all. Your grandpa Joshia had been awakened to the promise as a young boy of only five years old. He understood the silent cues and he knew of nature's ways. That night, sitting alone in the cold, dark woods, he knew. What it was, he couldn't say. But he knew."

Thomas peered into his son's eyes, which had grown wide with wonder. He lowered his voice to continue with the story. "He cocked his head to listen more intently to the voices of the night. I remember him tellin' me that he said out loud, even though there was nothin' there 'cept the trees to hear the words, he said, 'This ain't right. Somethin' ain't right.'"

His papa said, "Ya know, son, snow cover magnifies sounds in the woods. And sounds channeled through frigid air reveal their intent to those who know how to listen." He stopped for a moment to look at his son to make sure that he understood these words.

Tyoga did.

"Well," his papa continued, "it started as just the faintest echo of crunching branches and leaves and then grew into the unmistakable sounds of a chase. Mocassined feet were pounding through the snow, landing hard on the frozen ground. Many feet. Moving fast. Following the deer path straight toward Grandpa's campsite.

"Grandpa stood up, threw off his buffalo robe, and began scooping snow onto the fire with both hands. He managed to pile enough snow to stop the rising wisps of smoke that would surely have given him away. He threw the buffalo robe around his shoulder and crouched down behind the hedgerow and waited."

Thomas stood up, stretched his back, and relit his pipe. This was the place in the story where he always paused.

Tyoga remembered that when he and his brother were very small children, the next part of the story scared them so thoroughly that neither one was able to sleep for the entire night.

His papa sat back down on the hearth and began again in a loud excited voice this time.

"The screams that accompanied the charging hoard sent chills up your grandpa's spine. Were they war cries? No. These were different. The screams were taunting—almost bemused. The warriors were chasing a kill—but one in which the end would surely be an agonizingly slow, deliberate, and tortured death. Grandpa peeked through the branches of the underbrush and what did he see?" he asked while looking at Tyoga. "He saw an Indian Brave staggering to keep his feet."

At this, his father stood up and pretended to stagger around Tyoga's rocker, clutching his side to fit in with the part of the story to come.

"This lone Indian was ahead of the mob, but not by much. They were closing fast. Grandpa Jo could see the Indian's bloody right hand holding the shaft of the arrow that pierced through his right side. The Indian veered from the deer path and headed directly toward the camp-site. He stopped short of stepping through the hedgerow and leaned against the walnut tree. Just at that moment, Grandpa sprung from the underbrush, clutched the Indian around the waist and dragged him into the shadows of his camp. He muffled the Indian's mouth with one hand and with the other held the brave firmly to the ground. I remember Grandpa telling me that he would never forget the look of panic in the bloody warrior's eyes. Exhausted by the chase and weak from loss of blood, the brave passed out in Grandpa's arms. Just then, the war party flew over the crest of the rise about fifty yards to the south. So what did Grandpa do? He grabbed his buffalo robe, covered the Indian with his own body, and threw the robe over the both of them. Only yards away he could feel the bloodthirsty war party streak past his campsite. Thundering feet and wild screams filled the air as the warriors streamed past the two of them. I'll never forget Grandpa's description; he said the warriors flowed past them like a 'torrent of muddy water loosed from the breach of a mighty earthen dam.'"

His papa paused only long enough to appreciate the mental pic-ture his father had painted with words. He smiled ever so slightly before continuing, "The Sioux warriors—they were Sioux, Grandpa said—were so caught up in the hunt that they didn't even notice that the tracks of the man they were chasing had completely vanished. Once they ran past the chestnut tree, any hope of picking up his tracks was all but lost.

"Now, Grandpa stayed under that buffalo robe with the Indian for a long time. The heat from their bodies kept them pretty warm, so he didn't get cold even though it had started to snow again."

Tyoga's father stopped talking again and fell silent. The story always got to him at this point. The courage of his father risking his own life to protect a stranger was testament to an internal strength of character that few Virginians would have been willing to match. That the man was a Native American from an unknown tribe who, in other circumstances, may have taken his scalp and left him in agony to bleed to death made the gesture all the more magnanimous.

Thomas took a deep breath and started again. "I remember your grandpa telling me in vivid detail his recollections of the time he spent under the buffalo robe with the Indian brave. He was surprised at how the Indian smelled, I recall. Even though he was covered with sweat from the long distance run, Grandpa said he smelled of tobacco, pine, and newly worked leather. His face was painted with red and black patterns and the bridge of his nose sported a long dark streak that expanded over each nostril and stopped at the crease of his cheeks. Crimson red extended from under each eye all the way up to his temples. Grandpa said that he could tell from the scars on his face that this was not the first time this man had been chased, and it certainly wasn't his first brush with death. This man had fought hard, often, and for most of his life. Each ear had been pierced in several places and was adorned with shells and beads. The right side of his head was cleanshaven. The long hair on the left side of his head was tied in a knot and had feathers and a bird's foot attached. Grandpa reckoned that the man was older than he, maybe in his mid-forties. He wasn't sure, you understand—so maybe he wasn't that old. Grandpa said that he remembered that the Indian's body was hard and muscular. He must have been a powerful man in his younger years. It was a good thing that he was so strong because he was hurt pretty bad. But your grandpa thought that if he could tend to his wounds quickly, he just might make it.

"Well, about another hour passed before he felt fairly certain that the war party wouldn't double back in search of the Indian. Grandpa peaked out from under the robe and saw that the sun was about to set. He knew that meant the temperature would be falling and fast. He threw the buffalo robe off and stood with the bloody warrior lying unconcious at his feet.

"In the pitch blackness of the freezing night, there was no choice but for Grandpa to re-start the fire. He knew that it was risky but both he and the wounded brave needed the fire for warmth and light and to clean the warriors's wounds.

"Papa knelt down next to the brave and saw that the arrow had entered from the back and exited about eight inches to the right, just above his belly button. Even though the wound had bled a lot, it appeared that the arrow had passed only through flesh. Grandpa reckoned that out because he could see the shaft of the arrow running along just under the skin. The feathered end of the arrow had been broken off. Grandpa figured that the Indian did it himself as he ran to escape the war party of Sioux. But he could see that the arrowhead and about 4 inches of the shaft were sticking out from the brave's belly. It would be easy for him to remove the arrow by giving it a good tug—an' better to do it while the Indian was still unconscious."

At this Tyoga's father got up again from his seat on the hearth and knelt down on the hardwood floor. Tyoga smiled because he remembered that even as a little boy, he would do exactly the same thing every time he told the story. He acted out the next scene in every detail.

"Grandpa grabbed the shaft of the arrow with this right hand— ya see?" He looked up to make sure that Tyoga was watching. Playing along, Tyoga stopped rocking and was sitting on the front edge of the rocker's seat. "To give himself some leverage and to steady the Indian's body against the force of the pull, Grandpa placed his left palm over the exit wound so that the shaft of the arrow protruded between his middle fingers." He slid his right index finger between the middle and ring finger of his left hand.

He looked up at Tyoga and continued, "He pulled fast, firm and with all his might. With a horrific scream that shattered the night, that Indian sat straight up just as the arrow shaft was freed. He reached out and grabbed Grandpa Jo around the neck with both hands and threw him to the ground. Granpa could see right off that the Indian was frightened, confused, and in terrible pain. He didn't know where he was, how he had gotten there or why this white man was kneeling over him holding a bloody arrow. But there was something more. And this was something that Grandpa Jo remembered to his dying day. Besides the fear and pain—he told me that the Indian's eyes seethed with a hatred that needed no words. He had a white man by the throat, and his instinct was to kill. Like an animal cornered in his own den, the Indian's reaction was to fight to the death to keep himself alive. Grandpa Jo had to act fast."

At this, Tyoga's father got up off of the floor and sat back down on the hearth. He grabbed the bandana that was in his right front pocket and mopped his brow. He was sweating as if he had lived the experience himself.

Tyoga sat back in the chair and began to rock slowly.

His father began again, "O-gi-na-ni-li." *(Friend)* "'O-gi-na-ni-li,' your grandpa said while poking his chest so hard with his finger that it made a thumping sound. He felt the Indian relax the choke hold he had on his neck just a bit. Now, Grandpa Jo didn't know a great deal of Tsalagi like you and me. But he did know a few commands, so he said to the Indian sittin' on top of him, 'Ha-le-wi-sta. *(Stop)* E-lo-wi-hi. *(Be still)* E-lo-wa-hi.' *(Be quiet)*

"Well, at hearing his own language, the Indian looked around and Grandpa Jo said that the adled look began to leave his eyes. He looked down at Grandpa's face and slowly released one hand from around his neck. The Indian didn't get up off of him, but sat back on his haunches—keeping Grandpa's body firmly pinned to the ground between his legs. He was bleeding badly again and when the pain got to be too much, he clutched his side and rolled off of Grandpa.

"Right away Grandpa got to his feet, stepped over to the fire and dipped his bandana into the water that he had boiling for coffee. He let it cool for a few seconds and then wrung it out. He knelt down next to the Indian who was in too much pain to protest, and placed the soothing warmth of the cloth on the bleeding wound.

"Well, that Indian lay there for a long while and let Grandpa tend to his wound. After awhile he picked his head up off of the ground and looked up into your grandpa's face. Grandpa smiled and pointed to himself and repeated, 'O-gi-na-ni-li. Joshia. O-gi-na-ni-li.'

The Indian propped himself up on his elbow, pointed to himself and said, 'Openchanecanough.' He looked down at his wound, and then back at your grandpa.

"An' I'll never forget your grandpa tellin' me this. He said that the Indian looked away from him and said in almost a whispered voice that had no emotion in it all, 'O-gi-na-ni-li.' *(Friend)*"

Tyoga's father stood up, moved a chair from the table and sat next to his son to stare into the flames of the fire. After a long silence, he added, "Five days after Grandpa had left the cabin to go hunting, your grandma heard a dull thud against the cabin door that startled her awake. She jumped up, ran to the door, and pulled it open. Your Grandpa Jo fell at her feet like a sack of grain. Wrapped in his arms under the protection of the buffalo robe was the near lifeless body of Openchanecanough, the brother of the Chief of the Powhatan nation. Your gandpa carried him through the back county for two days to reach the front door of that tiny cabin nestled in the grove of trees along the banks of the James. And when Grandpa fell through the door with that Indian wrapped in his arms, he saved the lives of generations of Weathersbys to come."

He turned and looked at his son and said, "You wouldn't be sittin' here with me if it hadn't been for your grandpa's wisdom, courage and strength. All of that—and more—is coursing through your veins. You're born of fearless stock, boy."

The story was over. The two sat in silence, wrapped in the warm glow of the fire for a very long time.

By March of 1622, the injured Powhatan brave that fell through the cabin door wrapped in Joshia's arms had become Chief of the Powhatan nation. The man that Rebecca reclaimed from death and nursed back to health came to realize, just as his brother, Powhatan, had before his death, that the Englishmen had settled in Jamestown to do more than trade with the Indians. Openchanecanough understood that nothing short of complete domination of his people, and possession of their lands would satisfy the invading force.

In defense of his land, people, and way of life, Openchanecanough carried out a well-orchestrated attack on all English settlements. In a highly coordinated series of attacks, the Indians killed 347 settlers, one fourth of all of the English colonists in the New World.

Wolstenholmes Towne was one of the hardest hit settlements. The attackers killed men, women, children, and livestock. They destroyed crops and burned every home, except one. The Weathersby's log and earthen cabin nestled in the shallow glade along the fresh water run on the banks of the James River was left untouched.

When Openchanecanough realized that his plan to wipe out all of the settlers in his tribal lands had failed, he knew that the price to be paid at the hands of the white eyes would be devastatingly cruel. They would not fight alone. Their bitter enemies in the Sioux nation would be paid to fight with the English to punish the Powhatans, and the English would have no control over the renegade Sioux after the battles began.

The Weathersby family, who had nursed him back to health, had no chance of being spared an agonizing death at the hands of bloodthirsty Sioux warriors. He made hasty arrangements to save their lives.

The Ani-Unwiya had not participated in the Powhatan raids on the settlers, so their villages would be spared in the brutal battles of retribution that were but weeks away. In the dark of night, a party of Powhatans moved Joshia and Rebecca Weathersby and their children three days to the west to the Amansoquath village where they would be safe from the genocidal attacks that were sure to come.

Openchanecanough would never see the Weathersbys again. A hard man who ruled with an iron fist and meted out justice with merciless cruelty had repaid the debt he owed to Joshia and Rebecca Weathersby. He had no way of knowing that their bloodline would one day live among his decendents and save their lands from the grasp of a king.

Part Two

1696

The Power and The Promise

H.L. Grandin

Chapter 12

Mount Rag

Several years after the battle on the escarpment, Tes Qua's leg had healed well enough for him to walk again. But he was still many months away from being able to accompany Tyoga on his overnight trips into the backwoods, or his week-long forays to distant mountaintops and hidden valleys deep within the Shenandoah. In his place, Sunlei became Tyoga's constant companion.

It was a glorious fall day.

With a fractious shag of glorious yellow-gold, the sugar maples blanketed the gentle slopes of the foothills leading to the rocky summit of Old Mount Rag. Sugar maple gold yielded to matted amber hues at the intersection of foothill and mountain. The edges of the lower elevations burned with a brilliant coyfish orange before soaring to the heights where the foliage surrendered to a Georgia clay red.

Tyoga and Sunlei were on their second day of a three-day journey to visit with Sunlei's mother's sister, Sky Dove, who lived with the Mountain Creek Clan of Ani-Unwiya Cherokee. Sky Dove had been given to the son of the chief of the Mountain Creek Clan after the confederation council of 1666. Their union was a marriage of political convenience that united the clan in a familial bond to guarantee cooperation in times of peace, trade in times of need, and unquestioned loyalty in times of war. The practice was an age-old custom that reconciled the heartache of loveless unions by the stability and peace that served the greater good.

Sunlei and Tyoga were both anxious to get to the Mountain Creek village. Her cousins, Walks Alone and Night Sky, were favorite childhood friends, and had grown very close with Sunlei, Tes Qua, and Tyoga over the years. Oftentimes, after arriving at Mountain Creek, Tyoga, Tes Qua, and Walks Alone would spend the entire week in the freedom of the mountains, while Sunlei visited with Sky Dove and Night Sky in the comfort of their lodge. The boys had many wonderful memories of camping, fishing, and hunting together. They would miss not having Tes Qua there with them to enjoy this visit.

Tyoga and Sunlei paused at one of the many falls cascading from the higher elevations. As the water flowed over the polished surface of an enormous slab of granite, it was fractioned into a lacey curtain by interrupting lichens, moss, and glassy-edged quartz.

Sunlei knelt at Tyoga's feet and cupped her hand to bring the cool mountain water to her lips. Her eyes darted from side to side to check the underbrush on the rise to the East as she drank from her hands.

Tyoga knew that she was uneasy. He understood why.

"Ty," she said in a hesitant whisper.

He did not answer.

"I feel … something. I don't know …" She tried to give voice to her trepidation.

Tyoga looked around and smiled when he knelt down in the stream next to her. He reached his cupped hand into the coursing water to get a drink and noticed the water skimmers skating across the surface.

The odd little bugs darted about in a random—yet determined—display of senseless frenzy while relying with absolute certitude upon forces about which they had no knowledge to keep them afloat—and alive. Chaotically scurrying about on spindly oar-legs, some of the water-walkers desperately struggled against the current to gain access to the serenity of a calm, quiet eddy where they could skate and float and rest. Some had won their hard fought goal. They took no notice of their brothers' plight.

Tyoga wondered if the entrance to the tranquil haven was purely serendipitous or by design.

"Ty, did you hear me?" Sunlei repeated with a hint of the 'you never listen to me' tone purchased in the currency of a secure and devoted relationship.

"I heard you, Sunlei," he replied. "It's okay. We're safe."

"Then you feel it, too? But what is it? What is here with us?" She continued to look around.

He splashed his face with water, stood up, and peered up over at the ridge. Glancing down at his moccasins, he rolled some stones with his toe. "I see him all the time. He's never far. At first, I'd catch a glimpse of a gray and white shadow passing real fast through the brush. When I didn't see the shadows I'd hear him walking off the trail along side of me. It scared me the first time I saw him since that night. Wasn't sure what to make of it. I didn't know what he wanted." He wiped the water from his face with his shirt.

Sunlei moved closer and put her arm around his waist. Cocking her head, she looked up at him. Noticing the jagged scar on his left bicep from the battle with the wolves, she caught herself and quickly looked away. It wasn't the Indian way for a woman to dwell upon a brave's wounds. While Indian Braves could—and would—touch and examine with great interest, and near jealousy, the battle scars warn as badges of courage by their owner, a woman looking at a war wound with pity or concern was a sign of deep disrespect.

In the quiet of the moment, Sunlei took stock of the young warrior standing by her side. He was a remarkable young man, and she was proud to be with him—in him. She understood his silence, and revered his need for contemplation. It was in the quiet that the spirits spoke to him. It was only in solitude that his great medicine was revealed.

The People spoke of him as if he had changed after that night on the escarpment. She didn't think so. Sometimes, there were sides to him that he saved for himself—and for her.

They were quiet things. Little things. Things upon which others placed no value at all. Perhaps there was none to be found except in the eyes of Tyoga Weathersby. The reticence of water. The sigh of the clouds. The canvas that is the sky. The impossible colors of sunset. The uselessness of envy. The waste of worry. The gift of courage and fear. The scourge of cowardice. The shame of want. These things did not matter to others. That they existed was enough for most. But to Tyoga, their worth was in the pondering. Their value was in their truth.

Her eyes welled with tears when she thought of the great joy these gifts brought to her life. As is the want of all humankind, the glow of the glorious connection, was suddenly shattered by the demonic thoughts that linger beneath the protective veneer waiting for the slightest breech to impose their irrational sabotage.

The 'what if's' that so rarely come to pass shattered her delight.

Closing her eyes, she allowed the gut-wrenching horrors constructed on the fragile nothingness of scenarios imagined to hijack the moment's true joy.

What if he should fall out of love with me and just leave me one day?

A wave of nausea built in her belly. She swallowed hard.

What would happen to me if circumstance or situation prevented us from being together? Her hands grew cold and numb. She shook them slightly to reverse the unpleasant sensation.

A tear streamed down her cheek. She wiped it away before it reached her lips. She was certain that she loved him beyond the power of words to express.

Tyoga said, "Sometimes at night, when I'm alone in the woods, cooking my supper or lying down for the night, I hear him breathing just beyond the light of the fire. I hear him lie down—real close to me. I sometimes think that I can reach out and touch him—he's so close. The very first time I heard him rustling around my campsite, I stayed awake all night just waitin' to see what he was going to do. He looked at me for a good long while. After some time he yawned, laid down, closed his eyes and went to sleep." He chuckled. "I think I bored him to sleep."

Tyoga reached around and took hold of the hand that Sunlei had resting on his hip. Still holding her hand, he wrapped his arm around her so that their hands came to rest in the small of her back. He drew her near. "He doesn't show himself when I'm with Little Bull or Stands With Rock. He never shows himself when others are with me. But when it is just him and me, well, we get along pretty fair together."

He gazed down into her beautiful black eyes to see if she understood what he had been saying. Her eyes were calm, and her hand was holding his gently. She understood. "Yeah. I'm not exactly sure what he's doing hangin' around, but I know that I don't have to be afraid when he's near. Kind of nice knowin' he's close. I suspect that he'd let me know if there's somethin' ain't right."

After letting go of her hand, he took off his moccasin and shook it to dislodge a pebble.

"Come on. We better get moving. Gonna git dark soon. If we move fast, we can make camp on the top rock. Beautiful up there. A-he-na."

The trip to the summit of old Mount Rag would take them almost three hours.

Traversing a trail thousands of years in the making, they followed a path that had been defined by the millions of mocassined feet before theirs. The trail followed the natural contours of the land. In places along the route, it would meander around enormous granite monoliths jutting up from the forest floor like sentinels stationed at the palace gates. In other spots, the trail seemed all but lost in a tangle of matted roots. Ancient trees dispatched sinewy tentacles from just below the surface to ensnare rocks in a living prison. Trapped for eternity, the granite prisoners proved worthy adversaries as a millenia of twisted ankles and bloody toes would surely attest.

The trail periodically surrendered to the urgency of mountain runs that required a barefoot balancing act to gain the other side, or the resignation of making the rest of the trek in the discomfort of soaking leather moccasins. At more forgiving fords, the creeks were willing to yield no more than dry stone tops. They climbed a series of flat boulder stairs that led them through a narrow tunnel lined with slime. Framed by a triangular sculpture of enormous granite stellae, it exited onto a narrow, moss-covered ledge that provided an unparalleled view of the Blue Ridge Mountains to the south.

They passed under sharp-edged overhangs, curtained with ivy, moss, and ferns where the trail narrowed dangerously close to precipitous edges. In other places where the cost of distance and time trumped ease of travel, the path ascended steep vertical walls.

Even though Sunlei was a strong, seasoned traveler, the difficult vertical inclines required the pair to stop to rest every ten steps.

The mountain rewarded those strong enough to make the journey to the top where the trail would break into Greenwald's Overlook, a plateau of lichen encrusted rock from which the entire Shennandoah Valley could be seen at a glance. From the overlook, it was only another twenty minutes through Hanzel's Pass to the top of Mount Rag, fresh water, a warm fire, food, and rest.

The two reached the ragged summit rocks before sunset.

One of the highest points in the Appalachian Mountains, the top of Mount Rag is a rocky outcropping, crowned with a spherical boulder that the Cherokees and others used for centuries as a prayer rock—or odalvi. The Native Americans revered the heights for their proximity to the gods and for the unfettered view of the land—from horizon to horizon, and thousands of feet below.

For all of time, Shaman and Medicine Men brought offerings to Summit Rock on behalf of the People. They prayed for the ground to be fruitful, game to be plentiful, and peace to reign over the land. The geography of Summit Rock had a great deal to do with its stature as a blessed place from which the holy men prayed.

The concept of "oneness" is central to Native American beliefs. They considered themselves to be children of the universe—not separate, but a part of the divinity of being. The universe mirrored the People, and the People filled that universe with the innate and unique gifts of every other person, animal, plant, and thing given to their use by the great spirits. To separate or account for themselves in terms that set them apart from the natural world was a concept foreign to the Ani-Unwiya. They considered themselves a divine creation no less miraculous than the stars in the sky or the gift of the rising sun. To be closer to that divinity on Summit Rock was an occasion that required respect and reverence.

They were camping at a holy place. Tyoga and Sunlei would treat it with respect.

From each direction of the compass, except the North, three trails converged at the top of Mount Rag. The summit outcropping emerged abruptly from thick stands of pine, birch, and oak, which provided plenty of firewood. Scruffy blueberry bushes, heavy with the sweet fall fruit, blanketed the ground with a carpet of thorny woody branches. The bushes edged the summit trails with clearly defined borders, their dense growth discouraging veering from the path. The tired travelers kept a close look out for the numerous black bears that liked to gorge them-selves on the calorie rich berries to fatten up before the winter snows.

Tyoga started a fire using pine needles and desiccated cones for kindling, then collected enough firewood to keep them warm and safe through the cold autumn night. Sunlei opened her de-ga-lo-di, which held their provisions, and spread a deer hide on the ground in front of the fire. Deer jerky and a mash of dried beans and corn would serve them well for the evening meal. She set the foodstuffs out on the hide, and then went back down the trail to pick some sweet blueberries.

The beginnings of a stream percolated up through the rocks and bubbled into a tiny clear pool a little ways down the trail that went to the west. Kneeling down, Tyoga filled their travelling gourd with the mountain water. His eyes wandered to the lip of a pool and he watched the first hesitant drops of water breach the wall to begin the journey to the sea. His focus silenced the forest around him and allowed him to open his mind to watch and listen.

Once over the lip of the pool the drops of water disappeared into a swampy patch of mud and moss, decaying leaves, and loamy peat. The lost drops emerged out of the ooze by adhering to the edges of a decaying branch. As if joining hands in a more determined march, the drops spilled into a pool of more resolute structure and function. Tiny traces of water of similar birth poured into the same pool from all directions. The trunk of a sapling elm dammed the down-slope edge of the pool. The water bubbled over the lip of the dam in a frothy curtain that spit and spewed in a joyous celebration of birth. The trace would grow into a rivulet. The rivulet would be joined by others downstream, and together they would form the Rapidan and the Rappahanock—and finally the Chesapeake Bay.

Slowly, Tyoga rose to his feet, threw the filled gourd over his shoul-der, and headed back up to their mountain top camp. Recognizing the gift that he had been given, he became lost in thought about what the promise had revealed as he made the climb up to the peak.

A single drop of water—like a man alone—is lost in the swampy mire until hope is found in the company of others of its kind. Working together, combining strengths, resting to regain momentum, and begin ning the journey anew was the course set for the water even before it emerged from the spring to begin its journey to the sea.

What does the message mean for me and my life? What am I to take away from these precious moments at the spring? Why was I permitted to see, but not given the gift of understanding? Why am I, like the drops of water, powerless to change my course?

He wondered at the aloneness that seemed to define him.

Cresting the last rise in the trail, their summit rock campsite came into view. His heart skipped a beat at the realization that he wasn't really alone—ever.

Sitting on the deer hide, Sunlei was tending the fire and preparing their evening meal. The sun was setting to the West and, like a gossamer orb bowing in approval, the shadow of the summit rock was rapidly enveloping their campsite. In the crisp autumn air, the sun danced off of Sunlei's raven mane with an almost blinding brilliance. Curled up on the deerskin hide, her bronze legs to one side, she reached around and placed both tiny hands in the small of her back. She arched her back like a stretching kitten, threw her shoulders back and tilted her face to feel the warmth of the setting sun kiss her delicate lips good night. Her shadow poured over the rocks in sensual undulations running from the course of the setting sun.

Stunning, she took his breath away

It was no wonder at all that the Chiefs of the tribes from the Great Lakes to Georgia had tried in vain to broker a deal with Nine Moons for his daughter's hand in marriage to their first born sons. That no union had been forged with one of the propsective suitors was not for lack of trying by Nine Moons. Sunlei was adamant and would not be swayed. She would not be given as chattle to one she did not—and could never—love. Her heart, her future, and that of her children was with Tyoga.

Tyoga understood that Sunlei was prized by the Indian nations for more than her beauty, and that her continued rejection of powerful suitors may one day set the stage for taking by force that which they could not obtain in trade.

The temperature dropped rapidly as the sun set, and Tyoga stoked the fire into a roaring blaze. Enjoying the astonishing view of the heavens, they wrapped themselves in a single blanket to share their body heat before the fire.

There was no moon, and the stars lit up the night sky with a brilliance untarnished by the natural world. They pointed out the constellations—the same stellar patterns described for millenia by the Babylonians, the Aztec, and the Egyptians—and retold the stories they had heard dozens of times while gathered around the fire in the village's long lodge. They wondered at the clearness of the night when the bowl of the big dipper became filled with so many stars that its outline was lost in the celestial bounty.

In the hollows below, two owls teased with gentle enticements of the carnal pleasures to be had just a short glide away.

Sunlei rested her head on Tyoga's shoulder. She was content—and tired—and at peace.

Tyoga took her face in his hands and looked deep into her eyes. Before he had a chance to say a word, Sunlei threw her arms around his neck and hungrily drew his lips to her own. They kissed long and hard with an animal passion that had been caged for far too long. Sunlei's tears of joy salted their kisses with an acrid tinge that electrified their tongues and prepared them in other ways for what was to come.

They had saved themselves for one another far beyond the cultural norms of the Cherokee way. Many of Sunlei's friends were spoken for, promised, or married. Any of three understandings was license enough for couples to consummate the arrangements.

That Tyoga had not been more sexually demanding with Sunlei was a subject discussed around many an Uni-Unwiya lodge fire. But there was an understanding among the Cherokee that their ways were not always shared with the white world; moreover ever since Tyoga's battle with the Runion wolves, he was allowed a degree of respect that would not permit ridicule of any kind.

Sunlei got up, threw one leg over Tyoga's crossed legs, and straddled him where he sat on the deerskin mat. She kissed his lips, his cheeks, his forehead and his neck, but quickly returned to his mouth where their tongues could explore the mysteries of their desire. Slowly unlacing his deerskin frock, she pulled it over his head, and tossed it to the side. She stood upright and lifted her doeskin tunic to her thighs. Swaying seductively, she reached down and grabbed the hem to pull it over her head, but stopped and let it fall back into place when she heard the rustling in the underbrush.

Sunlei wasn't a skittish camper by any means. Used to the sounds of the night, she was as comfortable sleeping in the open air surrounded by the old growth forest as in her father's lodge. Being a seasoned Appalachian traveler, she too recognized the rhythms of the night. The danger from a step carefully placed to maintain cover concealed a threat more grave than that betrayed by the errant snap of a dried pine branch.

"Ty," she said with a whispered urgency.

"Yeah, I heard it. Seems we ain't alone up here," he replied in a conversational tone incongruent with her level of concern.

She knelt back down next to Tyoga and he drew her near. Pulling a blanket around her shoulders, she nestled herself close to Tyoga's chest. They listened quietly—not moving—barely breathing. A few yards away, behind a boulder, they heard three steps, lithely placed, seemingly meant to avoid disturbance rather than conceal presence, followed by the clumsy placement of a fourth step that slid into place rather than set.

Sunlei felt Tyoga's body relax. She saw the tension in the set of his jaw disappear.

He had his arm around her and he shook her gently. "Don't be afraid, Little One. Wahaya is here with us."

She looked around hestitantly. "Where is he, Ty? Close?"

Tyoga flicked his chin in the direction of boulder and said, "He's over there. Quiet now. He don't mean no harm."

Carried upon the gentle updrafts from the south, the call of a lone wolf, filled their campsite with its doleful petition. It was a long, mournful call. Pleading. Passive. Comforting in its solitude. A second wolf answered from the northwest. The cry was the same tone, pitch, and duration. It was somehow a reassuring sound—not unlike the midnight watchman's cry of "All's well."

As the cries collided and echoed off of the granite parapets and along the valley streams below, Tyoga felt Sunlei relax in his arms. She understood.

"Ty, what do you think he wants? What is he going to do?"

"I don't know what he wants," he replied. "But he won't hurt us. I know he won't hurt us."

Sitting on the deerhide with her legs crossed, Sunlei thought about his assessment of the wolf's presence. After several minutes she said with some measure of authority, "Ty, chase him away. I want you to chase him away from here. I don't want him here with us tonight."

Reaching across her, Tyoga pulled a strip of deer jerky from their knapsack. "No, Sunlei. I won't chase my brother away. He will keep his distance and guard us while we sleep. Funny though—" Knowing that her natural curiosity wouldn't allow her not to challenge the open ended pause, he stopped.

"Funny? What's funny?"

"He doesn't get this close when I have someone with me. He usually stays far enough away to keep out of sight."

Sunlei said, "Well if he is going to stay, you make him stay behind that rock." She noticed the little smile begin to brighten up his eyes in that mischievous way that she found so endearing. She asked more than demanded this time, "Will he stay behind the rock?"

"It's not up to me, Sunlei," Tyoga said. "He goes his own way. He's never shown himself to anyone but me. Are you afraid?"

"No. I was, but I don't think that I am now. I feel … safe."

"Shhh. Look."

From out of the blackness, the wolf's head and front legs rounded the boulder. He stepped into the light of the fire. The silver hairs that punctuated his thick winter fur reflected the firelight, and created an effervescent radiance that gave his body an other-worldly glow. He held his head high and erect. His stance was commanding; like an emperor dethroned, he would give no orders. His eyes were brilliantly alive, but deferential. They flashed with a reserved confidence in an as of yet untested ally. He sniffed the air and looked to the north.

He fixed his eyes on Sunlei.

His stare was so intense and purposeful that she gasped.

Tyoga's armed tightened around her shoulders. "It's okay."

The wolf focused his stare from Sunlei to Tyoga.

"O-si-yo, Wahaya." *(Hello, wolf)* "O-sti-nu-ga-wi. As-shi-no." *(You can stay. Sit down.)*

The wolf cocked his head, and looked back toward Sunlei. He took two careful steps toward them, and his whole body emerged from behind the rock. Though battered and slightly lame, he was still a magnificent creature.

Sunlei stared in disbelief at his majesty. "Ty," she said with a tone of awe in her voice. "I had no idea. How did you …"

"Shhh. Let him be. Let's let him be. He's never shown himself to anyone but me before. He's got somethin' in mind. Let's just let him be a minute."

The night was completely still. The night birds stayed their nervous chatter. The crickets quelled their incessant buzz. The fire stopped spitting ash. Nothing moved.

Tyoga's eyes lit with the spark of an idea. "Sunlei, I'm gonna take the blanket off of us. Don't move. Just sit still. Let's let him get a good look at us."

"Ha-wa," she replied.

The wolf tensed and stepped back when Tyoga slowly removed the blanket from around them. "It's okay, Ditlihi. It's only us."

Emboldened by the wolf holding his ground, Sunlei sat up on her knees and leaned toward the tentative animal. Reversing his slow retreat, he stepped closer to the fire. He sniffed the air again, and sat down two steps away from them.

Tyoga wrapped the blanket around the two of them. "He's okay, Little One." He picked up a stick and stirred the fire into a gentle, hot burn.

The wolf stood up, circled twice, and then stopped to face the trail leading up to summit rock from the south. His ears piqued and he sniffed the air. The scent flared his nostrils, and his eyes burned with the sensation of the night. Nervous, anxious, and filled with life, he circled once more and lay down in the direction of the pungent signals that would not let him rest. He turned his massive head to look at them one more time before placing it on his forepaws. He did not close his eyes.

Tyoga and Sunlei turned their eyes skyward to gaze up at the stars.

"A-silo, gitsi." She got up and walked into the woods beyond the fire's light.

Tyoga watched her emerge from the woods.

The moonlight danced off of her naked breasts. Her skin glowed in the light of the fire.

He had prepared their bed and was lying on his back covered with a soft black bearskin blanket.

Completely at ease with her nakedness, she knelt beside him and giggled when she lifted the blanket to see that he too was naked, and very much ready to forge the bond of a committed couple.

It was well after midnight before they fell asleep in each other's arms.

The Shawnee warriors camped on the overlook down the south trail were still wide awake.

Chapter 13

The Spirit Dog

Tyoga awakened to the first drops of rain and the steel gray skies of a gloomy Appalachian morning. Nestled in the rocky crags of Summit Rock, they had been protected from the light drizzle that preceded the storm. Without the brilliant sunshine that usually flooded the mountain peaks to wake them at dawn, they had slept later than was their usual custom.

Sunlei was startled awake by Tyoga's hand covering her mouth. Bringing a finger to his lips, he indicated for her to be quiet. She heard the voices, too. So muffled at first that they were unable to discern any words. As the voices grew louder, they looked at each other with eyes wide with fright. The voices were speaking an Algonquin dialect that while unfamiliar to them both, conveyed a meaning that they clearly understood. Shawnee. Tyoga did not have to explain what it would mean if they were found alone on the summit of Mount Rag by a Shawnee hunting party.

It would be horrible. Especially for Sunlei.

The Shawnee had been driven out of the upper Ohio valley by the Iroquois in the 1660s. The Cherokee allowed one clan of the Shawnee to settle in South Carolina to serve as a buffer between them and the Catawba tribe with whom they had been feuding over a political rebuke. Another Shawnee clan was permitted to locate in Tennessee to serve a similar purpose with the Chickasaw. But the Iroquois were fierce warriors and extremely protective of their lands. The transgression that caused them to chase the Shawnee from neighboring territory had never been forgiven, and the Iroquois pursued the Shawnee deep into Cherokee territory. The raids were brutal and cruel. Crops and lodges were destroyed, men and boys were tortured and killed, and the women and girls were taken by the Iroquois to serve as slaves and concubines.

Because the raids occurred on Cherokee lands, the Amansoquath were quickly drawn into the skirmishes with the Iroquois. Many Cherokee braves died fighting side by side with the Shawnee against the marauding tribe from the north. The bonds of battle secured the peace and friendship between the Shawnee and the Cherokee nations for years.

In the late 1680s, there was fierce competition between the French and the English for vast tracts of land in the New World. Bribery and treachery were common tools of diplomacy in the claiming of lands. Neither the French nor the English were above pitting tribe against tribe if the outcome suited their purpose.

In the early 1690s, the Shawnee aligned themselves with the British, and the treaties struck between them were codified with the exchange of money, whiskey, and guns. When commodities for which the English were willing to trade began to lose their caché, the Shawnee devised a plan to acquire a new line of goods for which they were certain the English would gladly trade, Indian women.

In 1692, while the Cherokee braves of Tessuntee were away on a winter hunting trip, a rogue party of Shawnee dog soldiers raided the village, killed the male children, and captured the women and girls as slaves to trade with the English. The cowardly raid on the unprotected village destroyed any trust or friendship that existed between the Cherokee and the Shawnee. From that day on, the Shawnee took their place alongside the Iroquois as the sworn enemies of the Cherokee nation.

When Tyoga was certain that the voices he heard were Shawnee, he was frantic to get off the summit of Mount Rag. He had good reason to flee in haste. The Shawnee were fierce warriors, whose cruelty in battle was legendary. War parties were known to fillet captured warriors alive, beginning with their thighs. Their adversaries would die in agony as they watched their captors cook their flesh and dine on it for their evening

meals. Those prisoners who endured the savage torture without screaming were rewarded with a quick death after the meal by having their
throats cut. Those who could not contain their suffering were left alive—
limbs stripped of meat down to the bone—to suffer for hours on end.

While Tyoga hurriedly kicked sand and dirt on the dying embers in
the fire pit, Sunlei put on her doeskin tunic and boots, and gathered up
their blankets and supplies.

When she was getting to her feet, her hand went to her chest to grasp
the sacred amulet she wore around her neck. Her eyes were wide with
despair when she looked up at him and whispered, "My amulet. Ty, it's
gone. I took it off last night when we—I can't leave this place without
my amulet." The totems contained in Sunlei's amulet pouch were powerful medicine. The objects had been given to her at milestones in her life
and they were imbued with the power to protect and guide her through
life's journey. To leave without it was unthinkable.

Tyoga understood its importance. "Where could it be?"

On her hands and knees, she searched the ground next to where she
had slept. "It has to be right here. Ty, help me look. Quickly!" She felt
his hand on her shoulder. She looked up into his eyes and he motioned
for her to look down at the ground. The prints of the commander were
clearly stamped into the wet sand next to where she had been sleeping.
"Ty, the wolf?"

The voices and laughter of the Shawnee braves were getting louder.
They were rapidly making their way to Summit Rock. Unaware of the
prize that awaited them at the summit, they approached the campsite
with casual indifference. They were but moments away.

Leaving all of their supplies behind, Tyoga snatched Sunlei by the
wrist and raced from the summit with reckless abandon. They had not
gotten a hundred yards down the mountain when they heard the voices
of the Shawnee braves replaced with bloodthirsty war cries.

Discovered, they ran for their lives.

The light drizzle to which they had awakened was but the harbinger
of a fierce storm moving in from the west. As the shower turned into
a steady rain, Tyoga could tell that the storm's intensity was growing
rapidly.

In the mountains, gullies and hollows serve as conduits to channel the force of colliding air masses into winds of unimaginable power. The currents build from the valleys below to pick up speed as atmospheric pressures crush the massive volume of air against the upward slopes of the mountainside. Like tributaries of a mighty river adding their contents to the downstream flow, each ravine contributes its volume in turn until the tons of pressure force the wind up and over the mountain peaks in a thunderous roar.

From the higher elevations, Tyoga could hear the roar begin miles away and thousands of feet below as a sound akin to that of muffled canon fire. They both felt the need to pop their ears. With the pressures bearing down from miles up in the atmosphere, Mount Rag felt like a mountain thousands of feet taller.

When he heard the first torrent begin its crescendo from below, Tyoga knew that they were only minutes away from being immersed in a power so violent that it would be impossible for them to continue their frantic charge down the mountain. The deafening roar that would engulf them would be so intense that they wouldn't be able to hear one another no matter how loudly they screamed.

The Shawnee would face the same challenges.

With the storm's help—Tyoga and Sunlei would have a chance. With the wind whipping the trees in violent convulsions to distort direction and distance, and the deafening roar blocking out the sound that gives away prey, they had the cover necessary to make an escape.

But Tyoga would have to make a bold and daring move.

The terrain on either side of the trail was rocky, muddy, and terribly steep. If they stayed on the trail, the Shawnee warriors would be sure to overtake them. They would make him watch while they raped and ravaged Sunlei before they tortured him to death. It was too horrific to even contemplate.

Leaving the trail to brave the naked raw terrain of the mountainside was a risk that he was willing to take.

They galloped another two hundred yards down the trail, and with an animal-like bound—pulling Sunlei like a soaking blanket—Tyoga dove into the forest to leave the trail behind them.

The wind let out a thundering roar as it raced toward them at incredible speed.

Jumping over a downed giant pine, he tucked Sunlei between the ground and the trunk of the tree just as the first blast of wind hit the summit. Like buffalo stampeding over the western plains, the earth shook when the force of the raging wind crushed the tops of thirty-foot saplings to the ground. The explosive fury of massive century old trees cracking in two added a lightening bolt dimension to the violence of the storm. Dirt and leaves filled the air with a blinding shrapnel that disoriented and confused.

Tyoga heard the party of Shawnee shouting while trying desperately to keep track of each other and refocus the chase. He raised his head above the trunk of the enormous pine to see where the braves were on the trail. Out of the corner of his eye, he caught a flash in the underbrush. It bound straight up the side of the mountain at a speed that rivaled the wind.

He grabbed Sunlei by both arms and screamed, "Sunlei, grab my shirt. Don't let go no matter what happens. Just hang on. We're gonna move fast. We're goin' straight down this mountain."

She clutched the tail of his shirt and he took off down the mountain.

Another salvo started to build in the valley. As the roar increased, growing louder and louder as it flowed up the mountain slopes, he did not stop to hunker down to take the blast. They had to keep moving.

The Shawnee were right behind.

Before the blast exploded overhead, they heard a horrifying scream above and behind them. The roar of the wind drowned it out.

Unsure of what to make of the distant cry, they paused for just a moment to look into each other's eyes before continuing the run for their lives.

While walking speed is increased when traveling down a mountain trail, the degree of difficulty in traversing the terrain isn't diminished in the least. Climbing down uses different muscles than climbing up, and those used going down aren't nearly as strong.

Blinded by the wind and the rain, and with no trail to point the way, Sunlei and Tyoga tripped and slid their way down the treacherous slopes. They stumbled over downed trees, roots jutting out from the black wet loam, and rocks greased with a thin film of mossy slime. The branches whipping in the wind lacerated their faces and arms, and their hands were bloodied by the bark of trees and jagged rocky outcroppings they used to brace themselves while sliding toward the valley below.

Running more on instinct than visual cues, Tyoga kept moving down. Down.

Sunlei held tight to his shirt. Wherever he could, he would hoist her over obstacles too large for her to handle on her own. Yet, she was strong and held her own.

In another hundred yards, they would be far enough down the slope so that the wind would no longer explode overhead. Once the wind subsided, he would be able to listen. Since hearing the terrifying screams, he had lost track of the Shawnee. He didn't know if they were still following them.

He stopped long enough to turn around and look at Sunlei. Her eyes were frantic and she was breathing hard. He knew that she would not complain, and would do nothing to slow them down, but she couldn't go on much longer.

Not hearing anyone behind them, and with the fierceness of the storm abating, he sat her down on a rock to rest. In the fog and haze that had descended upon the mountain, he gently touched his forehead to hers.

"Are they still following us?" she asked in between gasps for air.

"I don't know." He was breathing equally hard. "I don't know how they could track us in this storm."

"Ty, what will happen if they catch us? We can't let them catch us, Ty. They're Shawnee. You know what that means."

"I know. I know, Sunlei. Just be quiet now. Let me think."

Sunlei could tell that he was worried, and she understood his shortness with her.

They remained silent in the driving rain, the buffeting wind, the cold and the fog.

They were getting their breath and bearings when they heard the sound of someone—or something—stumbling through the brush. Whatever, or whoever, was still following them was moving very slowly. Unsteady. Stumbling. It wasn't clear which direction the person, or animal, was headed. Whatever was there—out of sight in the woods—was too close for them to be able to make another run down the mountain without being overtaken.

Tyoga gently lifted Sunlei from the rock upon which she was perched and nestled her down to the forest floor. He put his finger to his lips. "Stay here. Don't move."

"No, Ty. Don't go." She begged while holding onto his forearm with her trembling, cold hands. "You don't know how many are out there, or where they are, or if they are setting a trap. Ty, what if? Don't leave me. Promise you won't leave me here."

He took her face into his mighty hands, gently brushed the wisps of soaking hair from her eyes, and calmly said, "Sunlei, look into my eyes."

As she did, she saw the gentle hazel green dissolve away. The amber glow began to build from deep within the recesses of his eyes. The gentleness was replaced with focus, and resolve and glassy-eyed sting.

The pitch of his voice had deepened ever so slightly when he said, "I'll be back for you. Don't move."

She managed a smile and a nod. He would be back.

Tyoga had placed her beside and behind the rock upon which she had been sitting. Her back was pressed uncomfortably against the trunk of a downed oak tree, and her neck was bent awkwardly so that her chin was close to her chest. She was soaked from the rain, cut and bruised from their run down the mountainside, and shivering uncontrollably from the cold—and from the terror of their ordeal.

Tyoga had left her alone.

She did not know what awaited him back up the trial, but he would return for her—if he could.

She thought it peculiar that at that moment she would think about the sounds of her family as they gathered around the warmth of the fire pit in their cozy, comfortable lodge. She longed to hear her mother's voice. True Moon's voice was soft, reassuring, and filled with love and patience. Sunlei was a lot like her mother.

They didn't look like mother and daughter. Sunlei's height and shape set her apart from nearly every other girl in the tribe. But her smile was the same.

So were their eyes. Her mother's eyes were expressive and candid. They revealed her emotions without pretense or apology. Sunlei's eyes were more subtle in what they revealed. They spoke to those whom she permitted to hear. They told Tyoga all that he needed to know when he left her on the forest floor.

Slowly, Tyoga started to make his way back up the mountainside. The slope was incredibly steep and he had to pull himself up by grabbing on to trees and branches while he moved upward. He had to crawl on hands and knees in some places.

He came to a junction where the trail intersected the slope. He hid behind an outcropping where he could see both ways along the trail. The sound of whatever it was that was staggering through the woods grew louder. It was close. He hunkered down and waited.

When the rain picked up again, Tyoga wiped his face to get a better look at the ghostly figure stumbling toward him about twenty yards away to the east.

Through the summit mist and driving rain, it appeared to be one of the Shawnee braves who had been chasing them down the mountain. He was staggering back and forth across the trail, struggling to stay on his feet. His arm outstretched in front of him, he looked like a blind man trying to find his way. His other arm was hanging at his side. His hand appeared to be clutching a war club.

Tyoga guessed him to be in his late teens or early twenties. He would wait until the warrior was closer, and then spring out from his hiding place to take him down.

Before the warrior could advance to where Tyoga was waiting, he stopped, collapsed to his knees, and crumpled face first to the ground. Tyoga remained concealed behind the outcropping to see if the Shawnee's companions would come to his aid. After several minutes, and hearing no sound of a chase in the woods around him, he was confident that the others were not nearby.

Tyoga cautiously stepped from his hiding place and onto the trail. He slowly moved toward the warrior who was lying face down in the muddy trail. He got to within two feet of the warrior before he saw the growing pool of blood oozing from the Indian's head, turning the muddy loam into a sticky purple soup. He nudged the young man's shoulder with his foot.

He did not move.

Tyoga squatted down next to the bleeding man, and saw that he wasn't breathing. Standing back up, he rolled the dead man over with his foot. Gasping, he took two quick steps back at the sight of the butchered man at his feet. He had never seen anything like this before.

The Indian's face was hardly recognizable as human. The vicious attack had ripped his cheek and lips from his face. His left eye was hanging from the socket. All that was left of where his nose used to be was a gaping hole. His right ear was completely gone. The arm that was holding the war club was severed above the elbow. His artery hung like a bloody straw from his upper arm. His rib cage was torn open and his small bowel bulged from the hideous tear.

Whatever had attacked him had torn him apart. It wasn't even a fair fight.

Tyoga sat on his haunches next to the dead Shawnee.

Only the gentle sound of the rain and the muffled caw of a solitary crow filled the hollow.

He stood and turned to walk back down the slope to Sunlei. He walked slowly—deliberately. He knew that there was no need to hurry or to hide.

When he reached her, she was crying. She jumped up and threw herself into his arms and held him close.

The piercing howl descended from the summit of old Mount Rag to fill the valleys and hollows below with an icy declaration that was viscerally understood.

This battle was over.

Tyoga and Sunlei looked into each others' eyes before glancing up toward Summit Rock.

The rising sun peaked through the clouds of the passing storm to outline the silhouette of the wolf standing tall on the alter of old Mount Rag.

Putting his arm around her, Tyoga led Sunlei along the trail to the valley below.

He glanced over his shoulder to look up at the summit one more time before rounding a bend in the trail.

The wolf was gone.

The three of them began their journey home.

H.L. Grandin

Chapter 14

Frontier Intrigue

The early 1700s were tumultuous years in the Appalachian Mountains. The divisive pressures from the British, French, and Spaniards took an ever increasing toll upon the natural resources, and the lives of the Native Americans living in the territory from the southern Ohio Valley, western Tennessee, and on eastward to the Carolinas. Relationships between tribes were tenuous and fragile as political intrigue and deals with the Europeans for goods, especially for whiskey and firearms, fractured long-standing alliances, and established new ones that would ultimately be the demise of a proud and prosperous people. As the tribes vied for the weapons of war that would forever alter the balance of power, oaths of allegiance see-sawed wildly to gain the favor of—and firearms from—the French, or the British, or Spain. Weapons of flint and stone, obsidian and quartz, were no match for firearms and gun powder, iron and steel.

Members of the same tribe independently brokered deals with warring factions so that braves from the same tribe, sometimes even brothers, would unwittingly end up facing each other on the battle-field—some fighting with French against the British, or with British against the Spanish.

Unaccustomed to the deceitful ways of the foreign invaders, and imbued with a natural trust in the integrity of even their adversaries, the

Native Americans were easy pawns in a deadly game in which the stakes could not have been more consequential.

The treachery foisted upon the Native Americans by foreign countries competing ruthlessly for the bounties of the New World were less egregious, and in a sense more manageable, than the day-to-day injustices the Indians tolerated at the hands of the settlers who they had come to call neighbors. Not only did the white trespassers cheat them out of the fair market value of the land, but in establishing their homesteads, they chased away the game upon which the Indians depended for food, clothing, shelter, and sustenance. Even these transgressions the Indians bore without making war.

What tipped the balance in the early 1700s was the growing practice of stealing Indian women and children, and selling them into slavery, mostly to the northern colonies. The practice became so extensive that in 1705 the Pennsylvania legislature passed a law against the further importation of Indian slaves from the Carolinas. Unfortunately, the price to be had for such an easy venture was too hard for the southern colonists to resist. The practice would continue until the morning of September 22, 1711, when the Tuscarora Indians indiscriminately slaughtered virtually all of the white settlers homesteading along the banks of the Neuse and Trent rivers in eastern North Carolina.

The pressures of encroachment were pervasive and not confined to any particular region or territory of the frontier. The white tide had risen until it had breached the Appalachian Mountains, and flooded the pristine valleys and forested basins. The Ani-Unwiya Cherokee and the South Fork Shawnee were not insulated from the scourge of slavery. Both tribes had their women and children stolen and sold by the white man.

The Shawnee raid upon the unprotected village of Tessuntee in 1692 to steal Cherokee women and children while the men were away on the winter hunt, placed them squarely in the same category as the slave traders. The Native American code of civility decreed that when the men of any village were away on the winter hunt, the women and children of the tribe were to be left in peace. A breach of this code was an atrocity few were willing to own.

The Cherokee had never forgiven the callous treachery of the heinous deed. War between the tribes had been averted only through the tenuous bonds of arranged unions that had been orchestrated in times of peace. Even though no formal declaration of war had been issued from either of the feuding tribes, their braves kept a sharp eye out for one another and took every opportunity to skirmish and harass each other at virtually every encounter.

The deaths of the four young Shawnee braves on the summit of Mount Rag were not the first deaths to have occurred between the tribes since the raid in 1692, however, this attack was more than simply another assault on members of the Shawnee tribe. In the eyes of the Appalachian tribes, these deaths came at the hands of a single white settler who was accompanying the most beautiful and sought after Indian maiden in the land. To have killed Tyoga and captured Sunlei would have been an enormous coup for the Shawnee nation, even though it would have meant all out war with the Cherokee nation.

That one white man, or the magic over which he had control, could defeat four Shawnee warriors was an affront that the tribe could not reconcile nor abide.

The fact that there were no witnesses to the mauling deaths added a dimension of intrigue upon which legends grow and flourish. It was an occasion of historical significance that solidified the iconic stature of Tyoga Weathersby.

In protecting his spiritual brother, and the woman he loved, the wolf had set into motion a series of events that would tear two lovers apart, and break alliances that had kept a tenuous peace for decades.

Chapter 15

Camp at the Confluence

At eighteen years old, Tyoga and Tes Qua had grown into their magnificent prime.

Tyoga Weathersby was a mountain of a man. Powerfully built with broad muscular shoulders tested by the oppressive struggle that was life in the Shenandoah Valley in the 1700s, his rugged upper body reflected the agonizing work of clearing the land. His hard, rippled abdomen and finely sculpted torso recalled every swing of the ax. His massive upper arms and broad muscular chest were testament to the miles marched while wrestling teams of draft horses and plowing mules. The years of galloping the mountain trails and leaping cat-like along the bouldered spines of the Appalachian's outcroppings had sublimely chiseled his buttocks into smooth muscular orbs of granite perfection. His soft weathered buckskins—second-skin tight—softly sighed in protest at the flex of his thighs when he haunted the obscure back hollows and lush hidden valleys known only to him.

His face was set in the determined mold of generations of Weathersbys before him. Resolute. Single-minded. Hard, some would say. Friends and family would more kindly describe the look as intense and focused. The telltale etchings of his grandfather's facial creases were forming on his bronzed weathered skin. His nose belied his English roots. While regally structured, his face carried the gauntness familiar to those living on the frontier where time between full-meals was measured in days, not hours. He brandished several days growth of dense, coarse stubble, bear-like in its fullness and magnificent when spared the assault of the blade.

In a week's time, he looked more animal than man.

As the years had passed since the legend was born, Tyoga's eyes became his most distinguishing feature.

Like generations of Weathersbys before him, they sparkled with the courage of an adventurous heart. They echoed the restlessness that compelled Weathersby men to blaze trails through the wilderness, cross the Appalachians more than a century before the discovery of the Cumberland Gap, and settle in an unnamed glade in the Shenandoah Valley.

Rich in texture with a hint of caprice and unpredictability, Tyoga's hazel eyes were translucent portals that revealed the content of his character, and reflected an unvarnished appraisal of others. When content and satisfied, his tranquil green eyes calmed with an unexpected gentleness; when threatened or provoked, they glowed with the blinding amber brilliance of white-hot coal. Like a cup of black coffee turned cappuccino brown with the first drop of lily-white cream, the transformation was complete.

What was there was gone.

The gentleness replaced with an animal deliberateness and lethal intent. His brilliant amber eyes hardened into balls of cold unforgiving malevolence. Inhuman. Indifferent to death. Frightening.

The name Tyoga Weathersby was spoken in reverent hushed tones. Since the battle with the Runion pack, and the mauling on Mount Rag, deeds, shrouded in mystery and intrigue, had been attributed to him that blurred the divide between man and beast. Depending on who was telling the tale, Tyoga Weathersby was either an honorable rogue or a murderous assassin.

He was known throughout the Appalachians, the Ohio Valley, the Carolinas, from Charleston to Middle Plantation and Hampton Roads. He was both admired and feared for his mystical power over his brother the wolf—the creature revered above all others for his connection with the spirit world. Though the legend was borne of violence and death, and had morphed Tyoga into a fictional persona immersed in battle and blood, he in truth remained a gentle man of intuitive understanding and quiet confidence. While he had never raised a hand in anger toward any man, the legend that now surrounded him was enough to keep all but the most foolhardy at bay.

Tes Qua Ta Wa's foot had been saved by Yonevgadoga, the medicine man, and the skills of Tyoga's mother, Emma. Despite the severity of his injury, Tes Qua moved with the rhythmic sway of his Indian brothers—fluid currents of motion—with only the slightest crease that betrayed the horror of that night so long ago.

He had assumed the signature stature of the Ani-Yunwyia: stocky, low, and barrel-chested. His arms were powerfully sculped, but lithe rather than knotted with mass. His thick wrists were attached to surprisingly delicate hands. Storied with scars, his hands reflected the calloused honesty of a man tested beyond his years. The weathered ruddiness of his complexion proclaimed his Cherokee heritage with pride. His prominent eagle-like nose bestowed his countenance with the discerning incredulity of a suspicious schoolmaster. His deep set eyes, shadowed by a lightly feathered disciplined brow were diamond black—at once exposed, yet revealing nothing at all.

He had grown into his name: Tes Qua Ta Wa, The One Who Opens the Door, and his mettle had been tested according to the Indian tradition. He had taken his place around the council fires next to his father, and his opinion was often sought as his command of the English language and understanding of the ways of the whites was far beyond that of any other Native American in mid-Atlantic colonial America. A wise and thoughtful young man, he understood the value of compromise and the power of negotiation. Well known throughout the Appalachians as an even-handed, fair-minded arbiter, Tes Qua was called upon to help settle disputes in neighboring villages of the Choctaw and Chickasaw.

He was also known as the blood brother of Tyoga Weathersby.

The young men had reached the age where they were expected to shoulder the responsibilities of adulthood, so their free time was more limited than in their youth. Still, they found time to enjoy the freedom of the frontier. Their hunting and fishing trips deep into the rolling hills of Appalachia to harvest game for their tribe were excuse enough for exploration and adventure. Creatures of the forest, as naturally at home on the pine-covered slopes and rocky mountain outcroppings as the animals they would encounter along the way, they spent days at a time camped in a make-shift hunting lodge nestled in a hollow or on the bank of a mountain stream.

Life had changed dramatically for the Indian tribes of Appalachia since that night six years ago on the escarpment. When they were young boys, they traveled in relative safety with little more than a knife and a stout piece of hickory for protection. They gave wide berth to rival Indian clans, and avoided unpredictable trappers in their travels. For the most part, they did not have to worry about the intentions of the reclusive mountain folk. Now, at the turn of the century, they never traveled without their flintlocks primed and close at hand.

Tyoga and Tes Qua were on their way back to Tuckareegee from Dahlgren where they had traded some sassafras root for fishing hooks and a bolt of linen cloth.

Two days away from the Ani-Unwiya village, with the skies overcast and threatening, they stopped early in the afternoon to make camp on a spit of land located at the confluence of the Rapidan and the Rappahannock rivers. An ominous cool breeze blew down the river gorge from the north. They anticipated a long windy night of cold rain. Usually more comfortable sleeping out under the stars, they constructed a shelter of pine boughs and animal hide to protect them from the elements. They would be warm and dry through the night in the lean-to. Seated under the shelter, well within the warmth of their blazing fire, the young men sat cross-legged on deer skins and a thick black bear pelt.

It was the quiet time just before sun set—but the roar of the two mighty rivers colliding just a few yards from their campsite robbed them of the cleansing quiet they both so enjoyed.

They had dismantled their flintlocks to clean the pans and cocks and lock plates, and to do some minor repairs.

Several days earlier, they had come across the site of a skirmish in the woods. Many hard soled boots had disturbed the ground, and the underbrush was trampled and torn. Several rucksacks, a utility belt and a bloody, torn jacket rested near the discarded, broken stock of a Hudson Valley fowler.

They were removing the trigger guard from the fowling piece to replace the broken one on Tes Qua's rifle.

"Eh ya, adanedi gilasulo," Tyoga said to Tes Qua while reaching for his moccasins to place at the opening of the shelter near the fire for them to warm and dry.

Tes Qua handed his moccasins to him. "Galieliha."

"Welcome."

"Hey, ya ta we tsila uv do la, Ty."

"Okay," Tyoga said. "Here, use this for the screw lock."

"A-ho."

"How close do you think we are to South Fork and Seven Arrows?" Tes Qua asked.

"Oh, about a half day. Northwest."

Tes Qua slid the round pan back toward the butt and lifted it off the broken stock. Tyoga held the octagonal barrel of Tes Qua's Mackinaw while steadying the rifle in his lap.

The fire popped and a glowing red ember flew into the air like an angry firefly and landed on the thick fur of the bear pelt. Tyoga slapped at it several times with his open hand.

"I hope we don't come across him, Ty. He's never forgiven you for So-hi, Dawson's Creek—or for what happened on the Rag."

"The Rag. Damn the Rag, Tes." Tyoga was uncharacteristically annoyed. "Nobody knows what really happened up there. Not even me. It's just wild talk. We never saw no four dead Shawnee. We never saw nobody get mauled. I didn't do it. The wolf was there with us sure enough—but I didn't tell him to tear those boys apart. Nobody saw nothin' I tell you. It's plain old crazy talk. Don't nobody know nothin' fer sure."

"Ty, Seven Arrows's brothers, Spotted Calf and Running Elk, were killed up there. Everybody knows what happened. You can say whatever you want—but Sunlei told us what happened. Everybody knows about you and the wolf. Some say that you're one and the same—ever since that night—that's what the people say."

"An' what do you say, Tes 'A?" Tyoga asked. "Tell me what you think. Come on."

Tes Qua stopped working on the trigger guard and looked out toward the glowing fire.

"I think you are my brother," he said to Tyoga smiling. "And you only eat like a wolf."

They both laughed and continued working on their rifles. Tes Qua was rubbing the pans of both flintlocks with bear grease and lubricating the cocks. Every so often he would look up at Tyoga who was working on removing the trigger guard from the broken stock. He noticed Tyoga jerk his head up and scan the underbrush beyond the light of the flames.

"What is it, Ty?" Tes Qua asked.

Without answering, he shook his head.

"He's here with us now, isn't he, Ty?" Tes Qua asked. "I know he's here. I can smell him. Where is he?"

Ty handed Tes Qua the swan neck cock, and the set screw.

"He's over there. Behind the rocks, by the water," Tyoga said.

Tes Qua shook his head in annoyance and began securing the trigger mechanism to the stock.

Tyoga understood his good friend's sign of frustration, and teasingly asked, "What's wrong with you?"

"What?" he asked goadingly.

"It's Wahaya."

"Well, what about him?"

"It's funny that he won't show himself to me," Tes Qua said. "After all this time he still keeps hidden from me. I don't understand. Why won't he let me see him? He shows himself to Sunlei. He protects her like he watches over you, but he won't even show himself to me."

Tyoga listened to his friend, and thought quietly about what he had said. Truth be told, he had wondered the same thing. He and Tes Qua were together almost all of the time. Wahaya always let them know he was with them, yet he would not show himself to Tes Qua. Then, one day, he realized that the answer was in the question.

"I think it's because you are the only one who knows." He looked down at the work waiting in his lap.

"What?"

"Think about it, Tes. You are the only witness to what happened between us six years ago. Not another living creature saw the proud leader of the pack battered, broken, and bloody." Tyoga paused and took in a deep breath. "Tes Qua, do you ever think about that night?"

Tes Qua didn't answer.

"Don't you wonder why he let it happen? He could have killed us at any time. I'll never forget him stretched out there at my feet with his bloody head on the ground, his eyes staring up at me. I held that stone over my head and I was gonna bash his skull clean in two—and he didn't move. He just kept looking at me. I remember looking into his eyes and seeing my own reflection as clear as if I was lookin' in a mirror. I felt his eyes fill me with ... with ..." At a loss for words, he stopped. "I watched my reflection disappear into the blackness of his eyes ... and it was over."

Tes Qua didn't answer. He looked up and saw Tyoga staring out into the darkness.

Tes Qua looked back down at the work in his lap, and continued wrestling the stubborn set-screw. The Mackinaw stock wasn't exactly like the Hudson fowler. He had an elk bone awl in his rucksack that he could use to drill a new hole in the stock of his rifle to make the trigger guard fit, but it was late. It had begun to rain and he was getting tired.

Seeing that Tes Qua was finished working with his rifle for the evening, Tyoga helped him collect the parts and place them aside for in the morning.

Both rifles were in pieces—and useless.

It was a mistake.

Chapter 16

Thoughts that Young Men Share

The night was crisp, and the cold rain was unrelenting. The swiftly flowing water that chiseled the banks on both sides of the young men's campsite spilled over the rocks to course through the narrowing channels toward the confluence at ever-increasing speed. Like quicksilver Spartans in a game of musical chairs, the rivers collided and boiled in convulsive disarray until finally melding into a single channel of disciplined power heading southeast toward the Chesapeake Bay.

Warm and dry in their shelter, they listened to the rain pelting the oiled hides they had spread out over the pine bough roof while sharing the thoughts that young men share in the dark—in the woods—all alone.

Tyoga said, "Listen to that river roar."

"Yeah, it's moving fast," said Tes Qua. "Won't be doing any fishing tomorrow."

"That's all right. We have plenty to eat."

"Hey, Ty. Let's go west in the spring."

"I don't know, Tes Qua. Times ain't right for travelin' west just now. The French have the Sioux all worked up, and it just ain't safe. I'd hate to see your long black braids hangin' from a Sioux lodge pole. OUCH!" Tyoga exclaimed at the kick that caught him in the thigh. "'Sides, I promised Sunlei that I would take her east. Maybe we'll visit York Town. Hampden Roads, maybe."

"Ty, you should ask her to be your wife before you go?"

"I don't know," Tyoga said. "Maybe. I'll ask her sometime soon."

"Soon?" Tes Qua replied. "The People laugh and say that 'soon' will never come. They all wish Sunlei to marry."

"What do the People say about her marrying a white man, Tes?"

"They say a union binding the Wolf Clan to the Weathersbys would be a good thing. But, Ty, you cannot wait forever. Sunlei has refused the sons of many chiefs. The People speak of unions with the Chocktaw and the Chickasaw that might have been. The peace made by these joinings would have been good for the People. Soon Chief Silver Cloud will force my father to make Sunlei marry. You must not wait too long, my brother."

"I know, Tes Qua. I know."

The young men lay on the bear skin with their hands locked behind their heads staring up at their pine bough ceiling. Each was lost in private thoughts. Tes Qua was trying to imagine what it would be like to have his sister marry a brave from another clan or tribe. Tyoga was trying to imagine the same.

Sunlei was the most sought after maiden in the Shenandoah Valley. Her allure went far beyond the physical beauty with which she had been blessed. Her eyes sparkled with the excitement of constant discovery.

Gentle of countenance, Sunlei had cared for most of the children in the village as newborns. Recognizing the fluid curve of her forearm and breast from when she had cradled them in their first days of life, they flocked to her side whenever she passed through the well-worn alleyways of Tuckareegee.

Soft-spoken and warm, she was a frequent visitor in the lodges of the tribal elders. She comforted the infirmed with a compassionate confidence that sent many on their final journey secure in the love of their tribe.

Even-tempered and self-possessed, she adapted easily to situation and circumstance without abandoning principle or belief. She was always willing to politely listen to opposing points of view, confident in her intuitive strength to remain steadfast when petitioned with deceit, and in her courage to be swayed by reason when presented with fact. Yet, those who knew Sunlei well understood that her willingness to listen was not to be confused with agreement. It was a mistake to equate her tender heart with weakness of character.

With long legs and a lean torso, she was taller than the other Ani-Unwiya. Her athletic build bore witness to her tomboy adolesence of following in the footsteps of Tyoga and Tes Qua while they glided along the mountain trails of Appalachia.

On the brink of womanhood, Sunlei no longer roamed the village nor ran through the woods in the joyous freedom of naked abandon, but wore the mid-calf length doeskin tunic common to young maidens. She walked with a steady, confident gait that without effort or design produced a seductive rhythmic sway as enchanting as the gentle swells of the tidal bay. Through the softness of her doeskin tunic the sensual curves of her exquisitely muscled buttocks were clearly defined. Her sculpted thighs tugged at the deer hide dress with each determined step. Her voluptuous breasts bubbled from the neckline of her tunic to keep time with her silky cadence. The creamy softness of her butternut skin shimmered with a honey glow in the noonday sun, and scented the night with a loamy musk. She could not move but that all eyes fell upon her.

"Ya know, Tes, I don't know what I would do without her," Tyoga said. "We've been together our whole lives. When I'm without her, it's like part of me is missing somehow. When she's not around I feel like … I feel like the eagle without wings. The stars are silent, the sky shares no secrets, and the wind whispers no truths. It is as if the promise is with me no more."

"Have you told her these things, my brother?"

"Ahhh, there ain't no need, Tes A," Tyoga replied.

"I don't know, Ty. She isn't the little girl who used to follow us through the woods. Sunlei is a woman and a woman likes to hear the words."

They were still for awhile as Tyoga contemplated the wisdom in Tes Qua's reply. He knew that he should tell her how he felt, but somehow the legend that he had become made it all the more difficult for him to speak the words of love he knew that she longed to hear.

He thought about how his soul had melded with that of Wahaya-wacon. He knew it to be true, although he would never say the words out loud—not even to Tes Qua. The revelation that his feelings for Sunlei were somehow mirrored by his connection with the wolf caught him completely off guard. Before he could think to check the words, he blurted out as if talking to himself, "It's the same as when I watched my reflection dissolve away into the eyes of the wolf. She reflects me."

Tes Qua understood exactly what Tyoga was trying to say. While neither young man could fully comprehend the meaning of Tyoga's connection to the wolf, the mysterious alliance described in terms of the dissolving reflection provided a context that somehow made sense. "I understand, Ty. But if you feel this way, my brother, why do you not ask her to be your wife?"

"Because I am afraid, Tes 'A. I am afraid of what the future may hold."

"Afraid!" Tes Qua propped himself up on his elbow. "Ty, you have nothing to fear from any man. You are Tyoga Weathersby. Wahaya-Wacon, the wolf, is your spirit guide. From every valley, from every mountain top, your name is honored by the white man, the Cherokee, the Choctaw, the Arapaho and even the Osage."

"My fear is not for any harm that could come my way at the hands of another," Tyoga replied. "I am afraid because the world that we have known all of our lives, Tes Qua, is coming to an end. The end of that world will mean that our children will belong to neither the white man's world, nor to that of my red brothers. They will be torn between two worlds. They will be shunned as half-breeds. None of us—not me, not Sunlei, not our children—will be welcome in the white world. And, my brother, that is the world in which we will all live one day."

"But your family will always have a home with us," Tes Qua replied. "Your children will not be shunned by the People. You are a member of the Wolf Clan just as if you had been born an Ani-Unwiya. Your children will grow up to be strong and respected braves, and you will have everything that you could ever need or want."

"I will have everything except the respect of the white world. And that will be everything in the years to come."

Tes Qua was struck by the honesty with which Tyoga had expressed his conviction that one day, the world that he had known—the world that defined the Ani-Unwiya since the beginning of time—would one day exist no more. All that he and his ancestors had known would be replaced by a world of symmetry and design, the measures by which the English, Dutch, German, and Irish settlers gauged a culture's civility.

Tyoga was torn between despair and reconciled acceptance. He knew more intimately than most the terrible price that would be exacted by the white wave that would flood the ancient lands of the Cherokee, Choctaw, Iroquois and Chippewa. Like the ocean ceaselessly pounding the sandy shore, the footprints of the Native Americans would be wiped clean by the waves of white settlers who would wash over the mountain in torrents. With their advance, the stories told around campfires would be replaced by books in white clapboard school houses; clergy in steepled churches would supplant the shaman, spirit guides, and the sweat lodge; and wheel-rutted roads would replace his beloved mountain trails. The ways of living in, and as part of, the natural world would be lost forever.

After some time had passed, Tes Qua began the conversation anew.

"What about Praire Day, Ty?"

"What about her?"

"She wishes you to take her. All the People know that she wants you very much."

"Tes Qua, she is Chief Silver Cloud's daughter. He will arrange her marriage and he will choose Wind Rider or Stands with Fist."

"Be careful, my friend. She has you in her sights, and she is a very good shot with a bow."

They laughed. Tyoga not as hard as Tes Qua.

Alone in the silence of the night with their thoughts, the patter of the rain lulled them to sleep.

Chapter 17

Seven Arrows

The young men began to stir shortly before sunrise. The rain had stopped during the night and the morning air was damp and brisk.

Tes Qua was the first to hear the mocassined feet clumsily shuffling through the leaves and carelessly breaking branches as they approached the makeshift shelter.

Whoever was approaching their campsite was not concerned about a steathly approach. They had the young men trapped. The spit of land upon which they had camped was surrounded by the raging waters of the Rapidan on one side, and the Rappahanock on the other. There was one path in and only one way out.

"Ty!" Tes Qua exclaimed in a whisper that was louder than he would have wished it to be.

"Yeah." Tyoga was already reaching for his rifle.

The reflexive reach for his weapon was the instinct of a seasoned mountain man. The blood draining from his head with the panicked realization that their flintlocks were dismantled and that they had no firepower between them was a response more primal still.

He looked at his companion. "Tes, the rifles."

They were unarmed and defenseless.

The sanctuary of their lean-to had been transformed into a trap.

The footsteps grew louder and closer. The voices of the men approaching indicated a party of more than two.

They grabbed their knives. Tes Qua picked up his Cherokee tomahawk.

"Nay a, Tes Qua. Don't let them see the tomahawk. Put your knife in your belt under your shirt. We'll go out like we're unarmed."

They heard the footsteps stop just outside of their shelter.

A booming voice thundered "Eh ya taho, indea a ho, eh alo"

"What did he say, Tes?" Tyoga knew only a little Shawnee. However, Tes Qua was a good speaker of the language.

With the water roaring at full volume into the confluence of the two rivers, it was difficult to hear the words. The voice from outside repeated, "You in the shelter. Come out."

The giddiness of the voices surrounding the spokesman indicated that they were perhaps in for some hassle, but not in any real danger. A second miscalculation.

"Eta ho, Tes," Tyoga said calmly. "Let's go see how we can entertain our guests." He shot Tes Qua a crooked grin.

Tyoga's nonchalance encouraged Tes Qua, and he flashed back a nervous grin.

They put on their dry moccasins, and climbed out of the lean-to on their hands and knees.

Tes Qua was out first. Tyoga crawled out of the shelter, rose to his feet, and stood alongside his friend.

When he turned to face their "guests," he stared into the smirking, painted face of Seven Arrows

The Indian's eyes opened wide in amazement at the sight of Tyoga Weathersby standing, a prisoner, before him. Although they had not seen each other for many years, Seven Arrows recognized him right away. He had listened half-heatedly to the tales of the legend growing up, but more importantly, had felt the sting of Tyoga's alpha male domination on more than one occasion.

Seven Arrows's reputation had grown along with that of Tyoga, but his was rooted in fear and loathing. As the overindulged eldest son of Yellow Robe, Chief of the South Fork Shawnee, he was pampered as a child, tolerated as an adolescent, and feared as a ruthless young adult who wielded the power of his station with disregard for collateral consequence. He bullied his way through childhood with a cadre of obedient pawns who understood the important role that he would one day play as the result of nothing more than accident of birth. Torturing and killing for the shear joy of being acknowledged for the deeds, he carried on with the slaughter of innocent animals that he had started with the baby ducks at So-hi pool.

The Shawnee called Seven Arrows, Puta Loga, which translated loosely to "strangler of life," and he lived up to the sobriquet in every possible way. He snatched joy from celebration, squelched laughter from festivity, and quelled honor from sacrifice and courage. His savagery knew no bounds and his ruthlessness no limitations.

The only person who had been able to keep him in check was Tyoga Weathersby.

Ever since the incident at So-hi pool when Tyoga shamed him into submission with no more than his words, Seven Arrows had made him and Tes Qua the target of his special attention. A few years younger than Tyoga and Tes Qua, Seven Arrows and his Shawnee companions would follow them as they traveled through the mountain passes, disturbing the game they were stalking, harassing their campsite through the night, and stealing from them whenever they could. Their game came to an abrupt halt one late July afternoon when Tyoga and Tes Qua had turned the table on Seven Arrows's plan to raid their campsite along Dawson's Creek. Waiting in ambush to catch him and his companions as they made off with Tes Qua's best bow and nearly all of their provisions, Tyoga and Tes Qua forced them to walk home, eight miles along the Appalachian Trail, completely naked and empty handed. At thirteen years of age, they were well past the time that young boys covered themselves with loin clothes. Their naked entrance into South Fork was far less an insult to their pride and machismo, than the fact they had been forced to surrender their bows, arrows, and knives. It took Seven Arrows months to reestablish his position and stature. Those accompanying him never rebounded from the shame.

Tyoga had not encountered any members of the South Fork Shawnee since the misadventure on the summit of Mount Rag. He learned long ago that two of the Indians mauled on the mountain top were the sons of the Chief of the South Fork Shawnee, and Seven Arrows's younger brothers. That the older brother of the two dead Shawnee Braves would be the first person from the tribe Tyoga should come across was but an unfortunate happenstance of fate. He was sorry that it should be so.

As the morning fog greeted the new day with its timeless descent to the floor of the river gorge and an icy mist shrouded the young men in a cape of chilling gray, Tyoga said with indifferent dismissal, "A-ho Sesche picqua."

Tes Qua began to shiver when the muddy ground soaked through the leather soles of his once dry and warm moccasins, and the breeze from the rushing water slapped the saturated air against his naked arms.

Tyoga's feet were equally cold and wet, but he did not allow himself to shiver. Steely eyed and with no hint of concern, he remained calm, cool, and collected. His eyes left Seven Arrows for only a split second to scan the underbrush to their right along the shoreline. He saw what he needed to see.

Three young Shawnee braves were with Seven Arrows. They appeared to be in their late teens to early twenties. Their faces and bodies were painted with the colors and designs that clearly identified them as a marauding band of dog soldiers out to rob, kill, and scalp any unfortunate passers-by be they Indian or white settlers. In deference to his age and rank, the three remained a respectful distance behind Seven Arrows who stood directly in front of, and very close to, Tyoga. The condescending smirk left his face as he leaned forward and sniffed at Tyoga's head and neck—a sign of disrespect.

"Tey a taya ucun skinuka," Seven Arrows said with obvious disdain, and then spit on the ground.

The braves with Seven Arrows slapped at the air, and at each other, as they laughed out loud in a rowdy chorus of consent with his remarks.

Tyoga, who had riveted his gaze on Seven Arrows until that moment, looked away and turned his body so that he was not facing him. This was understood by the Indians as an insult of equal disdain.

Still looking away, Ty asked, "What did he say, Tes?"

"You don't need to know, Ty."

The slight of averting his gaze and turning away deeply offended Seven Arrows. He expressed his agitation by pacing randomly about the campsite. He was a powerfully built young man. His broad shoulders and upper arms were painted in black, and his biceps were accentuated by the leather adodas that encircled each arm. His left eye socket was painted black from mid-cheek to above his eyebrow, and his head was shaved save for a bristly brown stripe from his forehead to the nape of his neck. As he nervously paced, he never took his eyes off of Tyoga. Filled with years of festering rage at his disgraceful naked march through the woods to South Fork, the recent loss of his two younger brothers on the summit of Mount Rag, and the disdain with which he was presently being treated, he was unable to contain his anger any longer. Exploding in a convulsion of rage, Seven Arrows screamed so that the words spit into Tyoga's face, "You killed my brothers!"

Raising his fist as if to strike Tyoga, he took two determined steps in his direction. As he stepped forward he pushed Tes Qua out of the way, which nearly threw him to the ground.

Recovering from the shove that turned him completely around, Tes Qua caught a glimpse of a hazy gray presence darting through the underbrush. Righting himself, he looked again toward the thickets beyond the bank. He saw nothing.

Seven Arrows approached Tyoga with his fists clenched high over his head and murder in his eyes. His charge was so fierce that he fully expected Tyoga to cower in fear, move out of the way, protect his head from the blow or run for cover in the woods. But he didn't flinch or even uncross his arms. Standing tall and strong in the face of Seven Arrows's attack, he allowed him to get as near as he dare.

When Seven Arrows got close enough to see the ominous sizzle of Tyoga's piercing golden eyes, he found himself frozen in place. A tiny, nearly inaudible gasp accompanied his quick step backward toward his companions. At that instant, he realized who had been shamed into cowering with fear.

Tyoga had done it again.

With his fists still clenched and held over his head, Seven Arrows screamed out loud in anger and frustration at the indomitable bearing of this powerful adversary. Turning quickly away from Tyoga so as to avoid the menacing glare of his transforming eyes, he began pacing once again.

He didn't know what to make of the change in Tyoga's eyes. For years he had heard the story of the boys' encounter with the Runion wolf pack as it was retold around countless lodge fires in the Shawnee village. He was young when the battle with the commander had occurred, and he had discounted the stories as fanciful yarns told by the elders to entertain the women and scare the young braves. But the savage slaughter of his two brothers on Mount Rag had forced him to consider the possibility that the stories were true. Could he be at this very moment tempting fate by facing down a living legend? Staying a safe distance from Tyoga, Seven Arrows yelled again with less intensity, "You killed by brothers. They were only young boys."

"I never killed anybody, Seven Arrows," Tyoga replied. "I never even saw who was up on the mountain. We never set eyes on who was chasing us. Alive anyway."

"Liar! You tore them apart." He was near tears. "It was I who led the party to recover their bodies. You left my little brother, Spotted Calf, without a face."

The three braves with Seven Arrows had stepped away from the two warring Titans. The battle between their leader and the Legend of Tyoga Weathersby was an encounter of more intensity than they wished to stomach. Standing off to the side, close to the underbrush that ringed the campsite, was the better part of valor.

Abruptly, they looked at each other and cocked their heads inquisitively as if questioning the silent signals they both were sensing. Their years in the wilds of Appalachia had taught them to read the air and smell the wind. An unaccounted for presence never went unnoticed. Whispering to each other, they reached over their shoulders and pulled arrows from their war quivers. As they each notched an arrow in their bowstring, they bent at the waist while peering into the underbrush behind them and to either side.

The bushes were still. The ground undisturbed. It was as if the presence was part-of rather than separate-from the very air that surrounded them. It was everywhere—and nowhere at all.

In a low, controlled voice Tyoga said to Seven Arrows, "I told you that I didn't hurt anyone."

Tyoga's chest and arms swelled with the blood rushing to his muscles and engorging them with the power of Wahaya. The final tinge of hazel drained from his eyes to allow the hot yellow-gold to penetrate the morning mist with indifferent resolve.

The transformation, though subtle, was readily apparent to Seven Arrows. He would tell his grandchildren that on that day he witnessed the transformation of man into beast. He would go to his grave swearing that the legend of Tyoga Weathersby was no legend at all. He trembled with fear.

He heard one of his companions say, "Eh no tuta lo eh alo. Reshkulu na tay ya."

"A – ho. Le nasht tsy la."

Seven Arrows instinctively understood that he could not run from the encounter. To do so would be to turn himself into prey. He wasn't sure if he was dealing with man or beast, but he would not risk triggering the predator's attack. His mind raced as he tried to think of ways to quiet the demon bubbling up from deep within Tyoga's soul.

Assuming a more apologetic tone, he said to Tyoga, "So maybe it wasn't you who killed my brothers. Maybe it was your spirit wolf. Maybe it was your Wahaya."

As Seven Arrows slowly backed away, he continued to stare into Tyoga's vacuous amber eyes. He could not break away from the haunting glare that penetrated his façade of bravado and peeled away his shallow veneer of bravery. The blood draining from his head and hands, he stammered. "Or maybe … maybe you are the spirit wolf. Maybe you can't control it. You don't want these bad things to happen. Is that it, Tyoga Weathersby? Is it true what they say about you? Answer me! Why won't you answer me?" His words were swallowed by the icy gray gorge.

A deep guttural rumble filled the campsite from the forest floor to the tree-top canopy high above. Filling the space with the chilling pall that accompanies inevitable finality, its presence was palpable. Nearly inaudible at first, the rumble grew into a growl of such unearthly intensity and volume that its meaning was discerned not by sound, but by the visceral interpretation of heart and lungs and bowel.

Bow strings drawn ready to fire their obsidian-tipped arrows into whatever evil lurked in the shadows, Seven Arrows's braves pivoted on their heels in search of the source of the warning.

The sound saturated the scene with a paralyzing terror that awakened a palpable recognition that nature's power unchecked is devastatingly cruel in its dominion and finality. It was the terror. It surrounded them, penetrated them, and became them in its rawness and truth.

Eyes riveted on Seven Arrows, Tyoga allowed the truth to be heard before issuing the command, "Nay-ya Wahaya-Wacon." He said to the wind, "Etsola."

The growl stopped. Its echoes receded into the morning mist.

"So … it is true," Seven Arrows said. "The spirit wolf does watch over you."

Tyoga took two steps toward him, and bowed his head so that his chin was nearly resting on his chest. "Leave us," he whispered in a voice that was no longer his own. "Leave us in peace."

Tyoga's fists were clenched but at his sides. His focus never left Seven Arrows. He took another menacing step forward so that he was only inches away from his painted face.

Lifting his head so that he was staring straight into the eyes of his foe, Tyoga whispered again in a low measured other-worldly voice, "Go. Now. Before something terrible happens to you and your men."

Leaning into Seven Arrows so that his lips almost touched the Indian's pierced ear, he whispered nearly inaudibly, "I won't tell you again." When Tyoga was finished speaking, he did not pull his lips away. He remained bent at the waist, his face menacingly close to Seven Arrows.

Seven Arrows was forced to back away from Tyoga's threatening posture. The deferential retreat caused him to quake with a shame that emptied him.

"We will go, Tyoga Weathersby. But this day is not over. This day will not end until my brothers are avenged. I will find a way."

The three young Shawnee braves with Seven Arrows had preceded him in backing down the path toward the woods with their bow strings still drawn.

Before they disappeared into the woods, the wolf could contain himself no longer and loosed a deafening howl that pierced the shadowy fog, and shook the trees with its power and might. The overpowering force of the haunting scream caused all of the men, save Tyoga, to clamp their hands over their ears. The Shawnee braves, still covering their ears, ran as fast as they could toward the woods and away from the oppressive howl.

As Seven Arrows backed down the trail, his gaze never left Tyoga's eyes.

"Your life may not be the price that you are forced to pay Tyoga Weathersby. But the day will come when you will know that your life would have been a bargain." He turned. And they were gone.

Chapter 18

Green Rock Cove

Three days later, when the young men arrived at Tuskareegee, the unsteady stares from those they passed gave clear indication that something was amiss.

They kept up their deliberate pace toward Nine Moons's lodge. "Ty, what do you think is going on?" Tes Qua asked. "Why is everyone staring at us?"

"Don't rightly know, Tes," Tyoga replied, "but somethin' ain't right."

When they passed by the council lodge, nine-year-old Paints His Arrows Red came running up to Tyoga with a prideful grin on his face. He had been the one chosen to go forth to ask the question of the great warrior. His friends peered from around the corner of the lodge while watching the scene unfold from afar. "Is it true, Tyoga?" the young boy asked walking with a sideways skip to keep up with them. "Did you do it? Did you send Wahaya to do it?"

Tyoga looked down at him and said rather brusquely, "Go away. I don't know what you're talking about." The young boy skipped away toward his friends with his chest puffed out, swollen with the pride of having spoken directly with Tyoga Weathersby. He was greeted with congratulatory slaps on the back.

"What was that about?" Tes Qua asked.

"I don't know, but I reckon we're gonna find out right quick," Tyoga replied.

They entered Tes Qua's father's lodge. Nine Moons rose to his feet as soon as he saw them. "Good. You have arrived. Are you hurt, my sons?" he asked while hurriedly embracing them both. "I was afraid that you had been injured."

"No, Father," Tes Qua said. "We are fine. Why would you suppose that we had been injured?"

"So you do not know what has happened?" Nine Moons asked. "That is both good and bad, my sons."

"Why, Father?" Tyoga asked. "What has happened?"

"We have heard of your trouble with Seven Arrows two moons ago." Looking toward the lodge fire around which Tes Qua's mother, True Moon, was cooking, Nine Moons added, "Two of the men that were with Seven Arrows were found dead in Fifer's Pass. They were torn apart in a savage attack, much like the braves who were killed on Mount Rag." He paused to take a deep, slow breath. "Chief Silver Cloud wishes to speak with you in the council lodge."

Tes Qua said, "My father, we will go speak with Chief Silver Cloud, but I want you to know that neither I nor Tyoga had anything to do with the deaths of these Shawnee. If they were attacked by wolves, it has nothing to do with us."

Nine Moons held up his hand as if to stop Tes Qua's words. "We will see, my son. Sometimes the truth is not nearly as persuasive as what appears to be." He added, "We will see."

The gravity of being summoned to the chief's lodge was not lost on Tyoga and Tes Qua. They had been in wilderness campsites for the past six days. They were dirty, smelled of smoke and ash, and Tyoga's pelt-like beard concealed his face from below his eyes to his collarbones. He appeared more animal than man. Before presenting themselves to the leader of the clan, they both needed to wash and change into clean clothes.

True Moon told them, "I will get you both clean clothes. Tes Qua, you wash in the basin. Tyoga, go to the river and fetch more water so that you can clean up when Tes is finished. Hurry now. You don't want to keep Silver Cloud waiting."

"Mother," Nine Moons said, "let the boys eat some food and rest a bit before going to the council lodge. They are hungry and tired, and Silver Cloud will wait. Get them something hot to eat."

"Tes, you go ahead and use the water in the basin," Tyoga said, "I'll go to the river to bathe and shave. If e-tsi *(mother)* is good enough to fix her son a plate of her venison stew, I'll be back in plenty of time to eat and rest a bit before we go to Silver Cloud."

True Moon smiled. "Go clean up, my son. Your stew will be here for you when you return. Go."

Tyoga removed his sweat soaked doeskin shirt, threw it over his shoulder and headed for the river.

The sun was warm, the sky was clear, and the temperature unseasonably mild to make for a beautiful fall day.

There were two coves in the river that the villagers frequented to bathe. Flat Rock was the inlet closest to the village, and the one most often used for communal bathing.

The Cherokee were a vibrant people who recognized few barriers to sating their sexual desires. There were very few taboos. Tribal norms permitted couples to pause along a mountain trail for a sexual tryst for nothing more than the shear joy of the experience. Men and women bathed together without any regard to their nakedness. It was as natural to the Ani Unwiya as eating together, sleeping together, and making love in the family lodge.

Unmarried maidens often used the pond or stream to take advantage of a solitary brave. The young girls were sexually aggressive. Bearing the child of a particularly brave or strong warrior out of wedlock was not considered a social faux pas. On the contrary, the bearing of a child from such a union, especially if it was a male child, was seen as an honorable accomplishment for which the woman was held in high regard.

When Tyoga arrived at the Flat Rock, Lone Dove, Morning Sky, and Walking Bird were bathing together. Sisters, Morning Sky and Lone Dove were taking turns washing each other's back.

Finished with washing her hair, Walking Bird was quietly braiding her wet locks when she noticed Tyoga along the trail. "Eh ya, Ty," she said to her companion bathers while flicking her head in the direction of the stunning young man.

The maidens' dark eyes riveted on Tyoga's naked muscular chest. Their heads gently swayed in rhythm with the roll of his broad shoulders and swing of his powerful arms. Morning Sky and Lone Dove stole an impish sisterly gaze before making their way out of the deeper water. They reached water shallow enough to expose their breasts as Tyoga rounded the bend.

"A hey-yo, Ty," Morning Sky called to him while seductively arching her back and reaching her arms toward the sky. "The water's warm. Coming in?"

Lone Dove did not stay in the waist deep water, but continued her alluring glide to shore to expose herself all the more. With both hands over her head, she squeezed the excess water out of her thick lustrous hair. Brilliant sunbeams streamed through the swaying branches of the willow trees on the shore to halo her exquisite form with a radiance that matched her seductive beauty. Her taut breasts and erect nipples framed in the sunlight invited Tyoga to join her.

"A hey-yo, Ty," she said. "Come in and join us, Ditlihi. You look like you could use a good rub down."

"I don't think so, Lone Dove." Glancing at her breasts, Tyoga added, "Seems like the water is pretty chilly from up here!"

Walking Bird and Morning Sky covered their mouths and giggled out loud.

The open invitation to join the beautiful young ladies brought a smile to his face. "Thanks, but I think I'll give you girls some privacy. I'll head on down to Green Rock Cove. Besides, I know the kind of rub down you're talking about. Not that I couldn't use one, by the way," he said with a smile.

Seeing the bulge in his tight leather breeches assured the young ladies that their little game had achieved its desired intent. They weren't willing to let the opportunity simply walk away.

"Ah come on, Ty. You used to swim with us all the time," Walking Bird teased.

"Yeah ... well ... I've grown as you can plainly seen," he said.

Walking Bird, who had remained in waist deep water suddenly stood up. She cupped one melon-sized breast in each hand. "Have these grown too, Ty?"

Laughing, Lone Dove and Morning Sky ran back to the deeper water and splashed Walking Bird. They grabbed her arms and pulled her back down into the water. Walking Bird's voluptuous breasts were the envy of all of the girls in the village, and the focus of attention wherever they went.

Amused with their playful teasing, Tyoga waved his arm in the air and departed over the rise.

Green Rock Cove was a smaller, but deeper, inlet ringed by birch and maple trees. Boulders served as diving platforms on the far side of the cove, while the near side had a gentle slope of pebbles and sand that descended gradually into the deeper water. He hoped to find some privacy and calm here.

He stood for a long moment on one of the diving boulders while gazing into the reflections of the clear, cool water. After letting his doe skin shirt drop from his hands, he untied his leather adodas to let them fall to the ground. He placed the palms of his hands in the small of his back and bent backwards to stretch long and hard in the warmth of the sun. His muscular upper arms knotted and flexed in a sensuous dance that was perfectly timed with the rhythmic arching of his lower back. He locked his hands together behind his lower back, and stretched while reaching both arms as far back as he could. His triceps bulged as his chest exploded forward to release the pent-up power stored in his magnificent pects. The beads of sweat coursing along the chiseled contours of his abdominal muscles sparkled in the sunlight like tiny diamonds while drizzling past the hair below his belly button to continue their journey down the front of his leather britches. He squatted down close to the water's edge, filled his hands with the cool water swirling gently in the quiet cove, and flung it into the air to soak his hair, shoulders, chest, and back. He stood up slowly, and peeled off his deer hide breeches.

Closing his eyes, he stood naked in the sunlight to revel in the moment of oneness, silence, and inner peace. He quickly opened his eyes and cocked his head while listening intently. He wasn't alone. He paused only for a moment and dove into the cool water.

In the bushes on the rise just above the cove, Praire Day, the eldest daughter of Chief Silver Cloud, was quietly kneeling while watching

Tyoga's every move. Biting her bottom lip, she laid her left hand upon her chest in a futile attempt to quiet her pounding heart.

The sensuous joy of the crystalline water caressing his tired body buoyed his weary spirit. Holding his breath, he dove down and effortlessly glided over the pebble and sand-bottomed pool, while turning over stones in a playful hunt for concealed crayfish and salamanders. With a push off the bottom, he flew skyward to breach the water's surface like a dolphin in the bay.

Wiping the water from his face and eyes, he paused only long enough to catch his breath before rolling back down to the bottom to resume his critter search.

He was still underwater when he heard the splashing coming from the shallow sandy shoal. He looked toward the direction of the sound and recognized the long lean legs of Praire Day gingerly walking toward him. Before he had time to surface, she dove to the bottom of the pool and cupped his head in her hands. The surprise of her nakedness in Green Rock Cove left him with no defense save a sheepish underwater smile. The playful broad smile she returned put him momentarily at ease. But her eyes told another story.

They broke the surface with their arms and legs intertwined in that gangly awkwardness that accompanies balancing on wet stones.

"Praire Day, what are you doing here?" Ty asked even though he knew all too well the answer.

"What do you think, Ty? I've been following you." Her chestnut eyes sparkled.

They both laughed out loud when he lost his footing on the moss covered rocks and began to tumble backwards. She hooked her leg around his thigh to prevent his fall. He grabbed her shoulders to steady himself. Pulling her toward him—they looked into each other's eyes. The laughing stopped.

Praire Day was slightly built, and a few years older than him. Her long lean torso supported full breasts that seemed disproportionately large for her petite frame. Her well-defined waist hinted at the child that she nearly carried to term. Although her legs were long, the top of her head only came to Tyoga's chest.

When the laughter stopped, she did not raise her head to look him in the eyes, but floated in the water in front of him with her eyes locked on his upper chest. He looked down at Praire Day's wet hair cascading off her shoulders and floating in a tangle of gentle softness at the small of her back. Drops of water shimmered in the sunlight on her forehead before forming ribbons of water that streamed lazily down her nose and over her prominent high cheeks. Dewey drops softly drizzled over her full lips and she stuck out the tip of her tongue to arrest the flow. Pausing to rest in the cleft of her chin before dropping to her chest, thread-like rivulets careened over and between her breasts. She held herself far enough away from Tyoga's chest so that he could watch her breasts float in the crystal clear water of the cove.

Summoning her courage, she looked up into his eyes as her nipples grew in response to the urgency she felt between her legs.

"Praire Day," he whispered.

"Don't speak, Ditlihi. I have ached for this moment to come. More than you can ever know."

Placing her hands on his shoulders, she hooked her ankles together in the small of his back and lifted her forehead to his lips. As his lips gently brushed her skin, she shivered while her hips convulsed in a primal yearning that defied temperance or restraint.

Praire Day had been a widow since her husband was killed more than a year ago. At his death, one of his brothers would have been expected to take her into his lodge, care for her, and tend to her sexual needs just as he would satisfy the desires of his own wife. Praire Day's husband had no brothers. Even though she was the daughter of the Chief of the Ani-Unwiya, she had moved into her father-in-law's lodge, and was cared for by his family.

Usually a widow was not released from mourning until a brave asked for her hand in marriage. The village knew that Praire Day wanted to be Tyoga's woman, and no brave would dare to ask for her hand until he had made his intentions with Sunlei clear.

He and Sunlei had been lovers since the night on the summit of Mount Rag. The sexual freedoms of the Cherokee placed few constraints upon where, when, and how they were able to express their love for one another. As teens, their lust was unquenchable.

While the fact that Sunlei never became pregnant was a source of concern for her and her family, it had been a God send for Tyoga. The sexual freedoms practiced by the Native Americans were not acts that were open to the judgment of others. There was no good or bad, right or wrong associated with the joys of sexual union. There was the utility of procreation and the necessity of keeping the tribe strong with the blood of new warriors and wives.

Such was not the case in Tyoga's world.

The white world was shackled by traditions mandated by the zealous dictates of societal taboos and religious dogma. Sexual union out of wedlock was an immoral act that condemned the offender to burn in the fires of hell for all eternity. Fathering a child with an Indian woman would ostracize the Weathersbys from the few white families who formed the loosely knit neighborhood of the American frontier. They would be outcasts who would garner no help in times of need.

Tyoga was a young, strong, unmarried man who had been faithful to a single woman. He was torn between his love for Sunlei and the growing demand to take Praire Day, whose gorgeous body was draped so sensuously around his own. Feather soft, her nakedness floated gently against the coarseness of his masculine form, and her scent filled his head with a flood of emotion that engorged his senses with disarming abandon. He struggled to reconcile all that he thought he knew about his character and integrity.

What would my Cherokee brothers think of me if word got out that I had rejected the daughter of their Chief?

They will not think that it was the honorable thing to do. They will think it a dishonor and a disgrace to the tribe—the tribe of which I am a member—the tribe that saved my family's life.

His resolve waned with every beat of his pounding heart, as the natural curiosity shared by young men since the beginning of time overwhelmed reason and sensibility. Afterall, it would be little more than a physical act of intense pleasure lasting only seconds. How could such a simple and joyous moment jeopardize his relationship with the woman he loved? He was certain that after their coupling, he could walk away and leave the act in the waters of Green Rock Cove.

What about Prairie Day? Can I trust her to keep our tryst a secret?

It was not an act of which an Anu-Unwiya maiden would be ashamed. Any woman who could claim to have been taken by Tyoga Weathersby would be held in high esteem. Bragging about the liaison would be the natural course, and yet he somehow felt that she understood the need for discretion.

Lifting her gently to his lips, they delicately explored the taste of each other's mouth. Her fruity sweetness surprised Tyoga as he savored the fullness of her bottom lip. He kissed her cheeks with increasing urgency as he felt himself grow in response to her thrusting hips.

Praire Day pushed away from Tyoga and looked into his eyes in a way that Sunlei had never done. It was a look of resolute confidence borne of an acceptance of destiny's cruel injustice.

He watched her eyes as they traced the contours of his face as if committing to memory every line and nuance. She kept her eyes wide open and slowly inched her lips toward his in a gesture of intimacy that he had never known.

Without kissing, barely touching at all, she floated her parted lips over his in a feather soft sharing of breath and essence and life. The sensuous expression of passion filled him with an ecstasy that he had never known, and emptied him of resolve.

Releasing the hunger that burned within, he pulled her to him and kissed her long and hard. He reached around and cupped Praire Day's hard round buttocks in his strong shaking hands. With a gentle lift, Praire Day floated onto him.

Chapter 19

The Summons to South Fork

Tyoga was still soaking wet when he came rushing into Nine Moon's lodge. Tes Qua's mother met him with a bowl of hot venison stew in her hands. Sunlei was also waiting for him. Tes Qua was no where in sight.

Sunlei got up from tending the fire, grabbed her brother's ceremonial deerskin leggings and shirt that True Moon had gotten out for him to wear, and ran over to give them to Tyoga. "Look at you, my strong one. You are soaking wet, and your face and chest are all red. You are late. Get dressed. Hurry. Tes Qua has already eaten and is waiting for you in Silver Cloud's lodge."

"Thanks, Sunlei," Tyoga replied without looking at her.

"Ty, look at me," she demanded. "What is the matter?"

"Nothing. Just gotta hurry. Hand me the fringed moccasins."

She ran to the far side of the lodge, picked up the moccasins, and hurried back over to give them to Tyoga.

He reached for them without looking at her and was on his way out of the lodge with a hurried, "Thanks."

Sunlei reached out, grabbed him by the arm, and pulled him to her.

Looking up into his eyes she said, "Tyoga, listen to me. There is trouble. Traders from Bennett's Creek tell of two Shawnee braves who were killed on their way back to South Fork village. Their bodies were found in the rocks at Fifer's Trace. They were torn apart like the braves who hunted us on Mount Rag."

Pulling him farther to the side out of hearing range of the others, she whispered, "Ty, did 'he' do this terrible thing?"

Tyoga put his hands on her shoulders, and held her slightly away from him. "Sunlei, I don't know if he was there or not. I don't know what happened to those men. Seven Arrows and his men were looking for trouble at the confluence, but I didn't hurt anyone. If the braves were killed by," he looked around to see if anyone was within ear shot, before continuing, "'him' then he did it to protect me. That's all I know."

"You can tell me later. Silver Cloud is expecting you. Hurry now. It is not wise to keep him waiting any longer."

Silver Cloud's lodge served as the ceremonial meeting house for the conduct of official tribe business and the less formal gathering place where the People discussed the events of successful hunting trips or the courageous acts of their braves during a raid on an enemy's village. One end of the lodge had been arranged to accommodate those gatherings. Fifty or sixty tribe members would assemble to mete out justice, make laws, or laugh at a hunter's tale of a missed opportunity at an eight-point buck. That end of the lodge featured a stone-ringed ceremonial fire pit, and a raised podium upon which the Chief and tribal elders would sit to hear testimony and pass judgement. The ground was covered with reed mats, buffalo hides, and elk skin covered cushions to make the men comfortable during long hours of discussion and deliberation.

The remainder of the lodge was designed for daily living and was appointed in much the same manner as the lodges of the rest of the tribe members. Native Americans devoted great portions of the day to matters of nourishment and providing for the creature comforts that permitted them to live in harmony with the natural world. Harvesting, gathering, hunting, preparing and storing food stuffs for use in lean times were of primary concern to all members of the tribe. Their homes were little more than pantries for food storage, kitchen areas for food preparation, and industrial zones for the manufacture of tools, weapons, clothing, and the other survival truck essential for living in the 1700 Appalachian wilderness.

When Tyoga entered the lodge, Silver Cloud was crossed-legged on buffalo hides before a council fire. Two of the tribe's senior leaders, Night Bear and Not Afraid of Knowing, both dressed in their formal tribal attire, sat on either side of him. This was a clue to Tyoga that the call to the lodge was a summons with an important purpose.

Tes Qua was standing silently in front of the three seated elders. When Tyoga entered, Silver Cloud's wife and children promptly left the lodge, and Silver Cloud motioned for the young men to have a seat before the council fire. Choosing his words cautiously, Silver Cloud began speaking in Tsalagi.

"My sons, you have been as brothers since your birthing time. I have watched you grow into proud young men. Strong, brave, and wise. Tes Qua Ta Wa, son of Nine Moons, you have become powerful in your knowledge of the white man's ways. You speak their tongue and understand even their thoughts. For this, we have to thank your brother Tyoga-eh-alo. You will one day be a great leader of the People.

"Tyoga Weathersby, son of Thomas, and brother to all Unwiya, you have grown in our ways and are one of the People. You speak our tongue, and you have helped the People understand the ways of the white eyes. But, my son, you are more than of the People. You became more on that day when you defeated Wahaya-Wacon. You became part of the spirit world and you will be guided by Wahaya all of your days. You cannot turn away from the path you have been given. Where your journey will take you, we will only know when it is done. And when your journey will be done—no man can say."

Chief Silver Cloud paused to let his words of introduction and hommage pass from the lodge before beginning again.

"The People believe that you have learned to control the spirit of Wahaya that is within you. But the beast that runs wild and free is like the fire that comes from the sky. He strikes with a power of the spirit world that knows no mercy or restraint.

"Others say that you and Wahaya are the same spirit. They say that he strikes at your command, and when you must fight, you are filled with the savage fury of the mighty beast. He fights through you and you through him.

"But, my son, whether or not you and the unchecked beast are one and the same is of no matter to the People. You are one of us and we will protect our kind.

"It is said that Wahaya has caused great sorrow to come to the hearts of our Shawnee neighbors to the south. The Shawnee say that the deaths of six young braves have come at your hands. In the old days, they would have attacked our village and killed many of our men, women, and children. If not for the unions forged in times of peace, they would be striking us this very day. But we no longer wish to fight in the old ways. If words can spare life, then we must speak. Their Chief, Yellow Robe, has asked for a council to discuss these matters in peace. We will meet at their village at South Fork in three moons, to listen to what they have to say. I fear, my sons, that beaver pelts, skins of the bobcat and mountain lion, corn, pottery, and tools are not the price they will ask to be paid. While there is much that we have that they can demand of us to give, there is even more that they can demand of us—that is not in our power to give away."

Tyoga and Tes Qua exchanged glances.

Tyoga began to speak but Silver Cloud held up his hand, indicating that the counsel was over. "We will leave in two moons," was all he said.

Chapter 20

The Hidden Gifts of the Promise

The trip to the Shawnee village at South Fork would take two days. While only about ten members from the Ani-Unwiya clan would be making the trek, the entire village was involved in the preparation.

Silver Cloud, Night Bear and Not Afraid of Knowing would represent the Cherokee clan as official spokesmen. Their wives and Night Bear's son, White Wolf, would accompany them on the journey. Tes Qua, Tyoga, and Sunlei would travel as Nine Moon's family unit.

It was about a twenty-mile journey to the Shawnee village, and the trip wasn't terribly difficult. There was a single mountain pass through which the group would have to travel, and the rest of the journey would be in the lowlands along rivers and streams. There would be no need to hunt along the way because they would be able to pack enough food for their one night camp. The Shawnee would provision them for the return trip.

Nine Moons, Tes Qua, Tyoga and Sunlei gathered in Silver Cloud's lodge with the rest of the party making the trek to the Shawnee village. Communal packing allowed for women to inventory provisions and share resources. Portage of unnecessary truck was an inefficiency that Native Americans were loath to make.

The delicate bouquet of dried herbs and spices filled the air, as recently dug sassafrass root lay on shelves and sheaves of sage and wild thyme hung from the walls. Dried deer jerky tempted from the low wide bench along the south wall with its aromatic allure and peppery sting. The strips of smoked salmon released a more pungent scent that would become much more appealing during the long, lean winter months. Two dispatched quail awaited plucking and the pot, and three baskets of dried corn on the cob were ready for milling into flour and meal.

Along the north wall a recently tanned bear hide rested in a heap next to partially finished leather boots. A half-strung necklace snaked from an ornately decorated clay bowl filled with colorful glass beads. Two broken clay pipes rested next to a third in good working order. A sheaf of spider-veined dark brown tobacco leaves cradled an open pouch of its crushed cousins. Chips of quartz and dark black obsidian sat in a heap next to a striking stone, deer antler, and elk hide flecking-chap placed atop a small mound of newly quarried stones and slate.

Sunlei asked, "Will we make it through Cormack's Pass on the first day?"

Tes Qua answered, "I'm pretty sure that we will."

Tyoga disagreed. "We may not make it that far, Tes. We will have to see how fast Silver Cloud and Wind Song can travel. They aren't as young as they used to be."

Sunlei was on her knees packing cornmeal and pimih kan (pemmican) into a rucksack. "Don't worry about the old ones, Ty. They are still strong. Besides, Wind Song is not coming along." Folding an extra elk skin robe, she added, "It will be cold on the pass. Make sure to pack your winter leggings."

Tyoga and Tes looked at each other and rolled their eyes.

"Sunlei, you worry too much," Tes Qua said. "Ty and I have been up there in the dead of winter with our mocassins and a buffalo robe. We'll be fine. Why do you worry so much?" He continued, "I didn't think that Wind Song would come along. She is getting too old to venture so far over the mountains. We can take care of Silver Cloud. Sunlei, you don't mind caring for one more old man, do you?"

"I do not mind," she said. "But I will not have to take care of our Chief. Prairie Day is coming along to care for him." She reached for a neatly folded beautiful red blanket, and tossed it to Tyoga. "Ty, she brought this extra blanket over and asked me to give it to you. She seems concerned that you stay warm along the way. You'll thank her if it is a cold night on the summit."

Without a reply, Tyoga kept his head down and packed the blanket with the rest of his gear.

Tes Qua said, "Ty, I worry about staying in the Shawnee village. I do not trust that they will be content to just talk."

"I know, Tes. I ain't too anxious to camp with 'em either," Tyoga replied. "Until this business on the Rag, things have been pretty quiet between us since the Shawnee raided Tessuntee. There have been skirmishes when our paths have crossed in the woods, but they ain't amounted to much. The deaths of the two braves that were with Seven Arrows—that's what's got them riled. Yellow Robe invited us to parlez—so I don't think they mean us no harm. Still, we'll keep our flintlocks close."

"You men and your fighting," Sunlei said. "Why we cannot live in peace, I do not understand."

"Sunlei, you did not see Seven Arrows at the Rapidan," Tes Qua replied. "He wanted trouble. He was itchin' for a fight. If it had not been for the wolf—"

Tyoga looked at Tes Qua and shook his head.

Seeing the interaction, Sunlei stood up and put her hands on her hips. "Ty, I asked you if Wahaya was there. You said that you didn't know for sure. Why did you lie to me?"

Tyoga rested his hands on his thighs. "Sunlei, I didn't tell you because I didn't think that you would want to know." Thinking more about his feeble answer, and tapping into the honesty that he had so recently forsaken, he said, "No, that ain't true. I didn't tell you that Wahaya was with us at the Rapidan because I didn't want you to know. It is more 'n that, Sunlei. If he is responsible for these killin's, then ... someway, it feels like these deaths fall on me, too. I don't know how to explain it, or to make you understand. Worst of all, I don't know what to do to make him stop. It's like he takes my place. He fights so I don't have to. He won't abide no harm comin' to me. But ..."

Tyoga stopped packing and gazed far away. He hesitated to finish his thought because even though deep within his soul he knew the truth, he had not reconciled the knowing even unto himself. He was not ready. All he could manage was, "What if it isn't him doin' this alone. What if I have a part in it—and don't even know?"

"Ty, look at me," Sunlei said.

After what he had done at Green Rock Cove, Tyoga could not find the honesty required to accept her loving gaze. A nearly imperceptible crease of her brow revealed an intuitive suspicion that she would reckon with later.

She said only, "Don't ever lie to me, Ty."

Tyoga continued packing. He felt sick in the pit of his stomach at the realization that he did not leave the act in the clear, cool water of the pool, and would have to carry it with him—perhaps for the rest of his life.

Tes Qua and Sunlei were surprised at the openness with which Tyoga confessed his lack of control over the actions of the wolf. His suspicion that the wolf wasn't operating independent of his own thoughts and emotions was couched too deeply for them to understand. It conjured realities that neither were prepared to face.

There was another fear that Tyoga did not share with them. It was of a nature that could only be understood by those with whom the promise had been shared. He was not concerned about the safety of the group while they were with the Shawnee, nor with the matters of food and lodging and travel. He had come to realize that there was a chasm of consciousness between those to whom the promise had been revealed and those from whom its realities had remained concealed. Neither words nor experience could reconcile the divide.

When Chief Yellow Robe, and the Shawnee tribal elders, weighed the circumstances surrounding the deaths of the six young braves, they were sure to be swayed by the testimony of others for whom the gifts of the promise remained unseen and unheard.

Nine Moons's words, "'Sometimes the truth is not nearly as convincing as what appears to be,'" kept haunting Tyoga's thoughts.

The measures by which nature accounts for seasons and time, the benchmarks separating justice from tyranny, the cruelty that ignites courage and strength from smoldering brave intent, these are the shadow truths hidden from those who cannot see. Payment would be exacted according to the judgment of others for whom the rules remained a mystery.

Chapter 21

A Sigh in the Brush

The sun crested the foothills to the east and its life-giving rays showered the land with the newness of the day as the travelers began their journey to South Fork. The gray morning mist was rising specter-like toward the bluing sky as the savory scent of corn meal mush flavored with elk fat filled the morning air with the affirmation of community, safety, and home.

Many in the village had gathered outside of Silver Cloud's lodge to walk with the group as far as Keyser's Fork. As is the Cherokee custom, many brought items to offer to the travelers to make their journey more comfortable: blankets, leggings, food, and weapons. It was understood that the gifts could not be taken along, but the thoughtfulness of the gesture was in keeping with the custom of sharing with and caring for one another.

After packing and preparing their supplies the day before, the travelers gathered once again in Silver Cloud's lodge and were waiting for him to signal that it was time for the journey to begin.

The Chief never did anything in haste. A deeply religious man, his inclination was to allow events to unfold according to the plans of his spirit guides. "These things we cannot understand," he used to say to Tyoga and Tes Qua when they were little boys excited about accompanying him on a wild turkey hunt or fishing in the river. "We will know when it is time to go. To go before it is time is to act like the dog who barks bravely in the night at enemies that he cannot see, and runs away when they are revealed in the light of day. We will know when it is time." The boys knew to sit patiently and wait.

When Silver Cloud rose to his feet, the men lifted their rucksacks onto their shoulders, and cradled their flintlocks across their chests.

The women were more burdened with necessary truck for the journey. It was their job to make camp and to keep the men fed, comfortable, and healthy along the way. Their responsibilities were the consequence of necessity because women could neither travel nor survive in the backwoods alone. They depended upon the men for navigation, food, and protection. They understood that their very survival depended upon the men remaining strong, healthy, and alert. The men's hands had to remain free in order to defend against attack or the charge of a wild animal, which could happen at lightening fast speed. A rapid response could make the difference between life and death. They accepted their lot because it had proven to be an arrangement that had stood the test of time.

The Cherokee custom was uncomfortable to Tyoga for in the white world the men carried the heavier load. He stepped forward to help Sunlei arrange the wooden frame that carried their goods onto her back, and slipped the leather handle of their water gourd over the harness. "How's that, Little One?" he asked sheepishly, knowing full well what an honest answer would be. She did not reply, but looked up at him and smiled faintly.

White Wolf helped his sister with her pack, and then helped Silver Cloud with his quiver of arrows and longbow. With a confident nod that signaled the beginning of the journey, Silver Cloud led the group out of the lodge and into the day.

After walking the ceremonial send-off gauntlet, politely refusing the many gifts, the group was on their way. It was a sign of respect to allow the Chief to lead the way. However, his age and pace made it more practical for the younger braves to take the lead. As they rounded a bend and the village disappeared from sight, Tes Qua and Tyoga sped up their pace to move to the head of the procession.

When Tyoga passed Sunlei, she reached out and touched him on the arm. "Praire Day?" He turned around and noticed that she had not come around the bend with the others and was nowhere in sight.

"She must have forgotten something. She'll be along," he said while continuing toward the front to take the lead with Tes Qua.

"Ty, don't leave her," Sunlei implored. "Go back for her."

Ty looked around as if searching for an excuse not to go back to fetch Prairie Day. Finding none, he nodded his head in reluctant agreement. "Okay, Sunlei, I'll go back for her."

Tes Qua was a few paces in front of him. Using the unspoken signs the two had developed over the years of traveling together through the woods of Appalachia, he motioned to Tes Qua that he was going back. A quick glance to the back of the pack revealed to him who was missing. He nodded that he understood. "A-Ho."

Tyoga broke into the loping pace at which he was most comfortable traveling through the woods. Not a full run, but much faster than a walk, it had served him well as he could travel for hours on end without breaking stride or a sweat. When he rounded a bend in the trail, he nearly tripped over Praire Day who was squatted down in the middle of the path. Her backpack was on the ground between her knees. She was fiddling with a knot in the waist sash, which held the pack high up on her back and transferred the weight to her thighs so that her strong legs could carry most of the burden.

Ty squatted down next to her. "You okay, Praire Day? What's the matter?"

"My pack." She held it away from her as if examining it at different angles would force it to confess its intent to make her as miserable as possible along the trail. "The frame is digging into me and my sash won't stay tight."

"Here, let me do that." He took the sash from her hands, unknotted it, and took a closer look at her pack frame. Removing a deer hide that was bundled in her pack, he fashioned a square cushion that would fit between the frame of the pack and her back. He secured the pad to the pack frame with some strips of leather.

While he was working, Praire Day did not stand up, but remained kneeling by his side looking up into his face. He turned toward her and smiled.

The two were working in a clearing surrounded by sugar maples and towering birch trees. The leaves were in their full autumn glory. The bright October sun streamed through the upper branches to beam the colors to the ground in blazing shafts of brilliant orange, crimson, and yellow-gold.

The air was filled with the magic crispness of pre-winter chill. The natural rhythms command men to hunt and women to nurture and sustain. The imperative to couple in order to survive winter's callous reckoning runs deep and strong. Its lure entices and binds in a mysterious alchemy as old as time, and as palpable as opportunity.

Holding the pack and facing Praire Day, he said, "Stand up and turn around."

She did and he placed the pack on her back.

Holding it high on her back, he said to her, "Tie the sash. Pull it really tight low around your hips."

She grabbed the ends of the sash and tied them around her waist. "Okay."

When Tyoga let go of the frame of the pack, it slid down her back and came to rest on her derriere. "Praire Day, you have to tie it really tight so that the weight stays high. Here. You reach back and lift the pack. I'll tie the sash."

She reached back and grabbed the vertical stays of the frame and hoisted it up toward her shoulders. He moved around so that he was facing her, got down on his knees, and reached around behind her, and gathered the ends of the sash that were hanging at her sides. He knotted the sash once and pulled it taut. The knot tugged at her doeskin tunic as it came to rest just above her pubic bone.

At the urging of the knot, the sack-like tunic assumed the shape of Praire Day's seductive form. The softness of the deer hide was coaxed by the sash to reveal the gentle curves of her waist and thighs. She softly exhaled a tiny sigh when Tyoga pulled the sash tighter.

He looked up into her eyes and said, "You all right?"

"I'm fine." Smiling down at him with sparkling impish eyes, she asked, "Are you?"

Tyoga began to make the second knot, and stared straight ahead into the gentle mound of her abdomen. The seductive roundness beckoned to him, as it does to every man, and speaks of the life—his life—that could be contained and nurtured within.

The primal needs to protect and defend, to covet and control, to seduce and violate collide in an internal disharmony that quiets only after conquest or surrender. Surrender is frequently the path that most readily yields.

Praire Day let go of the frame and brushed the hair back out of his eyes.

At the same instant that she said, "Tyoga," he said "Praire Day."

They giggled nervously at their synchronous thoughts.

Tyoga pulled the second knot tight, and, before rising to his feet, rested his forhead against her abdomen for the briefest of moments.

At that very instant, Sunlei rounded the bend.

"Oh, there you are. I—" She turned away as if she had intruded upon a private moment before continuing, "I mean, we ... we were worried. Come on." She hurried away.

Before Tyoga could call her name, she was gone. He did not give immediate chase, but paused to look at Praire Day. Their eyes locked before she looked down at her feet. Instead of running after Sunlei, Tyoga went up the trail at a slower pace with Praire Day following close behind.

ᛒ ᘓ ᛒ ᘓ

The blazing fire warmed their campsite on the leeward side of Cormack's Pass. The glow enveloped the party in the comforting blush that has—through some magical conjuring as ancient as campfires themselves—convinced the species of its impenetrable protection despite all evidence to the contrary. The flames were allowed to billow because they did not need a bed of hot coals for cooking.

The pemikhan the women had packed served nicely for their evening meal. A pasty, dry bar of mashed meats and fruits, pemikhan had served as a food staple for American Indians for millenia. Its nutritious, if not tasty, sustenance kept warriors strong in battle or on the hunt, and tribes alive through the snows of winter.

As had been the case for thousands of years, the Cherokee campsite was safe, warm, and inviting. It was arranged so that family members would be close to one another through the night. The bed for Chief Silver Cloud was made ready next to White Wolf and Praire Day. Night Bear's and Not Afraid of Knowing's blankets were placed next to their wives. Considered a separate family unit, Tes Qua, Tyoga, and Sunlei were bedded together.

The night was clear and cold. The stars were shining brilliantly in the sky as there was no moon. From a bed of glowing red and white coals, the fire warmed the night.

Tes Qua and Tyoga were the only two left awake. Next to the fire, Sunlei had fallen asleep with her head in Tyoga's lap.

"Tes Qua," Tyoga said in a soft voice. "Tomorrow's a big day."

"Yes, my brother, a big day. I fear what the Shawnee will demand of us."

"I'm afraid, too, Tes, but we can't let them know." Tyoga stroked Sunlei's head in his lap. "We gotta stay strong, no matter what happens."

"Ah-ho, Ditili," Tes Qua replied. "We will stay strong."

Tyoga picked up Sunlei, who was feather light in his powerful arms, placed her on the bear skin she had spread out for her bed, and covered her with extra blankets. Tyoga and Tes Qua lay down and covered themselves with deer hides and blankets. Awake together in the dark and cold, they gazed up at the stars. They both heard the rustling in the brush about twenty yards away and recognized the ritualistic circling to make a bed in the leaves. The loud "end-of-the-day" sigh brought a smile to their faces.

Neither one said a word.

Chapter 22

South Fork

The sun floated in a crystal clear blue sky, warming the crisp autumn air into another beautiful fall day.

The party hiked along the mountain trails surrounded by ancient hardwood forests. They descended a western slope, and entered a deep gorge through which a feeder stream coursed on its way to join the Chapawanna River. Shafts of sunlight pierced the tree top canopy to sprinkle the trail with powdery pools of dazzling white. They rounded a bend in the river that curved lazily to the south.

The bank on the far side of the river abruptly broke to the west, widening the river's course so that its flow was nearly imperceptible. The cattails bordering the west shore disappeared into grassy meadows, framed by the Blue Ridge Mountains beyond.

The river's expansion created a mirror smooth surface and the rising sun's rays reflected off of it with a blinding intensity. The travelers shielded the left side of their faces from its glare as they continued on their way. With his hand deflecting the sun's rays, Tyoga squinted to bring the far side of the river into focus.

The Shawnee village came into view when the travelers exited the woods that edged the shoreline of the river. Nestled in a grassy, gently sloping plane, the village was ringed by dense woods to the north and east, and grasslands to the south. The river ran the length of its western edge.

The Shawnee lived in wood framed long houses with tall sides and rounded roofs. The wood frames were covered with tree bark or hides. The houses were arranged in a roughly circular pattern with the Chief's house in the center. Their villages were not ringed with a protective palisade. Their warriors were known for their fierceness in battle, and did not fear a raid from any neighboring tribes.

The Cherokee were announced by a gang of whooping adolescent braves who had been stationed all along the perimeter of the village to watch for their arrival. Running with reckless abandon, the boys raced toward the village with their bows and arrows posting off their backs like drunken jockeys. Their high-pitched juvenile war cries were quickly replaced by the more sobering beat of ceremonial drums.

Chief Silver Cloud, Night Bear, and Not Afraid of Knowing were at the head of the travelling band. Tyoga, Tes Qua and White Wolf fell in behind them, and the women brought up the rear.

Silver Cloud told the group, "We will walk straight to Chief Yellow Robe's lodge. Show no fear. A-hey-o. "

They followed the Chief's directions without question.

Staring straight ahead, Tes Qua said, "Bigger village than I thought it would be, Ty."

As they crossed the open field, voices chanted a song of welcome that floated on the late morning breeze.

"I've seen this village before, Tes," Tyoga replied. "More people 'n I remember. Keep walkin'."

As the sound of the drums and the song grew in volume, they heard the *CHING-cha-CHING-cha-CHING* of ankle bells strapped to the lower legs of the women while they stepped in time to the beat of the drums. The counter point of the larger bells on the squaw's right ankles and the smaller bells on their left, filled the air with an eerily seductive staccato refrain. In perfect unison, their mocassined feet stomped the hard-packed earth. *CHING-cha-CHING-cha-CHING-cha-CHING.* From a distance the sound was inviting and warm. At close range, its meaning became clear.

"Sounds friendly enough," White Wolf said.

Tyoga and Tes Qua looked at each other. They understood the intimidating undercurrent that the bells and chant conveyed.

The smell of roasting elk and bear wafted through the air as they made their way into the village proper.

The metronome beating of the deer-hide drums, chanting of the villagers, and jiggling of the ankle bells, combined with the aromas of the roasting meats, nearly overwhelmed the senses when the tiny band of Ani-Unwiya from Tuckareegee was swallowed up by the Shawnee village.

The sing-song chant broke into a chorus of welcoming whoops and hollers as the group made their way to the entrance of Chief Yellow Robe's lodge. When Chief Silver Cloud came to the lodge's doorway, the drums, the bells and the greeting yelps stopped short.

In quiet, they waited for Chief Yellow Robe to formally greet the guests. The silence was interrupted only by the occasional barking of wandering dogs and the nervous giggling of the young boys. Like an armless maestro conducting a maraca quintet, the gentle breeze rattled the seedpods topping the tall grass into a metreless chorus of monotone buzz. The sizzle of fat dripping from the elk haunch onto the hot stones and ash punctuated the hush with a menacing hiss.

Chief Yellow Robe finally appeared at the threshold of the lodge and filled the doorway with his presence. True to his name, the buffalo robe draping him from his shoulders to the ground was dyed a brilliant yellow-gold. Teased by hand into feathery tufts of silky florets, the fleecy wool shimmered in the autumn sun. His head was wrapped in a crown of lavishly folded red and yellow cloth ornately festooned with brightly-colored quail feathers, tightly spiraled pink cowry shells, and the dried puckered scrotums of enemy combatants.

His face was not painted with the black and red war paint that was the trademark of the Shawnee warriors. Rather, his right temple was marked with a single white dot representing the color of wisdom. His left temple sported a single golden dot—the color of illumination and understanding. A single green dot was placed on his chin to indicate honor and trust. These markings clearly meant that Chief Yellow Robe was interested in talking things out rather than fighting to defend honor.

"Ay-Ho Ug-wi-yu-hi," *(Welcome)* Yellow Robe said to Chief Silver Cloud. Speaking in Tsalagie, he continued, "My people welcome you to our village. We will care for you as our own. While you are with us, no harm will come to you or your people."

This was the traditional welcome extended to visitors who seek shelter and food at a foreign village. While the warm words were welcome, Silver Cloud and his party remained on edge.

Chief Silver Cloud spoke in an unusually loud voice. "Chief Yellow Robe, we have traveled far to talk with the Shawnee about matters that have come between our peoples. It is good that we speak of these matters like men. It is good that we do not kill one another as in the old ways. The union of your daughter, Winged Woman, with Grey Owl of the Mountain Clan forged a bond of peace between our peoples that must not be broken. Your grandchildren are of the Cherokee nation, and your wisdom to talk rather than fight is welcome by the Ani-Unwiya and all of the People."

Chief Silver Cloud paused. He understood that what he had to say next would be difficult for Chief Yellow Robe to understand. Looking into Chief Yellow Robe's eyes, Chief Silver Cloud continued, "We must speak of things that belong to the spirit world. It will be difficult for us to understand these things. My heart is heavy at the loss of your children. I, too, have lost children. I understand the tears of a father who cries in the night for his sons."

As a sign of respect for the dead his words now called to mind, Silver Cloud paused again.

Continuing in a more somber tone, he said, "How these things have come to pass are difficult questions to answer. Some say that the death of your sons has come at the hands of our white Cherokee brother." He pointed to Tyoga. "Others say that their deaths did not come at the hands of any man, but that the spirit-dog Wahaya-Wacon caused these terrible and tragic events. However we answer these troubling questions, Chief Yellow Robe, I must tell you that which you already know. Your sons will not return from the embrace of your ancestors. What has been done, has been done."

Chief Yellow Robe and the other tribe elders nodded in recognition of the words Silver Cloud had spoken.

"Chief Silver Cloud is a great chief of the Cherokee People," Yellow Robe replied. "His words are wise. The Shawnee have lived in peace with our Cherokee brothers to the north who allowed us to settle on this land. The peace that was broken by the dog soldiers who raided the village of Tessuntee many moons ago when the men of the village were away on the winter hunt, was broken by Shawnee braves not of the South Fork Clan. They did terrible things at the bidding of the white eyes in exchange for whiskey and thunder sticks. They were bad men, and they were punished."

Chief Yellow Robe now paused as Silver Cloud had done to indicate that his next words were of added importance. "What has come to pass has cost my people the lives of six young braves. Two of these braves were my own sons, Spotted Calf and Running Elk. Whether the lives of my sons and those of the other Shawnee braves were taken by the one you call your white brother, or by the spirit dog, Wahaya-Wacon, they are deaths that rest at the entrance to your lodge. Payment must be made for the lives we have lost."

Recognizing that he was speaking with more passion in his voice than he had intended and to continue in such a manner would be considered an offense to their invited guests, Yellow Robe reined himself in. In a more gentle tone of voice, he said, "We will not speak of such matters now. Tonight, we will gather around the council fire in the great lodge. Now, you and your family need to rest and eat. We will meet after the setting of the sun."

Chapter 23

Colliding Truth

The Shawnee had constructed a shelter on the outskirts of the village in which the Cherokee visitors were invited to stay. The campsite was located in a grassy plain about two hundred yards south of the village. A substantial structure, the lean-to even contained an inside fire pit for cooking and warmth. The campsite was comfortable, but did not afford the protection that being within the compound would have offered. Someone would have to stay awake on watch throughout the night.

The women unpacked their provisions and prepared the interior of the shelter for their overnight stay. They were meticulous in the preparation of a campsite, even if it was for a single night's stay. The lean-to had to be arranged in accordance with Cherokee customs, and the women set about the task in silence.

The men started a fire outside of the shelter, and took stock of their weapons while speaking about the council that would take place that evening.

Chief Silver Cloud began, "I fear that Chief Yellow Robe will demand much in payment for the lives he has lost." He reached into his adoda and removed a small pouch of crushed tobacco leaves. Placing the end of a long stemmed clay pipe into his mouth he blew hard to remove remnants of burnt tobacco.

"His demands will be much because he has lost much. It is right that it should be so," Night Bear said.

"If he asks for weapons, rifles, and knives, we do not have these things to give," White Wolf said. "Even if we did, it would be foolish to give weapons to those who would use them against us."

Nodding in agreement, the others did not respond out loud.

Taking a firebrand from the firepit, Silver Cloud touched the flame to the bowl of the tan clay pipe and sucked mightily to ignite the coarse cut tobacco leaves. Looking at Tyoga between puffs, he asked, "My son, is your spirit wolf with us this day?"

Tyoga glanced at Tes Qua, picked up a dried pinecone lying on the ground at his feet and began tearing it apart. "He has been following us on our journey, A-do-da (*father*). He is in the bushes down by the river." He nodded his head toward the west.

Clouds of acrid smoke engulfed the chief's head, and drifted slowly toward the open side of the lean-to. Drawing deeply on the stem of the pipe, Silver Cloud asked, "Will he remain with us?"

"He will watch over us through the night, and keep us safe." Tyoga looked into the eyes of each of the elders. What he had been asked was intended to solicit a response to a more important question. He pinched what remained of the pine cone into a powdery dust, and watched it slowly disappear into the grass. "But, a-do-da, I cannot stop him from killing."

The men acknowledged his answer with a chorus of noncommittal grunts.

Night Bear said, "It would not go well with us if he choses this time to kill again."

"Night Bear speaks the truth," Not Afraid of Knowing chimed in. "My son, you must do all that you can to make sure that he does not harm any Shawnee while we are here."

"Adoda," Tyoga addressed Not Afraid of Knowing with the title of respect. "If I knew how to stop him, I would."

All the men bowed their heads in deference to Tyoga's reply. There was nothing more to be said.

While the men sat around the fire in silence, pondering what Tyoga had said, a group of Shawnee women appeared walking toward the shelter from the village. They had removed the bells from their ankles and they approached the campsite quietly and in a manner that conveyed friendship. The women were carrying baskets and bundles wrapped in bright, colorful blankets.

"Hey-Heya." In response to Tes Qua's alert, Prairie Day and Sunlei came to the entrance of the lean-to to greet the women.

The Shawnee women nodded as they passed by the braves. The young lady in the lead who spoke a little Tsalagie greeted Prairie Day. They laid their baskets and blankets on the ground in the lean-to, and quietly turned and walked away. The baskets were filled with deer and bear jerky, cooked squash, beans and corn, and a variety of dried fruits. The council feast would not begin until after sundown, and the travelers had not eaten since their morning meal of beans, dried fish and ga-du (bread). The gift of food was a kind gesture of welcome.

While the men watched the Shawnee women dissolve into the distance, Sunlei appeared at the doorway of the tiny lodge to invite the men in for a late afternoon meal.

"A do fi la hitse a-lista-yuni-ti," *(Our hosts have brought us food to eat)* she announced. "Gi-yu-ha." *(Come in)*

The men stood up and began making their way inside to eat and rest.

Tes Qua turned to see Tyoga getting to his feet, but instead of heading in the direction of the lean-to, he was turning back toward the river. "Coming in, Ty?"

"You go ahead, Tes Qua. I'm going to go to the river to sit a spell. I'll be back after a while."

Tes Qua smiled, nodded and went inside.

The sun was making its slow decent to the western horizon, and the temperature was dropping rather quickly. Tyoga had noticed the open space of the river's wide expanse when the group walked along the river bank on their way to the Shawnee village.

It called to him now.

In the woods and along the mountain trails, one sees only what the immediate surroundings permit. Unless standing on a rocky outcropping or perched upon a summit rock, the view is bound by the density of the underbrush and proximity of the trees.

Outcroppings and summit rocks were Tyoga's favorite places in the mountains. The outcroppings permitted him to see from mountain range to valley below, and the summit rocks open the vista from horizon to horizon. Absent the confines of space and time and place, his spirit was free to soar. Open space beckoned to Tyoga like the glow of a flame to a maple moth in the evening shadows.

Even more than the openness of the river's wide expanse, it was the rhythm of the water that lured him with overpowering necessity.

If Wahaya was Tyoga's spirit-guide, water was the shepherd of his soul.

The integrity of its eternal ebb and flow was as apparent to Tyoga as the cycles of the moon that made it so, and the rhythm of the rising sun that blessed its journey anew at the start of every day. The honesty of the images its surface reflects are as true as the seasons and time itself. Pretense and charade are absorbed by its depths revealing the truth, unvarnished and raw, to be reconciled or denied. The water will abide no lie nor suffer injustice. The water tells only the truth.

The banks of the Chappawana River were only about one hundred yards away from their campsite.

The winding path that led to the river was lined with briar and berry patches, and Tyoga stopped to pick and eat some of the remaining dew berries. He was hungry. Fussing to claim a comfy perch for the night, the birds were scurrying about in the upper branches of the large oak trees. Gazing up into the trees while he maneuvered the path, Tyoga mimicked the repetitive crescendo of the darting cardinals. He smiled as they enthusiastically answered his ruse.

He turned his attention back to the path when it dipped into a ravine. He scurried along the downward slope, and put his back into the three steps needed to get him to the top of the rise on the other side.

As he crested the slight ridge, he stopped short in his tracks.

Twenty-five yards from the water's edge, Seven Arrows stood in the middle of the path. "Ay-ho, Wahaya," he sneered through the cruel grin that skewed his thin lips. He was standing where the safety and cover of the woods ended.

Tyoga did not reply.

The path to the river broke into an open meadow of grass and wild flowers. The Shawnee village was about two hundred yards to Tyoga's right. To his left, open meadow and a turn in the river redirected its course to the south.

Seven Arrows noticed him taking stock of the situation. Holding his arms out to his side and looking around, he asked in a taunting tone of voice, "So, Tyoga, you are alone? Where is your Wahaya?"

Tyoga stared into his eyes, but said nothing.

A derisive smile tightened Seven Arrows's lips. "It does not matter. Even he could not stop what will happen to you at council tonight." His demonic smirk broke into a toothy grin. "Tell me, Tyoga, Sunlei came with you to South Fork, yes? Is she back at camp preparing your bed? Do you think that you will be lying next to her this night? Will the softness of her body keep you warm? Hmm?"

Tyoga's hands began to clench into steely fists. He felt his heart begin to race and his breathing become shallow and sharp. He recognized the focused stare that presaged the transformation. On most occasions he fought the invasion of Wahaya-Wacon, but today, he lowered his chin to his chest and welcomed the spirit to enter. He extended his arms out to his sides ever so slightly and felt his muscles engorge with the naked abandon of the wild. His pupils ignited as the world around him came into sharp focus and the crispness of contrast stripped the world of color and hue.

"I told you that the day would come when you would pay for what your spirit wolf has done." The smile left Seven Arrows's face and he took two fast deliberate steps toward Tyoga. He threw both fists into the air and screamed with all his might, "That day has come!"

He stepped back and pretended to listen intently. Cupping his hand around his ear, he said, "No distant howl. Perhaps your spirit wolf has left you, Tyoga Weathersby. Or maybe only you are able to hear him. Is that it? Or are you truly alone?"

Without lifting his chin from his chest so his eyes were concealed from Seven Arrows, Tyoga said, "He is here, Descota."

"Oh? He's here? Where? Show me." Seven Arrows barked with growing confidence at seeing no sign of the wolf. "Show me this fearsome beast that protects the soul of Tyoga Weathersby. Call him out. Make him show himself."

Tyoga raised his head and stepped toward Seven Arrows with determined measured steps. "He is here, Descota," he repeated in a demonic voice that was no longer his own.

Seven Arrows stumbled over himself backing away from the frightfully cold glowing eyes that were filled with hatred and murderous intent. He fell to the ground, but quickly rose to his knees before the advancing Wahaya-Wacon. He got to his feet and ran as fast as he could for the safety of South Fork.

Tyoga watched the coward retreat in horror at what he had witnessed. When Seven Arrows was no more than a speck in the distance, he turned and headed back through the woods. His visit to the river's edge to quiet his soul would have to wait for another time. He did not want to face the horrible truth that the river's surface was sure to reveal. The water would accept no mask nor suffer disguise. It would reflect the naked truth that tethered him forever to his spirit guide.

The reconciliation of colliding truths would have to wait.

Chapter 24

The Call to Council

The evening shadows were filled with the thunderous beat of the ceremonial drums. It was the signal that Yellow Robe and the Shawnee elders were ready to receive the Cherokee delegation.

Silver Cloud and the others were on edge. Their brief welcoming encounter gave no hint about the true nature of the Shawnee's invitation to council. The parlez would be about the death of six Shawnee braves, and reparations would surely be demanded for the loss. How the meeting would end, and what repayment would be demanded was anyone's guess.

The sound of the drums poured into the Ani-Unwiya's lean-to with a thunderous roar that filled the Cherokee with dread. Seated around the fire, they looked into each other's eyes and recognized the fear they each harboured within their own trembling hearts.

Chief Silver Cloud stood up. With confidence in his eyes and courage in his heart, he looked at each member of the tribe seated at his feet. His gaze paused at each one in turn. He nodded his head, and the group rose in unison. Exiting the lodge, they headed for South Fork.

The sound of the drums grew in intensity as the small band approached the village. The space between the staccato beats filled with the resonating sound of the drumheads until the thunderous noise melded into an atonal cascade devoid of measure and beat.

It was obvious that the entire village had turned out to mark their arrival. The Shawnee stood shoulder to shoulder to create a wall through which there was no discernable opening for them to pass. There was no mistaking this pageantry for a welcome greeting. It was an intimidating display made all the more ominous by the deafening roar of the repetitive drums and the rattlesnake sizzle of ankle bells and cowry shells.

As they neared the human wall, Tyoga and Tes Qua feared for Silver Cloud's safety.

What if the people would not part to allow him to proceed into the village?

The act would be a gesture of disrespect and hostility so intolerable that propriety would demand nothing less than all out war.

"Tes Qua, ech ta eh alo," Tyoga said while quickening his pace.

Just as they got to either side of Silver Cloud, the Chief held out his hand to indicate that they were not to pass in front of him. They slowed their pace, but stayed within striking distance of their chief.

Without slowing his pace, Silver Cloud marched defiantly up to the wall of Shawnee. With but two steps left between him and the human stockade, the sheer force of his dignified presence caused a gap to open. The human wall yawned a widening pathway that led to the edge of the ceremonial fire ring. Silver Cloud stopped and stood in the glow of the bonfire. Surrounded by the deafening, threatening din, the Cherokee waited.

The haunting chant continued to build in intensity and volume until it broke into a wild chorus of howls, hoops, and high-pitched screams when their chief made his appearance.

With pompous excess befitting his station, Chief Yellow Robe stepped out of the darkness, and into the amber glow of the enormous fire. The Shawnee chief had been transformed from the man that they had met earlier that afternoon. Underneath the glorious yellow buffalo robe, the Chief wore a beautiful doehide tunic with matching leggings that glowed a powdery butternut in the light of the flickering flames. The luster of a dozen necklaces strung with chickpea-size fresh water pearls bridged the deep V of the chamois-soft chemise. Bathed in the fire's amber glow, the pearls cleaved the light into beams of dazzling color that danced from the ochre painted skin of his broad muscular chest. Deer hide fringe and tufts of feathery fox fur were sewn into the seams of each sleeve of the tunic. The mid-thigh bottom hem was ringed with red squirrel tails. His leggings were similarly fringed. The length of the fringe from the waist to mid-calf decreased as it descended his long muscular legs. His tunic was ornately appointed with elegant needlework patterns made of tiny puka shells, bone shards, and soap stone. The talons of an eagle were outlined on his left breast, and five bear claws decorated the right. Metal bracelets fashioned from various ores were wrapped around his wrists, and multicolored leather laces looped around both forearms.

The most striking difference between the Yellow Robe that greeted the group earlier in the day and the man who stood before them now was the black war paint that covered the top half of his face. From a line that ran laterally from each nostril to the lobe of each ear, and all the way to the top of his shaved head, his face had been smeared with bear grease infused with the coal and ash of burned walnut wood. The umber pigments contained in the heartwood of the walnut tree gave a reddish tinge to the black bear grease to add a demonic dimension to the chief's appearance.

Accentuated by the blackness that surrounded each socket, his eyes flashed an incredulous expression of surprised intent, which was oddly disconnected from a premeditated plan. A two-inch stripe of red ochre ran below the blackness of the top half of his head across his cheeks to his upper lip.

He wore a crown made from the antlers of a white tail buck. Like pleading hands begging the heavens for mercy, the ten points reached to the heavens in a magnificent display of nature's symmetry and balance. The breathtaking crown added nearly two feet to Yellow Robe's already impressive stature.

He raised the scepter that he was carrying in his right hand high into the air.

The drums stopped.

All grew deathly silent.

In a tone and volume that seemed inappropriately mild for the occasion, Yellow Robe said, "I welcome the members of the Ani-Unwiya Cherokee to the land of the Shawnee and to our homes at South Fork. You have come in peace and you will be treated as our honored guests. There is much for us to discuss. First, we will eat."

Silver Cloud only nodded at the end of the welcoming speech and stepped aside when Yellow Robe and the other Shawnee tribal elders made their way through the crowd to the place of honor where they and their Cherokee guests would eat the evening meal. Silver Cloud followed behind the last of the Shawnee elders and took his seat next to Yellow Robe. The rest of the delegation sat down behind the elders on the pallet of bear, beaver and elk hides.

As they took their seats, Tyoga said to Tes Qua, "Do you see them in the shadows? They are along the tree line to the north."

Tes Qua answered, "Yes, I see them. They are down along the river too."

Sentries were posted all around the circumference of the village.

"I guess they reckon that we're both pretty dangerous fellas," Tyoga said to Tes Qua with a wink of his eye. Tes Qua managed only a nervous grin as he took his seat behind the elders.

Sunlei sat down in between Tyoga and her brother.

Praire Day, who had taken a seat between her father and White Wolf, got up and sat down on the other side of Tyoga.

Taking notice of the move, Sunlei fidgeted nervously and moved closer to Tyoga.

The elders ate in silence while staring straight ahead into the darkness of the night. The Shawnee villagers ate with vigor while laughing over friendly conversation, and dodging the children who were allowed to run wildly through the crowd chasing dogs and chickens. The Shawnee served generous portions of elk and bear, maize and beans, and a pleasant beverage made of a blend of fermented peach and apple ciders.

While the crowd ate and drank with ever increasing revelry, Tyoga sensed a disquieting agitation growing in the young Shawnee braves. The others felt it, too.

"Ty?" Sunlei's questioning tone indicated her nervousness at the boisterous advances of the crowd.

"It's okay, Sunlei. They don't mean no harm. They're just hoping to make us uneasy, that's all. No need to worry."

Sitting on the outside edge of the dining group, Prairie Day was the closest to the Shawnee mob. She moved in closer to Tyoga so that their knees were touching.

He turned to her. "It's okay, Prairie Day."

Tes Qua said, "Ty, you see the one with the eagle feathers in his braid and the scar on his face?"

"Yeah, I see him, Tes," Tyoga replied.

"You see the way he is looking at Sunlei?"

"Easy, Tes Qua."

Tyoga watched the young brave who was drinking more than he was eating while grinning lustfully at Sunlei. He was stroking his crotch vulgarly while his companions egged him on with their drunken laughter and taunting.

Recognizing the sensations that presaged the sizzle that would drain his eyes of hazel-green, Tyoga took slow deep breaths. "Tes, do you see Seven Arrows?"

"Nay-ya, ditlihi," Tes Qua replied.

As the crowd of young braves grew in size and revelry, the Cherokee women were getting more and more upset. Some of the braves started a slow seductive dance around the ceremonial fire while the Shawnee women kept time with their ankle bells.

When he saw Sunlei's eyes well with tears, Tyoga knew that he needed to do something to divert her attention to more pleasant thoughts. He leaned over to her. "Sunlei, you sure were right about packing some extra blankets for our trip over the mountains. It got pretty cold last night."

"See. You should always listen to what your woman has to say." She wiped the tears from her eyes and lightly pushing him with her left shoulder.

Prairie Day took the opportunity to move even closer to him.

"You're right," he said playfully pushing her back with his shoulder. "I would have frozen if you hadn't covered me with that red blanket in the night."

Putting another mouthful of beans and squash into her mouth, Sunlei replied, "What are you talking about, Ty? I didn't cover you with a blanket last night. I was sound asleep."

Tyoga said no more.

The women who had been keeping the beat with their ankle bells as the men danced around the fire, now joined them in a more vigorous stomping dance. The CHING-cha-CHHING-cha-CHING of their ankle bells grew in volume as more and more women entered the circle and joined the slow walk-dance. Some elderly women started a quiet chant that the younger girls did not seem to recognize. The men made their way over to the ceremonial drums.

Abruptly, Sunlei stopped chewing, furrowed her brow, and looked over at Tyoga. "I didn't cover you with a blanket last night."

Prairie Day's fingers lightly tapped Tyoga's left knee. He glanced over at her and saw the gentle smile dimple her cheeks.

They all looked up as the drums began the staccato call to council.

Chapter 25

The Price

The crescendo of the drums' cadence built to a deafening roar while a lone chanter uttered a high-pitched soliloquy about Chief Yellow Robe's bravery in battle.

When the song of tribute ended, the chief rose to his feet. The drums quieted to a slow rhythmic pattern devoid of accent or measure. The Shawnee elders slowly rose after their chief and faced the enormous ceremonial fire.

The Cherokee delegation remained seated, and rose to their feet only after the Shawnee elders followed Yellow Robe toward the ceremonial lodge.

Concerned for the safety of their women, Tyoga, Tes Qua, and White Wolf lagged behind the elders. They did not want them to walk unescorted through the dark, moonless night to their temporary lodging on the south perimeter of the village. Fortunately, the same group of women who had brought the food and blankets to them earlier in the day stepped forward and gathered the Cherokee women in a very loving and gentle way. They indicated that they would take care of them in a nearby lodge, and that they would stay with them until the men were finished with their parlez.

Sunlei let go of Tyoga's hand reluctantly when they were gently led away.

Prairie Day was the last to follow the ladies into the lodge. Before entering the lodge of Runs With Elk, she turned toward Tyoga and with the faintest head nod of affirmation, she flashed a confident smile. Her subtle gesture said, "I trust in you. Do not be afraid. You will do the right thing at council."

He nodded in recognition of the message her smile had sent.

The ceremonial lodge was actually Yellow Robe's home. Larger than all of the other lodges in the village, the ceremonial portion was built at the north end of the structure in recognition of the wisdom represented by that direction of the compass. The buffalo was the medicine animal of the Shawnee and its majesty signified wisdom and deliberation. Hides of the mighty beast covered the ground surrounding the ceremonial fire that was already ablaze in the pit. Thirty wide and three deep, the buffalo robes were luxuriously warm and comfortable to allow the men to sit and talk late into the night.

Stands on Rock, the Shawnee Shaman, escorted each member of the Cherokee delegation to their seat around the council fire. Direction playing an important role in Native American deliberations, random seating was rarely permitted at formal gatherings.

Chief Yellow Robe began.

"Ey ya chinco sa *(My brothers)* ye yo tsalagia *(of the Cherokee nation)* sota loge ey alo *(have gathered with us)* this day to discuss matters that have caused my people to suffer. While the heart in my chest continues to beat, it is a heart that is filled with sadness and pain. Two of my own sons have been lifted to the sky. They walk no more in this world."

Yellow Robe paused to reach for a long ceremonial pipe with a bowl in the shape of a bear's head. "My sons have been taken from this world in a manner that we do not understand. It is certain that the fangs of a spirit dog released the life that was in them to the heavens. What we do not know is if the spirit dog was guided to kill by the command of another. I light this pipe and pray that the smoke that rises from our lips is lifted up to the spirit gods that it might please them with truth and wisdom. I ask my Ani-Unwiya brothers to smoke this pipe so that the truth of these matters will be revealed to us this night. I pass it in peace."

Yellow Robe lit the peace pipe and passed it from his lips to Silver Cloud, who took the pipe and inhaled deeply of the rough-cut harsh tobacco that burned hot and tasted bitter. No one spoke until the pipe had been passed to all present, and the smoke exhaled from the last elder had risen to the roof of the lodge.

Yellow Robe continued, "All of us at this council fire know of the stories that have followed these two braves since that night so long ago." He pointed to Tyoga and Tes Qua. "Your white brother defeated the mighty leader of the Runion wolf pack, Wahaya-Wacon. He saved Tes Qua Ta Wa, son of Nine Moons, from the jaws of a terrible and savage death."

Yellow Robe paused to acknowledge Tes Qua and Nine Moons as a sign of respect for the gift of his life. "But when the white eyes had the chance to put an end to the mighty wolf, he did not. He allowed the killer Wahaya to live. Why?"

He directed his gaze at Tyoga. "What did the young white eyes demand of the beast in exchange for the gift of his life?"

He paused for dramatic effect. "It is said that the spirit of the wolf came out of the beast." He gestured with both arms as if picking up a sleeping child. "I tell you, my brothers, that the cruel and savage spirit of Wahaya-Wacon left his own body that night, and now lives in the heart of the white eyes." He pounded his right fist over his own heart.

"Nay ya ho, ey a lo!" Tyoga shouted rudely to interrupt the chief.

Chief Silver Cloud raised his hand to stop Tyoga from speaking and motioned for Yellow Robe to continue.

"The young white eyes wishes Yellow Robe to stop because he knows that I speak the truth," Yellow Robe said with a disdainful tone in his voice. "There is more."

Tyoga saw the smirk on Seven Arrows's face grow while his eyes lit up in anticipation of what was to come.

"While the mighty wolf gave up his spirit to keep his own life, he took from the white eyes the medicine of his Beginning Gift."

At these words the Ani-Unwiya rocked backwards and looked at each other in disbelief.

The Beginning Gift was the most powerful medicine bestowed by the God of all creation. It was the life essence that determined the very nature of a man. It was seen by the Native Americans of Appalachia as the source of the fundamental truths of being. The Beginning Gift predetermined the degree to which a man is able to experience love, friendship, generosity, and compassion, or greed, hatred, deprivation, and inhumanity.

He was saying that Tyoga Weathersby had been stripped of his soul.

At this, Chief Silver Cloud could remain silent no longer. "Yellow Robe speaks the truth about the battle our white brother had with the spirit wolf," he said in a measured, strong voice. "You are right that his courage, strength, and devotion saved the life of Tes Qua Ta Wa. But you are wrong that in sparing the life of Wahaya-Wacon, he surrendered his Beginning Gift."

Angered at being told that he was wrong, Chief Yellow Robe interrupted Silver Cloud by pointing at Tyoga and demanding loudly, "Am I wrong that four Shawnee braves, two of them my sons, were torn apart by the jaws of Wahaya while camping peacefully on Mount Rag? Am I wrong that two more of our young braves were butchered by the spirit wolf after my son, Seven Arrows, stopped at his campsite on the Rapidan to ask for some food?"

Unable to sit silent in the face of such accusations, Tyoga replied to the chief's angry incriminations, "Chief Yellow Robe, it is true that your braves were killed by some—"

"I speak the truth!" Yellow Robes cut him off with a furious retort. Rising to his feet, he screamed, "And here is another truth. You, Tyoga Weathersby, are the spirit wolf. You killed my sons."

Leaping to his feet, Tyoga turned to his chief. "It is not true, Silver Cloud!"

He quaked with anger. The color drained from his eyes.

Collecting himself, he spoke in a calmer, more measured tone of voice, "Chief Yellow Robe, your Shawnee braves on Mount Rag were chasing me and Sunlei, daughter of Nine Moons, like wild dogs. They would have killed us if they had caught us. I don't know how your men were killed on Mount Rag, or what killed them. Something tore them apart, that is true—but it wasn't me."

He faced Yellow Robe. "Your son did not come in peace to our camp at the Rapidan. He did not ask us for food. When he called out to us while we were asleep in our shelter, he did not know that Tyoga Weathersby," he said pointing to himself, "and Tes Qua were inside. He was out to rob whoever was in the shelter. When he saw it was me—his eyes filled with hatred. He would have tried to kill me and Tes Qua if he had not been frightened away. He ran from our campsite like an old woman."

At this, Seven Arrows leaped to his feet, his eyes filled with rage.

Tyoga continued, "And the proof, Yellow Robe, is that the two braves that were with him that day were found dead at Fifer's Pass. The same pass that Tes Qua and I would have crossed if we had not suspected that Seven Arrows and his companions would be waiting to ambush us along the trail. We took the trail through Tonkin's Trace instead. Something found them as they lay in wait along the trail. Whatever it was ripped them apart."

Turning to Silver Cloud, he said, "My father, I have never killed any man."

Across the fire from him, Seven Arrows saw that Tyoga had not been able to keep his emotions in check, and that his eyes were beginning to glow ominously in the firelight. He pointed at Tyoga and said, "Look, Father. It is happening as we speak. Wahaya-wacon."

Still seated, Tes Qua reached up to touch him on the arm. "Ty, sit back down."

It was too late.

Tyoga's muscles began to fill with blood, and the hazel in his eyes had bled away.

He struggled to control his voice, but he could not. In a malignant tone devoid of caution and dispassionately aloof, he inquired, "What is it you want of us?"

This flagrant breach of etiquette and protocol called for Silver Cloud to demand Tyoga to take a seat and allow the negotiations to occur between the two chiefs. When he looked over at him, the chief saw for himself the stinging feral eyes of amber-orange and thought better of interceding.

Seven Arrows continued, "You see, Father? You see with your own eyes that I have spoken the truth. There is no spirit wolf. Tyoga Weathersby is responsible for the death of your sons. The killer stands before you."

Tyoga demanded once again, in a gutteral voice that was, and was not, his own, "What is it you want of us?"

Yellow Robe gained his composure and returned a callous gaze of indifference into the other worldly eyes that challenged from across the room. "What the Shawnee have lost cannot be repaid by goods or possessions. How many bushels of corn do we demand for the lives of my sons who suckled at the breast of their heart broken mother? How many rifles will replace the joy of their laughter? How many barrels of the white man's whiskey will replace the game they would have provided to feed my people?"

Yellow Robe paused. Unable to continue to stare into Tyoga's vacuous eyes, he diverted his gaze to the ceremonial fire.

"Stands on Rock, our medicine man, tells me that the will of the great spirit, gijudiva, and the law of the civilized people, demand that a life must be paid for a life. But a life taken will not replace a life lost."

The fire crackled and spewed bits of coal and ash high into the air. As if following a string of knotted yarn, the smoke and ash coursed along the superheated updrafts of air with deliberate intent until exiting the lodge through the vent in the roof.

The night was still and quiet. It was as if the entire tribe had suddenly vanished. No drums sounded. No sizzle of ankle bells. No talking or laughter. Not even the whisper of the wind could be heard.

The crooked smile-sneer creased Seven Arrows's lips once again. This was the moment he had been waiting for.

Yellow Robe said, "To replace that which we have lost, I, Yellow Robe, demand only one life in return. Six times over this one life will repay the debt owed to me and to the women of the Thawegilas tribe who weep for the others lost at the hands of Tyoga Weathersby." He looked up from the fire to stare straight into Tyoga's icy yellow eyes, and spat the words. "Wahaya-wacon."

"Sunlei A-wi, daughter of Nine Moons, will be taken by Seven Arrows. Together, their bodies will replace the lives we have lost."

With a blink as if to awaken, Tyoga broke away from Yellow Robe's stare, and refocused his gaze on the flickering flames of the dying fire.

Seven Arrows rose triumphantly and marched from the ceremonial lodge with the confident stride of a victorious general.

His laughter followed him into the night.

H.L. Grandin

Part Three

Abandoned Hope

H.L. Grandin

Chapter 26

Surrender

The party did not stop to camp at Cormack's Pass, but walked through the night to return to Tuckareegee. They arrived before the rising sun, tired, hungry, dirty, and desolate at what had transpired the day before in the Shawnee village.

As word spread throughout the village of Yellow Robe's horrific demand, the people gathered in Chief Silver Cloud's lodge to discuss the matter among themselves and to hear what their chief had to say.

In the family area of the lodge, Wind Song was preparing a basin of warm water for Silver Cloud and Prairie Day to wash off the dirt of the trail. She had already laid out the Chief's everyday tunic and leggings, and steam was rising from the bowls of deer stew she had prepared for them to eat.

Not speaking, Silver Cloud and Prairie Day exchanged loaded glances while putting on their clean clothes. Prairie Day had expressed her thoughts about Yellow Robe's demands to her father throughout the night as they trekked along the dark mountain trails. There was nothing left for them to say.

Four years apart in age, Prairie Day had cared for Sunlei as a sister when they were both no more than children. It was she who had taught her to braid her hair, macramé twine, scale a fish and sew rabbit skin mocassins. More than anyone else in the tribe, she recognized the gift that Sunlei was to the Ani-Unwiya. She understood that her light skin and command of the English language would one day elevate the Wolf Clan to a position of power in the coming white world. But more than that, she loved Sunlei. Taking Tyoga in Green Rock Cove was an act separate and apart from her relationship with her. She could not deny her love for Tyoga and found no shame in their sexual triste—it was their way. She loved Sunlei no less. She would do anything to secure her happiness even if it meant denying her own.

As she pulled her doe skin chemise over her head, she saw Tyoga and Tes Qua enter the lodge. They had not changed their clothes, washed, nor had anything to eat. Their faces were smeared with the smoke and ash from the Shawnee's ceremonial fire. Tyoga's face was covered in thick black stubble. Prairie Day noticed that while his eyes were alive with anger, they retained their gentle hazel hue. She feared that would not last for very long.

Sunlei, her mother True Moon, and her father Nine Moons had arrived in the lodge before Tyoga and Tes Qua.

Despondent and inconsolable, Sunlei sat in a far corner of the lodge cradled in her mother's embrace. True Moon rocked her gently while smoothing her hair with her soft touch. Eyes red and swollen, Sunlei stared blankly into space while allowing her mother's cradling arms to surround her in some measure of safety and peace. She had no more tears to shed.

Nine Moons, Tes Qua, and Tyoga went to the ceremonial end of the lodge where the others were discussing the terrible price that had been demanded for the loss of Yellow Robe's sons and the other Shawnee braves.

Nine Moons spoke with some of the men and women of the tribe while waiting for their chief. On most occasions, only men were allowed into the ceremonial end of the lodge. This day, the council session was open to all members of the tribe who wished to listen to the discussion.

After the Chief finished his bowl of stew, he stood up and walked slowly through the crowd to take his seat on a mound of buffalo robes. When he was settled, he gestured to Nine Moons to speak.

"My wise and brave Chief. We, your people, come to you at the rising of the sun to honor your courage and strength. I traveled with you to South Fork and listened at the council fire as Yellow Robe de-manded my daughter as payment for the Shawnee braves his tribe has lost to Wahaya-Wacon. I plead with you now not as my chief, but as my brother, to not allow this thing to come to pass."

Nine Moons paused while the crowd reacted with approving chatter. "Since our beginning time, we have been together. We have hunt-ed and supplied our people with food in times of plenty. We have fished the rivers and streams in the dead of winter in times of want. Together, we have defended our land, and shed blood to protect our women and children. Together, we have even taken the lives of those who would hang our scalps on their lodge poles. You are Sunlei's a-do-da–eh-alo (*godfather*). You held my daughter to the sky on her naming day. You presented Sunlei-Awi to the great-spirit and introduced her to the People. She is as your very own. Silver Cloud, I know that it is not in you to stand by and watch her walk into the arms of the Shawnee dog, Seven Arrows."

While Nine Moons was addressing Silver Cloud, many of the People had awakened to the news of the meeting in the council lodge, and rushed to take part in the discussion. A large crowd had gathered behind him to listen to his words. A woman yelled out, "Nine Moons is right. We cannot allow this to happen to our daughter!"

A brave chimed in from the back of the lodge, "We will not let them take her. We will fight!" At this, the braves raised their tomahawks and bows, and let out with war cries that shattered the silence of the morning.

Silver Cloud rose to face the crowd. With an expression of anguish contorting his weathered face, he addressed the crowd. "Eh ta tee chi tu no eh alo. Be-chi. E yo *(We)* et a *(have)* lish a lo come from a council called by Chief Yellow Robe of the Shawnee nation. He and his people have lost six young braves, two of them his own sons, they say at the hands of our brother and son Tyoga Weathersby."

He paused to carefully compose the next few lines of his address to his people. "That our brother is of the spirit world there can be no question. His power is real. The spirit of Wahaya-wacon lives within him. He possesses the courage and strength of Wahaya, but also the wisdom of the wild that guides the power he owns. My son, Tyoga, vows to me that he has never taken the life of any man. My son has always spoken the truth. His words are true. I believe them. But I also believe that the Shawnee braves were killed by Wahaya-Wacon. Where my son Tyoga ends, and the spirit dog Wahaya begins, I cannot say."

As Silver Cloud spoke, the people continued to pour into the council lodge. When he had finished speaking, the room was filled to capacity and the crowd was spilling out onto the ceremonial grounds outside of the lodge.

Silently, Prairie Day had made her way to where True Moon was holding Sunlei in her arms. She knelt down next to Sunlei's mother, put her arms around her and held her while she rocked her daughter. She rested her cheek on top of True Moon's head. With the rest of the crowd, they had listened to Silver Cloud's words in respectful silence. They waited quietly for him to resume.

Pockets of murmuring between the braves in the room caused Tyoga and Tes Qua to turn around and scan the crowd. The tone of the hushed whispers conveyed an anxious restlessness seeking rancor rather than resolution.

Silver Cloud continued, "Chief Yellow Robe has demanded that his son, Seven Arrows, be joined with Nine Moon's daughter Sunlei Awi. It is his wish that together they replace the six lives that have been taken from the Shawnee by Wahaya-Wacon. In seven moons, the Shawnee will arrive to take her."

"When they arrive we will kill them! We will kill them all!" a voice rang out. Once again a loud chorus of war whoops, punctuated with fists thrown in the air and tomahawks raised by muscled arms, erupted through the crowd.

Silver Cloud raised his hand to quiet them. "My People. We must not interfere. We must not allow any harm to come to Seven Arrows and his men when they come to take Sunlei. For many years, we have lived in peace with our Shawnee neighbors. The unions made between our peoples have allowed it to be so. Cherokee and Shawnee blood runs in the veins of our children, and because of this we will not risk a war."

Chief Silver Cloud paused to allow this edict to be understood by all. "Yellow Robe is a wise and powerful Chief of the Shawnee. Once before a renegade band of dog soldiers defied their chief's orders and wiped out a peaceful village of unprotected Cherokee. If the Ani-Unwiya do not pay what has been demanded, I do not know if Yellow Robe is strong enough to stop them from making war. If Seven Arrows and his party do not return to South Fork with Sunlei, the Shawnee may rise up against the will of their chief. If they come, they will butcher our men and torture our sons. Our women, our wives, they will rape and enslave. The Shawnee will leave no footprint of a single Ani-Unwiya."

A hush fell over the crowd as if the wind had been knocked out of every brave in the room.

The good of the many was the credo by which the Native Americans lived their lives. Self-sacrifice was an unquestioned obligation that was given freely by members of any tribe. In battle, in a dangerous hunt, or in matters of state, the willingness to sacrifice oneself for the sake of territory, honor, freedom, or peace was an expectation rather than a duty. The imperative was to continue, to persevere, and to survive. If one must be given up so that the destiny of the many is fulfilled, then it must be so. Native Americans gave of themselves freely so that others might live.

But giving up Sunlei would not be an act to which the People would freely bow.

Sunlei had grown into so much more than merely one of the People. She was "the" one of the People. While it was true that her physical beauty was spell binding, and that her strength of character and personal charm were unequaled in the land, those attributes played only minor roles in her value to the Ani-Unwiya people.

Sunlei Awi *(Morning Deer)* was their hope for a future rooted in the respect and reverence for their past. It was she who was destined to fulfill the imperative to continue, to persevere, to survive.

From the northern snowy hollows of the Caughnimaw Valley to the humid southern swamps of Okeefenokee, the entire Cherokee nation had placed their hopes for bridging the growing chasm between the colliding worlds of the white man and the Native Americans upon her delicate frame. Enough white blood coursed through her veins to chisel her facial features and sculpt her lean body into a package that would one day be accepted in the white man's world. If not as an equal, then certainly as an acceptable partner in civil discourse.

Her command of the English language and a hoped-for marriage to Tyoga Weathersby would make her a formidable presence in managing the white avalanche that was poised to bury the Appalachian frontier.

To surrender her to the Shawnee was to abandon their hope for the future.

Stepping from the crowd, Calling Owl, a strong and respected warrior, said, "Tyoga Weathersby, Yellow Robe believes that you and the spirit wolf are one and the same. It is of no matter to the People if this is true. What matters is that Sunlei Awi will be taken from us because of what Wahaya-Wacon has done. Because of the spirit dog, you may never feel her touch again in the night. Her voice you will hear no more. Wahaya-Wacon has not only broken your heart, but the heart of the People as well. What have you to say about your spirit guide now?"

Tyoga rose and faced the crowd. Before he could begin to speak, Tes Qua rose to stand by his side.

"E ya a ho, Wahaya-Wacon eh a to wa e alo," Tyoga said. "That Wahaya-Wacon is my spirit guide is not a choice that I have made. His spirit has chosen me. Why this has happened, I cannot say. I only know that it is true. He tested me on that night on the ridge because he knew that I, like the Weathersbys before me—Joshia, Joseph, and Thomas, my father—had been awakened to the ways of the natural world by a promise spoken to me by our earth mother. She has revealed her secrets to me in ways that others cannot understand. The rising of the sun speaks to me not in words but in textures, colors, and hues. The rivers and streams do not reveal themselves to me as water coursing to the bay, but as whispers carried on the wind that speak of abundance and want. The pine trees swaying in the mountain breeze disclose their courage and strength in terms of time, generations, and fleeting chance."

His meager attempt to make the crowd understand having been for naught, Tyoga stopped and bowed his head. The promise spoke to him in a language understood only by those who had been awakened to its presence. While they heard his words in Tsalagi, he may as well have been speaking in Cheyenne. "I do not expect you, my brothers and sisters, to understand these things. I only wish that you know them to be true. The spirit of Wahaya found a willing soul when he chose mine to share. He lives in me and has shown me the ways of mother earth even beyond the revelations of the promise. Now, his deeds—or mine—have caused us to lose Sunlei forever."

At hearing these words, Prairie Day stood up at the far end of the lodge. She looked at Tyoga not with the hurt eyes of an angry, jealous woman; but with eyes filled with compassion and heart wrenching pain. More than anyone, she understood his words. It would take great courage for him to carry on.

Wanting him to see that she was there, she stood proud and strong. He did.

As the crowd listened to Tyoga's words, they understood his acceptance of Yellow Robe's demand as the only prudent course. As much as they would have stood by him had he called them to arms to protect Sunlei, they knew that he would not risk their lives and the lives of the entire Ani-Unwiya clan for the sake of his own happiness. Their understanding made them no less angry. The restlessness of the crowd grew in intensity. The People abandoned the hushed tones of their private conversations.

"You ask us to stand quietly and surrender Sunlei to the Shawnee dogs?" a brave screamed from the back of the lodge.

"How can you allow her to be taken by Seven Arrows without a fight?" a female voice chimed in.

Another cried out, "Are you an Ani-Unwiya warrior or a scared woman? Call on us to fight and we will stand by your side." With bows and tomahawks raised high into the air, the crowd again erupted into a chorus of war cries, screeches, and screams.

Sunlei had been lying in her mother's arms in an exhausted trance that mercifully dulled her senses to the horror that awaited her as a Shawnee squaw. The gentle touch of her mother's loving hands as she stroked her thick black hair and the sound of her soothing voice in her ear had lulled Sunlei into brief periods of sleep. Hearing her fate the evening before at the council in South Fork, and walking through the night to return home had been too much for her. She was strong and brave, but still a young woman not yet hardened by the unexpected trials of life on the frontier.

The braves' war cries shook her awake. Caught in the boundary between sleep and consciousness, it took several seconds for Sunlei to sort the imagined from the real. As her eyes cleared, she slowly lifted her head from her mother's lap. Gently peeling away the fold of her mother's arms, she rose to her feet.

The crowd hushed when they saw her stand.

Straightening her tunic, she righted her shoulders and walked through the crowd straight toward Tyoga. Her measured, deliberate steps were spaced to keep her on her feet while her mind raced with the intoxication of exhaustion and disbelief. While her focus was on Tyoga's eyes, she saw—yet did not see—her childhood friends embracing each other with tear-stained faces and trembling hands; her aunts and uncles clutching each other; and Lone Dove, Morning Sky, and Walking Bird holding each other. As she walked by them, they reached out to her and called her name. She heard, but did not hear. When she got to the front of the crowd, she turned and announced in a voice quivering with emotion, "Seven Arrows will come to Tuckareegee in seven moons. When he comes, I will go with him in peace."

Some of the women in the crowd began to cry, and others called out, "No! We will not let you go!"

Turning to face Tyoga who was standing at her side, she took his hands in hers. Looking up into his tear-filled eyes, she said, "Tyoga will never ask you to risk your lives to secure his happiness, nor to ensure mine. While we could easily defeat Seven Arrows and a small band of Shawnee Braves, it would be a battle that would only buy time. The South Fork Shawnee will come with all of their warriors to wipe us out. I beg you, do not ask Tyoga to carry the deaths of his brothers with him for the rest of his life. Do not ask him to suffer the nightmare screams of our children as they are butchered by the Shawnee."

Sunlei stopped to hang her head as she shook with the effort to contain her sorrow. She looked back up at his face, which was now streaming with tears, and said for all to hear, "I do not ask this of him. Even if I did, he would refuse."

A body wrenching sob contorted her tiny frame so that she was barely able to speak her final words. Her knees grew weak and she drew herself closer to Tyoga, who supported her more earnestly. Gathering herself, she turned to the crowd and said in a voice strangled by emotion, "He is Wahaya-Wacon. He is filled with the wisdom to know what must be done, and with the courage to see it through. His spirit will give him the strength to carry on."

Tyoga pulled Sunlei to him as her body convulsed in heart-breaking resignation of the horror that was to come. They stood for a long moment entwined in each other's embrace. With monumental effort, she stepped away, turned to the crowd, and said, "I am but one soul, and I will go with Seven Arrows of my own free will. I do this so that my People will live in peace."

The tears streaming down Sunlei's and Tyoga's faces spread through the gathered crowd. The women hugged each other while they wept in disbelief at what was to come to pass. When the eyes of the braves began to fill, they turned to exit the lodge so that their tears would not be seen.

"Wait, my brothers," Tyoga cried out before many could leave the lodge. "Hear me. When Sunlei is taken from Tuckareegee, my heart will be torn from this place. A man cannot live without his heart. I cannot bear to stay here without Sunlei by my side. I cannot bear to stay among you as the cause of your grief. I will leave my Ani-Unwiya family, and find my own way."

No one uttered a sound. No one cried out, "Stay."

In the back of the lodge, Prairie Day wiped her eyes, clenched her fists, and walked out alone into the dawn.

Chapter 27

A Reckoning

The entire village spent the next several days helping Sunlei's family prepare for her departure. They moved through the alleys of Tuckareegee as if in a trance. Silence filled the usually vibrant town with an eery pall that would not abate.

Gifts flooded the lodge of Nine Moons and True Moon while families gathered to say their private goodbyes to Sunlei. Tes Qua stayed with Sunlei and his parents while they were receiving visitors, acknowledging their gifts, and embracing well wishers in long painful partings filled with tears.

To make the parting all the more difficult, Seven Arrows and a band of Shawnee braves arrived three days ahead of schedule and camped only about a half-mile to the south of the Cherokee village. It was a calculated taunt designed to provoke the grieving citizens of Tuckareegee.

Since announcing his impending departure at the meeting in the council lodge, Tyoga had made himself scarce. His rebuke at not being encouraged to stay among the People after Sunlei's departure was a painful reminder that he was indeed a brother to the Ani-Unwiya, but not a son. Although he had lived among the People all of his life and was accepted as a member of the tribe, no Cherokee blood ran through his veins. His color, build, and cultural heritage were barriers too conspicuous to be erased by ceremony or time.

He had made camp on an overlook from which he could see Sunlei's lodge. The People could see his campfire burning brightly in the night sky. Alone in the wilderness, with Wahaya by his side, he thought of the journey that had brought him to this place and time.

He recalled that day with his papa so long ago when he stood on Carter's Rock on a chilly summer morn and he saw the beams of sunlight that exploded from the peaks to the east to fuse with his soul and lift him from the confines of time and place.

That precious moment released him from the burden of questioning why and filled him with the intuitive truth that the answer made no difference at all. The knowing freed him from the imprisonment of doubt, uncertainty, and fear. The liberating wisdom permitted unfettered action and uncompromised certainty.

Why have I been chosen to receive the promise?

Events in his life had unfolded so that the distinction between gift and curse had been more than marginally blurred.

What sense does it make for my journey to unfold so that the woman I love should be taken away from me by an adversary whose life has inexplicably intersected with mine in such devastating ways?

His faint smile revealed the awareness that he had caught himself asking "why?" He chuckled and whispered out loud, "The answer makes no difference at all."

He remembered the horrific night on the escarpment when he very nearly died saving the life of his brother Tes Qua Ta Wa. He shivered when he looked upon the mighty beast lying so docilely at his side and recalled the moment that the gift was given to him on that fateful night. He understood that he had been chosen to receive the power from Wahaya-Wacon, but he struggled still to understand the hand that had guided the melding of their souls. He reached out and gently touched the wolf's left shoulder.

The wolf picked his majestic head up off of his enormous forepaws and turned to reassuringly gaze into Tyoga.

Tyoga remembered growing up wild and free with the Ani-Unwiya and running naked through the woods with Sunlei and Tes Qua, White Wolf, and Four Bears. They had all grown into young adults. The joys and dreams of childhood had been sobered with age and tempered by experience.

Hearts broken as puppy love crushes yield to the caprice of emotions as unpredictable as the flight of a feather in the wind.

That moment when Sunlei floated so lightly in his arms in the swimming hole was the first time that he noticed that she was leaving behind those things of childhood and accepting nature's call to focus on those inescapable demands that herald the advent of womanhood. The eyes reflecting his own were that of a woman. He recalled the loss of his tomboy friend. That brief exchange of a knowing glance changed their relationship forever.

He thought about Prairie Day. Her eyes reflected a part of him that he did not see in Sunlei's eyes. She radiated an unyielding confidence in the rightness of his words and deeds; like an adoring mother reassuring a reticent child, her gaze unerringly filled him with the confidence he needed to succeed, conquer, and command. She was a remarkably strong woman whose maturity anchored him in ways that Sunlei could not. That she loved him was beyond question.

His fists clenched and his jaw tightened with the realization that circumstances had conspired to spiral his life out of control and strip away from him the independence and self-reliance that had defined him as a man. Like a flock of doves whose course is determined by the prevailing winds, his destiny was being determined by the unpredictable villainy of a single man determined to do him harm.

How is it that everything that has come to pass has been so closely linked to Seven Arrows? Why were his brothers among the warriors chasing me and Sunlei on Old Mount Rag? Why was it my camp that Seven Arrows stumbled upon on that gray cold morning along the Rapidan? Why is it me, so in tune with the ways of the natural world, being inexorably guided down this destructive path that will only end in heartache, loneliness, and despair?

He stood, raised his arms to the heavens, and released an anguished cry that filled the mountain tops, echoed off of the canyon walls, and descended into the village as a melancholy pall foreshadowing the events to come.

Tyoga listened to his own voice die away as it was consumed by distance, time, and indifferent dismissal. When there was nothing left but the sound of the whispering wind in the pines, he dropped his arms to his side and bowed his head in dismay. He stood for a long time. When he sat back down, he found that Wahaya was no longer lying down, but was sitting erect and looking up at the moon. Tyoga reached out to reconnect with the primal energy of the wolf.

Sitting side by side, the wolf was a full head taller than Tyoga.

He dropped his hand into his lap, looked up at the wolf, and said, "Wahaya-Wacon. What more do you know? Tell me what to do."

Wahaya-Wacon stopped gazing up at the moon, and looked down into Tyoga's eyes. The power of his stare startled Tyoga for a moment, but the calm of the quiet knowing transcended the wolf's momentary position of dominance and command. His eyes stayed riveted to the wolf's golden-brown eyes. Falling ever deeper into the abyss, he surrendered to their spell as the warmth of knowing washed his senses free and cleansed the confusion that muddles reason and paralyzes action in the chains of second guesses.

Tyoga closed his eyes and heard a whisper in a voice so tranquil that he knew it wasn't his own say. "You know what to do. We will not let this stand. Together, we will find a way."

With his head still cocked toward the heavens, he heard his own voice say out loud, "I know what to do. This time—the 'why' matters. This time—the answer makes a difference."

With his eyes still closed, he reached out to touch Wahaya.

He opened his eyes to see his hand flailing in the blackness of the night.

Wahaya was gone.

Sitting alone on the outcropping, Tyoga shook his head and said, "I know."

Chapter 28

Farewell, My Love

The outcropping upon which Tyoga had made his camp was about a half mile to the southeast—and a quarter mile straight up—from the site Seven Arrows and his band of Shawnee Braves had chosen for their campsite. They had set up camp within earshot of the village because they wanted the People to hear their jubilation at the horror they were to visit upon them in three days time.

When they heard Tyoga's anguished scream in the night, they looked up toward the outcropping and began to joke with one another saying that the cry was probably Tyoga making love to Sunlei for the last time. That they could make light of such a thing days before they were to take Sunlei away from the only home she had ever known laid bare their cold, callused hearts.

The agonizing thought that she would be separated from her family and friends, perhaps forever, was of no concern to Seven Arrows. What filled his spirit with a soaring joy was the knowledge that she would be torn from the arms of his unconquerable adversary, Tyoga Weathersby. She was the most beautiful woman in all of Appalachia, and she was to spend the rest of her days pleasuring him in ways that only Tyoga had known.

It was a tremendous coup for Seven Arrows and the Shawnee. He was going to relish every moment.

The whiskey Seven Arrows and his party had traded for with some French trappers they met along the way to Tuckareegee was taking its toll on their judgement and behavior. With whiskey-induced bravado, one of the braves screamed into the night, "Sunlei, we have brought many gifts for you."

As laughter and war cries echoed from their campsite in the valley below the village, Seven Arrows's voice could be heard above the rest, "Don't be sad, my Little One, soon you will know the joys of a real man being inside of you. I hope you are saving yourself for me. I do not wish you to be covered with the stench of that dog-man Tyoga Weathersby."

At this, one of the braves fired a rifle shot into the air and the war cries and screams reached a fever pitch.

"Maybe you do not wish to wait to begin your new life as a Shawnee squaw," another voice screamed. "Maybe we will come and take you now." Another rifle shot shattered the night air.

The icy howl of the wolf descended from the mountains and engulfed the partying band of Shawnee braves with a sombering dispatch. The sound was not terrifying in the way that it had paralyzed Seven Arrows at the campsite at the confluence. This call did not penetrate their bodies with a quaking resonance borne of proximity and mass. This call was hauntingly plaintive and eerily prescient.

While the first howl's echo was dying in the distance, the second crescendoed through the night blanketing the Shawnee's camp with a decree that ordered quiet and demanded peace. The Shawnee looked up from the valley floor toward the Ani-Unwiya village. Their eyes were drawn farther up the mountainside to the billowing flames from the outcropping where Tyoga had made his camp. Without saying a word, they put down their weapons, corked the whiskey bottle, and gathered quietly around their fire.

At the sound of the doleful howl, Tes Qua and Sunlei stepped outside of their family's lodge into the cool night air. They, too, gazed up at the overlook where Tyoga's fire lit up the night sky. It was a clear night and the heavens were filled with stars and a smiling crescent moon bejeweled the northern sky.

Tes Qua put his arm around his sister and held her close to him. "Wahaya-Wacon is up there with Tyoga, isn't he, Tes A?"

"They are never far apart, Little One," he replied. "I suspect that they are together now."

"Will you take me to him, Tes?" Sunlei peered up into her brother's tired eyes.

"Are you sure that you want to go, Sunlei?" her brother asked. "Tyoga has separated himself from the village for a reason. Do you think that it is the right thing to do?"

"I know why he has stayed away. I understand." Sunlei was rolling a small stone on the ground with the toes of her left foot. She threw her gaze toward the fire lighting the tall pines that framed the outcropping. "Tes A, Tyoga told me that he will be leaving before the Shawnee take me away. Maybe he will leave tomorrow morning. This may be the last night that we will ever have the chance to be together. Take me there, my brother. Please."

It was only about an hour's climb to Tyoga's campsite, but the trail was steep and traveling in the dark slowed them down. It took them about two hours to reach the outcropping.

As they approached the camp they could see Tyoga, wrapped in a buffalo robe, seated alone by the fire. When he saw them approach, he sprang to his feet and raced toward Sunlei.

Bounding toward him with unbridled emotion that erupted into squeals of delight, she threw herself into the air to land in the embrace of his loving arms. Burying her face into his chest and neck she cried and laughed uncontrollably while he smothered her head and face with hard kisses of impassioned urgency that knew no bounds. With a yearning more demanding than expressed by a kiss, she wrapped her legs around his waist and painted his neck and chin and cheeks with her mouth and lips as if tasting his manhood would extinguish her need. Consuming her scent, he inhaled the heady musk from her hair and savored the sweet salty sweat from her brow filling his senses with her carnal bouquet. He held her so tightly that she could barely breathe and still she was not close enough.

Placing her feet on the ground, she gazed deeply into the eyes of the only man she had ever loved. She examined his face the way a mother lovingly searches her child's countenance for nuanced truth. She smiled at his futile attempt to conceal himself from her, and seared his image into her brain.

She had stopped crying and her eyes reflected the stars and the image of the crescent moon.

Without saying a word, she took Tyoga by the hand and led him toward the shelter. She stopped to allow Tyoga to pull the hide flap aside before she stepped in.

Tyoga turned to Tes Qua, nodded, and followed her inside.

Tes Qua went back to the lodge alone. It was after midnight when Sunlei rolled out of Tyoga's arms to spoon in his loving embrace. Naked, warm and satisfied, she listened to him breathing for several minutes before giving him the lover's nudge and asking, "Are you awake?"

Tyoga took a deep breath and responded, "I am now. What is it, Little One."

"My cousin, Walks Alone, is coming to see me."

"Walks Alone is coming here?" Tyoga asked propping himself up on his elbow.

"Yes. He wants to see me before …" She did not finish her thought.

"That's great news," Tyoga replied.

Sunlei rolled over so that she was facing him. "Great news?"

"We haven't seen Walks Alone for a long time and it will be good to see him again."

Sunlei wondered at his enthisiasm for reconnecting with Walks Alone, but other matters were more pressing so she left it alone.

"Sunlei," Tyoga said, "stay with me until he gets here."

"I should be with my family, Ty," Sunlei replied, but quickly added, "but I want to stay here with you. I just can't stand staying in my father's lodge listening to those Shawnee dogs camped below." She paused for a moment, rolled on her back and gazed up at the ceiling of the lean-to. "Yes," she replied. "Yes, I will stay here with you."

Tyoga rolled her into his arms and held her close to him for a long time. "We will move my camp today."

"Why, Tyoga? Why do we need to move."

"At the council I told the people of Tuckareegee that I would leave the mountains and never return. Now that we can stay together for two more days, I do not wish them to think that I have not kept my word. The People—and Seven Arrows—must think that I have left the mountains. They must not see my fire at night, or any movement during the day. It must be as if I have disappeared."

"My brother will come to get me this morning," Sunlei replied. "He can help us move."

"Yes, Sunlei. Tes Qua can help. But no one else must know that I am here. Seven Arrows must think that he has driven me from the mountains and that he will never see me again. I will leave this place when he takes you away."

"Okay, Ty, if you say so," Sunlei said with some question in her voice.

Tyoga sat up and said, "Sunlei. This is important. He must think that I am already gone."

"I understand," she replied. "But you must promise to stay close until he takes me away. Will you promise me?"

"Yes, Little One. I will stay close."

CB ℰℭ CR ℰℭ

The sun had not risen yet when the two stood on the outcropping folded in each other's arms. Their nakedness was wrapped against the cold in a bright red blanket.

Holding both of her hands in his, he looked into her eyes. "Dohiyi, tsigeyui *(Peace, my love)*," he whispered gently to her forehead.

Tyoga closed his eyes. The words he was about to speak would be as painful to hear as they were to say. "Sunlei, even though we have the next two days to be together, what I must say cannot wait."

Pushing away from him, Sunlei asked, "What is it my love?"

"When Seven Arrows comes to take you away, I must remain out of sight. I will be watching, my love. But, whatever happens, I will not be able to make myself known. I want you to be strong, Little One. Always remember that even though distance and time may keep us apart, you are forever here." He pointed to his heart. "And here." He pointed to his head. "You take me with you wherever you go."

Peering up into his eyes, she said, "You are my love and my life. I breathe with you all of your days. When you listen with the promise, you will hear my name in the whispering of the trees, in the song of the brook. My love is as the sun rising, warming you with each passing day. That I am forever yours is as true as time, and as unwavering as the mountains and the sky. You can never leave me."

Tyoga pulled her to him and whispered in her ear, "Look." He motioned with his head in the direction of a rocky ledge high above his campsite. Standing there was Wahaya-Wacon, neck extended, ears back, staring down at the Shawnee camp.

"I promise you, my little one, you will never be alone."

Chapter 29

The Rebuke

Three days had passed since Seven Arrows and his band of braves had arrived to make camp near Tuckareegee. Their whiskey had run out, their food supplies were running low, and the men were tired and bored.

Finally, the day had arrived for which they had been waiting. The coup that they were about to deliver to Tyoga Weathersby put them in reasonably good spirits.

Although it was not to be his wedding day, it was to be the day when Seven Arrows would take Sunlei for the first time—and that was reason enough for celebration.

The men used the early morning hours to prepare themselves for their entrance into the village by donning their finest ceremonial attire. The braves who attended Seven Arrows dressed in their best buckskin vestments. The doeskin from which their fringed tunics and chaps were made was of a dark chestnut hue, which indicated that the skins had recently been cured and tanned. They painted their shaved heads a bright crimson red from the top of their foreheads to the nape of their necks. Their foreheads and the skin around and below their eyes was painted an ashen gray. The braves painted two vertical black stripes on their left cheeks. Necklaces made of glass beads, seed pods, shells, and bone adorned their necks, and bracelets of metal, leather and fur encircled their wrists. Each brave wore an anklet of bells on their left leg. Marching in step, the rhythmic cadence of the bells proved a reasonable musical accompaniment for the tiny band of men entering the village as conquerers collecting the spoils of war.

Seven Arrows was dressed in full Shawnee wedding attire. A beautiful full-length overcoat of beaver and fox fur covered a butter colored elk skin tunic with matching chaps. Long strips of leather fringe dyed brilliant gold, forest green, lavender, blue and peach lined the tunic's sleeves. His leggings had no fringe, but were decorated with intricate beadwork from waist to mid-calf. His bearhide boots sported side welts trimmed with bobcat and coyote fur. Both of his ankles were collared with bells so that his lone belled foot striking the ground served as a solitary counterpoint to the downbeat of the groups marching procession: *CHING-ching-CHING-ching-CHING-ching.*

Smiling and waving their arms while crying out in a joyous tone of voice, "Osiyo oginali, osiyo *(Hello, friends),*" the band of Shawnee braves paraded grandly into the village. Expecting a ceremonial reception accompanied by a formal welcome from Chief Silver Cloud himself, they marched into the village.

They were greeted by no one at all.

The People of Tuckareegee went about the business of their daily lives without acknowledging, or even looking at, Seven Arrows and his wedding party.

The deliberate shun wiped the smiles from the painted faces of the Shawnee braves, and their voices fell silent with a growing rage. The flagrant contempt being shown to Seven Arrows and his men was more than the Chief's son could endure. Abandoning the cadence of their in-step knell, the bells dissolved into a discordant mockery of their ridiculous procession.

"Eh ya ho *(Come),*" he demanded of his men.

Advancing now at a much more determined pace, Seven Arrows quick-stepped his men to Chief Silver Cloud's lodge. Pausing at the threshold, Seven Arrows made a motion as if to advance into the inner sanctum of the chief's home. Wrestling with the urge to enter, Seven Arrows stopped short at the entranceway. To enter the Chief's lodge unannounced was a breach of protocol of which even Seven Arrows was not prepared to stand accused.

He bellowed in a gruff, menacing voice, "Osiyo, Wiyuhi *(Hello, Chief)*."

When there was no response, he called out again. This time he abandoned the title of respect. "Silver Cloud. It is Seven Arrows. I have come for the daughter of Nine Moons, Sunlei-Awi."

Many minutes of silence passed before Chief Silver Cloud's wife, Wind Song, appeared at the door to the lodge.

The Shawnee braves looked at each other with wide-eyed disbelief. Seven Arrows took a step back at her sudden appearance at the doorway. To send a woman to conduct business with the son of a chief, even if casual in nature, was an insult of epic proportion.

Wind Song did not look up at Seven Arrows when she said, "You are too early. Sunlei is not here. You will have to wait."

Seven Arrows did not reply. Unwilling to accept the slight, he remained standing at the door, and refused to budge until Chief Silver Cloud acknowledged his presence.

The mid-morning hours passed. The scent of venison, pork, and porridge filled the air when families enjoyed the breakfast meal. The sounds and smells teased the senses of Seven Arrows and his party of braves, while they remained standing stoically on the stoop of Silver Cloud's lodge.

The midday hours filled the village square with the warming rays of the autumn sun.

People with business to conduct with Chief Silver Cloud entered his lodge while passing right through the Shawnee party without acknowledging their presence or even looking their way.

Still, Seven Arrows and his braves remained standing like sentinels to the court, posted at the entrance of the lodge. The passage of time did little to mitigate the horrific treatment they were being subjected to at the hands of the entire Ani-Unwiya tribe.

Seven Arrows was seething with anger.

Sunlei had not been seen in Tuckareegee for the past two days. Tes Qua had not even told his mother and father that she was with Tyoga. It was well after noon when Sunlei and Tes Qua came walking into the village square. His arm around his sister's waist, Tes Qua appeared to be supporting her while they slowly walked toward their parents' lodge.

Certain that she would never see him again, Sunlei had just parted from Tyoga for the last time. As they staggered past the Shawnee braves standing outside of Silver Cloud's lodge, Seven Arrows bellowed, "Haliwista! *(Stop!)*"

Practically carrying Sunlei, Tes Qua stopped, but did not turn around to face him.

Seven Arrows ran up to Sunlei and grabbed her gruffly by the wrist, "You have kept me waiting too long, woman." He pulled her toward his band of men. "You will learn respect when you are a Shawnee squaw."

Like a coiled rattlesnake, Tes Qua's muscled arm struck out at Seven Arrows's neck. His large hand enveloped his throat in a vice-like grip. He had only to squeeze to shatter his voice box and windpipe.

The Shawnee, though unarmed, moved menacingly toward Tes Qua to protect their leader.

At the threatening move, a dozen Ani braves appeared from the surrounding lodges with their bows drawn ready to riddle Seven Arrows and his party with a deadly barrage.

While Tes Qua's grip was closing and Seven Arrows's eyes were bulging with panic at the finality of his impending demise, Chief Silver Cloud stormed out of his lodge and screamed, "Nahya Ditlihi! Put your bows down. Tes 'A, release Seven Arrows. There will be no blood spilled this day."

Tes Qua released Seven Arrows and threw him backwards, while saying, "Leave our village and go back to your camp. You will wait for my sister some more. We will bring her to you when she is ready to leave. Go. Now."

He put his arm around Sunlei and guided her to their father's lodge.

The color drained from her face as she slowly backed away from her brother to take her place by Seven Arrows's side. The sparkle bled from her soft, dark eyes as the reality of abandonment emptied her soul.

Her family and friends had relinquished their familial responsibility to protect and defend. Her knees grew weak at the finality of her discharge, and with the primal understanding that from that moment on, she would be completely alone. She could rely upon no one but herself to maintain her physical well being, sustain her spiritual strength, and nourish her need for love.

Her eyes filled with tears for only a moment.

Pity was—and would forever more be—a luxury on which she could not waste a single minute.

One by one her relatives and friends made their way to her to say their final goodbyes. Lone Dove, Morning Sky, and Walking Bird hugged each other in a group embrace that quaked with the trauma of parting. Nearly inconsolable, Morning Sky and Walking Bird had to pry Lone Dove's embrace from Sunlei, and support her as they slowly went back along the trail to the village.

When Walks Alone stepped up to Sunlei, his eyes betrayed a knowing that at once puzzled and yet fortified her fragile resolve. He held her close and whispered in her ear, " Eh ya to hey-yo. *(He is very near.)* Et ta se gee. *(He is watching.)* Eh ya net yaho."

She grasped the sleeves of his shirt and held him away from her for just the slightest moment.

He kissed her hurriedly on the cheek, turned, and walked away with a stride that was anything but that of the conquered.

Nine Moons took his daughter into his arms as he had done a thousand times before. Her head fit under his chin. He gazed off into the distance. "When you were but my baby girl, we would sit together beside our lodge fire long into the night. We would speak of many things," he softly whispered into his daughter's ear.

"Yes, Adoda. I remember," Sunlei replied.

"One of your favorite stories was that of the firefly," he continued. "Do you remember?"

Sunlei smiled.

"Aukawak, the firefly glows in the night hoping to attract the perfect mate. Flying over the calm, cool waters of Silver Shore pond, she flashes and flashes her beautiful light, hoping to find a mate with the biggest and brightest light of all. After many hours of searching for the one firefly whose light equals the brilliance of her own, she sees on the opposite shore the most glorious flashing firefly she has ever seen. The brightness of the light is illuminating the darkness of the night, and she is certain that he is calling her name. She flies toward him, and his light is getting closer to her. It seems as though they have found one another."

"But he never makes it across the pond to her," Sunlei interrupted him.

"That's right, Little One. The light that he cast was also seen by the pond's biggest fish. He became a meal before he could become a husband. They would have had many beautiful babies."

Nine Moons stopped as he felt his daughter begin to shake with the effort to stay strong. He kissed her on the top of her head and continued.

"Do you remember the lesson of the story's ending, my Little One?" he asked.

"Yes, Father," she said. "Aukawak's light does not go out at the loss of her chosen one. She continues to glow until she finds another. Her light never goes out."

Nine Moons stepped away from his daughter and held her shoulders in his strong hands. "Be strong, my daughter. Never let your light go out. Glow brightly. Remember me."

He took two steps back to allow True Moon to approach her daughter.

She cupped Sunlei's face in her trembling hands and looked helplessly into her sad eyes. Managing a little smile, she said, "You are the light of my life. My body sustained your life and my heart beats within you forever. We can never be apart, my little one. Remember what I have taught you. We will see each other again someday."

True Moon turned to Seven Arrows and said, "Be kind to her."

He nodded once.

As the final group of well-wishers disappeard on the trail leading back to Tuckareegee, Seven Arrows reached out and roughly grabbed Sunlei's shoulder to turn her toward the trail to South Fork. "Eh ya," he commanded when she turned and followed.

The Shawnee had already packed their belongings in preparation for the trek home. They had only to throw their packs over their shoulders to be on their way.

Seven Arrows stopped at a large pack filled with his own belongings. He looked at it, and then at Sunlei.

Pointing to the bundles her people had carried from the village for her to take with her, Sunlei said, "My things. Who will carry my belongings?"

With no change of expression, Seven Arrows raised his hand and struck Sunlei across the face.

She fell to the ground and turned away covering her cheek with her hand. She had never been struck before in anger. More than the pain of the blow, it was the feeling of shame and worthlessness that accompanied the strike.

How was it that I have done nothing wrong, and yet it is I who bears the shame of being struck?

Though it was his hand that had committed the assault, it was she who would bear the mark of fault and disobedience. It was not the pain of the blow that brought a tear to her eye, but the injustice and entrapment that left no recourse or hope.

She wiped away the tear not wanting him to see, and got to her feet.

"Your trinkets mean nothing to me, and you will have no use for them as a Shawnee squaw," Seven Arrows barked. "You will learn to cook in *our* ways, prepare hides in *our* ways, dress in *our* ways, and obey in *our* ways."

He walked over to his large and cumbersome pack and pointed to it.

Sunlei walked over, stooped down, and struggled to lift the heavy pack onto her back.

As Seven Arrows walked away into the woods, he kicked over the bundle in which the chinaware given to Sunlei by Emma Weathersby had been lovingly packed.

She closed her eyes when she realized that the shattering china represented so much more than the loss of ornate place settings. It was the shattering of the hope for an entire nation of people. It was the destruction of dreams and promise and possibilities. It was the crumbling of peace and the collapse of a culture thousands of years in the making.

As she kneeled on the ground, struggling to get an arm through the leather shoulder strap to hoist her burden onto her back, she gazed back up at the outcropping where Tyoga's camp had been. In utter desperation and total despair, she screamed into the shadows, "Tyoga! Help me! Please. Help me!"

Seven Arrows turned around, hurried to where she was squatting on the ground and lifted her to her feet by her hair. Laughing derisively, he spat into her face, "Your wolf-man is not here. He has abandoned you like the rest. You are mine now. All mine." He raised his hand as if to strike her again, but was satisfied at her cringing and holding up an arm to block the threatened blow.

One last time, she turned her head to look up at the mountainside where Tyoga's camp had been.

With her right eye swelling and the other filled with tears, she was not able to discern the silver grey outline of the Commander framed by the granite majesty of the outcropping. He was standing stone still with his eyes riveted upon her every move. He watched her struggle to stand under the weight of her enormous burden. He saw her snatch a small leather pouch containing a few of her personal items from one of the bundles strewn on the ground. He observed her staggering behind the band of Shawnee braves as they led the way to South Fork. He watched her melt away into the woods.

And so did he.

Chapter 31

Coarsened Cowardice

Seven Arrows decided not to take the route over the mountains through Cormack's Pass to get to the Shawnee village at South Fork. Although he was fairly certain that the unspoken threat of annihilation was enough to keep the Ani-Unwiya from trying to rescue Sunlei, he was wary of an ambush by Cherokee Braves who did not agree with their chief's decision to allow her to be taken without a fight. It was what he would have done. Always the schemer and enabler of misfortune to suit his needs or advance his standing, he trusted no one because no one could place their faith or trust in him.

He was disappointed that Tyoga had not been present when the Cherokee turned Sunlei over to him, but he reveled in the fact that he had beaten Tyoga so summarily that he had left the Appalachians with his tail tucked between his legs.

Still, he was suspicious and cautious.

He had been alone with him when Tyoga's eyes drained of humanity and the blood-tinged amber hue infused them with the darkness of the beast. More than any other, he recognized that Tyoga was more than a man and capable of near magical feats of courage and strength.

He had run away like a frightened child from his encounter with Tyoga by the river when there were no witnesses to his cowardice. He could not allow a repeat of the incident when other eyes were upon him.

Following the rivers and streams that snaked through the valleys and lowlands of Appalachia, he took the long way back to the village. Because of their late start, it would take them an extra day to reach South Fork. They would have to camp for two nights along the trail.

Sunlei was strong and her powerful legs had carried her hundreds of miles along the Appalachian trails while following in the footsteps of Tyoga and Tes Qua. But she had never been burdened by the enormous weight that Seven Arrows had strapped to her back. Her back ached and her thigh muscles quaked under the strain of the goods that hung from her shoulders.

There was no wooden frame to which the goods were secured and the absence of even a waist sash to transfer the weight from her shoulders to her legs caused the straps to dig deep raw gouges into the flesh of her soft round shoulders.

"Halewista *(Stop)*!" she cried out when they rounded a bend in the stream. "Da gi yo we ga *(I'm tired)*, and I am thirsty." She crumpled to the ground.

Seven Arrows called out to his men, "Keep moving. We'll catch up."

As his men moved out of sight along the trail, Seven Arrows turned slowly and walked back to where Sunlei had collapsed to the ground in a heap. She did not see the cruel smile stretched across his wicked lips.

Seven Arrows preyed upon the weak and defenseless. Careful to always pick as his victims those too timid or frail to fight back, he had bullied his way through childhood and adolescence. Young girls and women were favorite targets.

As a young boy, he recognized his innate superiority as a matter of stature and brawn. As a young man, the sexual gratification realized as the result of his complete domination and mastery of his victims compelled him to more frequent—and more violent—encounters.

"So my little princess is tired?" he said with a coldness in his voice that she had never heard before. "Thirsty too?"

He took the water gourd off his shoulder, as if to give her a sip of water. When he removed the stopper, Sunlei reached out with her trembling open hand. Seven Arrows crouched on the ground before her, and raised the gourd to his lips. He took a long drink of water. Sunlei's arm remained outstretched, certain that she would not be denied a sip of water. Seven Arrows raised the gourd to his lips again, took another long drink, and then spit what he did not swallow into her open hand.

Abruptly, he stood up, so close to her face that his knee nearly struck her cheek. He pushed her with his foot and barked, "Get up, you Cherokee dog. We have far to travel before we stop. You will learn to carry your burdens without complaint." When Sunlei did not budge, nor look up at her tormentor, Seven Arrows squatted down and hissed into her ear, "You are a Shawnee squaw. You will obey. Do you understand?"

Sunlei wanted to cry, but she refused to give him the satisfaction of seeing her broken and weak. She licked the wetness from the palm of her hand before struggling to her feet. She raised herself to her knees, but as soon as she tried to plant a foot to push herself upright, she crumpled under the shifting weight of her heavy load.

Her efforts were not good enough for Seven Arrows. Her inability to get to her feet could one day shame him because the strength of a man's squaw reflected upon his own status as a powerful warrior in control of his woman.

He dropped to his knees again and screamed into her face, "I said get up!"

Exhausted from her efforts, she remained motionless where she collapsed and did not try to rise again.

Seven Arrows stood up and removed the knife and tomahawk that he had tucked into a long, two inch wide leather strap that wrapped around his waist several times. Slowly, he walked behind Sunlei and carefully added the knife and tomahawk to the goods already weighing her down. Doubling over the leather strap and wrapping a loop around his wrist, he said in a viciously calm controlled voice, "I will begin your lessons in obedience now."

The Shawnee braves hesitated only for a moment when they heard Sunlei's horrific screams. Knowing exactly what was happening to her on the trail behind them, they smiled at each other.

Over and over again, they heard the snap of leather on flesh.

When they continued to hear Sunlei's screams after walking ten minutes ahead on the trial, the smiles had long since left their faces.

Their exchanged glances conveyed something more.

CB ED CR ED

The sun was beginning to set and the temperature was dropping fast, so the braves decided to make camp and wait for Seven Arrows and Sunlei to catch up. They stopped at a clearing surrounded by sugar maple and towering pines about thirty feet from the bank of the river.

The braves set to work on their campsite like members of a regimented team assigned specific tasks. Falling Bear and Sky Hawk collected stones to build a rock ring for a fire pit. Others collected firewood while Runs Too Long got a warm fire roaring in the pit. Several braves went fishing for their supper. Others spread out blankets and skins, and unpacked cooking utensils for the evening meal. Two Fox and Otter got to work constructing a makeshift lean-to for Seven Arrows and Sunlei. He would not be interested in waiting for a formal wedding ceremony to consummate the arrangement.

When Seven Arrows and Sunlei arrived in camp about a half an hour behind them, the men were taken aback at her appearance. The brutality of Seven Arrows's attack was far more severe than even they had imagined. They looked at each other, and then at him, with a new found estimation. That he was capable of such merciless violence—and to a woman yoked by the burden of backpack and gear—placed Seven Arrows in a category of regard that coarsened cowardice. Two Fox looked away and walked into the woods.

Sunlei's left eye was nearly swollen shut and the left side of her face was distorted with swelling and bruising. The back panel of her tunic was shredded, and the sticky dark stains of dried blood glued the leather to the open gashes on her back. The lashing had ripped open the flesh of her forearms and shoulders. Even her legs were covered with welts and bruises.

Seven Arrows had tied a leather collar around her neck and led her into camp on a leash made of the strap he had used to beat her. He had the backpack slung over one shoulder because Sunlei was barely able to stay on her feet.

He pushed her to the ground while he slung the pack off of his shoulder and said, "A-gi yosi. *(I'm hungry)* What's for dinner?"

Chapter 32

No Way Out

Sunlei had not slept in forty-eight hours. When Seven Arrows threw her to the ground she mercifully passed out from exhaustion and pain.

Loss of consciousness was a blessing. The swelling and open wounds she had suffered from the terrible beating would grow worse and more painful in the coming days. Her suffering would make it nearly impossible for her to get any sleep at all.

The gentle nudge of a moccasined foot against her back startled her awake. Not sure of where she was or how she had gotten there, she bolted upright while instinctively searching her surroundings for immediate threat and possible escape.

The searing pain in her back brought the terrible events of the past twenty-four hours into sharp focus. Through the spinning haze that the mind conjures as a protective shield between reality too cruel to comprehend and the dreams that make everyday life bearable, the living hell that her life had become hit her in the gut like an iron fist.

She saw the shadows and silhouettes of the Shawnee braves she would soon be forced to call "family." There was no stopping the bile she felt rising to fill her mouth. The vile mucousy froth made her wretch. She did not bend over, or even turn her head to the side. She let the foul humor course down her chin and dribble a viscous yellow-green slime onto her torn and bloody tunic.

A voice that was much kinder than Seven Arrows's said softly to her, "Get up now, Little One." Two Fox handed her a cold wet rag to wipe her face.

She was grateful to get the dried blood off of her lips and nose, and the cool dampness of the cloth felt good against her swollen face.

He handed her a gourd of fresh, cold water. She filled her mouth, swished it around, and spit the mucousy red froth onto the ground. She rinsed her mouth again before taking several small sips of the water. She looked up into Two Fox's face, and could tell from his expression that she had been hurt even more severely than she had thought.

Pointing toward the firepit, Two Fox said to her, "Pick out what you can of the left over fish. Then, you must go to Seven Arrows."

"Wa-do *(Thank you)*," she said barely above a whisper. Her lips were swollen and it was difficult for her to speak, but she managed to say, "Eh ya to batsh-te."

Two Fox reached his hand down and helped her to her feet. She shuffled-stepped away from the campfire, and squatted to relieve herself. She limped back to the fire pit and fell to her knees to search the ground for chunks of fish not consumed, or spit out, by Seven Arrows and his men. A large backbone still had a good amount of meat on it. After brushing the dirt and ash from the discarded fish carcass, she was able to salvage enough to stem her hunger.

Feeling a little stronger, she stood up, and looked around for Two Fox. He was nowhere to be seen, so she said to another of the braves, "I need to clean my wounds. May I go to the river to bathe?"

Without saying a word, Sky Hawk motioned for her to follow him down to the river.

Sunlei paused at the bundle she had been forced to carry to grab the tiny sack that contained the few belongings she had managed to bring with her. While following Sky Hawk to the river, she removed a bar of soap and a small towel from the sack. She felt the tears begin to well up in her eyes when she thought of how Tyoga's mother had lovingly packed these ordinary, everyday items for her to take with her to her new life. How horrified she would be to see her now.

Late evening, it was completely dark away from the light of the campfire, except for the light of the rising moon. Sky Hawk stopped about ten feet from the bank to allow Sunlei to continue into the river alone. When she turned to him to see if he was going to look away while she disrobed, she got her answer when he sat on the ground, folded his arms, and smiled.

The river was lower than usual, so she had to step down from the bank to reach the water's edge. She dropped her tunic to reveal her perfect figure in the moonlight, and bent down to wash.

Unable to contain himself at the silhouette of Sunlei's naked body glowing in the moonlight, Sky Hawk let out a little whoop that summoned his companions to join him for the show.

Grimacing from the sting of the soap in her open wounds, Sunlei paid little attention to the sound of the others running to join him. She had learned from helping Tyoga's mother care for Tes Qua's wounds after the battle with the wolves that keeping a wound clean was critically important.

The braves could only see Sunlei from the waist up, but it was view enough. Watching her in the moonlight lathering the cloth, washing her arms, her neck, breasts and abdomen was nearly more than they could stand. She would disappear when she bent down to the water to rinse herself off, and then emerge again to repeat the process.

One of the braves, stroking himself, got up as if to go over to her.

"Nay ya." Otter reached out to grab him by the arm. "Seven Arrows will kill you if you touch her first. He will share when he is through. Be patient. Your turn will come." At this the four braves laughed, stood up, and went back into camp.

Sunlei followed after them when she was finished bathing.

She pulled a clean tunic out of the leather pouch and threw the torn bloody one into the bushes. She unbraided her hair and brushed it out so that her long raven tresses curtained her shoulders in an ebony veil that simmered in the firelight. She felt better now that she had bathed and changed her clothes, but the sting of washing her wounds with soap and water made the lacerations even more painful.

Fighting to keep from thinking of her family and Tyoga, she moved closer to the fire and sat down to warm herself. How she longed to hear their voices and to feel Tyoga's strong arms wrapped around her in a warm embrace. She winced when she thought of the words that Walks Alone had whispered in her ear when he said goodbye.

How horrible it must have been for Tyoga to stay hidden in the glade while I was being handed over to Seven Arrows.

She shivered in empathy at the self-control and courage it must have taken for him to stand helplessly by and watch her disappear into the woods.

He could have killed them all. Wahaya-Wacon would have helped. He would have torn them apart.

She felt ashamed that she had called out to him in desperation.

How I wish they had just …

"Stop it Sunlei," she heard herself say. She looked around to see if anyone had heard her outburst.

Tyoga and Wahaya could not have saved her. To do so would have been to condemn all of the People to certain death. To rescue her now would do the same.

"Sunlei," she heard one of the braves call out. "Et ta ya ho."

The words cut through her like an icy obsidian blade slicing her heart into little pieces. She felt her entire body go numb. The horrible reality of what was to be dulled her senses and blackened her soul.

Seven Arrows would take her. It was inevitable and there wasn't anything that she could do to stop it. She searched her brain to come up with an excuse, an option, a way out. The anguish seemed to dull her senses and render her incapable of thinking clearly.

She thought of running—but they would catch her.

She thought of claiming her unclean time—but that would not stop him.

And then she saw the gleaming blade of a butchering knife embedded in the log upon which she was seated.

She knew that it was the coward's way out, but it would end her nightmare.

The gruesome thought oddly erased all others, as what her death would mean for her tribe seemed of little consequence.

Ever so slowly she eased toward the blade, moving so cautiously that her progress went unnoticed.

She reached out her hand, and closed her fingers around the elk horn handle.

The handle grew warm in her hand as she sat for a long moment staring at the blade as it reflected the light from the campfire. With one quick pull she could free it from its mooring and put an end to the nightmare her life had become.

It won't be a terrible thing for me to do, will it?

Warriors were known to take their own lives when they had been disgraced in battle. In some nations, it was expected when a chief had led his tribe to defeat in battle.

The pain of slitting my wrist will only last a moment. I'll just sit here on the log, close my eyes and feel myself grow sleepy.

A smile came to her face as she thought,

That will fix him. He will have no prize at all. All of his efforts, all of his bluster and the esteem in which he has fooled himself to believe he will be held, will be snatched away from him in an instant.

She nearly giggled out loud as she pictured the moment that he would discover that she had beaten him with such finality.

Tears streamed down her face when she thougth of never seeing her family, or Tyoga, again.

They'll understand, won't they?

At that very moment, the face of her father, Nine Moons, presented to her mind's eye as if he were standing right in front of her. When he came into focus, she gazed into his steely, grey, gentle eyes, and was struck by the fact that it was not Tyoga's or her mother's faces that she should see. When she heard his voice in her ear coming from the blackness of the forest night, she gasped and looked around her to see if he was truly standing next to her.

"Aukawak," he was whispering softly in her ear. She heard him repeat the word, "Aukawak," more loudly this time. A third time it pierced the night with an urgency that returned her focus like a bolt of lightening cleaving the night sky.

She released her grip on the knife handle and stood when she heard the cry of a lone, distant raven *"AUKAAWWWW"* carry across the river's surface and vanish into the mist of the dark Appalachian night.

She remembered the story her father shared with her at their parting.

Aukawak never let her light go out.

Clenching both of her hands into determined little fists, she said out loud, "Neither will mine."

The words that Tyoga had spoken to her, "You will never be alone," filled her with the resolve that steeled her spine and rekindled the fires of self preservation.

I must stay alive. He will come for me. I know he will come.

"Sunlei. Et ta ya ho," she heard the brave call out for her again.

There was no option. No way out. She could not save herself. This thing she must do for those she loved.

Sunlei had only made love to one man. Tyoga Weathersby. No other man had ever touched her—kissed her.

Will Seven Arrows want to kiss me? What will he taste like? What will he smell like so close? Will his hands explore where only one other's have been? Would he be gentle or gruff? Will he hurt me ? Would he want her to use her mouth?

She felt the bile rise from her stomach again, and she choked it back to keep from gagging with fear and loathing. The thoughts careened and collided in a cacophony of noise, emotion, and confusion.

As if from outside of herself, she observed, more than felt, herself slowly turn toward the lean-to where Seven Arrows was waiting. She watched herself move in the direction of the entrance. She paused at the doorway, pushed the hide covering to one side, bent over, and walked in.

Seven Arrows was lying naked on a buffalo robe, covered from his waist down with the beaver and fox fur overcoat that he had worn when he walked into Tuckareegee to get her.

"It is time, my little one," he said with an evil grin.

Paralyzed with fear, not knowing how to act, what to do or say, Sunlei stood at the entranceway.

Seven Arrows took the lead. "You look as beautiful as I imagined, Sunlei. Turn around. Slowly."

Sunlei turned to her left. He saw her stunning profile. Her firm breasts held the tunic away from her abdomen, and her soft shoulders were draped with her stunning black hair. She turned her back to him so that he could see her perfectly formed buttocks and the gentle curve of her waist, hips, and thighs. Her right profile revealed the side of her face that was not swollen from the beating he had given her.

The exquisite proportion of her delicate facial features made Seven Arrows shake with anticipation.

He threw the overcoat off and revealed himself in his readiness to violate her tender soul. He got up on his knees and motioned for her to come closer.

Looking straight ahead, she took a step toward him, and felt him bury his face in her waist.

Throwing his arms around her buttocks, he inhaled deeply of her natural musk. Kissing her tunic he reached up with his strong hands and caressed her ribs so gruffly that her sides ached.

He glanced up at her face fully expecting to see her head thrown back while encouraging sighs escaped breathlessly from her full inviting lips. Instead, he saw nothing but a stoic stare that revealed dispassionate acquiescence.

Reaching up, Seven Arrows tore her tunic off of her shoulders with all of his might. It crumpled to the ground while he cupped her breasts in his hands and brought her nipples to his mouth.

Still, Sunlei stared straight ahead with dead eyes focusing vapidly into the night.

Jerking her down to her knees, he kissed her hard on the mouth, neck, and cheeks.

Sunlei winced at the pain when he forced himself onto her swollen and bruised cheeks and lips. She tasted the blood when the split in her lip opened and began to bleed again. She would not look at him, nor respond to his touch.

Seven Arrows picked her up off of the ground, threw her onto her back, and spread her legs wide. The saliva was spewing from his mouth like an enraged dog when he screamed into her face, "Now, you will feel what it is like to have a real man inside of you!"

When Seven Arrows reached down to guide himself into her, Sunlei could stand no more. Exploding in violent rage that caught him by surprise, she fought back with everything she had. Thrashing her powerful legs and flailing her arms, she kicked at his abdomen and thighs, elbowed him in the ribs and chest, doing everything she could to push him off of her. Fighting with all of her strength to preserve her dignity and womanhood, she didn't care if he killed her, or if her refusal to be taken meant the death of her entire tribe, she would not surrender without a fight.

He grabbed her wrists to control her flailing arms, but was unable to restrain her strong kicking legs. "What is wrong, Little One? Don't be afraid." Seven Arrows taunted her as if he were enjoying the struggle. "Oh, I know what it is. You are used to mating with a dog. Okay. We'll do it the way you and your wolf-man used to couple." Grabbing her around the waist, he flipped Sunlei onto her stomach so that she could no longer kick and push him away.

Exhausted from a nightmarish day of excruciatingly painful events, Sunlei had no more fight in her. As Seven Arrows bent her legs and pushed her knees under her, she was overtaken by the involuntary retching that emptied her stomach onto the buffalo robe.

Sensing that she was no longer going to fight him, he became more gentle. "That is it, Little One. Rise up on your knees and spread your legs. Is this better? Is this how you like it?"

With her face smeared with half-digested fish, and her shoulders pinned down on the buffalo robe, she spread her knees wide, and prepared to receive him.

The splatter of the warm sticky fluid on her back and shoulders sent a wave of relief through her. She expected that the deed was done before he could enter her.

One squirt, then another, and another as powerful and voluminous as the last.

The gurgling sounds coming from behind her and the crimson red liquid now running down both of her arms made her turn around to see what was happening.

Seven Arrows was clutching his neck with both of his hands while the blood squirted through his fingers, down his arm and onto her lower back and thighs. She turned over, sat up, and moved out of the way as Seven Arrows collapsed face first into the buffalo robe now soaking wet with the warmth of his own blood.

Getting to her knees, she saw the blood continue to pour from the gaping wound under his right ear.

She heard the patter of bare feet running from the lodge.

Grabbing her tunic, she threw open the flap covering the entrance-way and ran naked after the footsteps she could hear in front of her on the trail.

In ten quick steps, the camp was out of site and she was running for her life.

Chapter 33

You Are Never Alone

Sunlei ran with all her might. It didn't matter that she hadn't really slept in nearly forthy-eight hours. It didn't matter that the gashes on her back from her beating were open and bleeding. It didn't matter that she had no moccasins on and that the rocks on the path along the riverbank were cutting the soles of her feet.

Sunlei ran.

She ran through the blackness as the branches of the trees and bushes lining the path whipped her face, arms, and shoulders. Breathlessly, she pursued her savior who was running only steps ahead of her. The steps were quick, short, and light. She desperately wanted to cry out, "Stop! Wait for me! I can't make it alone!"

Whoever was out in front of her was fast, silent, and not at all interested in being discovered.

Someone had ended the scourge of Seven Arrows, but left Sunlei alone and suspect. His throat had been brutally severed, and no one other than she had been anywhere near him. She would be blamed for the ferocious attack, and there was no talking her way out of the facts.

Her only salvation was escape. And so she ran.

When she heard the war cries from the camp, she knew that Seven Arrows had been found lying face down in a pool of his own blood. They would be after her, and she knew that she had no hope of out running the young, strong men.

The gravel and dirt trail followed the contours of the river to her left. The woods to her right became dense with scrub pines and thick with matted briar patches that made veering off the path to elude her pursuers impossible.

Beyond the underbrush that lined the trail, large granite boulders were scattered in disarray like sinful chess pieces banished from a massive board of disapproving squares. They would provide cover, but leave her no way out.

She jumped the rocky bed of a feeder stream emptying into the river when she heard Seven Arrows's men begin the chase. With only a two-minute head start on them, they would be upon her in no time at all. Breathless, she paused to search the woods around her for a rocky outcropping in which she could conceal herself or even a briar patch under which she could crawl.

The thundering of the warriors' mocassined feet hitting the ground left her no more time to consider concealment.

She turned and ran as fast as she could.

As her surroundings melted into the confusion of primal panic, her body shifted into the automatic rhythms of preservation that ward off waste, conserve energy, and focus on staying alive. Her legs flew over the rocky ground without registering the pain from her lacerated feet. Her eyes focused on the trail ahead and blurred her surroundings into a hazy distortion of time and place. Her breathing synchronized with the beating of her heart as the blood coursed through her veins with a regulated urgency recorded in rapid pulse and shallow breath. She floated in this magical space for another hundred yards before her body awakened to the pain of her pounding heart, the searing ache of air-starved lungs, and the knotting cramps in calves and thighs that signaled the end of flight.

Sunlei bent at the waist, placed her hands on her knees and whispered to the night, "Help me. Please, help me." Hearing the braves closing the fifty-yard gap between them, she stood upright to accept the reality of her capture.

She scanned her surroundings one last time to assess any means of concealment or escape. The landscape whirled around her like she was a child spinning in place. A reflective golden sparkle to the south halted the frenzied search and drew her attention down the trail.

Peering into the night, she blinked several times to bring into focus what now appeared to be two amber orbs about waist high, fixed directly upon her. She took several quick steps toward the lights and immediately recognized the glowing eyes of Wahaya-Wacon gleaming in the night twenty-five yards down the trail.

Glancing over her shoulder in the direction of the pursuing braves, she ran with renewed vigor toward the wolf. When she arrived at the spot in the trail where she had seen him, he was gone.

"Wahaya," she screamed out too loudly. "Wahaya-Wacon," she called again as loudly as she dare. She turned around and around on the trail while looking into the woods and up and down the trail. In desperation, she cried out, "Do not leave me here. Come back."

Collapsing to her knees, she placed her head in her hands and bent to the ground in utter despair. Certain that the witnesses to her final prayer were to be only the rocks, water, and wind, she said again into her hands that were covering her tear-stained face, "Don't leave me."

When she felt the gentle nudge of his cold wet nose against the back of her neck, she gasped—first in fear, and then in joyous relief. She raised her head to stare into the firey, urging eyes of Wahaya-Wacon.

Her prayer had not been in vain.

The Shawnee braves were getting so close that she could hear their footsteps slapping the trail. "Wahaya, what do I do?" she asked as if she expected him to speak to her.

The Commander took two steps off of the trail toward the dense woods and circled twice to indicate that she was to follow.

Silently nodding, Sunlei got to her feet and followed him into the blackness of the forest. He only ran about twenty yards into the woods before stopping next to a jumble of gigantic boulders that had cleaved from the smooth south face of a granite ridge and tumbled hundreds of feet down to the forest floor. Their landing created a shallow grotto into which the wolf ran.

Sunlei followed. She fell to the ground and pressed back as far as she could into the recesses of the damp refuge. The wolf moved to the front of the alcove, circled once and lay down facing toward Sunlei, who was curled up on the ground. His dark coat blended into the granite surroundings and concealed Sunlei in living camouflage.

Sunlei looked into the eyes of Wahaya. He stared back with a gaze of calm reassurance. The wildness could still be discerned in his eyes.

His ears piqued when the Shawnee stopped at the spot where she had left the trail to follow him into the woods.

"She must be just ahead," she heard one of the Shawnee say. The same voice ordered, "Sleeping Owl, run to South Fork. Tell Yellow Cloud what has happened. Tell him that we need help to carry Seven Arrows's body over the mountain. Tell him the Cherokee squaw has murdered his son." With that the men resumed the chase along the river bank.

If they had been discovered, Wahaya would have torn them apart with the dispassionate savagery that is the hallmark of the apex predator. Yet, the gentleness in his eyes when he looked into Sunlei slowed her breathing, quieted her panic, and calmed her soul.

All things in nature unfold only as they are meant to be. There is but one outcome, one end-point, one resolution, for an alternative ending cannot be. The wolf would see her through this, or he would not. He would allow her pursuers to pass in peace, or, if discovered, tear them apart. She would survive, or she would not. Her light continues to glow, or it is extinguished.

Quietly, the two of them lay facing each other until the wolf stood up, turned his back to Sunlei, and sat down in front of the grotto like a vigilante sentry standing guard.

Sunlei was overcome with fatigue. For the first time in many hours, she felt some measure of safety under the watchful eyes of Wahaya-Wacon. Secured by the pureness of the peaceful beast, she closed her eyes and rested her tired, battered body deep within the recesses of the quiet grotto.

After only minutes, Sunlei was reawakened to the reality of her nightmare by the loud voices of the Shawnee braves. They had figured out that she had left the path and had doubled back to see if they could pick up her trail.

They were very close.

The wolf was gone.

The realization that she was alone sent a frightening shiver up her spine. The respite in the grotto had cleared her mind of the panic that had kept her at a disadvantage. With renewed determination, she bolted from the shelter of the grotto and dove headlong into the woods.

Her first steps on the carpet of dried pine branches and cones alerted the Shawnee to her location. In a flash, they left the trail in hot pursuit of their prey. In the dense underbrush, there was no path for her to follow. She felt her feet flying through the briars and over boulders and stones strewn helter skelter about the forest floor.

"Ehya tola si wayho *(Quick. She went this way),*" she heard the warriors cry out.

Bounding up the jagged face of a boulder, she slid down the moss covered north side into a depression in the forest floor at the base of an ancient oak tree.

"Eh wa ta, eha lo," she heard another brave call out.

She could hear their footsteps and the crashing of the underbrush and the snapping of branches as they made their way closer and closer to where she lay. She fell to her belly and slithered along the forest floor while clawing through the dirt and rocks, crawling over roots and stones to the far side of the giant oak.

When she paused to listen, she noticed for the first time that she was completely naked. She was clutching her balled up tunic in her left hand. The realization that she was wallowing naked in the muck and rot of the forest floor was a blow to her person-hood more offensive than a slap in the face.

Rising purposefully to her feet, she wiped the sweat from her brow, and brushed the loose dirt and wet leaves from her naked shivering body with the crumpled tunic. Her quaking fingers explored the tunic's seams until she found its hem, and she gently shook it back into shape and form. Raising the tunic toward the towering tree tops, she extended both arms through the sleeves and felt the safety of its caress warm her as it slid over her battered, bruised, and sweaty body.

If they were going to find her, she was going to maintain some measure of dignity.

Just as her head popped out of the neckline, she felt the calloused hand cover her mouth, and a massive, muscular arm snake around her waist to lift her from the forest floor.

Struggling to free herself from the vice-like grip, she kicked and punched at her abductor with what little strength she had left. She was being carried deeper into the woods and farther away from the river and the trail. After the hijacker had carried her about thirty paces, he put her down, grabbed her by the shoulders, brushed the hair out of her eyes, and said, "Eh ya to, Sunlei. It's me."

She looked up into his eyes and collapsed into his arms. Overcome with fatigue, pain, and relief, she passed out in the fortress of his embrace without saying a word.

Chapter 34

Beaten to the Punch

When Sunlei awoke, she was swaddled in warm blankets. Her head rested on a soft, down-filled pillow covered in a linen casing.

She was lying on a thick mattress of buffalo hide suspended off the ground and supported on a wooden frame. It was a white man's bed. She threw the covers off. Realizing that she was naked, she pulled the soft red cloth blanket up to her chin.

She inspected the delicate weave on a corner of the blanket. She knew this work. She brought the corner to her nose. "Prairie Day."

Reaching behind her head, she felt that the wall against which the bed abutted was hard packed dirt and rock. Lifting her head, she saw that the other walls were constructed of uncut pine logs and mud daub. The floor was made of broad-cut knotty pine. The rough-cut oaken front door was swung wide open. Fuzzy-edged sunbeams danced through the opening. A gentle breeze caressed her face with its fresh, crisp earthy scent. The shutters of an opening next to the door, not really a window because there was no glass, were open.

It was a beautiful bright autumn day. Running water gurgled in a nearby stream, and chirping songbirds hidden in the tall trees seemed to safeguard the dark, cool cabin nestled in the recesses of the quiet glade.

Sitting up, she stretched and drew a deep breath to fill her lungs with the newness of the day. Throwing the red blanket over her shoulders, she got up and walked tentatively to the open door.

Peeking outside, she saw that the cabin was in a deep, green hollow surrounded by circular earthen ramparts. It was constructed into the side of a mountain. Towering over her head, enormous ancient trees appeared remarkably statuesque for she had to look up about thirty feet to see the rooted origins of the enormous trunks.

It was a beautiful, peaceful setting. She liked it very much.

The magic of the moment vanished when the blanket rubbing against her lacerated back forced her to recall the horrific realities of the last day. The memory of nearly being raped by Seven Arrows sent a shiver up her spine. She covered her mouth with her hand when she recalled the horror of being drenched in his blood while he knelt so close behind her. She remembered fleeing from the lean-to and running as fast as she could to catch up to whoever had slit Seven Arrows's throat. She covered her ears while the pounding of the Cherokee braves' moccasined feet echoed in her brain, and tears spilled from her eyes when she recalled the vision of Wahaya-Wacon standing majestically in the middle of the trail.

Her last memory was of how Tyoga had found her and rescued her in the night.

Inquisitively, and quietly at first, she called out, "Ty?"

When there was no answer, she cried out with more urgency, "Tyoga."

She began to fear that she had imagined her rescue when Tyoga crested the west ridge with an armful of firewood. Seeing Sunlei in the doorway, he dropped the wood and ran to the cabin door.

She threw open the blanket that was covering her nakedness to welcome him into her arms. He picked her up and held her close while she clung to his neck with a grip that wouldn't permit him to breathe. Tears poured from her beautiful black eyes.

She was unable to utter a sound. When she was able to breathe, her screams stilled the valley.

Tyoga held her close. "Shhh ... Sunlei. You're safe. I'm here and no one can harm you."

Releasing his neck, she wrapped her arms around his waist, buried her head in his chest and continued to weep.

They stood together for a very long time.

After gathering herself, she dried her eyes and face with the red blanket. "Is he dead?"

"I don't know for sure, Sunlei, but I think so," Tyoga said. "Leastwise that's what his men were saying when they were chasing you through the woods."

"Tyoga, it wasn't ... Did you cut his throat?"

"No," he said. "If I had slit his throat there wouldn't be any question about him being dead, and I sure wouldn't have left you behind, now would I? Someone beat me to it. I was on my way to get you and to kill Seven Arrows and all of his men, but someone got there first."

"So you weren't going to let them take me," Sunlei said in a tone of voice reflecting vindication of her belief that she had never been abandoned.

"No, my little one." Tyoga said as he gently folded her back into his arms. "From the moment he took you from me, he was living on borrowed time. You were being led through the woods by a dead man."

Sunlei pressed her face against his chest, and pulled the blanket tight around her shoulders.

He kissed the top of her head over and over again.

"But, Ty, if you were going to kill him, why did you let him take me from you? Why did you let him treat me so cruelly if you were going to kill him all along?"

"Don't you see, Sunlei? I had to allow him to take you. It ripped out my heart standing there a short run away, watching him tear you away from your family and from me, but there was no other way. The demand that Chief Yellow Robe made of the Ani-Unwiya had to be fulfilled. Seven Arrows arrived in Tuckareegee, Silver Cloud turned you over to him as promised, and he and his men were allowed to leave in peace. I could not interfere. Everyone had to believe that I left the Appalachians like I announced at council. That way, when I killed Seven Arrows, there would be no way for me or the wolf to be suspect."

"Now that Seven Arrows has been killed, Yellow Robe will demand more or make war," Sunlei said. "The six braves the Shawnee have lost because of Wahaya-Wacon will not be replaced. He will make war on us."

"If that is the way he chooses, Sunlei, our hands are no longer bound by decree. Now, we can fight. Our debt has been paid. We kept our part of the bargain. Whatever happened to Seven Arrows and his men after you were turned over to them is out of our hands. I did not kill Seven Arrows. Wahaya-Wacon did not kill him, nor did he harm his men. Only you saw Wahaya on the trail. Only you know that he was there. It is Yellow Robe's decision to choose peace or war. But if it is war that he wants, we will not stand by and allow him to butcher us without a fight."

"I knew that you would not let me go," Sunlei said. "I knew that I would not live the rest of my life as the wife of that Shawnee dog. I would have killed him myself, even if it meant my own torture and death."

The sun peaked over the eastern rampart to flood the hollow with the warmth of the new day. In silence, they held each as if they would never let go.

After the sun had risen to the treetops, Sunlei asked, "Ty, what are we going to do now?"

He was quiet for a long moment, thinking of what—and how—to say what needed to be said. Sunlei had been through so much, he did not want to burden her with the harsh realities of what was to come. As gently as he could, he said, "What we must do next will be even harder than what we have already been through. The important thing is that we will someday be together."

"What do you mean 'someday' be together. We are together now. I won't ever let you go." She pulled herself even closer to him.

He closed his eyes and breathed in her scent. He sighed. "You must be starving. I have much food inside. Let's get something to eat."

"A gi yo si."

As they both turned to step into the cabin, Sunlei stopped and looked up at him. "Ty, how did you know that I saw Wahaya on the trail? I didn't tell you that."

Tyoga kissed her on the head, put his arm around her waist, and led her into the cabin.

Chapter 35

Half a Man

The sun was setting. An early fall chill was in the air. The warmth of the cozy fire was made all the more welcome by a slight breeze out of the north, a harbinger of the winter weather soon to come.

Sunlei and Tyoga had eaten a large mid-day meal of fish and squash and bread. She had spent the remainder of the afternoon sleeping. She was still tired and her back was red and raw from the beating she had received at the cruel hands of Seven Arrows. Tyoga had anointed the wounds with a salve of bear fat and willow sap to numb the pain.

With the man she loved, she was warm and safe. Sitting side by side, they stared into the flames when the long shadows gave way to the descending darkness of the night.

It was the quiet time that Tyoga so relished. It was the time of day that the promise spoke most clearly.

This evening, it was silent. It had made the path clear long before this night.

Tyoga knew what he had to do.

"Sunlei."

She could tell by the tone of his voice that he had something to say and that there was no need to acknowledge her name.

"Y a to la gowi eh a lo. Tesa e ta leawo."

Lifting her head from his shoulder, she pierced him with incredulous eyes that rejected what he had said out of hand. "Why? Why must we part? I don't want to go away." Her eyes were already filling with tears. "I want to go back home. I don't understand."

"Sunlei, you've got to go away from here. You've got to go where you cannot be found."

The pitiful look of desperate confusion dulled the natural shine of her eyes.

Reaching out he enveloped Sunlei's tiny shoulders in his powerful hands and tried to explain, "Don't ya see, darlin'? You were the only one with Seven Arrows when his throat was cut. His men were right there when it happened. They will tell Yellow Robe that it was you for certain—sure. If I had gotten there before whoever beat me to it, no one would have been left to tell the tale. As it stands now, if you go back to Tuckareegee, the Shawnee will come for you and demand justice."

Uncharacteristically, Sunlei interrupted him. "Yellow Robe will demand justice whether I am there or not. He will kill my family and all of the People for an act committed by another. Tyoga, we cannot allow that to happen. No matter what becomes of us, we cannot allow others to die for what has been done."

"I know, Sunlei, but that won't happen." Tyoga turned away from her so that his eyes would not betray his tenuous resolve. "If you aren't at the village, then the Shawnee will start looking for you. But Yellow Robe will not order his braves to wipe out the village."

She pressed him further. "How can you be so sure that he will not order the massacre of our people?"

"Because, Sunlei, Yellow Robe is not a vengeful man. He is not a reckless chief. He knows that a massacre of Tuckareegee would bring the entire Cherokee nation to our defense. It would mean war for years. Besides, he would never risk the lives of his grandchildren."

"His grandchildren?" she asked.

"Yes, Sunlei. Are you forgetting the union of his daughter, Winged Woman to Gray Owl? Their two sons are Cherokee of the Mountain Creek Clan. To war with the Cherokee is to break the sacred bonds that were created at the union of his daughter and Gray Owl. Their bond protects the peace for all time. His hands are tied."

"But, Ty, won't they suspect that it was you who killed Seven Arrows to save me? They will be looking for you, not for me." She was searching for any way out of having to be parted from him.

"They may suspect me, but my tracks don't lead away from the lean-to where Seven Arrows was murdered. My tracks are no where to be found. Even if they look, they will not find them."

Tyoga got up and walked over to the pile of wood. He threw some large logs on the fire that would burn for a long time.

"Besides, I told everyone that I would leave Tuckareegee and that is exactly what I did. No one knows where I have been, or where I am now." He watched the newly ignited flames leap into the chilly evening air. "It is as if I melted into the Appalachians with Wahaya."

For a long time, Sunlei thought about what Tyoga had said. It all made sense. Her departure seemed the only way to proceed without bloodshed. The tears streamed from her tired, red eyes while she contemplated the journey that lay ahead for them.

With every fiber of her being she wanted to go home to be in her family's lodge, help her mother prepare corn meal, and sew seasoned leather into warm garments to protect against the coming winter chill. She wanted to be present at the birth of Lone Dove's baby. She had promised Takes Too Long, the old one, that she would help her with the winter wheat.

None of this was to be.

Staring into the fire, she wiped her eyes and mustered the courage to whisper, "Where will I go?"

"You are going to the Chickamauga Cherokee to the southwest."

"Will I be staying with my uncle and his family?"

"Yes. Lone Bear has promised to take care of you. He will keep you safe. You must listen to Lone Bear and do as he says."

"You will take me to Chickamaugua?"

"No, Sunlei. Your cousin, Walks Alone, has agreed to take you. He will meet me tonight at Kansaki Ridge. We'll be back here tomorrow morning. You must be ready to travel at dawn."

Sunlei could not hold the tears back any longer. She cried not the tears of fear or pain, but the quiet tears of promises unfulfilled, hopes and dreams unrealized, and the agony of a broken heart. Her eyes stared blankly through lifeless lenses submersed in pools of despair, want, and loneliness. A gentle blink of each tender eye freed the emotions in dewy pearls that breached her lower lids and coursed along each delicate cheek.

She made no sound.

Tyoga took her in his arms and rocked her gently. Staring into the flames, she said, "You have been planning this for sometime then?"

"Yes."

"Does Tes A know?"

"No," Tyoga said. "I thought it best to make the arrangements without his help. The less he knows, the less chance of harm coming to him and your family. Everyone had to believe that I was miles away. My Cherokee brothers must think me a yellow-bellied coward for not standing by you, but that is okay. All that mattered to me was getting you away from the Shawnee and Seven Arrows. I knew that he would not take you back to the Shawnee village through Cormack's Pass, so I circled in front and planned to ambush them in the night. I was about a mile off in my figurin' 'cause Seven Arrows's men stopped to make camp just short of where I thought they would be. I was on my way to kill them all when I heard them chasing you. Wahaya ran to you as fast as he could. It was hard for him not to attack and kill the Shawnee. He stayed in the shadows because if he had been seen, it would have ruined everything. If there was any trace of the wolf, then Yellow Robe would have had evidence that would have pointed right at me. As it stands now, we are free and clear of the whole thing."

"He did find me, Ty, and he protected me," Sunlei said in a tired voice. "He led me off the trail and into the woods without making a sound. He covered me with his body so that they would not see me when they passed by." She paused to listen for a moment to the gentle sounds of the night. "He knew not to show himself. Is that how you found me in the dark, Ty? Did he call to you and tell you where to find me?"

He did not reply.

She let it go.

"Then you will leave me alone here tonight? What if I am found before you get back?"

"Don't be afraid, my little one. No one knows of this place except your brother. Tes A and I found this spot when we were ten years old.

The entrance to the hollow is through a cave along the north wall over there. We have never found any evidence of any other people being here, or even finding the mouth of the cave. You will be safe. Besides, you won't be alone."

They stayed by the fire for a long time. Sunlei's head was in his crossed legs, and he folded her in his arms.

After darkness had engulfed them, the sound of the evening gave way to the silence of the night.

She sat up and looked at him. "This may be the last that we see of each other for many days."

"I will be back tomorrow morning with Walks Alone. We will say 'goodbye' then, my little one. But we will see each other again. Sooner than you think."

Sunlei gazed out at the darkness of the night. "No, Ty, I do not think that we will see each other for many days," she said with a halting voice. "Tyoga, I could not live knowing that you are alone. You must promise me that you will not live your life alone. If I thought that you were cold in the night with no one next to you to keep you warm, it would break my heart more than knowing that you have found someone else. Promise me that you will not live alone, because I …"

Tyoga stopped her, "No, Sunlei, I want to be with you. There will be no one else. I can't live without you."

She interrupted, "No, hear me."

"I ain't gonna listen, Sunlei—"

"Listen to me, Ty. You must listen." She reached up to stroke his worried brow. "Just as you have been awakened to the promise, I have been awakened to the ways of a woman. There are things that I know, just because I know them to be true, even if I cannot explain them to you. We must live our lives and seek to find happiness and contentment wherever our destinies may lead us. You do not want to hear it, my love, but I must tell you. I do not think that we will see each other again for many moons. I love you with all of my heart, and I know that you love me. It is because of your love for me that you will want nothing more for me than the happiness that all women feel holding their children in their arms. Don't you see, Tyoga? It is because of my love for you that I set you free."

Tyoga's strength was waning when he heard Sunlei speak these words. She was right. And he knew what she was asking of him. Despite his bravest attempts, he knew that he may not see her again for a long time—maybe never again. His eyes welled with tears. He turned away so that she would not see.

She reached up and gently touched his cheek. She turned his head so that their eyes met in an aching embrace.

A tear rolled down his face while he gathered the strength to speak. "Sunlei, the words that you speak may be true. I release you to find happiness in the arms of another, just as you have released me. But know this. If we are never to be together, I will wander through the rest of life as half a man. Without you by my side, I will never be all that I was meant to be. There will be a hole in my heart that no other can ever fill. It is the place where you belong. I will go on, and I will be brave and strong. I will blaze new trails across this land, and I will speak for my Indian brothers wherever and whenever they need my voice. You will hear the name Tyoga Weathersby spoken around the lodge fires from the Chesapeake to the Mississippi, but I want you to know that whatever you hear is only half of what the tale may have been if you had been by my side. I will love you forever and always."

They looked into each other's eyes for a long while before turning toward the fire once again.

Sunlei stood up. "When are you to meet Walks Alone?"

"We will meet at the ridge when the moon has set."

"Then there is time." She took him by the hand, and led him to the cabin door.

Chapter 36

Run!

Sunlei awoke shortly after midnight and reached for Tyoga who had been next to her when she had fallen asleep. She was alone. Recalling that Tyoga was on his way to meet Walks Alone, she sat up in bed to watch the shadows cast by the fire dance around the room.

The wetness that spilled from between her legs brought a contented smile to her face. She lay back down and clutched her hands over her heart. The gentle sounds of the night seemed to agree. This time had been different.

In the middle of the night, she arose to peer out through the shutters. It was very dark outside.

The moon has set. She noticed that the fire outside had dwindled to a bed of hot coals.

Wrapping the red blanket around her shoulders, she walked quietly to the cabin door. Tyoga had stacked some dried pine and hickory on the porch. Tiptoeing in her bare feet, she carried two logs to the fire pit and tossed them onto the white-hot coals. Standing quietly, she listened to the sounds of the night while waiting for the logs to ignite into billowing hot flames.

As soon as the flames lit up the darkness, she noticed the haunting eyes on the far side of the campsite piercing the blackness, staring straight at her. Gasping out loud, she brought her hand to her mouth before realizing it was Wahaya-Wacon that was standing watch over her.

Remembering Tyoga's words, "You won't be alone," she dropped her shoulders and allowed herself to relax.

Walking to the far side of the fire, she squatted down and said, "Come, Wahaya-Wacon. Come to the warmth of the fire. It is okay. Come on."

The wolf never took his eyes off of her. He dropped his head the slightest bit, looked first to his left and then to his right. He took one halting step toward Sunlei before searching the air with his nose. Satisfied that Tyoga's scent was in the air, and that Sunlei was the only other human he could detect, he took two more steps in her direction.

Every time Sunlei had been in the presence of the magnificent creature she was taken aback at his majesty and grandeur. He was indeed an imposing figure, especially in the blackness of the night. He was astoundingly thick and large. His head easily came to her waist. The confidence in his stature radiated from his eyes with an eloquence that needed no words and demanded no homage. The honor was in its being.

That was enough.

Sunlei had only been alone with the wolf when he saved her life on the trail. That they had bonded so strongly while gazing into one another's eyes in the concealment of the grotto was little comfort to her as she stood alone in the woods with the naked rawness of the massive predator but two steps away.

Wahaya-Wacon was the wildest of wild creatures and Sunlei knew instinctively that there was no "tame" in him save that which he granted of his own free will.

Summoning her courage, she crouched down so that his head was above hers, and extended her hand toward him.

He took a step closer.

Frightened, she reflexively pulled her hand back into her lap. He could curl up at her feet as easily as he could rip her apart. Reaching her hand out toward him again, Wahaya took two more steps toward her until his nose touched her hand. It felt as cold and wet as it had when it brushed the back of her neck as she knelt on the trail crying for him to return to her.

He sniffed her hand with more intent, and gently brushed the palm of her hand with his muzzle and lips. When he licked the tip of her fingers with this coarse pink tongue, Sunlei smiled at the noble gesture of acceptance.

When she stood up, the wolf did not back away. "Stay by the fire, Wahaya," she said to his now gentle eyes as she walked back into the cabin.

He followed her to the threshold and watched her lie back down on the bed.

Lifting her head up from the pillow, she saw him circle thrice before lying down to face the blackness of the night. She pulled the soft red blanket up close under her chin, hugged her cool, down-filled pillow and fell into a deep, peaceful sleep.

She was safe.

Ꮳ Ᏽ Ꮮ Ᏽ

Sunlei woke with a start just before sunrise.

The muffled sounds descending the ramparts that encircled the grotto were difficult to decipher. Men's voices. Loud voices piercing the silence of the dawn. Branches breaking. Many feet pounded the leaf-covered forest floor.

Springing from the bed, she put on her tunic and moccasins and ran to the door. The wolf's hind quarters were inside the door, and the hair between his blood-engorged shoulder muscles was standing on end. His ears were piqued, and his gaze was intently focused on the north rampart.

"What is it, Wahaya?" Sunlei asked. "What do you hear? Is it Tyoga?"

The wolf lowered his head, threw his ears back and crouched ever so slightly toward the ground. His growl was more menacing and sustained. His gaze never left the path leading into the hollow from the north. With a quick chirp-like bark, he bounded off in that direction and disappeared in the morning mist.

Stepping quickly back inside the cabin, she quietly closed the leather-hinged door and placed the bar across the jam. She closed one of the window shutters and left the other cracked open enough to peer in the direction that the wolf had gone.

She could hear the cries in the distance more clearly now. They were war cries mixed with voices, some of them giving commands others calling out, "This way. They went this way." The loud voices were the Shawnee tongue. She heard other voices, too. Cherokee speaking Tsalagie. She was certain that she heard Tyoga's voice, but she couldn't make out what he was saying. The voices got louder and louder.

They were coming straight for the campsite.

Tyoga had said that there was only one way in and one way out of the hidden hollow, and that the entrance to the cave that led the way in was well concealed. When she thought that the voices were practically on top of her, she saw her cousin Walks Alone running toward the cabin with Tyoga behind him. Even though Walks Alone had been traveling through the night to meet Tyoga on the ridge, his powerful build gave no hint of fatigue. He, like Tyoga and Tes Qua, was a seasoned mountain traveler. They were both covered in sweat and nearly out of breath, but both men could have continued to run for their lives for as long as necessary. It was the urgency in their eyes that warned Sunlei that there was no time to lose.

Lifting the heavy oaken bar from the door jam, she threw the door open and ran toward the breathless men.

"Ty, Walks Alone, what is happening?" Sunlei quietly asked.

Tyoga put his finger to his lips, and turned toward the tiny opening to the cave. The distance of the passage tunnel muffled the sounds coming from the woods, but the Shawnee braves were thundering through the underbrush just beyond the cave's opening. The three of them held their breath and stared intently at the portal until they heard their pursuers footsteps disappear into the morning shadows.

Tyoga grabbed Sunlei by the shoulders. "Go with Walks Alone, my little one. Don't look back. Run!" He looked at Walks Alone with wild eyes that conveyed the urgency of his message and repeated, "Just run!"

He kissed Sunlei brusquely on the forehead and started back toward the cave; unwilling to surrender the final touch of his skin, Sunlei held tight to his hand as he moved away.

He paused at the tender tug for only a moment. Then, without turning around, allowed their intertwined fingers to slowly release in a final, silent kiss goodbye.

Walks Alone grabbed her by the arm. "Come, Sunlei. We must go." When her feet would not obey, he jerked her arm and commanded. "Sunlei! Now!"

Walks Alone was pulling her away to lead her over the rampart to the south, but she kept her eyes riveted on Tyoga while he jogged away. With her arm still extended, her fingers alive with the sensation of their final touch, her lips formed the words, "Goodbye, my love."

No one saw. No one heard. Only the promise registered the pain.

She turned toward Walks Alone, grabbed his hand, and ran as fast as she could.

Chapter 37

Destiny Designed

Bending at the waist and protecting his head with his hand, Tyoga ducked and raced through the length of the dank, dark tunnel. Concealed in the cover of the underbrush that hid the mouth of the cave, he emerged into the woods.

Wild grape vines, dense clusters of thick, broad-leafed ferns, and thorny rose and berry bushes made the two-by-three foot opening virtually invisible. The Shawnee had run right by without noticing it.

The wolf was standing like a muscled statue waiting for him to arrive when Tyoga stepped out onto the path.

After exchanging a quick glance with him, Tyoga quickly turned his attention to the direction that the Shawnee had taken.

Looking anxiously into Tyoga's eyes, Wahaya took several energetic prancing steps in that direction. He stopped short and circled back to indicate that Tyoga should follow him so that together they could put an end to their tormentors once and for all.

Tyoga understood. But instead of following, he got down on one knee. "Nah-ya, Wahaya. You can't stay with me. You must go with Sunlei."

The wolf stopped his anxious circling, sat down, and stared up at Tyoga. His expressive face conveyed an understanding of Tyoga's words, but that their meaning remained a mystery was evident in his eyes. He was to follow after Sunlei and Walks Alone. He had no way of appreciating the importance of the task he was being assigned, but he would do this thing for the one who asked. Stepping gently up to Tyoga's side, he touched his cool wet snout to his cheek and lightly tasted his salty skin. It was the first time that they had shared such a moment of intimacy. But as Tyoga lifted his hand to place it upon Wahaya's head, he lithely stepped back out of reach.

Stepping reluctantly toward the mouth of the cave, Wahaya turned a final time to gaze upon the one to whom he had given the miraculous gift.

"Take good care of Sunlei," Tyoga commanded his mate. "Don't let any harm come to her. I'm countin' on you, Wahaya-Wacon."

With that, Wahaya disappeared into the cave.

Unexpectedly, Tyoga felt himself well up with tears.

So much had happened over the last two days. He hadn't slept. He had released the love of his life to keep her safe and free. He may wander the rest of his days as a hunted man by the South Fork Shawnee, and now he had ordered his spirit guide to leave him to protect the one he loved. Wiping his eyes, he took a deep breath, and took off at a run to catch up with the Shawnee.

The jog through the woods brought Tyoga back to life.

The fresh, clean morning air filled his lungs and he felt his spirit soar as the power of Wahaya filled his blood with the call of the wild.

He had only traveled about half a mile when he spotted the marauding pack in an open glade under a stand of willow trees. Stopping short, Tyoga ducked behind a moss-covered boulder wedged between two large pines.

He and Walks Alone didn't have a chance to see how many Shawnee braves were chasing them. This was the first time he was able to get a good look at his pursuers.

He counted nine warriors. All them were in their late teens or early twenties. Their faces were painted with the black and ochra pigments of battle. They wore the leather leggings and breech clothes of deep woods warriors.

They were not outfitted to take prisoners, but to murder and defile. They carried full quivers of arrows and hickory long bows. Some had war clubs and others had iron-head tomahawks.

It was obvious that the Shawnee had figured out that Tyoga and Walks Alone had somehow eluded capture. They had stopped in the open glade to discuss their next course of action.

Tyoga couldn't hear the braves' conversation because they were just out of earshot. It was too risky to try to get any closer, so he hunkered down and waited to see what they would do next. He was certain that they would double back to see if they could pick up his tracks. When that happened, they would be coming in his direction.

The quiet of the dawn was suddenly shattered by the long, lonely howl of Wahaya-Wacon. The cry of the wolf was subdued and the tenor muted to convey a sadness that was palpable. It filled the morning mist with a pall of barren aloneness that stifled the Shawnee's conversation and quieted all of the morning birds.

Tyoga knew that Wahaya was calling him back to the cave. *Something must be wrong.*

Upon hearing the wolf, the Shawnee ducked down where they stood in an attempt to conceal themselves as best they could.

Taking advantage of the diversion, Tyoga slowly backed away from his hiding place. In ten carefully placed steps, he was beyond the Shawnees' line of sight. Turning toward the mouth of the cave, Tyoga ran as fast and quietly as he could toward the howl of Wahaya.

When he arrived at the entrance to the hollow, Wahaya was nowhere to be seen. Afraid of alerting the Shawnee to his whereabouts, he called out no louder than in his normal speaking voice, "Wahaya. Wahaya, lo ta tok talo?"

Bending at the waist to enter the cave, he looked down to see Sunlei's leather amulet lying atop a smooth, round boulder ringed by rainbow ferns. It was the amulet that went missing from the campsite on the top of Old Mount Rag.

Tyoga knelt to pick it up.

Smiling toward the West, he whispered to the wind, "Yes, Wahaya, it will protect me until you return. One day, I will tie it around the neck of its rightful owner."

Tyoga tied the amulet around his neck. He turned and took two steps to resume his hunt for the Shawnee braves before stopping in his tracks. He pivoted toward the cave, and entered the dark cavern. He emerged moments later with the red blanket draped over his shoulder, and tied to the opposite side of his waist sash.

Standing to his full height, he stretched out his mighty arms and felt them swell with the power of the earth and sky.

Time seemed to stop as his tomorrow had already come and gone. Listening to nothing at all, he heard every sound. Seeing nothing but blackness, the world was illuminated in stark and frightening detail.

He turned to the east and ran toward his destiny.

Chapter 38

Savage Retribution

Renewing his pursuit of the Shawnee, Tyoga ran at full speed along the uneven trail until he came to the spot under the willow tree where he had seen them before Wahaya beckoned him back to the cave.

Instead of doubling back as Tyoga had suspected they would, the war party had forged ahead thinking that he and Walks Alone were still out ahead of them. Not only didn't they realize that they were no longer chasing anyone at all, but they had no idea that they had become the hunted.

Tyoga knew this area well. He and Tes Qua had spent many days in their youth exploring the pristine acreage from the safety of their secret hollow. About a half a mile up the trail, the path veered sharply to the north and descended precipitously to the cut of Dobson's Run.

Leaving the trail, he dove into the woods and headed north. Moving silently through the thicket, the shortcut made it easy for him to flank the war party and beat them by ten minutes to the spot where the path crossed Dobson's Run. While well concealed in the underbrush and reeds, he prepared himself for the first murderous deed.

Tyoga was tired, hungry, and filled with an assassin's contempt born of loss, entrapment, and desperation. He was dirty and smelled of smoke, sweat, and the musky reminders of Sunlei's final goodbye. He had not shaved in over a week and his eyes had long since abandoned any pretense of their docile hazel hue. He had surrendered to the sizzling amber glow that annihilated reason, steeled resolve, and obliterated the ethical lines that separate the moral discipline of human sensibility and the savage ferocity of animal instinct to protect and defend.

Tyoga Weathersby was gone.

The transformation was complete.

What was there had vanished, replaced with an animal deliberateness filled with inhuman intent. Indifferent to death. Frightening. He would do what had to be done with ruthless abandon.

He heard the mocassined feet approaching from the south well before they came into view.

When they passed by him not an arms length away, he stopped breathing and froze stone still. He lay in wait like the bear trap that had ensnared his friend all those years ago. Silent. Cold. Cocked. Lethal. His massive arms were engorged with blood in anticipation of the strike.

The next brave in the line placed his foot on the first stepping stone to cross the Run when Tyoga struck. Lifting the young man completely off the ground with his left arm, he covered the brave's mouth with his right hand before he could cry out. Laying the brave on his back, and placing his knee in his chest, Tyoga returned the terror in the man's eyes with the cold blank gaze of an alpha predator. As easily as filleting a roe-filled shad, Tyoga slit the warrior's throat from ear to ear with a single stroke of his butchering blade.

The clear, cool water in Dobson's Run turned a pinkish brown as it continued its journey to the sea.

Tyoga glanced over the swaying tops of the tall reeds across the creek to see if he had been discovered.

The last warrior in the line did not turn around or give any sign that he had heard the silent murder of his friend.

In a single deer-like bound, Tyoga cleared the width of the Run and landed silently on the balls of his feet. Taking two quick quiet steps, he placed his hulking hand over the mouth of the warrior in the back of the line, and slid the razor edge of his knife along the soft spongy tissue of the young man's jaw line. The war party kept moving forward without noticing the loss of their two companions.

Tyoga was dragging the body of the second warrior he had killed across the creek when he heard the others in the party call the names of their missing friends.

"Sheshotahey *(Looks Within)*. Entowata *(Bull Song)*. Eh ta eeta wa lo?"

Receiving no reply, the eldest in the group asked, "Talking Bear, weren't they walking behind you?"

"Yes, River Claw, they were right behind me."

"Did you not hear anything?"

"No, Ginsata. I heard nothing."

"What shall we do, River Claw? Do you want me and Winged Bear to go look for them?"

"Nay ya. They will catch up. Eh ta ho."

Searching for any sign of Tyoga and Walks Alone, the Shawnee braves continued on until noon. They made camp in a clearing next to a spring surrounded by large willow trees. They had covered about eighteen miles since they had begun chasing Tyoga and Walks Alone before dawn.

They were tired and hungry.

"We will make camp here," River Claw announced to his men. "We will eat and rest. We will resume our hunt tomorrow when Looks Within and Bull Song have rejoined us. If they have not returned by nightfall, we will build a great fire so that they can find their way to us in the dark. Stay together. Do not leave camp for any reason. When it gets dark, stay within the light of the fire. Wahaya may be near. "

"River Claw," Talking Bear protested, "let me circle back to look for Bull Song and Looks Within. I will take Yellow Stone with me and we will not go far."

"Talking Bear, it is a brave thing that you ask to do," River Claw responded looking at the others to reinforce his message with affirming nods. "But I have seen many days more than you in the woods. The trees are telling me that this is a time to stay close to camp. These things you do not know now. But you will learn."

"I do hope to know what you know and to hear what you hear some-day, River Claw. But now my friends are missing and all that I hear is the wind through the pines. Let me go find our friends, your nephew."

"My son," River Claw replied, "you have heard of the legend of Tyoga Weathersby. I have seen your eyes as I have told the tale many times around my lodge fire. You cannot understand the power of his magic. He is neither man, nor beast, but something else that we cannot know. We all will stay here in camp. That is my final word."

Like the wolf that singles out a victim from a roaming herd before making the kill, Tyoga had already picked out his next two victims. He watched and waited throughout the evening hours. When the Shawnee fell asleep, he silently rose to his feet.

The war party awoke to a scene of utter horror.

Looks Within and Bull Song were swinging in the morning breeze from the trees surrounding their campsite alongside the mutilated bodies of two additional braves murdered in the night. The Braves had been disemboweled, their entrails dangling from their swaying corpses.

Blood, mucous, and feces pooled to make a putrid soup on the ground below their bodies.

When the first Shawnee brave awoke to relieve himself before the sun had risen, his horrific screams alerted the others to the carnage that surrounded the camp.

Springing from their blankets in the pre-dawn chill, the remaining members of the party ran for their lives from the hellish sight. They left behind their provisions, their clothes, and most of their weapons.

Like a panicked herd stampeding in fear, their frantic flight worked to Tyoga's distinct advantage. He was already waiting for them as they entered an open meadow.

After Tyoga hung and mutilated the bodies of the four dead Shawnee, he had plenty of time to get far ahead of the frightened five remaining young men who were now frantically trying to make their way back to South Fork. Lying on his back in the tall grass surrounding the meadow, Tyoga casually plucked a long stemmed blade of grass that was topped by a heavily laden seedpod and absent-mindedly stuck it in his mouth. Thinking of Sunlei, he wondered if Walks Alone had delivered her to Lone Bear's family safely. He wished his best friend Tes Qua were by his side. He thought about the night that he had defended Tes Qua's life by battling the marauding Runion pack while his defenseless friend was caught in the massive jaws of the bear trap.

Furrowing his brow while he chewed on the grass, he considered how much like the trap he had become. While the bear trap that imprisoned Tes Qua had retained its size, shape, form and function, its intent was magically transformed by circumstance from a weapon of destruction into an implement of protection securing Tes Qua's foot and ankle in place.

Like the trap, Tyoga recognized that he had changed, too. His transformation had been completely in reverse. The gentle young man who battled so courageously to preserve his friend's life and struggled through the night to get him safely home, now lay in wait to murder terrified young men fighting to accomplish the same goal for which he had once so dearly fought.

The recognition did not deter his purpose.

Hearing the war party running from the protection of the woods and into the north end of the open meadow, he picked up the bow and arrows he had taken from their campsite, and repositioned himself to get a better shot.

The flight of the arrow pierced the morning shadows with a menacing "zzzzzttttttt", before the first brave silently dropped to his knees. So true was the shot that the arrow punctured his voice box and cleanly severed his jugular vein.

The horrific sight of their friend wildly clutching at the blood spurting from his neck and mouth sent the remaining braves scattering in a panic-stricken canter for their lives.

The second Shawnee fell with an arrow through his heart.

The two running behind him fell over his lifeless corpse. They picked themselves up off the ground and followed River Claw into the protective cover of a shallow ravine.

As they stumbled to the bottom of the gulch, they found the elder's body lying belly down in the tall grass. They paused only long enough to turn him over to check for signs of life. They jumped back at the horror before their eyes.

Rather than being scalped, their leader's face had been completely removed from his skull. While the practice of removing the scalp was accepted as a keepsake that honored a fallen enemy's courage in battle, removal of a warrior's forehead, nose, cheeks, lips and chin was seen as defilement beyond contempt.

Tyoga dropped the final two warriors where they stood even before they had the chance to recover from the abomination that had paralyzed them in place.

Strolling from the shadows, Tyoga pushed at the lifeless bodies with his foot. Sitting down in their midst, he slipped off his right moccasin and shook out an annoying pebble. Rubbing the back of his neck, he stretched out his lower back and felt the blood drain away from his engorged and tired muscles.

As the gentle hazel hue slowly replaced the feral amber sting in his eyes, his body relaxed. He felt himself return. He pushed back from the spot in which he was sitting when the blood draining from the warrior's neck to his right soaked into his britches. He drew his knees to his chest, and looked beyond the three dead men and out into the open meadow they had crossed.

Tyoga understood the brutality of the murders he had committed. He also knew that when the bodies were found, the degree of cruelty and mutilation would be the measure by which time would be purchased for Sunlei and Walks Alone to get away.

Ultimately, those sent to find Sunlei and bring her back or kill her would always remember the carnage visited upon the first party sent to recover her. Their enthusiasm for the hunt would undoubtedly be tempered by the fireside tales of the gruesome scenes created this day. He had taken advantage of the legend that had grown around him and calculated that the terror evoked by the savage revenge of the wolf-man he had become would serve to protect him and those that he loved.

This time, no one was left to tell the tale.

He lay down in the grass and went to sleep.

☙ ❧ ☙ ❧

In the Shawnee village of South Fork, Two Fox and Sky Hawk and the others who Yellow Robe had sent to carry his son home placed his cold, pale body at his Father's feet. With tears streaming down his cheeks, he gazed at his son lying motionless on the floor. He remembered the pride he felt at his son's first deer kill and the celebration that lasted all night after he had taken his first woman. His father's eyes would not allow him to see the wretched human being that Seven Arrows had become. Blinded by parental bond, he remembered only the joy that his son had brought to their family in his younger years.

Falling to his knees in desperate grief, Yellow Robe gently placed his strong, calloused hand under his son's blood soaked head. Bending at the waist he touched his tear stained face to his son's chest.

At the low, shallow exhale, Yellow Robe's eyes opened wide, and he sprang to his feet.

Chapter 39

Chickamaugua

Sunlei and Walks Alone arrived in the Cherokee village of Chickamaugua in only two days.

It had been an arduous trip along some of Appalachia's most rugged trails. The route had taken them through Indigo pass and over Shorts Mountain, just south of Mount Mitchell, the highest peak in the Blue Ridge. By creating an inhospitable environment for all but the most sure-footed creatures, the tall jagged peaks of the Blue Ridge resisted intrusion. The deer trails followed by Native Americans were intuitively the lines of least resistance; they were steep, narrow, and provided few spots to make camp. The deep, flat lowland valleys provided little respite because the next steep climb was but a ridge away. Above the timberline, rocky peaks jutted straight up into the clouds and the trails up the nearly vertical slopes became little more than treacherous sheets of slippery shale.

They did not stop to make camp or to sleep through the night. They only rested for half-hour intervals; for sustenance, they sliced meat from the carcass of an elk and ate the flesh raw.

When they entered the village of the Chichamaugua Cherokee, Walks Alone was carrying Sunlei like a child—sound asleep in his arms.

Her clothes were torn and tattered, and she was covered with scratches from the thorny brush through which they had trekked.

Walks Alone placed Sunlei into the arms of Lone Bear's wife, Blossoms in Spring, and fell to his knees, completely spent. Lone Bear's sons rushed to Walks Alone's side, lifted him to his feet, and escorted him into the lodge where he collapsed onto a pallet of soft bear hides. They slept for two days straight.

Lone Bear's family took turns sitting with Sunlei so that someone would be with her when she finally awoke. She did not arouse to eat or drink. She did not awaken even to relieve herself. While she slept, Blossoms in Spring washed the dirt and blood from her wracked and battered body, and cared for the still open wounds on her back. Most importantly, her soft touch allowed Sunlei to sleep.

On the third day, Sunlei awoke to the smiling face of Standing Bird, Lone Bear's eldest daughter, who asked, "Agi yo si?"

Rubbing her eyes and stretching, Sunlei replied, "Yes, I am hungry and thirsty."

When Standing Bird announced to the lodge that Sunlei was awake and hungry, it set off a whirlwind of activity that was so orchestrated that it seemed rehearsed. Lone Bear's daughters rushed to prepare an enormous plate of food, while others scrambled to be the first to present Sunlei with the new doeskin tunic and sandals they had made in anticipation of her arrival. Lone Bear's three sons pushed and shoved each other to be the first to enter the lodge to gaze into the open eyes of the beautiful Indian maiden that they had heard so much about. Blossoms in Spring walked over to greet the new arrival in a more measured, maternal way.

"There, there, my little one, how tired you were." Blossoms in Spring sat down next to Sunlei's bed and folded her in her massive loving arms.

There was magic in her touch.

Blossoms in Spring was a huge, fertile woman who had not only given birth to thirteen children, but had extended her maternal compassion to all the children in the village. Her smile enveloped with love and her hands comforted with a sense of security and trust that made everything right in the world. "You have had a long hard journey, but you are safe with us now." She combed Sunlei's tangled raven mane with her pudgy weathered hand.

Sunlei was in the midst of swallowing her second bite of food and could only look up at Blossom with gratitude.

"That's it, my little one," Blossom said while Sunlei continued to place handfuls of venison stew into her mouth. "Eat until you can eat no more." Throwing her head back, Blossom let loose a roaring laugh that filled the room with cheer.

The infectious lilt captured all within earshot. A chorus of raucous laughter spilled beyond the lodge and into the communal square.

Sensing that there was no need for words of thanks, Sunlei dug into her plate of food with a gusto that triggered another round of hearty laughter.

Over the next several days, Sunlei enjoyed the comfort, companionship, and safety of her new home. She told Lone Bear and his sons the story behind her being turned over to Seven Arrows, and the details of her rescue as best as she could recall. She recounted her harrowing escape, running naked through the night while trying to catch up to whoever it was that had slit Seven Arrows's throat, and of being hidden from her pursuers in the recesses of the moss-covered grotto by Wahaya-Wacon. Tears filled her eyes when she told of being miraculously delivered into the safety of Tyoga Weathersby's strong arms.

Her mention of Tyoga and the wolf opened the door to a barrage of questions about him and Wahaya. This was the first time that Sunlei had been exposed to Cherokee people who were not of her immediate family or village. To witness the regard in which they held the man who she knew only as a gentle loving soul astonished her.

"We have heard that Tyoga Weathersby is more wolf than man," Lone Bear said while they sat around the lodge's fire pit. More of his family gathered around. "It is said that when he becomes angry, Wahaya-Wacon is awakened within his soul. The spirit wolf changes this man into a savage beast that thirsts for blood. Is this not so?"

"No, Lone Bear. You do not understand," Sunlei blurted out before she was able to consider her words. "Tyoga is a good, kind man who seeks to harm no one unless they threaten those he loves. It is true that he saved my brother, Tes Qua Ta Wa, from certain death at the jaws of the Runion wolves. It is also true that he spared the life of

Wahaya-Wacon. That the story has given rise to the legend of Tyoga Weathersby is not of his doing, nor by his choice."

"The legend holds that Tyoga is—and is not—of this world," Lone Bear continued. "It is said that the spirit of Wahaya has caused him to see the world through the eyes of our animal brothers. Is it true that he sees like the eagle, hears like the owl, and fights with the savagery of the wolf?"

For a long time, Sunlei thought about her answer to Lone Bear's question. Her answer was important because the boundaries between animal and man were as important to the Cherokee as the connections that made them one with the Medicine Wheel. Her words must not do any harm to Tyoga, the man, but must not denigrate his connection to the spirit world.

"In return for sparing his life, Wahaya-Wacon has shared his spirit with the man," Sunlei replied. "The spirit that he has shared has opened the door to visions of the world that reflect its truth and the rightness of nature's judgement. Tyoga is guided by these visions of truth and honor and justice. It is difficult to explain, but you must believe that the strength of Wahaya fills him with restraint and wisdom and a knowing of things that are hidden from his Cherokee fathers. It is a wonderful gift. And he uses it well."

Lone Bear did not reply, nor did any members of his family. So passionate was Sunlei's defense of the man—and the beast—that no one dared question her explanation. They spoke of other matters.

On the fifth day of her stay, Sunlei awoke to the not surprising news that the South Fork Shawnee had gotten word of her whereabouts. While the Appalachians can guard a secret for eternity, those who understand her ways are rarely fooled. She walked over to the lodge fire to find Blossoms in Spring crying and Lone Bear deep in thought.

"What are we to do," Blossoms was asking her husband.

Squatting down next to Blossoms, Sunlei lovingly wrapped her arm around her and rested her head on her shoulder.

Staring into the fire, Lone Bear said, "It is not a decision that we can make alone. I have sent Stands with Rock to the Chief to ask for a council this very night. We must decide as a People what is best to do." He looked over at Sunlei, and then back into the flames.

Sunlei stood, and looked down at Lone Bear who would not return her gaze. "The decision of the council will be just. Tyoga told me to listen to you. I will do as you say." Turning toward the entrance to the lodge, Sunlei headed toward the door to go outside.

Lone Bear glanced over at his son, Runs Long, and jerked his head in her direction.

Runs Long stood up immediately and grabbed his bow to follow Sunlei outside.

"Where do you go, my child?" Lone Bear asked.

"To check on Wahaya-Wacon, my father," she replied. "He must remain strong. I fear that we will be traveling again very soon." She ducked her head and left the lodge.

That night at tribal council, the People of Chickamauga rallied to Sunlei's defense. They vowed to take up arms to protect her and to put an end once and for all to the merciless hunt for her that was threatening to tear apart the Appalachian confederation.

As she had pleaded before at the Cherokee Council in Tuckareegee, Sunlei begged that others not be asked to sacrifice their lives for her sake. She remained adamant that others should not be punished for the deeds of an unknown assailant, and that killing in her name was a burden that she was not willing to bear.

The council agreed to steal Sunlei away in the night, and to let the information leak that she was no longer with the tribe. A party of five Chickamauga braves accompanied her to the land of the Osage.

In three week's time, Sunlei's travels were lost to the realities of frontier life that distanced occurrence and news by weeks, months, and sometimes years.

Chapter 40

Confession

After the mutilated bodies of the Shawnee war party were discovered, the legend of Tyoga Weathersby grew in stature and consequence beyond that associated solely with the presence of the spirit wolf. Nine Shawnee braves had been butchered without a single witness to tell the tale.

This time, the tracks of Wahaya-Wacon were nowhere to be found.

Stopping only to rest when his legs would carry him no further, and eating only some pemikan that he took from the Shawnee war party's camp, Tyoga arrived at his tiny makeshift lodge on the overlook at Tuckareegee after midnight of the second day. Pushing aside the deer hide entrance flap, he stumbled across the milled plank floor, and collapsed into a heap of buffalo robes.

He awoke to the scent of roasting venison wafting into the shelter on a cool autumn breeze. Someone had removed all of his clothes, and bathed him. He found himself lovingly wrapped—toes to chin—in the warm red blanket that had been his traveling companion since leaving Sunlei with Walks Alone at the secret hollow.

Even before Tyoga had the chance to clear his head and rub the sleep from his eyes, Prairie Day was at his side holding a steaming cup of asi.

He looked up into her gentle eyes, the first kindness he had beheld in a week's time, smiled faintly, and whispered through parched, crusty lips, "Prairie Day."

"Shhhh," she replied gently pushing his thick brown hair away from his eyes. She stared at him with sad eyes full of compassion and unquestioned devotion, as a tiny smile parted her full lips. Softly, she cooed in a voice as comforting as his own mother's. "Drink this, Ditlihi. Rest. You have been asleep for two days." Getting to her feet, she went to the entrance of the tiny lodge, and pushed aside the deerhide flap so that the sunshine streamed into the lodge.

Tyoga held up his hand to block the sunlight from his eyes and brought the clay bowl filled with the piping hot dark caffeine-rich asi to his lips. The bitter, strong drink had the effect of rousing him to his senses almost immediately. He realized that he had not had anything to drink for several days, and before he could ask for water, Prairie Day was once again at his side with a clay urn filled to the brim with clear, cool water. He emptied the urn and asked for more.

Tyoga sat up in bed and stretched. Wincing in discomfort at an unexpected pain, he reached around to feel behind his left shoulder. He fingers smeared the sticky bear fat poultice that had been applied to the wound on his back. He remembered that River Claw, the leader of the Shawnee band who he killed in the ravine had not submitted to his fate without first delivering a forceful blow to his back with his tomahawk.

"Hurt much?" he heard the familiar voice call as his leather britches hit him in the face.

"A-ho, Tes Qua. Ne chitela a yeaho e alo," Tyoga responded with a smile.

Tes Qua took two steps toward the mound of buffalo hides that had been Tyoga's bed for the past two days, and knelt down just as his friend extended his arm.

The two clasped hands like they had done since they were children. The force of their grasp conveyed the arrogant confidence that solidifies male friendships in a baptism of forgiveness, understanding and uncompromised fraternity.

"I wish you had told me what you were up to, Ty," Tes Qua said with a sheepish 'you-left-me-out-of-this-one' tone of voice. "She is my sister, you know."

"I know, Tes. But I wanted to keep you out of this mess, and to tell you the truth, I didn't think I was gonna come out of this one with my hair," he said as he ran his fingers through his thick brown mane. "Besides, if Yellow Robe had the slightest notion that you or any member of the tribe was involved, we wouldn't be talkin' right now."

"Did you kill him, Ty?"

Tyoga shook his head. "I was on my way to kill 'im, but someone got there first. I thought maybe you?"

"Nay ya. Silver Cloud had a difficult time keeping a war party from striking out to rescue Sunlei. He even posted guards around the village to keep anyone from sneaking off to get her. He gave his word to Yellow Robe, and he meant to make sure that his word was kept. Works out pretty good this way, though. Silver Cloud kept his word. Payment was made." Tes Qua paused. "But now we have all lost Sunlei."

Tyoga slipped on his leather britches.

Tes Qua handed him his freshly laundered shirt.

As he was lacing it up he asked, "How did you know that I was here? Nobody knew that I would return. I didn't even plan to come back."

"Prairie Day," Tes Qua replied with a nod of his head in her direction. "She came up here every evening and would sit until after dark. She said that you would return. She was right."

"Any word?" he asked.

"We know that Walks Alone delivered Sunlei safely to the Chickamaugua. At least that's what Lone Elk said he heard on his way back from the Holston grade. Ty, they say that Wahaya is with her. Is that true?"

"Yeah, it's true. I sent him with her." Recalling the sad eyes that looked into his as he sent Wahaya away, Tyoga said, "He didn't want to leave me, though. I had to send him along to keep her safe 'til I can get to her." He put his hand to his chest to grasp the tiny brown leather pouch filled with Sunlei's totems. "He left this for me. I found it lying on the ground at the entrance to our secret hollow. I reckon he figures its magic will watch over me until he returns." He paused before adding, "I'm gonna miss him."

"What are you going to do now, Ty?"

Prairie Day called them to come out of the lodge for something to eat before he had a chance to answer.

Stepping out into the sunshine, Tyoga looked over at where she squatted by the fire to tend to the trout that were cooking over the searing heat of the hot coals. Smiling, he remembered Green Rock Cove.

"I was gonna go east for awhile, Tes," he said. "Spend some time out of the mountains. Go to Middletown, Fredericksburg, maybe all the way to Hampton Roads." As if answering the questions racing through his mind, he stopped to shake his head.

"I had it all set up," Tyoga told them. "I told the People at council that I would be leaving Tuckareegee, and as far as everyone in the village knows, I have. Only you and Priarie Day know that I am here now. But I can't leave the mountains now. I thought that going away for awhile would keep the People of Tuckareegee safe. Yellow Robe couldn't accuse you of hiding me. With me and Wahaya gone, he would have no cause to make any trouble. But I think now that my notion of leavin' the mountains may have been just a selfish way of keepin' me safe. That's a coward's way out—and I may be many things, Tes A, but a coward ain't one of 'em."

"No one would ever call you a coward, Tyoga," Tes Qua insisted. "You are the most courageous brave of all of the Ani-Unwiya. All of the People know that to be true."

"Just the same, I think that I was just takin' the easy way out."

Prairie Day was listening to the two men speak. In the tradition of the Ani-Unwiya, she kept her counsel to herself, but she wanted to know more. "Eh ya, Ditlihi. Eh ya ta ha ni gi?"

"I'm going after Sunlei," Tyoga said.

Prairie Day closed her eyes for the briefest of moments. Then, she stood and walked over to them with two plates filled with trout, beans and squash, a mash of corn and lima beans and corn bread.

In the late afternoon, there was a great deal of activity in the village below. Tyoga stayed close to the lodge so that he could not be seen by the people milling about the grounds of Tuckareegee. Used to seeing Prairie

Day at the campsite at all hours of the day and night, the villagers paid no attention to the smoke coming from the outcropping.

In horror, Prairie Day and Tes Qua listened while Tyoga described the methodical murders of the Shawnee war party. He disclosed unnecessary details of their demise and described the slaughter with neither pride nor shame. Watching his gentle hazel eyes as he told the story with a matter-of-factness that seemed to mitigate moral responsibility for the atrocities he had committed gave them both pause. Prairie Day and Tes Qua exchanged inquisitive glances while Tyoga told the tale. Each of them was sure that the other was thinking the same thought.

Tyoga had killed as deliberately and with the same degree of cunning and stealth as the wolf the legend said he had become. Perhaps there was more to the legend than either was prepared to accept.

Prairie Day took the shallow wooden bowl from Tes Qua's outstretch hand. She paused and turned toward Tyoga. He held his bowl out for her to take from his hand, but she did not reach for it.

Looking him straight in the eyes, she said, "Tyoga, you cannot go after Sunlei."

Tyoga raised his eyebrows and looked over at Tes Qua for confirmation that Priarie Day had spoken boldly and out of line.

Tes Qua did not return his look of surprise. Instead, he was staring intently at Prairie Day, which granted her silent permission to continue with her thoughts.

Without taking her eyes off of Tyoga, she said, "You must not go searching for Sunlei. Not yet. Not now. Chief Yellow Robe will not rest until you are found. If you go looking for Sunlei, his braves will know and they will allow you to draw them nearer to her. Your search to find her will only bring her harm. They will follow you and capture and kill you both."

"Prairie Day, you do not know these things to be true," Tyoga replied incredulously. "Another truth may be that I find her and take her far away from here. We will go to the Powhatan and live in peace."

"No, Tyoga!" Prairie Day demanded as tears welled in her eyes. "Hear me, Ditlihi. You must listen. If you go searching for Sunlei now, neither one of you will remain alive to see the spring." She paused to wipe her eyes and regain her composure.

Tyoga stared up at her gentle face. He had no words.

"There is more, my brave one." She referred to him as only Sunlei had in the past. She waited for him to reply.

"Tell me, Prairie Day." Tyoga looked down into the dirt between his crossed legs.

"Did you see Seven Arrows's dead body?" she asked. "Did you look upon it with your own eyes?"

Knowing what she was implying, Tyoga sprang to his feet and shouted at her as she turned to walk away, "I didn't need to see his dead body. I heard his warriors screaming of his death. Over and over I heard them say 'He is dead, he is dead'."

Prairie Day spun around to face Tyoga and planted her feet firmly to stand her ground. "He is not," she shouted back at him. She turned away, walked toward the fire, and repeated more softly, but no less firmly, "He is not dead."

At this, Tes Qua stood up and looked back and forth between them.

Tyoga reached out for her and turned her around by the shoulders. His eyes asked the question to which she replied, "There are things that a woman knows that you cannot understand. I tell you that his spirit lives."

"Tyoga, if Prairie Day is right, you cannot go after my sister. They will let you lead them to her and kill you both," Tes Qua said.

Turning away from them, Tyoga took several steps toward the shelter. He stopped to gaze into the woods.

Prairie Day saw the fabric of his shirt begin to tighten across his back. His breathing became deep and slow. She walked over to him and laced her arm through his and rested the palm of her other hand on his growing biceps. "No, Tyoga," she said quietly. "Now is not the time for Wahaya. Now is the time to think and act wisely." She stroked his arm lovingly and waited until she felt the tension drain away before leading him back toward the fire.

"Prairie Day is right, Tyoga," Tes Qua said. "You must do what is best for everyone. But, my brother, it will not be easy."

"And what is that, Ditlihi?" Tyoga asked. "What is it that I must do?"

"Leave," Tes Qua replied. "You must leave this place and disappear into the wilderness like Wahaya. You must go where no one will find you, and you must not return until I come for you."

The sun was setting over Keyser's Ridge. The first evening stars twinkled to life. The village of Tuckareegee was swallowed in stillness and calm. The forest came alive with the sounds of the night as the blackness enveloped the three friends—each lost in silent thought.

Once again, Tyoga was at a crossroads.

Feeling the coolness of mother earth through the boulder upon which he sat, Tyoga threw his head back to look up into the heavens.

Closing his eyes, he remembered once again that glorious moment on Carter's Rock when the awakening changed his life forever. Feeling his spirit meld with the blackness of night, like it had done in the brilliant light on that frosty morning so many years ago, he wondered if the promise had forsaken him when he needed it the most. He intuitively understood that when circumstances force us to make decisions that hold in the balance the choice between life and death, perseverance and renewal is the promise of nature's way. To choose otherwise is to be deaf to the whispers and blind to the subtle cues.

When fighting for Tes Qua's life in his battle with Wahaya, he had chosen mercy when the balance between life and death was held in his hands. Yet, he had callously dismissed compassion and had chosen death for the Shawnee braves.

Had the spirit of Wahaya muted the wisdom and truth of the promise so profoundly that I am no longer able to hear? Is the price to be paid for my savagery the loss of the whispered truth?

Wait. Perhaps I have heard. Maybe I did listen. Perhaps the murder of the Shawnee braves was no choice at all, but decreed by the truth of the promise. Maybe their murder and desecration was the path set forth for them from the moment of their birth. Maybe, just maybe, I was simply the instrument in nature's orchestra which understood the true commands of the maestro's baton.

His mind was flooded with the confusion of loss and the regret of compromise. Placing his hands on either side of his head to quiet his mind, he drew his knees to his chest and felt the tears stream silently down his cheeks.

Prairie Day stoked the fire with dry hickory logs and went over to where Tyoga was sitting. The smoke from the rising flames, caught in her current, followed her gentle sway and clung to her form while she leaned over to kiss the top of his head.

When she walked away, the smoke did not follow but swirled around his head and stung his eyes with its pungent bite. A puff of wind from the northwest cleared the smoke and blew the sandy locks of hair from his eyes. He blinked to stem the flow of salty tears, straightened his back, and rubbed both eyes with the palms of his hands.

Dropping his hands between his knees, he gasped when his eyes regained their focus. Putting his knuckles on the stone, he lifted himself up ever so slightly as if the heightened point of view would reset the focus of his eyes.

Looking across the gorge at the trees lining Wilfer's Ridge, he could see the individual leaves of massive oak trees in stunning clarity. He rose to his knees as the scent of the water running through the trace two hundred feet below was as clean and crisp as if he were standing on the bank.

The rising moon electrified his skin, and the hair on his arms and the back of his neck stood on end when he felt the wings of an owl cut through the evening shadows.

He was the night. He was the smoke and the wind. The water in the trace was the blood in his veins.

He smiled when he recognized the promise's embrace.

The answers were all around him hiding in plain sight. They drizzled from the granite walls and danced in the flames of the coal and ash. The answers rose in the smoke, condensed in the morning dew and were passed from pine to pine on the silent breeze.

He remembered.

In all things there are but two outcomes—and each is in keeping with nature's wondrous plan.

His choice was to kill the Shawnee or be killed by them. He would find Sunlei—or he would not. He would make the right decision now— or he would not.

In either case—the journey would end exactly as it was meant to be.

His decision would be right.

Tyoga stood and turned to face his friends who were sitting by the fire. With a clear, calm determined voice, he said, "I will leave this place. I will go tomorrow and stay away until you come for me."

Tes Qua and Prairie Day looked at each other with resignation in their eyes. The decision had been made. "Where will you go, my brother?" Tes Qua asked.

"Northwest, toward the land of the Iroquois. They will never suspect that I have headed for the lands of our enemy. I must lead those seeking to kill me far away from here," Tyoga replied. "There is much to do before sunrise. I must get ready."

Tes Qua went over to Tyoga. The men embraced.

Prairie Day rose, stepped into the shelter, and came out holding her leather travel bag. She folded the red blanket neatly and placed it inside the doeskin a-do-da.

"What are you doing, Prairie Day?" Tyoga asked.

"I am packing for the journey."

"Thank you. I will need that blanket where I am going."

"Then you had better pack one for yourself. This blanket is for me. I am going with you and there is nothing else to say." With a solitary tear running down her cheek, she stepped assertively toward the men.

Stunned at her adamancy, neither of them spoke.

"You will need someone to care for you. I will cook and carry your belongings. I won't slow you down. You can run ahead and I will catch up to wherever you are and make camp. I will not let you leave me behind."

Tyoga stepped over to her and caressed her cheek in the palm of his calloused hand. "Prairie Day, I would love to have you by my side, but you will slow me down. The journey will be hard and dangerous. I will not even be able to make a fire. I will lie down on the forest floor to sleep wherever I can find a soft patch to rest my head. I will eat only what I can carry and scavenge."

"Then, so will I." She threw her arms around him and pulled herself close to his chest.

Tyoga let her hold on to him for a long moment before gently clutching her shoulders in his strong hands and holding her away from him. "Prairie Day, you cannot come with me. I know that you want to help me, but don't you see that if you come along there will be two lives that I must protect. My feelings for you will make me reckless. There are no second chances out there." He tossed his head toward the wilderness.

At this, Prairie Day fell to her knees and clutched his thigh. "Don't leave me, Ty. Please, don't leave me here. I am not alive unless you are near to me. You will tear my heart out if you go without me."

Tyoga knelt down and held her close. He had no words.

He looked up at Tes Qua and motioned for him to come over.

Her head was hanging down as Tes Qua picked her up off the ground. She sobbed quietly into the palms of her hands.

Tyoga rose to his feet and put his arm on Tes Qua's shoulder.

"Goodbye, my brother," Tes Qua said. "If you need me, just send for me. Wherever you are—I will come."

"I know you will," Tyoga replied.

Tes Qua turned with his arm around Prairie Day's waist to begin the journey down the slope to the village below. They took two steps, before she stopped.

"No," she said. Standing up straight, she dried her eyes with the back of her hands. "Ty, you go rest now. We will go down to the village and I will get the supplies that you will need for your journey. I will come back and ready your gear and supplies and I will wake you when it is time for you to leave." She went over to where she had dropped her knapsack to the ground, picked it up, and went inside the shelter to prepare Tyoga's bed.

Tes Qua and Prairie Day made the hour-long trek down the mountain trail in the dead of night. Without the night watch even noticing her presence, Prairie Day slipped into Tuckareegee and collected the supplies that Tyoga would need for his trip. It was nearly midnight when she arrived alone back at the outcropping.

When her work was done, she stepped into the shelter and stood for a long time while watching Tyoga sleep.

Yearning to feel him once again upon her naked skin, she tiptoed over to the buffalo robe upon which he slept, slowly untied the shoulder laces of her tunic and allowed it to float silently to the floor. Lifting the soft elk hide blanket that covered him, she lay down beside him.

Propping herself up on her elbow, she leaned over and whispered softly into his ear while he slept, "What I have done, has been done for you, my love. If I must live the rest of my life with but half a heart, it is a small price to pay for your happiness. I will love you forever, and will be with you always." Closing her eyes, she moved so close to him that her lips nearly touched his ear. "Forgive me."

She closed her eyes. But did not sleep.

Part Four

Prosperity and Emptiness

Chapter 41

The Trek to Mattaponi

Shawnee Chief Yellow Robe had honored the treaty forged by the bonds of marriage between his daughter, Winged Woman, and Gray Owl of the Ani-Unwiya, and did not exact revenge upon the people of Tuckareegee for Sunlei's escape and the vicious attack upon his son.

The target of the Shawnee chief's fury remained Tyoga Weathersby. Yellow Robe was certain that Tyoga was somehow responsible for slitting Seven Arrows's throat even if it was not he who held the knife.

He had not been fooled by Tyoga's act to convince the People that he had left the Appalachians before Seven Arrows arrived to take Sunlei for his wife. At his order, war parties fanned out throughout the Appalachians to search for Tyoga. The Chief would not rest until his head was displayed upon a pike at the entrance to his lodge.

Tyoga headed northwest toward the land of the Iroquois. He remained hidden in the deep hollows and unnamed valleys of the Appalachians while traveling along narrow deer paths and oftentimes slogging along knee-deep in mountain creeks and streams.

As a means of escape, he traveled through the night, which was a dangerous practice used only by the most experienced woodsmen. The technique came at a high cost.

His body's demand for restorative nighttime sleep could only be denied for so long. When sleep finally did come, his slumber was so deep that it silenced the nocturnal cues that he relied upon to keep him alive. It very nearly cost him his life.

The third day into his trek, Tyoga could travel no more. Seventy-two hours without any sleep was as much as his body could take. He desperately needed the deep nighttime sleep that refreshes and restores.

The sun had set and the temperature was dropping fast when he came upon a damp, musty grotto hidden by evergreens and wild rose bushes. He found a dead pine bough and poked around inside the cavity to make sure no critters had made it their home. Dropping to his belly, he crawled inside, wrapped himself in the warmth of the red wool blanket, and slept past sunrise.

He awoke to the sounds of a Shawnee search party standing not two feet away from the entrance to the shrub-covered hiding place. He could have reached out and touched them. After several minutes, the Shawnee resumed their search without realizing that their prey had been but an arm's length away.

The close call made Tyoga realize that he could not continue traveling through the mountains like a hunted animal. He would most surely be caught if he continued on his present course.

Tyoga looked up from the shallow creek he was wading through and said out loud in a voice barely above a whisper, "I've got to change the direction I'm headin'. It looks like he's figured that I would head to the north, toward the land of the Iroquois. And that's where they're huntin' for me." He placed his hands on hips and skewed his mouth in annoyance. "Hmm. I never thought they would follow me north."

Tyoga surveyed the granite rise to the north. Deep within one of Appalachia's hidden gorges, it was even difficult to see the sky through the dense treetop canopy.

"Well," he whispered. "I reckon I've got to climb to the top of this ridge and map me out a new course."

The slope was steep and covered with loose granite shards which made it like a wall of solid ice. One wrong step would send him sliding down to the bottom of the gorge. He had to take it slow and easy. Half way up the slope, it hit him.

"They think that I'm headin' northwest. I'll go in the opposite direction. I'll head southeast toward the colonies. Heading toward the whites is the last thing they will expect me to do. It's the land of the Powhatans, the Algonquins and the Mattaponis. I'll be heading away from the mountains but toward my American brothers—and the colonies. It is the perfect cover. They will never follow me there."

When he got to the crest of the ridge, he saw a clear route to the tidewater in the east.

He had been to Middle Plantation in New Kent once with his papa. It was about two weeks due southeast from South Henge.

He had been traveling three days toward the northwest so that would add a couple of days to the trip. He calculated that if he pressed on he could make it before his supplies ran out.

With a spring in his step, he trotted along the ridge while thinking out loud. "I'll go to the Mattoponi just north of Middle Plantation. They are Algonquin. Papa said that they were once part of the Powhatan confederation. They will give me a place to stay and help keep me safe." With that said, he picked up his pace.

Along the ridge, footpaths were well worn and the slope varied little for the first few miles. The wind blew his long brown locks of hair out of his eyes and he recalled how Sunlei used to do that when she wanted to look into his eyes.

He was confident that she had made it safely to Chickamaugua and he knew that Lone Bear's large family would keep her safe. He had no way of knowing that she had left the safety of the Chickamaugua Cherokee and was lost to the wilderness. Certain that their separation would be for less than a year, he was already planning for their reunion in the spring.

Prairie Day's red blanket was draped over his right shoulder and secured to his waist cinch. He held onto it with his left hand while he ran.

He could not get Prairie Day out of his mind. The village mourned her husband Running Elk's loss in battle. Tyoga noticed how she watched him from afar whenever they were around one another. When she lost her son to miscarriage, she summoned Tyoga to her lodge. She held him close and cried. He dismissed it as nothing more than a lonely friend seeking comfort, but understood after Green Rock Cove that there was a great deal more to the summons and tears.

He was lost in thought about the magic in her eyes when it happened. It was so fast that he had no time to prepare himself for the fall. A loss of concentration, and one misstep sent him careening off the trail and onto the shard covered slope to his right.

His right shoulder hit first to send him tumbling out of control for the first twenty-five feet. He righted himself and was able to sit up so that his feet were in front of him while he continued sliding down the slope on his back and rear end. The granite shards were like razor blades cutting chunks of flesh from his hands, legs, back, and thighs. Faster and faster he raced down the slope with no way to control his speed or direction. His right foot hit a more substantial boulder, which spun him around so that he was sliding backwards down the slope. He watched bits of his clothing and hunks of his flesh speckle the slate gray slabs of rock bright red with his blood.

Tyoga saw some shrubs and bushes bordering the pine trees to the west. Throwing his weight in that direction, he changed his course so that he headed directly for the underbrush. He reached out a bloody hand and tried desperately to grasp a branch that would stop his fall. The branches whipped his already bloody hands and arms with the sting of a lash, but none would give him mooring. He was finally able to throw himself off of the slippery slope and into the woods. He passed out on the pine needle covered ground before he was able to assess the damage.

CB ED CR ED

When he awoke the sun was setting. He was on fire from head to foot. The fall had torn him apart. His shirt and breeches were shreaded into rags. His backside, arms, and hands were slashed as if he had tumbled down a slope covered in straight razors. Some of the gashes had stopped bleeding. Because of the clean-edged incisions, others continued to bleed profusely.

The lightheadedness he felt told him that he had lost a good deal of blood. He had to do something to stop the bleeding and he had to do it fast.

With herculean effort, Tyoga picked himself up off of the ground and staggered further down the slope. Struggling to stay conscious, he felt his way like a blind man through the brush in search of running water at the bottom of the gorge.

He hadn't gone more than fifty feet before he heard the sound of rapids and waterfalls. Moving ever closer to the sound of the mountain stream, he stumbled faster and faster through the pines. When he got to the bank of the stream he threw the blanket onto the shore, staggered knee deep in and fell face first into the icy water. A lazy eddy twenty yards downstream turned crimson red as it filled with his blood.

Tyoga lay in the water until he began to shiver. When he opened his eyes it was dark and the light of the moon guided him to the shore and his bloody blanket. The pain was too great for him to wrap himself in the wool blanket so he laid it on the ground, and went to sleep face down in the sand.

The night was cold and dark when the moon set behind the mountain peaks. The cold was exactly what he needed to clot the wounds on his back and keep the swelling in check.

Thankful for the gift, he shivered through the night.

C3   ℘   CR   ℘

When the sun rose, he discovered that he had lost everything in his fall down the shard covered slope except the red wool blanket and Sunlei's amulet pouch. His shirt was gone and what was left of his leather breeches did not even cover his crotch. Struggling to his feet, he stripped them off and threw them into the bushes. He picked the blanket up off of the shore, and wrapped it around him from the waist down. Securing it with his sash that was still in one piece, he began the agonizing climb back to the top of the ridge.

He hadn't been beaten yet.

Chapter 42

The Tidewater

It took nearly ten days for Tyoga to reach the rolling foothills that were the gateway to the Appalachians from the east. With the mountains fading away to the west, and the low, flat, wetlands of the tidal piedmont ahead of him, the traveling became much easier and he covered ground more quickly.

He had been able to recover his striker and flint from the bottom of the slope, allowing him to start fires for warmth and light. He was not able to hunt so he had been subsisting on what he could fine. Pine nuts, berries and carrion were his main staples. One day, he feasted on the remnants of a deer carcass. The remains of a rotting carp were less appetizing, but devoured with equal relish.

He had not bathed or shaved in nearly three weeks. With no people from whom to hide his nudity, he had abandoned wrapping the red blanket around him. It was all that he had left to remind him of home and happiness, so he carried it, tattered and torn, thrown over his right shoulder and tied to his waist with his sash.

Exhausted and nearly spent, he traveled on.

In five days he made it to the outskirts of Essex. In six, he arrived in New Kent. On the seventh day, he swam the Mattaponi River, waded through the marsh and broke through the rushes and cattails that bristled the east bank of the river.

There before his eyes, nestled between two giant oak trees, was the most beautiful grassy glade he had ever seen in his life. A brisk feeder stream creased the south edge of the open plot, and the north was protected from the wind by an enormous stand of birch and pine. The east perimeter abutted a forest of hardwoods, cedar, chestnut, and elm. Sturgeon and trout, shad and herring schooled in the shallows of the stream so that the surface boiled with life. Mussel shoals breached the mud flats of a broad estuary as ducks and geese fussed noisily over no particular spot to float.

Holding back a curtain of reeds in each hand, he stopped and gazed at the land with an expression that required no words. This indescribably beautiful patch of land burned its brand into his heart with a single moniker.

Home.

He dragged himself from the kneedeep marsh and wrapped the blanket around himself to provide a modicum of formality to the arrival. He picked up a long, straight staff of hickory as he marched up to one of the giant oaks. Stabbing the hickory into the ground, he declared to the trees, "This will do," before sitting cross legged on the ground.

Hanging his head down between his knees, he was overwhelmed with the events of the past weeks.

He had lost his love, his spirit guide, his family, friends, and home. He had crossed the Appalachian Mountains alone and arrived upon this piece of land in a country that he knew little about. He felt completely alone for the first time in his life.

Exhaustion and hunger threatened to shake the very foundations of his courage, strength, and will. His eyes welled with tears. Inside of him, he felt the beginnings of a body-wrenching sob over which he would have little control.

He placed his head in his hands to accept the cathartic cry when he heard a familiar sound drifting down from the mountain peaks far off to the west. Soft and low, it floated across the Mattaponi like a welcome whisper. Another followed, louder and more resolute. The howl grew in intensity and duration as it was answered from peaks unseen from the north and south.

The cries of the wolves buoyed his spirit to release the tears as sobs of joy and rejuvenation, rather than desolation and defeat.

As the tears streamed down his cheeks, he looked off to the east where the dense hardwood forest bordered the grassy plain. In the trees he saw the silhouette of a human figure, cast hauntingly aglow by the light of the setting sun.

He was anxious to make contact with another human being, be it friend or foe. Wiping the tears from his eyes, he looked again. He stood up and cried out in English, "Hey! Don't go. Don't—"

He took two steps toward the woods and fell to the ground.

He was spent.

Chapter 43

Salvation

Tyoga awoke to the aroma of venison stew, corn bread, and azi. He was lying on a bearskin and was covered with a soft doeskin hide. His had been bathed and his wounds were dressed.

When she came into the makeshift lean-to, he sat upright and pushed himself against the back wall.

She was dressed in a buff-colored doeskin tunic. Long fringe lined the back seam of the tunic's arms. Shorter fringe adorned the knee-length hem. Her long auburn hair was pulled to the side in a ponytail. Two eagle feathers hung from the leather tie. She wore puka and cowary shells around her neck. A thin gold necklace with a silver cross was peaking out from beneath them. She was bare foot.

She stopped short when she saw that he was awake. Reaching out a slender hand in a gesture of friendship, she said in broken English, "You ... safe ... here. Safe ... here," she repeated as if asking if her words had been chosen correctly.

"Who are you?" Tyoga asked.

When the young woman looked at him as if she did not understand, he repeated the question in Tsalagie, "So de tsa do a?"

Smiling with gratitude that he spoke her language, she said, "Da gwa do a Adohi Yutsa *(Forever Girl)*. My ... nem ... name," she pointed to herself, "mmmm … Trinity." Opening her hand she placed her palm on her chest and repeated, "Trinity … Jane … O'Do—O'Doule."

When she moved closer to him, he could see her sparkling blue eyes and angular, chiseled features. "You're a white girl," he said to her in astonishment.

"Yes," she replied in English that was obviously difficult for her to summon.

"But what are you doing here?" Tyoga asked in English. When it was obvious that it was easier for her to converse in Tsalagie, he repeated the question in her native tongue.

"There is plenty of time for us to talk about that later. Right now, you need to drink and have something to eat. Wait here. I will bring it to you." She smiled.

After she scurried out of the lean-to, Tyoga saw that he was in a structure built of birch frame lattice and mud-daub sides. The roof was made of pine boughs and oiled deer hide. He grabbed one of the sidewall stays and gave it a tug. Whoever built the shelter had done a good job.

Trinity Jane was ladeling deer stew into a clay crock at a stone-ringed fire pit that was about ten steps from the shelter's open west side. He watched her put down the crock, pick up a gourd, and run to the river.

She was a strong woman with shapely calves and arms that were used to work. She moved gracefully with a natural flow that was different from the posture and gate of the native women. She moved like Sunlei.

Re-entering the lean-to with the stew steaming from the earthen crock and the gourd brimming with clear, cool water, she handed Tyoga the gourd. "Here. Drink first. You must be thirsty."

He emptied the gourd and asked for more.

Showing her deep dimples and beautiful white teeth, she smiled broadly, handed him the stew and a piece of corn bread, and skipped to the river to refill the gourd.

"How long have I been asleep?" Tyoga asked when she handed him the gourd of water.

"Three days," she replied.

"Was it you that I saw standing in the woods watching me?" he asked.

"Yes, I watched you cross the Mattaponi and walk up to the tree. I could tell that you were hurt, and tired, and hungry; I was afraid to approach you because…" She stopped speaking and looked down at the ground.

Tyoga finished her sentence, "Because I was running around naked and talking to myself."

"Yes." They both laughed out loud.

When the laughter stopped, Tyoga put down the stew and reached out to take her hand in his. "My name is Tyoga. Tyoga Weathersby. And I have not laughed in a very long time. Thank you."

He watched her eyes dance when she searched for the next words. "You … welcome." She reached out and brushed his hair from his eyes. "We need to do something about your hair. Turn around now and let me dress your wounds."

Chapter 44

Trinity Jane

Tyoga rested for the remainder of that day. Wrapped in the dirty and tattered red blanket, he did get up to walk to the woods to relieve himself.

It felt good to be on his feet again. The salve or potion with which Trinity Jane had been treating the wounds on his back was working remarkably well. Ho noticed that she had not removed the amulet from his neck.

When he woke up on the fourth day, he found her at his feet laying out some clothes for him. "Et tey ya *(good morning)*," he said softly to her.

They kept their conversations in Tsalagie for the time being.

"Good morning," she said with a glorious smile. "I have brought these clothes for you to wear. I hope they fit." She added with an impish grin, "You are a very big man."

Tyoga knew what she meant.

"Thank you, Trinity. Where did you get them? Did you go to your village?" he asked.

"I could not find you new boots. We will have to tend to that later. Get up now. I have corn meal mush and venison warming. The azi *(coffee)* is ready, and we have a great deal of work to do," was her diversionary reply.

When he stepped outside of the shelter while wrapped in his blanket, he saw leaning against the giant oak a broad ax for felling trees, an adze for shaping logs, and two iron headed hatchets.

When Tyoga stretched in the warmth of the morning sun, the red blanket fell to the ground. Standing naked in front of her, he yawned, scratched his head, and said, "I see you were serious about the work that needs to be done."

Trinity Jane shook her head and poured him a piping hot bowl of azi.

The first day back on his feet, he and Trinity Jane worked to expand and fortify the shelter. They began by removing the pine bough and oil skin roof covering so that they could extend the sides upward to make some standing room inside the frame. It was hard work, but Tyoga found out quickly that she did not shy away from pulling her weight.

Tyoga felled birch trees while Trinity Jane trimmed off the branches and sliced them into long pliable slats to extend the sides of the shelter. By working together in such a fashion they had enough slats to extend the sides up three feet all around in about four hours time. They finished weaving the slats around the vertical stays just before night fall.

Muscles aching with the exhaustion that celebrates achievement and progress, Tyoga sat down by the firepit to watch the sunset while Trinity Jane cooked shad over the flames.

"Did you catch those yourself?" Tyoga asked.

"A-ho," she replied.

"What did you catch them with?" She answered by holding up her hands. They were scarred and calloused, but delicate in contour and size. Her fingers were long and supple despite the evidence of hard work and cruel treatment.

"You mean you waded into the water, reached down, and grabbed the fish?" he said in a teasing tone.

"Yes," she said. "That is exactly how I caught them. The shad are running in the rivers and streams this time of year. They are so plentiful that all you have to do is stand in the water and scoop them up onto the shore. Here. This one is ready."

While Tyoga was eating he looked closely at her face. She was tanned from being in the sun, and her face was smeared with the soot from the fire and dirt from toiling in the woods all day. When she leaned forward, the ponytail that was draped over the right side of her face fell in front of her shoulder to reveal a six inch scar that ran from just in front of her right ear along her cheek nearly to her chin.

Despite the blemish, she was a lovely woman.

"Where do you live, Trinity?" Because she was white, and had told him her name in English, he called her by her Christian name. She seemed to like it.

"I have been with the Nansmond Powhatan since I was eight years old, but I do not live there anymore."

Tyoga did not press further, even though she had more that she wanted to stay.

"I ran away from my village, my home, and my family. I was on my way to my sister's lodge in the Mattaponi village of Passaunkack when I spotted you from the woods. The village is that way." She indicated the direction of the village with a toss of her head. "I went there two nights ago and found these tools in the fields they are clearing for maize. I borrowed them. We must return them when I go to live with my sister. She does not know that I am here."

Seeing that she was not ready to confide in him why she had run away from home, he let that be for the time being. Instead, he asked, "Why did you stop to help me? You could have gone on your way."

She looked up from the fire into his face, and then gazed toward the mountains and the setting sun. Staring off into the distance, she answered, "I don't know, Tyoga Weathersby. You just called to me."

She turned her attention back to the other fish cooking over the flames and took it off the spit. "Besides, you were tired, hungry, hurt, and scared. You are white. So am I."

Tyoga thought that there was something in the way that she called him by name. Up until now she had given no hint that she knew who he was. It was all the same to him if she did not. But he thought it odd that a Nansmond Powhatan would not recognize his name and know of the legend.

Tyoga said to her in slow measured English, "Trinity Jane, you saved my life. Thank you."

The sun had set and their camp was shrouded in the quiet darkness of the early night. She sat down beside him in the glow of the firelight and answered him in Tsalagie, "You may have saved mine as well."

Chapter 45

The Mattaponi

Tyoga and Trinity Jane were felling trees to construct a more substantial shelter before the autumn chill set the Appalachians ablaze with the colors of fall. While Tyoga chopped down the tall, straight pines and topped the trees, Trinity followed behind trimming the branches from the trunk. After noon, they were eating a lunch of dried fish and pine nuts in the shade of an ancient chestnut tree.

Tapping Tyoga's thigh with her foot, Trinity tossed her head in the direction of the woods.

Appearing out of the shadows, thirty Mattaponi braves stepped into the sunlight of the glade. As they emerged from the cover of the forest, the braves did not remove their long bows from their backs. At the edge of the glade, they watched in silence while Tyoga and Trinity calmly continued to eat their lunch.

"What do they want, Ty?" Trinity quietly asked.

"Don't know, T.J., but it don't appear they're lookin' for any trouble," Tyoga replied. "They kept their bows on their backs and their arrows quivered. We'll keep eatin' and let them have a good look."

When they had finished their lunch, Tyoga stood up. "Let's see if they want to talk." He extended his hand in a gesture of peace, and began walking toward the braves. Two braves, whose heads were wreathed in eagle feathers, crossed the glade toward him with their open hands raised high above their heads. The three men met in the center of the field.

"A tey ya ho," the taller Mattaponi said.

Tyoga smiled. "A tey ya ho."

"I am Acuna-tunckala *(Gray Sky),* and this is Tuneesichealo *(Swift Wind).*" He pointed to his companion.

Tyoga nodded a friendly greeting while trying to buy some time.

He was hesitant to give his name. He was certain that his legend had made its way to the Eastern shore, but unsure exactly what the piedmont tribes had heard about him. While they would know his name, he was less sure what their reaction might be.

If he did not tell the truth about his identity and was caught in a lie later on, they would never trust him again. Native Americans never forgive a lie. Tyoga had always dealt with his Native American brothers honestly, and he was annoyed at himself for considering doing otherwise now.

"I am Tyoga Weathersby." He pointed over his shoulder to Trinity Jane. "She is Adohi Yutsa." Unsure of their reaction if they learned that they were both of the white world, he used the shortened version of her Indian name. "I have traveled many days across the mountains from the land of the Amansoquath. I—We wish to winter here near our brothers in Passaunkack."

Gray Sky and Swift Wind exchanged glances of enthusiastic glee. Shattering the afternoon silence with an eagle-like war cry that filled the forest behind them and sent the grazing geese into panicked flight, Gray Sky lifted his bow high over his head.

Suddenly, all of the Mattaponi standing along the north perimeter of the glade ran at full speed toward Tyoga while shouting wildly and lifting their bows high in the air. Their frightening screams and cries were nearly deafening.

Standing still, Tyoga did not know if the glance exchanged between Gray Sky and Swift Wind was joyful because a mighty enemy stood before them completely at their mercy, or the happiness they shared was in genuine friendship at recognizing the presence of an honored guest.

He felt his muscles swell and the life drain from his eyes.

It was a good day to die, but he would not go alone.

Trinity reached out and touched him on the arm when she saw what was happening. Tyoga knew at that moment, she understood clearly who he was. She also knew that there was no danger and this was not the time for Wahaya to appear.

When the war party was about to overtake the two of them, Gray Sky reached out his hand and patted Tyoga on the shoulders and back. He moved closer so that he would be able to hear his words above the shouting of the Mattaponi braves.

"We have heard of Wahaya-Wacon and his friendship with the Algonquin tribes. Stories are told around lodge fires to this day about the Great Powhatan Chief Openchanecanough who was saved by your ancestors. You and your woman are welcome here, great Wahaya."

The party of whooping warriors encircled and danced around Tyoga and Trinity Jane until Gray Sky held his hand in the air to ask for quiet. "To hey yo. Ichti a way ha, Wahaya-Wacon."

At this, the circle of braves crushed in to touch Tyoga's face, arms, hands and chest. It was as if they hoped that his legendary power would transfer to them by the mere touch of his skin.

When order was restored, Gray Sky stepped through the crowd of men toward the tiny lean-to as if to survey the scene. "You need food. And blankets. And pots and fresh water. All of these things we will give to you. But you must come to Passaunkack and meet with Chief Blue Coat. He will want to meet you and your woman—"

"She's not my woman—," Tyoga tried to interject, but Gray Sky kept on speaking over him,

"—and hear the stories of your many adventures."

Tyoga's interjection had not gone unnoticed by Trinity. Leaving his side, she went through the crowd of Mattoponi braves toward the shelter.

"We will come to Passaunkack to see Chief Blue Coat," Tyoga said.

"Good. Come." Gray Sky turned to lead them to the village.

"No, Gray Sky. Wait. We cannot come with you today." Tyoga stopped Gray Sky's determined lead into the woods. "We will come in two moons. There is much work that needs to be done here at Twin Oaks." He pointed out the two large oak trees that shaded the shelter. "We will come in two moons." This time, he held up two fingers.

"Eh ya ho," Gray Sky nodded his head in agreement. He looked around the campsite one more time, raised his bow, and trotted off into the woods.

Looking over at the lean-to, Tyoga slowly walked toward the shelter. It was obvious that he had done something to hurt Trinity's feeling, but he had no idea what it could have been.

"T.J.," he called from outside the shelter.

Trinity Jane had become too cumbersome to say, so he called her T.J. as a pet name between the two of them. She liked it. Very much.

She did not answer.

"T.J.," he said again softly. "Did I do something wrong?"

She still did not respond.

Tyoga bent down and entered the shelter.

Crying quietly into her hands, Trinity was facing the back wall.

He put his hands on her shoulders and whispered again, "I'm sorry, Trinity. What did I do?"

"You did nothing wrong, Tyoga." While tears streamed down her delicate face, she turned to face him. She pulled her ponytail over her right cheek and said quietly, "I have no one in my life. I am alone in the world. We have been together for only two weeks time—I know that. But, in that short time together, I have known a sense of family more intense that I have experienced in my entire life. Even though we have not slept side by side and you have not warmed me with the embrace of your strong arms in the night, it is not because I wish it to be so. You have never tried to touch me like that. I understand." She pulled again at her hair to make sure that her scar was hidden from view.

Tyoga reached out and brushed her hair aside. He cradled her scarred cheek in his huge strong hand and started to say, "No, T.J. You are a beautiful—"

"I am not!" she replied, removing his hand. "Let me speak." She looked into his eyes as if asking for permission to continue.

Tyoga nodded silently.

"My family—my mother and father—were killed by the Shawnee when I was only eight years old. We were on our way to Cumberland where my mother was to be the settlement's school teacher. My father was going to open a law practice there. It was just before noon when they struck. We had stopped for lunch. My baby sister was napping in her cradle and Mama was reading a book to me. The first arrow sliced through my father's neck. I remember the look in his eyes as he tried to make sense out of the blood that was pouring from his mouth. My mother screamed and got up to run and get my baby sister, but it was too late. A warrior had ripped her from the cradle and was galloping off through the woods with her in his arms. I haven't seen her since. I remember someone grabbing my head and feeling fire race along the right side of my face. I saw my own blood splatter off the trunks of the pine trees and turn the ground at my knees bright red. I heard my mother scream. And then everything went black. The Shawnee did not take me because they must have thought that whoever slashed my face had cut my throat and that I was dead. I woke up in the lodge of Kicking Deer. His wife was rocking me in her arms and all of his children were standing around me. I have lived with them for the past ten years. Now, I find the great Tyoga Weathersby—Wahaya Wacon—alone and hurt and crying in the woods. Your legend has been told around the lodge fires of the Nansmond Powhatan for as long as I can remember. I know what they say about you—the good and the bad. But I could not leave the legend to die alone on the shores of the Mattaponi. So I cared for you and nursed you back to health. I thought that perhaps we were building something together here at this beautiful place. And now? Now, I am all alone again."

Tyoga looked at Trinity with a new set of eyes. "Trinity, why did you leave Kicking Deer's lodge?"

"I ran away because I will not be traded like a gutted deer. I will marry for love—or not at all." Trinity's declaration was spoken with a passion that surprised Tyoga. He knew that she was a head-strong young woman, but the determination in her words was uncompromised and final.

"When I was a young girl," she continued softly, "Chief White Elk promised me to the son of the chief of the Chickahomony Algonquin, Night Hawk. Their land is very close to the colony of middle plantation. White Elk was certain that the white eyes would look favorably upon a chief that had allowed his son to marry a white woman. His son would be placed in a positon of power and influence."

"I begged my Father to not let this marriage come to pass, but he was powerless to help. The only way out was if a brave of our own clan claimed me for himself. No one would have me."

"Oh, as I was growing," she said looking down at her ample bosom, "I received plenty of attention from the Nansemond braves." Looking toward the back wall of the shelter, she added, "But no one would claim me for their own."

Trinity Jane turned to look into Tyoga's eyes and continued, "Do you know what it is like for a woman—a white woman—to be unclaimed? No, you couldn't know."

Prairie Day's face flashed in Tyoga's mind. He did not tell Trinity Jane that he understood more than she could know.

"My flight from my adoptive family may have been for nothing at all," she added. "Your words have made me an unclaimed woman once again. What I have run from, I have stumbled into."

Tyoga had not thought of the impact of his words in the context of the Native American's cultural norms.

Trinity was right.

He had openly declared that she was not his woman. Consequently, she was available for the taking. Women from other tribes were highly coveted commodities. Tribes depended upon a steady stream of progeny to keep their culture alive. That relied upon couplings outside of familial ties. Intermarriage was frowned upon by Native American cultures. When the pool of women of reproductive age was on the wane, cousins were sometimes allowed to marry.

The imperative was to replace the ranks of tribal warriors. If to do so, a taboo had to be relaxed to accomplish the desired purpose, then permission for the unions was readily granted. A woman from another tribe was seen as a source of strength and renewed vitality.

Tyoga slowly retreated from the shelter and went back to work felling trees in the pine grove.

After a while, Trinity Jane came out of the shelter and made her way toward him. She picked up her hatchet, went to the top end of the pine and continued removing the branches.

They did not speak.

In the silent understanding shared by those tested by travail, they re-connected through the rigors of common purpose, the reliance upon fidelity and the ethereal bonds that tether souls.

As the shadows grew longer and the temperature began to drop, they put down their tools and sat side by side while listening to evening's descent.

Trinity rested her head against Tyoga's arm, a gesture of forgiveness that both seemed to understand. Suddenly, she picked her head up. "Ty, do you hear that?"

"Yeah. People comin' this way. A lot of people." He stood and picked up the ax.

From the north side of the glade, where the Mattoponi braves had appeared earlier in the afternoon, a long line of men and women with baskets hoisted on their shoulders emerged from woods. Walking past the tiny shelter to the stone-ringed fire pit, they placed their baskets of beans, corn and squash, sacks of flour and salt and sugar gently on the ground. Iron kettles brimming with venison stew and succotash were placed directly onto the bed of coals, and loaves of unleven bread were set on the flat stones surrounding the fire pit. Wool blankets and skins and cloth shirts and deerhide skirts were placed on the ground inside the lean-to. Some Mattaponi women entered their shelter and replaced their coarse reed sleeping mats with a thick buffalo robe mattress. They set bees' wax candles in the corners of the tiny shelter and bowls of dried fruit by their bed. The Mattaponi spoke no words of welcome, but waved and smiled while dissolving into the shadows of the forest.

With a smile and nod of his head, Gray Sky was the last to leave the now darkening glade.

Tyoga and Trinity Jane looked at each other with astonishment. They ran to Twin Oaks and knelt before the pots of fresh food already bubbling on the coals.

It was their first real meal in many days.

Chapter 46

Passaunkack

It was a two-hour walk to the Mattaponi village of Passaunkack, but only twenty minutes down-stream by canoe. The Mattaponi had given a canoe to Tyoga and Trinity the day after they had delivered the food and supplies. They used it now to make their first visit to the village.

About halfway to the village, they were greeted by groups of young boys who kept pace with the speed of the canoe by running along the shoreline path. Several canoes joined in a celebratory flotilla to escort the guests the final quarter mile to the village.

Rounding a gentle bend in the river, the Mattaponi village came into sight. Set back from the water's edge about one hundred yards, it was surrounded by a circular palisade of rough hewn pine. Rather than a traditional opening through a gated entrance, the circle of the palisade folded over itself like a snail's shell to create a long, narrow passageway into the village that was easily defensible.

Chief Blue Coat was waiting for them on the shore with a group of tribal elders dressed in their ceremonial finest.

True to his name, the Chief was wearing a blue sailor's coat from which the buttons had been removed. He was bare-chested under the coat. A large loincloth fell nearly to his ankles to cover his leather leggings. A large cowry shell medallion hung around his neck. His head was shaved except for a long coiled top-knot that rose about 4 inches from the crown of his head.

"Et tay ya ho, Wahaya-Wacon," the chief said in a loud ceremonial voice. "We welcome you to Passaunkack."

Tyoga and Trinity Jane were wearing the clothes that the Mattaponi had brought to them two days earlier at Twin Oaks. It so pleased the Chief and the elders that they pointed and smiled at one another when they saw that the gift of their clothes had been put to such ready use.

Tyoga stepped from the canoe and turned to lift Trinity out so that she would not get her new moccasins wet.

She surveyed the crowd in hopes that she would see her stepsister, Grows Strong, racing to her through the throng. She was nowhere in sight.

Walking up to the Chief, Tyoga said, "It gladdens our hearts to be your guests on this beautiful day. I, Wahaya-Wacon—and my woman, Adohi Yutsa—thank Chief Blue Coat and the People of Passaunkack for the many gifts they have given to us. Your giving spirits have saved our lives."

Trinity's eyes met Tyoga's. Her dimpled smile was all the thanks that he needed for the announcement that he had declared before the People. Not many were there to hear his pronouncement, but it was enough to keep her safe from unwelcome flirtations.

Stepping toward Tyoga, the chief put his arm around his shoulder and escorted him toward the entrance to the village. "Wahaya-Wacon, brother to all Algonquin, the Powhatan tribes speak of your legend around their lodge fires. The stories are of a proud, strong man who has the heart and courage of Wahaya. That you have come to the Mattaponi at just such a time is a blessing from the great spirits. We are pleased that you will put our gifts to such good use. It makes our hearts glad. In the days ahead, these gifts will be repaid by the courage of Wahaya-Wacon. Come. Enter our village and let us give thanks for your deliverance to us."

Tyoga looked at Trinity, who returned his inquisitive gaze.

The Chief had something in mind, and whatever he asked could not be denied.

Passaunkack was very large. The palisade wall enclosed many lodges that housed roughly eight hundred villagers. Unlike the Cherokee lodges, their homes were round rather than long. However, they were spacious enough to house several family units. The sides of the huts were constructed of stick and mud daub latticework. The roofs were made of marsh grasses and reed interwoven into a waterproof matting.

While Tyoga, Trinity, and the party of elders made their way along the neatly landscaped central avenue, children ran out from the lodges and alley ways to present them with gifts and tokens of greeting. Trinity received many bouquets of wildflowers and a laurel of daisies to place on her head. They also presented her with dresses made of beautifully woven cloth and delicately cured leather, doe hide and elk skin boots, and more blankets and cooking utensils than she could carry. Tyoga received more substantial gifts of iron hatchets, metal knives, iron tipped arrows and ornately decorated quivers. Iron tools for clearing and working the land were placed at his feet while he went along the central boulevard. Young braves followed behind the procession to collect the gifts for them.

It was beyond anything Tyoga and T.J. could have imagined.

Being so near to Hampden Roads, Middle Plantation, and Yorktown, the Mattaponi were frequented by many white traders anxious to exchange tools and weapons for blankets, pottery, moccasins, and precious metal ores.

Their fire pits were rife with cast iron kettles, Dutch ovens, and copper pots, which were all in use baking, roasting, and smoking the food for the great feast that was being prepared in honor of Wahaya-Wacon.

Mattaponi women were roasting loins of elk, deer, and bear. Others were smoking herring and shad by the hundreds. Fires were roasting ducks, geese, and pheasants, while rounded earthen ovens were baking breads made from the coarse flour of various grains.

The men were tending a giant vat of wheat beer that was many times more potent that the ale consumed by the colonists.

Everyone in the village was busy preparing for the feast and dancing to come. Mothers stood in the avenues and lanes of the village admonishing their children not to get their ceremonial garb dirty as they chased after barking dogs and free range chickens and guinea fowl. While their sisters and friends brushed and decorated their hair, young Indian maidens straightened their finest doeskin tunics outside their huts. Musicians tuned their drums and flutes because music was a central component of any Mattaponi celebration.

The procession stopped outside of Chief Blue Coat's lodge, one of the largest huts in the village.

Turning to the Mattaponi elders, the Chief said something to them that Tyoga could not hear. Nodding in agreement, they turned and walked away.

"Come into my lodge," the Chief said to Tyoga and Trinity as he bent down to enter the building. "We have prepared a space for you to rest before the celebration. It will be a very long day."

Leading them to a place in the hut that had been cordoned off to provide some privacy, the Chief smiled broadly before leaving them alone.

The area had several buffalo robes on a wooden frame upon which they could sit or recline. A bowl of berries and nuts was on a three-legged stool next to some warm, flat bread. Elk jerky and dried sturgeon filled an ornate ceramic bowl, and a jug of asi was on the floor next to the stool.

Tyoga stretched out on the buffalo robes while Trinity Jane sat on the edge of bed and helped herself to some berries and nuts. Tyoga took her hand in his. They clenched each other's hand in the universal gesture of unity common to those placed in unfamiliar territory.

Tyoga asked, "What do you think he wants of me?"

"I don't know yet, Ty. We'll just have to wait and see. By the look of all those things they possess that are of the white man's world, my guess is that it will have something to do with the colonies."

"Maybe," he said. "If he wants me to translate for the Mattaponi in their dealings with the whites, I'll be happy to oblige. It is the least that I can do to repay their kindness."

"Don't be so anxious," Trinity wisely cautioned. "Much harm can come from words misspoken."

Knowing she was right, Tyoga did not reply.

The celebration began after noon and lasted well past the setting sun. After they had eaten and drank their fill, Tyoga and Trinity Jane took their seats of honor next to the Chief and the tribal elders to watch the dancing and listen to the music and songs. The Mattaponi danced around the enormous ceremonial fire in the village square, not in the exuberant fashion of the Cherokee or Choctaw, but in a more reserved, rhythmic walk/dance that was melodic rather than frenzied in its presentation.

When the circle of mostly women danced past the head table for a second time, Trinity grabbed Tyoga's hand and squeezed it hard. She jumped up from her seat and ran into the circle screaming, "Adelu (*sister*), adelu!"

When Grows Strong saw her stepsister running to greet her, she broke from the dance circle and ran into her embrace. "Adohi, Yutsa, adelu, adelu! What are you doing here, Yutsa?"

Trinity did not answer because of the tears streaming down her face. Instead, she glanced toward Tyoga who was now standing up next to Blue Coat. "Adelu, you are with Wahaya-Wacon? How can this be? Why have you come to me? Is father, or mother? Are they okay? Is it—"

"Adelu," Trinity interrupted. "Everyone is fine. I will tell you later how all of this has come to pass. For now, know that I am here and being well cared for. We will speak later."

Trinity returned to her place of honor next to Tyoga. He reached out and took her hand to help her step up to the dias. "Your sister?" he asked.

"Yes, that is my sister," she replied.

"She's quite beautiful," Tyoga said.

Trinity furrowed her brow and replied, "Yes. Yes, she is."

After several hours of dancing and more food and drink, Chief Blue Coat signaled that it was time for council. The men stood up and followed him into his lodge.

As Tyoga was standing, Trinity grabbed his hand and flashed her dimpled smile up at him. In English, she said, "Careful, Tyoga."

"Okay." He squeezed and then released her tiny hand.

She watched him follow the elders down the boulevard to Chief Blue Coat's lodge.

Chapter 47

Speak for the People

With Chief Blue Coat leading the way and Tyoga right behind, the elders entered the chief's lodge.

The inside of the lodge had been rearranged for the council. A ceremonial fire was burning in the middle of the lodge. Animal hides of buffalo, elk, deer, and bear had been arranged around the fire pit. The private area that had been set-aside for Tyoga and Trinity had been dismantled.

The council members took their seats as if prearranged. An ornately decorated pipe, with a two-foot long stem wrapped in fox fur and a bowl the size of a tea cup, was lit and passed to each man in turn. The braves held the pipe in their raised arms before bringing the stem to their lips and inhaling deeply.

Tyoga noticed that the tobacco in this pipe was very different from the tobacco passed around the Shawnee council fire. It was mild and sweet with a taste not nearly as unpleasant as he remembered.

This is another advantage the tribes living so close to the English colonies enjoy.

In the one hundred years since the colonists first landed at Jamestown, the white man's understanding of horticulture, and their ability to selectively breed-in desired tastes, had produced a tobacco that was remarkably mild. The robust trading that took place between the Mattaponi and the colonists truly had its advantages.

But at what price did these many gifts come?

Chief Blue Coat and all of the elders were eager to hear Tyoga tell the tale of his battle with the leader of the Runion wolf pack.

Tyoga was surprised by how much they already knew about him. They were very familiar with the battle on the ridge and his superhuman effort to carry his Cherokee brother to safety.

While recounting the battle on the ridge, Tyoga could see the disappointment on their faces at learning that the wolf did not rise from the dead after he had bashed his head in with the boulder. They were, however, impressed when he told them that he had spared the wolf's life in the same way that the wolf had spared Tyoga's.

The Indians understood and revered this benevolence.

Tyoga related the events that occurred at the Shawnee Council, and verified to them that the Ani-Unwiya Chief, Silver Cloud, had remained true to his word and had turned Sunlei over to Seven Arrows. They had heard about the Shawnee council and of Chief Yellow Robe's demand for Sunlei to become the wife of his loathsome son Seven Arrows. As the tales made their way across the mountains and to the shores of the Chesapeake Bay, Seven Arrows had become so demonized that he had been given the ability to change shape and to dissolve into nothingness like the rising morning mist. They wanted to know what had become of Sunlei after she had killed the chief's son, and where she was hiding now.

In a ruse that was more protective than deceitful, Tyoga disavowed any knowledge of Seven Arrows's demise or of the whereabouts of Sunlei.

"You do not know where your woman has gone?" Chief Blue Robe persisted.

"I do not know where she is, Chief Blue Robe," Tyoga said.

"The beauty of Sunlei-Awi is known to our people. Her understanding of the white man's tongue is a precious gift. How is it that you can lose such a woman?" he asked with outstretched arms inviting communal agreement with his amazement.

Tyoga did not reply.

Seeing that Tyoga was not going to be more forthcoming, Blue Coat continued, "So, Adohi Yutsa has taken Sunlei's place in your lodge?"

Tyoga continued to stare into the fire. Without averting his gaze from the flames, he said, "I have known Adohi Yutsa for only a short time. She saved my life."

Chief Blue Coat paused to look into the eyes of the elders around the council fire. "We know of this woman, Wahaya. She, like you, is of the white eyes. Do you not find it strange that in the land of the Powhatan and Algonquin you would be rescued by a white woman living among the Nansmond clan? Among all the people roaming the land that she should find you on that day is no matter of chance, my son. There is a reason that she nursed you back to health."

The elders grunted their approval of the words their chief had spoken.

Chief Blue Coat was not finished. He had one more thing to tell Tyoga. With the wisdom of his years, and the tone of a father advising his son, the Chief counseled Tyoga while he continued to stare into the flames, "My son, a warrior should not sleep alone. Your eyes tell me that Adohi Yutsa has not yet found a home in your heart. That, my son, is a burden that no brave can long carry."

The lodge fell silent for a long time.

"Chief Blue Robe, is there a service that you wish of me?" Tyoga asked while the chief's wife and daughters poured more asi into the buffalo horn goblets beside each council member.

"There is, my son," the chief replied, "The People need the wisdom and courage of Wahaya to do what must be done. More than that, we need one who understands the white man's tongue and can speak for the Mattaponi at their council fires."

Tyoga nodded his head in agreement.

"We have lived in peace with the white man for many moons. They are welcome in Passaunkack, and the Mattaponi walk the streets of Middle Plantation in peace. What the white eyes bring to trade with the Mattaponi are good for my people. The iron tools help us to clear the land, cultivate our crops, cook our food and hunt our prey. Yet, they are no longer content to trade for blankets and pottery and buffalo robes. They now wish to trade for our lands. If we do not agree to trade, they claim our land just as the beaver turns a creek into a pond."

Blue Coat stopped to look into the eyes of the Mattaponi elders. The nods of their heads emboldened him to continue with more difficult words

"The white men's ships arrive everyday. More and more of the white eyes pour onto our shores and demand land to build their homes, grow their crops, graze their herds, and raise new generations who will demand the same. In the wet season, a man called Carry came to Passaunkack to speak with Blue Coat. He said that the white eyes wish to build a town at Mattaponi because the water at our shores is deep and will allow many ships to unload more people and goods. These ships they will fill with our trees and hides and tobacco and corn and return to their homelands without paying for what they have taken from us. He wanted Blue Coat to make his mark on paper giving our lands to the white eyes. I refused. When he insisted that he would take our land with or without my mark, my braves entered the council lodge with their bows and hatchets. Carry and his men left Passaunkack shaking their fists at Blue Coat and screaming that they would return with many men and their thunder sticks.

"In the growing time, more white eyes arrived with a paper that said I must go to Middle Plantation to speak with their chief, Edward Nott. The Mattaponi council advised Blue Coat not to go. They fear that Chief Nott is setting a trap to keep Blue Coat away from Passaunkack. Without their chief, the white eyes would take our lands without a fight."

Chief Blue Coat paused to look at the elders seated around the council fire. If his words had not spoken the truth, it was their time to speak. They stared stoically at Blue Coat. Not one of them made a sound.

Blue Coat told Tyoga, "That Chief Nott has summoned me to his council fire is a good thing. It means that he will hear Blue Coat's words. This is a sign that he is a just and honest man. If he can stop the white eyes from taking our land, then I must go to Middle Plantation as he has asked. If I do not go, then he will sign our land over to this Carry and the others. There will be war and much killing. We will not allow the white eyes to take our land without a fight."

"How can I help the Mattaponi, Chief Blue Coat? What would you have me do?" Tyoga asked.

"Go with Chief Blue Coat to Middle Plantation. Speak for the Mattaponi. Tell Edward Nott that we will not give away our ancestral home and that we will fight to keep what is ours. Chief Blue Coat does not speak the white eye's tongue. If there is no one there to tell me what this man, Nott, is saying, how can I trust that his words are true? How will I know what is in his heart? You must go with Blue Coat to this place."

At this, the conversation ceased.

Tyoga stared into the fire for a long time. He had not been in a city or town for many years. He had not moved within the white world and he wasn't even sure what that really meant anymore.

What will I see? How will I react?

He was frightened at what he might discover, not only about the world beyond the Appalachians, but about the world within himself.

After many minutes passed without a response from Tyoga, Chief Blue Coat added, "Wahaya-Wacon, if you do this for your Mattaponi brothers, the land two days walk in every direction from your Twin Oaks will be yours to live on in peace, forevermore."

Tyoga said, "Chief Blue Coat, I will go with you to Middle Plantation to speak with this Mr. Nott. But I do not go for the gift of the land. I go to stop a war and preserve the way of life for the Mattaponi. The land is yours. No one should be allowed to take it away."

Chapter 48

Turnabout

The following day, Tyoga and Trinity waved goodbye to their friends and pushed their canoe into the cold clear waters of the Mattaponi River. It was an hour after sunrise, and a ghostly mist still hovered just above the shiny glass surface of the river. Their home nestled between the twin oak trees was an easy trip from the village so Trinity, in the front of the canoe, did not need to help Tyoga paddle. They drifted lazily along with the morning breeze at their backs and the rising sun in their eyes.

"How was your visit with your sister?" Tyoga asked.

"Wonderful, Ty. She said that I can stay with her as long as I want to."

A wry smile creased Tyoga's face when he used her Indian name. "Yutsa, why did you not stay with Grows Strong? Why are you sitting in the bow of my canoe, woman?"

Trinity was looking straight ahead so that Tyoga could not see her face. He could tell that she was smiling broadly when she answered, "Because I want to go home."

Tyoga grinned and did not answer. He paddled the canoe out into the middle of the Mattaponi River and let the current glide them along. Securing the paddle to the stern with his left hand, he allowed it to sink only blade-deep into the water and used it as a rudder to steer the canoe.

After a while, Trinity said, "Grows Strong told me some stories about the legend of Tyoga Weathersby that I had not heard before."

Tyoga did not reply.

"Sunlei was a beautiful, gifted woman," Trinity added without any prompting.

"Yes, she is," Tyoga replied using the present tense.

Trinity noticed and the smile left her face. She beamed again when Tyoga offered, "She is a lot like you."

The two floated quietly down the river. Their heads turned gently from side to side to gaze at the wonders of the cool Virginia morn. Deer by the dozens stood statue-like at the river's edge. The does hovered over their playful fawns. The willows, birch, and elm trees were filled with song birds incessantly chirping to proclaim their ground. A fox and her cubs scurried back into the cover of the reeds as they rounded a bend, and hawks, searching the river for fingerling fry, soared overhead.

Warmed by the rising sun they reveled in the joys of being—both of them thankful not to be alone.

On the sandy east bank of the Mattaponi, their modest shelter haloed in the morning sun came into view. Like a castle's sturdy parapets, the tall twin oaks stood powerful and strong, welcoming them home.

The canoe crunched ashore on the sandy bank. Trinity sprang from the canoe, lifted the bow, and pulled it out of the water so that it was secured on the shore.

Tyoga was climbing out of the canoe when the terrifying scream made him jump with fright. Trinity was crumpled on the ground clutching her right calf.

He was by her side in two steps. "T.J., Trinity Jane, what's the matter, what's wrong?" He barely finished the words when the second snake struck the hand she was holding protectively over the first bite.

"No!" He grabbed the snake behind its head and snapped it in two. "Water moccasins!" he cried out.

Trinity did not have to ask what that meant. Growing up in the tidewater of Virginia, she knew. With eyes wild with fear and pain, she asked him, "Ty. Ty, what are we going to do?"

Without saying a word, Tyoga scooped her up into his arms and ran to the shelter. He knew exactly what to do.

Davey was racing through his mind. He had watched his mother tend to his little brother when he was bitten by the snake. He was well aware of the consequences of not acting fast. His mother had gotten to his brother too late to save him. He wasn't going to allow that to happen now.

He lay Trinity on the buffalo mattress and felt her forehead. The poison was traveling fast through her system because her panic caused her heart to race and spread the vile toxin more rapidly. She was perspiring and having difficultly sitting up.

"T.J.," Tyoga said sternly. "T.J., keep your eyes open. Don't close your eyes. Keep looking at me."

He searched frantically for a particular basket that held a straight razor given to him by the Mattaponi. When he saw the basket, he kicked it over and the straight razor fell out onto the ground.

"Lie down, T.J." He pushed her gently onto her back. He grabbed a corner of a deer hide and placed it in her hand. "Bite down on this, Little One." He didn't notice that he had used the term of endearment previously reserved only for Sunlei. "Scream as loud as you want—nobody is gonna hear."

He knelt down by her calf, picked her leg up off of the ground, and turned his back to her. "This is gonna hurt, T.J. I'm sorry."

Working quickly, he opened the straight razor and wiped the fang punctures with the cuff of his sleeve. He hesitated when he remembered that his mother had always placed her instruments directly into a flame, or dipped them into his papa's peach brandy before lancing or cutting. He had neither.

Time was the determining factor. He went straight to work.

Placing the front edge of the razor over the first fang mark, he cleaved Trinity's skin with a single deft stroke.

As the clean red line opened and bled, he placed the edge of the razor into the cut and pushed harder to open the calf muscle where the poison had been deposited.

He turned to look at Trinity Jane. Tears were streaming down the sides of her face, but she made no sound at all.

He opened the second fang puncture in same manner, lifted her leg to his mouth, and sucked hard over both cut marks. His mouth filled with blood, serum and residual venom. He spit it out through the front opening of the shelter. Three more times, he sucked and spit. After the final time he filled his mouth with water, swished, and spit.

He then turned his attention to the bite on her forearm.

This bite was far more serious than the bite on her leg. The snake was larger, and wasn't surprised by Trinity's presence. He saw her, and aimed his strike carefully before lunging for her arm. He had latched on and delivered a full bolus of his venom.

Her swollen forearm was turning a deep purple and red.

Tyoga slashed open the puncture marks with the straight razor and extracted as much poison as he possibly could with his mouth. The sick feeling in the pit of his stomach told him that he had not tended to this bite in time.

He remembered that his mother had cared for his baby brother by placing hot cloths over the incisions to force the cuts to bleed. He ran to the fire pit, dropped to his knees and blew the ash off of the two day old coals. Placing dry pine needles directly on the red hot coals, he coaxed a flame to life with three gently breaths. The pit was ablaze in a matter of minutes. He filled a clay pot with water, placed it directly on the flames, and ran back to Trinity's side.

Her lustrous auburn hair was plastered to her head and her clothing was soaked with sweat. She was beginning to shiver.

He cradled her head and shoulders in his arms, shook her lightly, and said, "T.J. T.J., can you open your eyes?" When she did not respond, he held her close to his chest and rocked her gently. There was little else he could do.

As the hours passed, Tyoga kept the hot compresses over the wounds. He placed a cool cloth on her brow, neck and upper chest, and blotted away the sweat that pooled in her eyes.

Wiping her face and cradling her body against his chest, he looked closely at the soft young woman lying in his arms. She was beautiful in a way that was oddly foreign, yet hauntingly familiar.

He had never held a white woman in his arms before. Her skin was velvet soft and creamy white. Her lips were thin and smooth. When she swallowed, the dimples in her cheeks puckered to give her an oddly impish aire even while asleep. Her neck was long and supple.

Brushing her hair from the right side of her face, he saw the scar that ran the length of her jaw, from in front of her ear lobe to her chin. The laceration had been deep and jagged. It was easy to imagine how the Shawnee brave who had held the knife in his hand thought that he had slit her throat. That the war party left her for dead was no surprise.

Tyoga gently touched the scar with the tips of his thick fingers and shook his head in disbelief that she had endured such an injury and survived. His hand slid from her cheek to her soft shoulders. He lingered there for a moment and rubbed her gently.

He picked up her limp left arm in his muscular, calloused hand. She felt so frail, so light, almost as if she wasn't there at all. He placed her tiny hand in his and smiled when he brought it close to his face. The long delicate fingers had worked hard. Very hard.

The lot of a white girl brought into an Indian tribe at a young age was often difficult. Days were filled with work from sun up to sun down. Fetching water, scraping hides, planting and harvesting crops, milling grain, butchering game, cooking and caring for the needs of the young and old.

Those who survived the harsh realities of servitude and debasement were accepted as full members of the tribe. Their strength, courage, and stamina were unquestioned.

Just as Trinity had done for him, Tyoga did not leave her side for twenty-four hours.

On the morning of the second day, he awakened to his clothes wringing with sweat from Trinity lying against him through the night.

She was mumbling and shivering with fever. Remembering that this is exactly what had happened to his little brother, he threw back the blankets covering her lower leg, and beheld the sight that he hoped not to see. Her leg was so swollen that he could not discern her ankle or knee. If he didn't do something soon, her skin would tear like an old linen sheet.

Gently he laid her on her back, removed all the covers and lifted her blouse over her head. He stripped her doeskin skirt up over her head so as not to disturb her swollen leg.

For the briefest moment, he felt a catch in his chest at seeing a naked white woman for the first time in his life.

Scooping blankets and sheets up in his arms, he ran to the river. He stumbled into the river until he was knee deep and submerged the bedding in the cold water. With the wet sheets and blankets slapping at his arms and legs, he ran back to the shelter. When he fell to the ground, he crawled the final ten feet into the shelter.

He covered Trinity first with the soaking linen sheet and then with a cotton blanket. Startled at the sudden cold, she shuddered and moaned, but did not awaken enough to protest. He placed a separate sopping wet, cold compress directly over her calf. He did the same for her forearm.

Placing his hand on her chest, he felt her heart beat. It was strong and her breathing was deep and regular. Grabbing another armful of covers and sheets, he ran down to the river again and repeated the process. All through the day he made the circuit from shelter to riverbank and back.

The sun was setting when his legs grew weak from lack of food and sleep. He collapsed onto the elkhide next to Trinity, placed his hand on her forehead, and dropped his chin to his chest in relief. Her fever was down and she had stopped shivering. He laid down beside her and fell asleep in a pile of soaking blankets—completely exhausted.

಄ ಞ ಚ ಞ

He was awakened by a gentle nudge to his side, and a whispered request, "Esgihusi."

Propping himself up on his elbow, Tyoga rubbed his eyes and saw that it was dark outside. "T.J.," he said. "You're thirsty? That's good."

Trinity acknowleged with a slight shake of her head but did not open her eyes. Propping her head up with his hand, Tyoga held the water gourd to her lips. She drank slowly until it was nearly empty.

She struggled to open her eyes for just a moment and looked up at him.

Seeing a hint of surprise in her furrowed brow, Tyoga responded with a playful, "Don't run off. It's me! I just shaved off my beard. Had the straight razor out anyway, so I figured I'd put it to good use."

Smiling, he brushed her hair out of her eyes. Trinity had never seen him cleanshaven. He had not shaved during his trek through the mountains and he had been with her for nearly a month now. After nine weeks of not shaving, he looked more animal than man. He understood how the dramatic change would have startled her. He rubbed his cleanshaven face with his open hand and shrugged his shoulders.

Standing up, Tyoga stretched his back and discovered that he was starving. Before he could get himself something to eat, he had to make a fresh bed of dry pelts and wool blankets for Trinity to lie on. He took the wet covers off her, and dried her body from head to toe. Placing her gently down on the soft dry bedding, he covered her with a clean sheet, and leaned over to place a soft kiss on her sweaty brow.

The kiss caught him completely by surprise.

Tyoga stoked the fire, heated some venison stew, took off his wet clothes and put on a store-bought cotton shirt and trousers, which were gifts they had brought back with them from their visit to Passaunkack. He had worn a pair of cotton trousers only once before. His papa had bought him the pants on one of their trips to Yorktown. They weren't as durable as his doeskin britches, but he liked the way they felt against his skin.

Looking up at the stars, he thought of Sunlei, Tes Qua, and Prairie Day. He wondered if they were looking up at the moon at that exact same moment.

Are they thinking of me?

As two distant owls sang their haunting serenade, and nightbirds twittered overhead, Tyoga stretched and went inside to go to bed.

One side of the interior of the shelter was a muddy mess from where Tyoga had kept Trinity soaking in cool, wet blankets all day. The only dry part of the shelter floor was where he had placed her on a soft elkskin.

In the month that they had been together, Tyoga and Trinity had never shared a bed.

This never would have been the case had Trinity been pure Cherokee. Warming each other through the night with their shared body heat was an expectation rather than an act of intimacy. From the very first night, they would have slept together while keeping each other warm.

This was surely something Trinity would have done if she had been with a Cherokee brave. Somehow their "whiteness" dictated a contrary set of moral guidelines. That they wanted to snuggle through the cold nights was without question. It made sense to do so. That they did not, spoke to the power of societal dictate as the oppressor of natural inclination.

Tyoga removed his shirt. He reached behind his neck and untied the knot in the leather thong that secured Sunlei's amulet—and lay down next to Trinity Jane.

Chapter 49

Twin Oaks

Trinity's recovery was remarkably fast. She was young, and strong, and determined.

Tyoga had administered all of the prescribed treatments for snake bite. Thanks to the help he had given his mother when she cared for his younger brother, he had provided care well beyond what the untrained woodsman would have been able to do.

Tyoga steeped a tea of willow bark and yarrow to keep Trinity's fever in check. He managed her pain by using ginger root and wild mint that acted as a powerful sedative. He made sure that she drank water, even when she claimed that she wasn't thirsty. And, he was prepared to incise her leg from ankle to knee if the swelling had begun to rip her flesh apart.

While Trinity was recuperating, a great deal of time was spent helping her to remember the English language. She had been taken from her family when she was eight years old and already quite fluent in her native tongue. A schoolteacher, her mother had read to Trinity from an early age.

Trinity could read and write in English before that horrible day when she was the lone survivor of the Shawnee attack. As it turned out, the fact that she had only spoken and heard Algonquin for the past ten years diminished her recollection of the English language hardly at all. There were some difficulties with subject and verb agreement. Everyday items like the words for "fork" and "spoon" and "shoes" had to be relearned; but once they were, she never needed to ask again.

The summer of 1707 lasted well into the fall, and the tidewater stayed green and warm into the later weeks of October.

True to his word, Chief Blue Coat had assigned the task of marking Tyoga's property lines to four young braves who were instructed to walk two-days in each direction of the compass, and mark the corner trees with the Twin Oaks brand. Over two hundred square miles of pristine Virginia countryside had been claimed in the name of Tyoga Weathersby. All of the land, timber, minerals, streams, and lakes belonged to the eighteen-year old man. All of the fish and fowl, hides and pelts were his to do with as he pleased.

In forty-eight hours, Chief Blue Coat had made Tyoga Weathersby a wealthy man.

The Mattaponi men helped Tyoga build a sturdy log cabin with a door of solid hickory, and two large window openings in the back and front of the home. The back wall faced the forest to the east and the path to Passaunkack. The front faced the Mattaponi River, the Appalachian Mountains, and the setting sun. The roof was made of the woven thatch the Mattaponi had learned to rely upon for a watertight lodge covering because milled planking and shingles would have to be purchased and transported from Calvert County. Glass windowpanes would have to be shipped from Yorktown.

The cabin had a great room and an area partitioned off as sleeping quarters. A kitchen area for preparing and processing foodstuffs was along the north side of the cabin, and the majority of the south wall was taken up by an enormous stone fireplace.

The Mattaponi had seen chimneys before, but had never been involved in the construction of such a massive stone structure. The lean of the chimney to create the necessary updraft to keep smoke from filling the interior of the house had them a bit puzzled. However, they carried the stones, mixed the mud and straw mortar, and made the scaffolding necessary to construct a fireplace more grand than the one planned for the Governor's Palace in Williamsburg—the new name for Middle Plantation.

As warm and inviting as it seemed in the winter of 1708, the cabin, was only the beginning of what would become the magnificent estate along the Mattaponi known as Twin Oaks.

 C3 ⅋D C3 ⅋D

While the men were building the main house and out buildings, Trinity was hard at work learning the ways of the woodland tribes. She had grown up in the Nansmond Clan of the Powhatan, a tribe that lived among the estuaries of the Chesapeake. They grew corn, beans, and squash, and hunted the tidal basins for sturgeon, clams, mussels, shrimp, crabs, and shad. Their subsistence was based upon the harvesting of seafood rather than sowing and reaping vegetables and grains. While coaxing sustenance from the land was a talent not completely foreign to her, she had never had the opportunity to acquire the knowledge and skills of the inland Powhatan who were experts at planting, sowing, and preserving their crops.

Trinity Jane's sister, Grows Strong, and her family and friends were frequent overnight visitors to Twin Oaks. Although it was far too late to plant any crops, the women of Passaunkack taught Trinity how to store seeds, preserve bulbs, and winter tubors for planting in the spring. They showed her planting and sowing techniques that would allow her to enjoy an abundant harvest the following growing season.

The fall was the time when the women of the village were most involved in the tanning of hides and the preparation of skins to make warm winter clothing for the cold months ahead. This was a skill at which Trinity had a great deal of experience. She showed the women of Mattaponi more efficient ways of fleshing a hide and new ways of making stretching frames that allowed for a final product that was uniform in thickness and shape.

The women exchanged clothes patterns and sewing techniques that produced warm and durable clothing the likes of which neither had been able to manufacture before.

As the weeks and months passed, the aloneness felt by Tyoga gradually faded away with the growing admiration for Trinity's uncanny knack for teasing opportunity from adversity. The admiration born of shared hardship, misfortune conquered, and health restored blossomed into mutual trust that, over time, solidified into unshakable commitment.

Desperation, perseverance, and triumph are the ores from which the strongest bonds are forged. They revealed their devotion to one another in the transparency of a smile, the gentleness of a glance, or the open flirtation of a sensuous sigh.

Still, they had not touched.

One evening in late October, they were sitting around the campfire, watching the blazing orange ball of the sun slowly sink into the mountains to the west. Their bellies were full of turkey breast and trout fillets. The remnants of blanched watercress partially filled one of the two clay bowls. The other held a helping of creamed corn.

They were both very tired. Their muscles ached with the throb of accomplishment and progress. They were content and relaxed.

As the sun continued to set and darkness descended into the glade, Tyoga turned his attention to Trinity Jane, who was seated in front and to the side of him.

The transition from day to night strips the world of color and replaces the dazzle of reds and greens and blues with a pastel grayness that compensates for the loss with a clarity of its own accord.

In the dying light of day, the scar on Trinity's face transitioned from what might have been seen by others as a blemish, into a milestone of passage that was pleasing to his eyes. The mark accentuated rather than detracted from her beauty. Even at her young age, she radiated a wisdom and contentment of soul that are the rewards of living a life more accomplished at giving than coveting.

In the grayness of twilight, Trinity Jane virtually glowed.

When she turned and caught him staring at her, she smiled rather coyly and moved back so that she was next to his side. She put her hand on his thigh and rested her head against his shoulder.

"Are you thinking about her, Ty?" she asked.

"No."

"It is okay if you are. I understand," Trinity said.

"It is better if I don't," he replied. "If I imagine where she might be, what might be happening to her, and that I should be with her to protect her—it just becomes too much to bear."

"You made the right decision, Tyoga," she said. "You did what was best for everyone, you must know that."

"I did what was best for everyone when I left the mountains. I know that." He paused, and then added, "I don't think that I have done right by you, T.J."

She gently pushed away from him, and sat up on her knees so that they were eye-to-eye. "Ty, I am here by my own choice," she said. "You are not sorry that I am here, are you, Ty? It would kill me to know that you do not want me here with you. I have helped you, haven't I? I haven't been any trouble."

Rocking to his knees, he took Trinity's shoulders between his two strong hands and lifted her so that she was kneeling upright and they were once again face to face. "T.J." He waited for her to focus on his eyes. "I could not have made it without you by my side. Do you hear me?"

She knodded.

"Don't ever ask me again if I want you with me. Never again."

Overcome with the sincerity in his voice and the look in his eyes, Trinity released herself to him. She held his head in her hands and tenderly kissed him with her dewy lips. Before Tyoga even had the chance to respond, she said, "Wait here. I have a surprise for you." She kissed him again, jumped up, skipped up the stone steps, and disappeared into the cabin.

Outside, Tyoga watched the moon rise and the stars begin to shine.

The promise had been strong within him over the past several weeks. It had spoken to him, not in the usual way that alerted him to threat or peril, but in a whisper that allowed him to see the ordinary and mundane in new and different ways. The pattern of stones on the shore of the Mattaponi murmured truths about the journey that lay ahead. The dew on the cattails dribbled hints of birth and transition. The flocks of crows roosting in the pines to the east felt like an arrival unforseen.

He was shaken from his thoughts of the promise by Trinity's doeskin dress landing in his lap. From behind him, he heard her sultry voice say, "Ty."

He turned around.

Haloed by the light of the fire inside, Trinity Jane stood in the front door of the cabin.

Tyoga stood up and just stared. He had no words.

The sheer pastel linen dress flowed over her slender waist and taut abdomen nearly to the floor. The deep plunging neckline, filled with a gauzy lace bodice, revealed the cleavage between her ample breasts. She wore no shoes.

She had brushed her hair out from the usual side ponytail. The thick auburn waves cascaded past her shoulders to between her shoulder blades. She did not have bangs like the Cherokee or Powhatan women, but had allowed her hair to grow out at an equal length. Her forehead and brows where hidden behind an auburn veil of lustrous hair that was teasing, provocative, and alluring.

She took a step down from the threshold and onto the cabin's stone stoop. She shook the hair from in front of her eyes and said in English, "Well? Do you like my dress?"

Tyoga whispered, "Turn around."

Ever so slowly, Trinity lifted herself up onto her toes and turned around. The skirt flew out from her body to allow the glow from the fire to illuminate the silhouette of what was beneath.

Tyoga marched up the stone steps to take Trinity Jane into his arms. He enveloped her with his shear mass and kissed her hard on the mouth.

Trinity reached up and threw her arms around his neck and kissed him with an open mouth passion so intense that she cried out loud. He lifted her from the porch.

They stood in between the glow of the two fires for a long moment. The fire in the earthen pit outside of the cabin, where Trinity's Indian garb lay crumpled in the dirt, was dying out while the fire inside the cabin's stone fireplace roared with heat and light and life.

Tilting her head back, Trinity looked up into his eyes. "Well, Tyoga Weathersby?"

Swinging her like a ragdoll, he threw her legs over his outstretched right arm, stepped up over the threshold, and kicked the cabin door shut behind them.

It was well past midnight before the deer grazing in the grassy glade could do so undisturbed.

Chapter 50

The Trip to Middle Plantation

It was late in November when Chief Blue Coat arrived at Twin Oaks to tell Tyoga that he had been summoned before Lord Edward Nott, and that he was to travel to Middle Plantation in two days time. Tyoga told the chief that he would be at Passaunkack and ready to travel with him to see the Lord Governor of Virginia in two moons.

Tyoga awoke before sunrise to see Trinity Jane packing his knapsack for his journey to Middle Plantation.

Boiling over the firepit outside, the coffee's earthy scent filled the cabin with the warmth of home.

"Mmmm, smells good, T.J. That fancy perkin' pot sure makes good coffee, don't you think?" he asked.

"The coffee smells good," she agreed.

Tyoga had been conversing with her only in English over the past several weeks, and she was speaking it as comfortably as she spoke Tsalagie.

More comfortable dressing in the clothes of the white world, she had not worn her doeskin tunic or elkskin boots for sometime now. Anxious to go to Middle Plantation and the other nearby Virginia colonies, she wanted to dress and speak like a white woman when she went into their shops and boutiques.

"Shiata ney ya tees a lo *(It doesn't matter anyway)*," she replied in Tsalagi.

Recognizing an uncharacteristically short reply, and knowing that she only slipped back into Tsalagi when she was irritated, Tyoga went over to her and put his arms around her, "What's the matter, T.J.?"

"I don't know, Ty. I can't sleep even though I am tired all the time. I guess we have just been working too hard."

"Maybe. Why don't you sit down and I will go get us the coffee?"

"No. You sit. I will go." She got halfway to the firepit before she fell to her knees and wretched uncontrollably.

Tyoga ran outside and put his arms around her. "T.J., what's the matter? Are you sick?" Letting Tyoga support her weight for a brief moment, Trinity stayed on the ground. Slowly, she climbed to her feet and ran her fingers through her flowing auburn mane. "No. I am not sick. I will get the coffee. You go back inside."

Remembering the message of the promise about unforeseen arrivals, Tyoga turned to go back inside.

Ꭶ Ꮣ Ꮳ Ꮫ

Trinity Jane had them packed and ready for the short canoe trip to Passaunkack by sunrise. She packed very little for Tyoga's trek to Middle Plantation. The trip would only take two days each way, and the party would be well provisioned by the tribe. She did not need to pack very much for herself either because she would find all that she needed in her sister's lodge.

The morning chill had not yet been broken. Winter's embrace was choking the life from the leaves festooning the towering boughs of chestnut and spruce, hickory and elm.

They pushed off the rocky shore just as the sun crested the tops of the trees. By the time their canoe slid onto the shores of Passaunkack, Trinity's face had turned crabapple red from the cold wind blowing up the Mattaponi.

Trinity's sister, Grows Strong, and her two teenaged sons greeted them when they stepped ashore. The boys and some of their friends helped to carry their belongings into the village.

In half an hour, Tyoga, Chief Blue Coat, his sons Shield Maker and Thunder Bow, plus three young Mattaponi braves were on the trail headed south toward Middle Plantation. Large bundles of furs and hides were draped down the braves' backs.

The men hiked along the shores of the Mattaponi for about forty-five minutes before the morning fog lifted and the warmth of the sun broke through the low hanging clouds. The trail turned gradually toward the west. Soon, the sound of the rushing river was left far behind.

"Si too eh yetta wa heya *(We are heading west),*" Tyoga said.

"Yes, my son," Chief Blue Coat replied. "We go to Brick House in New Kent to trade our hides for cloth and knives. We could trade for these things in Middle Plantation, but trading is better at Brick House. Besides, these young men do not wish to carry their loads all the way to Middle Plantation."

The young men carrying the load of furs smiled and nodded in agreement.

The footpath broke from the woods to cut through an open glade thick with waist-high meadow grass. The path intersected muddy ruts that marked a wagon trail leading into the village of Brick House, the first colonial town established in New Kent. The narrow wagon wheel path fanned into a wider muddy lane along which the New Kent County Courthouse and several mercantile businesses had set up shop.

Outside of shabby, canvas-topped lean-tos supported by flimsy sapling frames, three half-naked squaws sat on the ground. Hair disheveled, their faces were rubbed red and raw from the coarse unshaved faces of mountain men and settlers. The cries and moans emanating from the damp, dark recesses of the prison-like structure left no doubt about the horrors taking place within.

Unable to look at the filthy, stinking little man standing at the entrance to the tent, Tyoga walked by. He had no way of knowing that around the corner, in front of the Kent County Courthouse, an even greater horror awaited him.

By the early 1700s, indentured servitude, the practice of working for merchants or landowners in exchange for the cost of passage across the Atlantic, was being replaced by the less costly, and more lucrative, practice of buying and selling slaves. Fortunes were made in the trafficking of human beings kidnapped from their native lands in South America, Africa, and the Caribbean Islands.

The African slaves came from many tribes: the spirited Hausas, the gentle Mandingos, the creative Yorubas from the Igbos, Efiks and Krus, the proud Fantins, the warlike Ashantis, the shrewd Dahomeans, the Binis, and the Senegalese.

The frontier farms had adopted the ways of the southern plantations. The mid-Atlantic estates filled their intense labor needs with slaves purchased at the harbors in Yorktown, Savannah, and the Mississippi delta.

When Tyoga saw the proud dark man standing on the auction block in front of the Kent County Courthouse, he had no way of knowing that the chance encounter would change both of their lives forever.

In his early thirties, he was old for a slave. Standing atop an old wooden wine barrel that was being used as a makeshift auction block with his legs and wrists manacled, the worn black man was the very picture of abandoned life and conceded hope. Head bowed, sweat streaming from his brow, clothes tattered and torn, he listened impassively to the auctioneer's plea for an opening bid.

When no bid over ten shillings was offered, the unacceptable measure of his worth condemned him to a fate even worse than if he had been sold.

The auctioneer, an unkept little man by the name of Darby, grabbed him by the wrist shackles and pulled him off of the wine barrel. The barrel tipped over. The auctioneer threw the black man against the courthouse's red brick wall.

The unclaimed slave sat down, leaned against the wall, drew his knees to his chest and rested his forehead upon them.

No one had bid for his services. Worse than being a slave was being a slave that nobody wanted. He thought that he had forgotten the exposure of shame, he was startled to learn that he was wrong.

While the auctioneer stooped over to right the fallen barrel, Tyoga was struck by the transformation the simple act engendered.

The wine cask in its intended employ was a vessel that once held the spirits of celebration and joy. Filled, the barrel's entry into a room would have been applauded and acclaimed. Its contents would have been coveted and shared with much fanfare and bally-hoo.

But now, empty and upright, its entry into the perverse pageantry unfolding in Brick House's town square mocked its very purpose and ridiculed its intent. Serving as a stage upon which men and women were bought and sold was in stark contrast to the promise of life and liberty its contents were meant to celebrate.

Yet, the barrel had not changed. It could once again hold promise and joy. It was only the will of man that debased its purpose and bastardized its employ.

Tyoga watched the man for a long time.

Sitting silently amid the sights and sounds of the human sale, the hopelessness embraced his massive frame like the sea enveloping a drowning man.

Children were running through the gawking throng, which was oddly composed of young ladies who had come to watch the strong black men and proud, steadfast women stand half naked on the barrel while the squires cast lots for their chattel. The ladies would cover their leering giggles with lace kerchiefs in hopes that the sins absorbed by the cloth would remain forever trapped in the delicate weave.

Vendors were selling boiled peanuts and beef jerky. Drams of rum were selling for two shillings and whiskey for five. A guitar, banjo, and flute trio played gospel tunes and religious anthems.

The black man seemed not to notice. When he lifted his head from his knees, the tears streaking down his face beckoned Tyoga to his side.

Looking down at the disheveled man crumpled at his feet, Tyoga asked, "What's your name?"

Without looking up, the black man rose slowly to his feet. He was a large man, taller, and more robust around the chest than Tyoga had thought. His upper arms were chiseled and nearly as large as Tyoga's. His forearms and hands were terribly scarred, and he was missing the ring finger on his left hand. Bearing the ritualistic facial scars identifying him as a member of the Ashantis tribe, his carriage and gate belied his once noble lineage.

Looking Tyoga directly in the eyes, he answered his question. "My name is Akuchi Akua. Massa call me Three-Toe Brister."

Noticing Tyoga inspecting the nubs that were once the three small toes on his right foot, he explained, "Fust massa wok Akuchi in quarry. Boots too small shoes. Make brister toes."

"Your toes got infected?" Tyoga inquired in an effort to help Brister with his speech. Staring at the man's foot, Tyoga opened his eyes wide, and touched the man lightly on the shoulder. His face broke out into a broad smile. "Oh! Blister toes. Brister toes. That's how you got your name."

Tickled by the obvious that had eluded him, Tyoga laughed out loud.

Staring at the laughing white man with his hand resting gently on his shoulder, Brister stood stone faced. He could not remember the last time he had allowed himself to smile, let alone laugh. He wasn't even sure that he knew how. Years of requiring permission to speak, to eat, to drink, to rest, and even move had taught him to squelch even the most fundamental involuntary responses. A sneeze could be grounds for a beating. A yawn meant the whipping post. The horror of his existence had stripped the very life from his eyes.

Looking at Tyoga Weathersby, who was laughing uncontrollably, and taking the silent cues that it was okay to share in his joy, Brister sensed the unfamiliar beginnings of a smile. He had forgotten that he had dimples. He looked down when he felt his eyes begin to shine with the remembrance of life as it should be led.

The auctioneer, Darby, hurried over to the two men. He grabbed Tyoga's forearm to throw his hand off of Brister's shoulder, and shouted, "Sit down there, boy! Who told you to stand up?"

When he swung his fist back over his head to strike Brister to the ground, his arm was stopped in mid-swing by the vice-like grip of the mountain man he had unfortunately misjudged.

As if hitting a stone wall, the force of the blocked blow swung Darby around so that he was eye to chest with Tyoga.

Darby was a disheveled, spongy man in his late forties with a pasty, wan complexion disguised behind untrimmed salt and pepper stubble. While his clothes were assembled to convey an air of importance and someone to be reckoned with, the food stains on his torn cravat rendered the pretense of an obvious sham. He smelled of beer, body odor, and urine.

He did not look up into Tyoga's face before chastising him for interfering with the coup he was about to administer to his property. "Here now. Take your hands off of me. This is no business of yours. I own this slave and I will deal with him as I see fit." Just as he finished the sentence, his eyes locked with Tyoga's. He swallowed hard.

"Ah. Well ah. Well, Mister," Darby stammered. "I mean, ah, I can see that you are a man with a keen eye for ah ... Perhaps you are interested in Brister here ... Just look at the chest on this slave, why he can ..." While he was speaking, Darby reached to rip open the shirt that Brister was wearing.

Again, Tyoga reached out his mighty left hand and held it between Brister's chest and Darby's sweaty, trembling hands. "I can see the man just fine with his shirt on."

"Well, sure you can ... sure you can." Darby dropped his arms to his side. "So what do you say, Mister? Ah—Oh, I know that it is a steal, but I could part with good ol' Brister here for say ... twenty shillings. Waddaya say?"

The thought of one man owning another was contrary to everything that Tyoga believed and stood for as a free man. Man was born to nature just as the bear, the deer, and the mountain lion. He was free as the wind and the sky and the rain. Man was no more tethered than a butterfly, bee, or bird.

The promise whispered to Tyoga of the shared oneness common to all living things. The simple fact of his being was not meant to be judged by others, as a man's worth is independent of judgement or review. A man could no more be owned by another man than Wahaya could be owned by Tyoga. As Wahaya could not live at the end of a leash, so, too, no man could live bound by chains.

Without removing his glare from the wretched little man, Tyoga reached into his adoda and pulled out two shillings. He pinched the coins between his index finger and thumb and held them in front of Darby's sweaty face.

Sensing the tension in the air, the crowd gathered around the three men standing behind the auction block next to the red brick wall.

Tyoga could feel the color drain from his eyes and the sleeves of his shirt begin to tighten.

Calmly, but loud enough for the gathering crowd to hear, Tyoga said, "You will take these two shillings and release this man. You will release him not to me or to any man, but to the air and the sky and the heavens above. These coins release this man from ownership."

Darby's gaze went from Tyoga's face to the coins he was holding in his hand. Seeing the life drain from Tyoga's eyes, Darby swallowed hard and sweated profusely. He did not respond.

Tyoga said, "Hold out your hand and take these coins."

When Darby did not do as he was asked, Tyoga stepped into the man and whispered, "I will not tell you again."

Darby held out his trembling hand.

Tyoga dropped the coins into his palm. "Now. Release this man so that all can hear."

Swallowing hard, Darby said, "I release this man."

"No, no," Tyoga said more forcefully. "I want to hear you give this man his freedom. Say it out loud for all of us to hear, 'This man is free!'"

Darby stammered to get the words out of his dry mouth, "Th ... This man ..."

"Come on. You can do it," Tyoga demanded.

"This man is free," Darby said in a frightened whisper.

"Louder. You can do better than that."

"This man is free," Darby repeated with more conviction.

Tyoga turned to the crowd. In a voice just slightly not his own, he announced, "Just in case you did not hear my good friend the auctioneer, he has given this man, Akuchi Akua, his freedom. Just sos there ain't no misunderstandin', and that no one take this exchange of coins as an act of ownership, I say to you now this man is a free man. No man may own him after this day. If I hear of this man being taken, the taker will answer to me."

Tyoga reached into the pocket of Darby's filthy vest and snatched the key to Brister's chains. In a menacingly quiet voice, he ordered a final humiliation. "Release this man from his chains." As Darby squatted at Brister's feet to do as he had been ordered, Tyoga headed back up the lane toward the mercantiles and the Mattaponi who had already traded their furs.

Startled at what had just transpired, Brister left Darby staring down at the two shillings in his hand, and ran after Tyoga. "Massa. Massa," he called out while he ran.

Tyoga stopped and turned around.

"Massa. Akuchi free?" he asked.

"Yes. You are free."

"Massa, where go Akuchi now?"

"Well, I don't rightly know," Tyoga said. "I suppose that you can go anywhere you want to go."

Akuchi thought before nodding his head.

Tyoga patted him on the shoulder and turned to walk away. He was not surprised to hear Brister's footsteps following close behind.

Chief Blue Coat and the Mattaponi braves had been watching the action at the courthouse steps. Their bows were in their hands and they had brought their quivers to their sides ready to intercede should the crowd turn against Tyoga.

When he reached them, Tyoga waded through the band of men without hesitating and made his way toward the cover of the woods.

The Chief turned and followed behind him.

Thunder Bow and the rest of the Mattaponi party backed away toward the woods while keeping an eye upon the crowd at the courthouse.

Two hours away from the town of Brick House, the men were once again following along the shores of the Mattaponi River. Leading the way, Chief Blue Coat turned to indicate that the band would stop at a clearing ahead to rest.

Squatting down on the banks of the river to take a drink of water, Tyoga saw that Brister was relieving himself along side of a giant chestnut tree down the trail. Wiping his hands on his sleeves, he stood up and walked toward the tired black man.

With a big smile on his face so as to reassure him that he meant no harm, Tyoga said, "So, Brister, where do you suppose you are off to now?"

"Massa, Brister got nowhere go. Me follow Massa. Me work for Massa. Brister belong Massa."

"No, Brister, you belong to no one. You are your own man. You can come and go as you please."

Tyoga had been thinking about what he was about to say to Brister ever since he first set eyes on him. The smile left his face. "You are welcome to come with me if you understand that I do not own you. Do you understand?"

Not really understanding the meaning of Tyoga's words, Brister nodded his head.

"If you come with me," Tyoga said, "you must not call me Master. My name is Tyoga. Tyoga Weathersby. You can call me Tyoga, or Ty, but you must not call me Master. Do you understand, Brister?"

Brister nodded again.

"You can come and help me build my homestead. I will feed you and give you shelter, but I cannot pay you for your work right away. After we have built Twin Oaks together, I will pay you for your work and give you land to grow your own crops if you choose to stay. If that is acceptable to you, then you may come along. Do we have a deal?" Tyoga extended his hand to shake on the agreement.

Brister looked at his extended hand and then looked into his eyes. No white man had ever extended his hand to him in friendship. No man, black or white, had ever trusted in him enough to seal a deal with the simple shake of a hand. He didn't know what to do.

Tyoga reached out his left hand, grabbed Brister's right wrist, and placed his right hand in his own. As the two men shook hands, a smile came to Brister's face.

"Deal?" Tyoga asked.

"Yes, Massa."

"Call me Ty."

"Yes, Massa-Ty," Brister replied.

The deal was struck.

Chapter 51

The Parlez at Middle Planatation

When Tyoga, Brister, Chief Blue Coat, and the Mattaponi entered the village known then as Middle Plantation, an act of the Virginia General Assembly had already been passed decreeing that the village would be chartered as a new city and renamed Williamsburg, "in honor of his Highness William Duke of Gloucester."

The meandering, muddy path upon which the men were walking would go on to become the Duke of Gloucester Street.

The cobblestones of the avenue would one day echo the buckle shoes worn by Thomas Jefferson, Benjamin Franklin, Sam Adams, and Patrick Henry when they briskly marched to Raleigh Tavern to plan a rebellion that would change the world.

The act also stipulated that the new statehouse would be constructed "somewhere at Middle Plantation, near His Majesty's College of William and Mary." It would take another four years for construction to begin on the Governor's Palace.

The news contained in the act passed by the Virginia General Assembly had not made its way to the frontier, so Tyoga and his companions saw nothing more than a muddy path along which Bruton Parish Church, a blacksmith shop, and a mercantile had been established. On the other side of the path were several brick homes owned by John

Page and his family. Beyond the village, the path rolled through swampy ravines and marshlands that separated the James and York Rivers.

Upon inquiring of the blacksmith, Tyoga learned that Governor Edward Nott, Henry Carry, landowner Henry Tyler, and several other wigged dignitaries were assembled in one of John Page's modest homes.

They were in the parlor having tea and sipping port when Tyoga and the Mattaponi were announced by a tall, pasty man wearing white gloves and a powered wig. The ridiculous chapeau was so infused with the branding chalk that a plume followed his every move like a comet's tail billowing though the void.

The valet asked, "Whom shall I say is calling?"

Tyoga looked around him and chuckled at the pointlessness of the query.

"Tell them we're here," he said with a shake of his head.

When he heard the distain in the valet's voice as he announced, "They are here, my Lord," Tyoga nearly laughed out loud.

Chief Blue Coat and the other Mattaponi had no clue what it was that Tyoga found so amusing, but they smiled anyway so as not to offend in case laughter was the appropriate reaction to whatever was going on around them.

Tyoga motioned toward the door with a nod of his head to invite the Native American contingent to step into the parlor ahead of him.

Before Chief Blue Coat could step up onto the pine boards of the entrance foyer, a forcefully extended arm planted an open hand to his chest to prevent him from stepping up into the house.

Henry Carry's voice said, "Not you. None of you." The sweep of his hand indicated the Native Americans. "Only the white man may enter to parlez with Lord Governor Nott," he announced in haughty tone.

Chief Blue Coat's face darkened with anger. Even without under-standing the words, the intention was clear. He took his foot down from the top step.

Some of the Mattaponi braves swung their bows from their backs and others placed their hands on their tomahawks secured in their waist sash.

Brister stepped from the side of the house and turned his imposing frame menacingly toward the stoop.

"Ees-ta ho," Chief Blue Coat commanded.

The braves reluctantly stood down. Tyoga held his hand up in the air to stay Brister a safe distance from the front door.

Tyoga, who was still standing in the street, climbed the two bottom porch steps and said to Mr. Carry, "I wouldn't advise you placin' yer hands on the Chief again. 'Cause he won't stop them a second time."

At this Mr. Carry, dropped his arm to his side and said with more embarrassment than contrition, "Well, then. Tell him that he and his men may not enter this house."

"No," Tyoga replied.

"No? No?" Mr. Carry replied. "My good man, it is the order of his Lord Governor that you and only you may enter this house to parlez. Now, I won't tell you again to instruct this man that he may not enter this house."

Tyoga felt himself begin to lose his patience. Chief Blue Coat and the Mattaponi braves were some of the finest men he had ever known in his life. They had taken him and Trinity Jane in, cared for them when they had no food, no clothes, and no shelter, and now they were being told that they were not worthy to be in the presence of his Lord Governor.

His heart pounded in his chest with that urgency that prepared him for battle. His eyes grew cold and his arms swelled. Still he kept control of his voice and demeanor. "I will not enter without the chief by my side. He is the man to which his 'Lord Governor' must speak."

While Tyoga was saying these words to Carry, Chief Blue Coat touched him on the sleeve. Stepping down, Tyoga leaned into the Chief to hear what he wished to say. A smile came to Tyoga's lips. He stepped back up to face Carry standing on the threshold.

"Chief Blue Coat says that no one will enter this house. Tell Nott that now he must come outside to speak with the Chief."

"He will not, sir!" Carry was indignant. "I have never heard such a thing!"

At this, Tyoga stepped back down to speak with the Chief. The other Mattaponi braves gathered around to hear what the funny little man standing self-righteously on the top step had said. The conference went on for some time before breaking up when the Mattaponi, led by Chief

Blue Coat, starting making their way up mainstreet toward the college grounds.

With his back turned toward Mr. Carry, who was still standing in the doorway of the house, Tyoga watched them walk away. Smiling, he turned to face him. "Mr. Carry, it seems that there will no longer be a— What did you call it?—Parlez between Nott—"

"Lord Governor Nott," Carry interrupted.

"—Lord Governor Nott," Tyoga repeated with a mocking bow.

"What do you mean no parlez?" Carry demanded. "You've come all this way to speak with Lord Governor, and now you will turn your back on an audience with my Lord without listening to that which he wishes to decree?"

"No. Not exactly that. No," Tyoga said. "But now, instead of a *parlez* there will be a *pow- wow*."

"A *pow-wow*?" Carry asked. "Just exactly what does that mean, sir?"

"That means," Tyoga explained, "if Nott wishes to speak with the Chief, he must now come to him. We'll be camped on the outskirts of the school, yonder. We'll expect Nott sometime after supper."

Dumbfounded, Carry made no reply.

When he turned to follow after the Mattaponi, Tyoga said to him, "You're welcome to come along if you want." He stopped and turned to him. "Least-wise, I don't think he'll object."

Motioning for Brister to follow, he laughed out loud, turned, and disappeared into the evening shadows.

Chapter 52

The Pow-Wow at Middle Plantation

They made camp outside of the manicured ground of His Majesty's College of William and Mary, south of the campus on a high spot of land that allowed a view of the village of Middle Plantation.

The campus proper was landscaped in keeping with English tradition of angular gardens filled with Coreopsis and Verbena bordered by cropped boxwood and vinca groundcover. Beyond the low brick walls were nothing but fields, forest, and swamp.

After the sun had set and the men had finished their dinner, they heard the sound of horse and carriage making its way along the center street toward their campsite. The carriage stopped beyond the light of the campfire, about twenty-five yards from the men. They heard the carriage door open and the sounds of the steps being lowered to the ground.

Like costumed apparitions, the soldiers of his majesty's royal guard marched into the light of the fire with their gleaming bayonets shimmering in the glow of the dancing flames. Crisply, the columns split by pairs to create a path through which the Lord Governor could make his appearance. At a single command, the soldiers of the guard extended their weapons at arms length and waited in silence while Governor Nott slowly paraded along the human corridor.

Tyoga, Chief Blue Coat, and the Mattaponi continued to stare into the fire. Thunder Bow spit a bit of dislodged pemikan to the ground as members of the governor's retine made their appearance. Brister was seated just beyond the light of the fire, pulling at some jerky.

Henry Carry came into the light of the fire first. He was followed by Henry Tyler, and Jerimiah Spotswood, and another local landowner. The dignitaries took their place in line before stepping aside to make way for the Governor himself.

He was a slight man. His diminutive stature was made all the more apparent by the members of his royal guard who were each a head taller than he. Dressed in formal attire, his cream-colored tunic, embroidered with a thick, gold brocade of elaborate and intricate design, complemented his tan breeches and vanilla stockings. The white ruffle around his neck indicated that he had every intention of impressing his audience with his own importance. He wore a round brimmed Tudor bonnet.

Marching with ridiculously exaggerated steps through the honor-guard column, his air of entitlement would have been embarrassing had it not been worn with such sincerity. With deliberate, measured steps, he made his way toward the campfire around which the Mattaponi were seated. Planting both feet disrespectfully close to Chief Blue Coat's crossed legs, he placed one hand on his hip in a sign that he was ready to be formally announced.

Stepping crisply forward, the royal guardsman at the head of the column announced to the night, "His Exellency, Lord Governor Edward Nott."

Nott bowed at the waist.

"Ja yo—siha—s?" Chief Blue Coat asked.

"Excuse me?" Governor Nott responded.

"He asked if you are hungry," Tyoga told him. "Do you want something to eat? It is how the Mattaponi say hello."

"Oh. Well then ... tell him ... 'hello' and that I have already eaten."

"Eh toya," the Chief replied knowing that the Governor did not understand his greeting and that he was not the least bit interested if he was hungry or not.

"Sit down," Tyoga told the Governor.

Without looking around, the Governor began to sit, seemingly on thin air. Before his knees were bent, a folding chair appeared into which he settled himself.

Acknowledging the Governor not at all, Chief Blue Coat continued to stare into the fire. Several minutes passed before the Chief rose to his feet. Thunder Bow rolled a large willow stump onto the bearskin he had been seated upon and turned it upright for him to use as a seat. It brought him eye-to-eye with Governor Nott.

"Eachta—eh-alo," the Chief announced.

"He is listening," Tyoga said to Nott.

"Oh, look here, my good man," the Governor began with a distinctively irritable tone. "It makes absolutely no sense me speaking to this man who has no idea what it is I am saying. Come over here so that I may conduct my business with you!"

"The land that you wish to speak about belongs to Chief Blue Coat and the Mattaponi," Tyoga replied. "Governor Nott, the Mattaponi have lived on this land for thousands of years. For generations, they have farmed the land, cared for the land, and treated it with reverence and respect. The land has provided them with everything they have needed to survive; food, clothing, housing, and a resting place for their ancestors. They do not see the land as a source of wealth or as producing commodities that can be purchased and sold. The land is alive to them. It provides for them as a mother provides for her children, and they care for the land just as they do their own mothers. They do it no harm and ask no more from it but what it can spare. If it is the land you wish to speak about, then your business is with Chief Blue Coat. I will tell him what you are here to ask of his people."

"What is your name, sir?" the Governor asked in a more amicable tone.

"I am Tyoga Weathersby."

"I have heard of you, young man," Nott said. "Quite a legend has grown up around you— something about being raised by Indians and wolves and what not. Hmm."

Tyoga smiled. "Somethin' like that."

"Well. You have a remarkable command of the English language for having been brought up with savages, and I dare say that your services will be of great use to His Majesty."

"Use?" Tyoga asked.

"Yes," Nott said. "We shall see, my good man. We shall see."

Losing patience with the haughty little man, Tyoga said with just a hint of exasperation in his tone. "What do you wish to ask the Chief?"

"I have no question to ask him, my dear fellow," Nott said. "I have come to tell him that the crown intends to procure his land along the Mattaponi River."

Being a seasoned negotiator, Tyoga knew better than to react immediately to the governor's statement. He remained calm and controlled. He would not interpret what the Governor said to Chief Blue Coat. His reaction would have to be more demure.

"Procure?" Tyoga questioned.

"Yes, my good man. Surely, you know the word. Acquire. Seize. Garner. The Crown intends to take the Mattaponi lands."

Tyoga did not reply. He stared into the governor's wan, fragile face with a look that at once commanded more information and implored an explanation to justify such a demand.

Nott seemed to intuitively understand that he was negotiating with a man the likes of which he had never encountered before in what he considered to be a savage land. The Governor had not found favor with the King of England by being naïve or petulant. He was skilled at reading people and appreciating intent. But he was at once intrigued— and confused—by this articulate, leather garbed mountain man with the insulating eyes that protected him from intimidation and steeled him against compromise of principal.

Tyoga's lack of pretense and disinterest in manipulating the facts to persuade or change opinion were based in the fundamental truths revealed to him on Carter's Rock twenty years ago. The nature of truth is not found in opinion nor is it subject to the interpretation or intrigue of man. It is beyond that which is available to contrivance.

Truth simply is.

The Governor was unable to understand discourse without pretense, but was astute enough to understand that a change in tactic was necessary.

Turning to face Chief Blue Coat, Governor Nott said, "Please convey this message to the Chief, Mr. Weathersby. Tell him that the Crown, er … the great father across the waters, or whatever he understands the King to be, is interested in creating a port—a town, as it were—on the site presently occupied by the Mattaponi."

Tyoga interpreted Nott's words for Chief Blue Coat.

Nott continued, "Tell the Chief that the site is well situated for loading boats—big ships—with furs, and trees for lumber, and tobacco and corn and all sorts of goods in demand in England. Tell him that for his land and the goods we take we will give him enough money … shillings … .no, errrr wampum to make him and his people very rich."

Again, Tyoga told Chief Blue Coat what Governor Nott had said.

Chief Blue Coat responded, "Itchta eh aho chi-chaho."

Tyoga said to Nott, "Chief Blue Coat has some questions."

The Chief continued, "Tell me, Chief Nott, why would I want to part with the gifts given to the Mattaponi from our mother earth, for the treasures you promise? What would the Mattaponi buy with this money? Tobacco? Furs? Corn? All of these things we already possess."

Governor Nott did not reply.

Chief Blue Coat continued, "These things you ask the Mattaponi to sell are not ours to give. They do not belong to us. The fur of the beaver and fox belongs to the beaver and fox. The trees belong to the mountains and plains and forests. Who do you ask if they are for sale? They are not for sale. We will not give them to you because we cannot."

His doughy face pinking with anger, Governor Nott rose to his feet. "Look here, Chief. His Majesty will have the land upon which your village stands and there is nothing more to be said about it. If you do not vacate the land peacefully, His Majesty's Royal Guard will take it by force. Many of your men, women, and children will die. And for what? For wild animals that roam the forests in numbers uncountable? For trees that grow without end for as far as the eye can see? Chief, if you do not relinquish this land, your people will die for nothing at all."

Chief Blue Coat rose to his feet and said, "We will not leave our homeland. If we die at Passaunkack, we will not die in vain. We will die to protect what is not ours to give—yet belongs to all of the People. We will die to revere the memory of our ancestors. We will die to save our way of life." He placed his weathered hand on the head of his tomahawk. "And, we will not die alone."

With a wave of Governor Nott's hand, the Royal Guard snapped from their ceremonial columns, reassembled into battlefield rows, and shouldered their arms.

At the same instant, the Mattaponi notched their arrows and pulled their bowstrings taut. Brister rose to his feet with a Cherokee war club clutched in his huge, scarred hand.

Tyoga stepped in between Governor Nott and Chief Blue Coat. Calmly, he said, "Wait. There is another way."

Governor Nott raised his hand and the soldiers reformed their ranks.

The Mattaponi lowered their bows, but did not quiver their arrows. Brister stood his ground.

Gesturing to their seats, Tyoga said to Governor Nott and Chief Blue Coat. "Please. Sit down. Sit."

After they were both seated, Tyoga said, "Governor Nott, His Majesty wants to have access to the natural bounty of this new land that he has claimed for himself and his people." His inquisitive look at Governor Nott indicated that he wanted a brief acknowledgement of his statement.

"That is correct, sir," the Governor replied.

"Is it not true, sir, that if these riches could be conveyed to His Majesty at an expense less costly than that anticipated if taken down the Mattaponi to the York River and through the Chesapeake to the Atlantic Ocean, His Majesty the King would be greatly pleased?"

"That too is correct, good sir," the governor again replied.

"Would not the person who handed these great savings to His Majesty be applauded for his efforts and be rewarded with position, power, and treasure beyond his wildest dreams?"

"Pray, to the point, sir." Governor Nott sat on the edge of his seat.

Tyoga said, "Governor Nott, there is a land to the north where the game runs wild ten fold more abundant than what one may find here in the tidewater and foothills. There are enormous trees so abundant that no man has set eyes on them and soil so rich that no seed planted can refrain from producing unimaginable crops."

"Where is this place?" Governor Nott demanded. "What good is it to His Majesty if there are not waterways easily employed for conveyance?"

"Wait, Governor Nott. There is much more to be had here than easy access to the Atlantic Ocean."

"What more could there be, man?" Nott asked.

Tyoga looked to his left and then to his right. He knelt down close in front of the governor's chair. Again he looked from side to side, and motioned for the governor to lean forward so that he could better hear what he had to say.

"Governor, you have heard of the Ohio and St. Lawrence River Valley?" Tyoga asked.

"Yes, of course, I have. Everyone knows of this land, but I don't see what—"

"Then, you are aware—Are you not?—that the French are laying claim to vast tracts of land, and enlisting the allegiance of the Cayuga, the Oneida, and the Huron to claim the territory for the King of France?" Tyoga asked.

Governor Nott brought his hand to his chin and nodded.

Tyoga let the information sink in before continuing. "The Iroquois braves will be leaving Kaniataro Wanenneh to go on their winter hunt. Only women and children will be left behind in the village. A battalion of British soldiers could take over the entire region without firing a shot. The French would be displaced. The furs and trees and fertile lands could be claimed for His Majesty, and the St. Lawrence waterway could be secured by British garrisons all the way to the Atlantic. The route will cut a full week off of the Atlantic crossing from the bay and save your king millions of pounds over the years. Think about it, Governor. You could be responsible for presenting to His Majesty everything that he has been hoping to secure from his new lands, and, in the process, stop France's ambitions to expand its holdings on the continent."

Tyoga rose to his feet and took a step back toward Chief Blue Coat. "All of this will be yours if you agree to leave the Mattaponi lands in peace."

Chief Blue Coat and the Mattaponi looked at Tyoga with stoic stares of confidence that whatever it was that he was negotiating would be in their favor. They did not understand the words, but they clearly comprehended the importance of the conversation that had just taken place around the campfire.

After several minutes, Governor Nott rose to his feet. "You make a strong case, young man. I am quite certain that the House of Burgesses will agree to your proposal. They were not greatly enamoured of building a port at Passaunkack in the first place. I will, however, have to discuss this further with His Majesty's Lords. Tell me, who will lead us to this 'Kanan—taro' place? We will need guides and interpreters and provisions—"

"Kaniataro Wanenneh," Tyoga interrupted. "Guides and interpreters will be provided to you, but only if you agree—here and now—that you will not bother the Mattaponi, nor move to take their lands, until we have spoken again. I leave it to your wiles to assemble the necessary truck for the expedition. I am certain that it can all be arranged."

"Yes," the governor responded with a smile. "I believe that it can. It may take several years, but I believe it can."

With that he turned and strode with confidence toward the carriage. Carry, Tyler, and Spotswood were taking their places in line to follow him, when he abruptly stopped and turned toward Tyoga.

"I will send for you at the Mattaponi village when I am ready to speak with you again. Until that time, no harm will come to your ... friends."

Bowing his head in agreement, Tyoga turned to tell the Mattaponi that for the time being, their lands were safe from the voracious grasp of the King.

Chapter 53

Consequences of the Accord

As the sound of the Governor's carriage wheels disappeared down Center Street, Tyoga turned back toward the campfire and sat down next to Chief Blue Coat. The Chief had pushed aside the willow stump and was once again seated cross-legged on the softness of the bearskin rug.

The agreement was celebrated by Thunder Bow and the younger braves as a distinct coup. The consensus was that Tyoga had beaten the Governor at his own game. The Braves slapped him and each other on the back while planning the celebration they would have when they returned to Passaunkack.

Tyoga would be proclaimed the savior of their way of life and the deliverer of the Mattaponi people.

Chief Blue Coat and Tyoga were not so sure. After the others had gone to bed, Tyoga and the Chief stayed up until nearly dawn discussing what had occurred.

"My son, what you have done this night will be celebrated by the Mattaponi for many moons," the chief said. "Your treaty with the white eyes has preserved the Mattaponi way of life, and that is good thing. But no one can tell what the future may hold. What this treaty means for the Mattaponi, and for the Algonquin nation will not be known for many moons."

"I know, Blue Coat," Tyoga said. "Even more than that, the consequences of what I have done this day will reach far beyond the land of the Algonquin people. I have purchased the peace for the Mattaponi at the expense of another Indian nation. That it is the Iroquois who will suffer as the result of my plan makes the treachery no less vile. It is true that the Iroquois ran the Shawnee out of their homeland in the Ohio territory. It is also a fact that they instigated the attack on Tessenatee that wiped out an entire Cherokee Village of defenseless women and children. They continue to this day to murder young Algonquin braves who are doing nothing more than hunting game to feed their families. Still, these trespasses do not make what I have done a right thing to do."

The two men sat in silence for a long time listening to the quiet of the night. The summer sounds had been stilled by late fall's chill. The call of a distant owl wrapped the blackness in its plaintive moan.

When the dawn approached, the men stoked the fire to keep them warm and dry.

"Wahaya-Wacon scolds himself too harshly," Blue Coat said after thinking about Tyoga's words. "What has occurred in the past does not make what you have done right, my son. But it makes what you have done less wrong. Here is the trouble with the accord you have struck." He poked at the fire with an elm branch and watched the ashes rise in the updraft and scatter in all directions around the campsite. "That is the problem, my son."

"What, Blue Coat?" Tyoga asked. "The rising ashes are the problem?"

"Yes, that is exactly it," he replied. "Today, you have jabbed at the coals with a stick. Unlike the fire, you do not have the luxury of knowing what will rise from the coals. Here, sitting by the fire, we see what rises into the air. We can watch where the embers fall, and, should they ignite a tiny fire in some dried leaves or pine needles, we can run over and crush the flames out with our moccasins."

"But, Blue Coat," Tyoga argued, "it will take years before the plan I have proposed this night will come to pass. Other events will surely be more pressing to the King of England than some plot of land in the Iroquois nation. More than likely, this will be forgotten and nothing will come of it."

"More than likely," Blue Coat said shaking his head in agreement.

He jabbed at the fire one more time. Again the embers rose into the sky, dancing and whirling on unseen currents of air. Some fell to the ground and died a quiet, silent death.

"Look up, my son," Blue Coat said to him. "Do you see that some of the embers go dark but continue to rise?"

"Yes," Tyoga answered.

"They remain hot enough to start a fire still. But they do not let us know where—or when—they will land."

Tyoga stared back down into the fire, and thought of home.

Chapter 54

A Very Wealthy Man

In the years that followed Tyoga Weathersby's negotiations with
Governor Knott, his legend grew to near god-like status among the
tribes of the mid-Atlantic. From the villages of the Seminole tribes
in the Carolinas to the Massachusettes Indians in New England, he
and Trinity Jane were welcomed as honored guests. Tyoga's counsel was
sought and his legend revered.

They wanted for nothing.

Their smokehouse was always filled with elk, venison, turkey, and
quail. Their root cellars overflowed with potatoes, yams, corn, and squash.
Native American clothes beautifully fashioned from fox, mink, beaver,
and bear filled an entire outbuilding from floor to ceiling. Their cup-
boards were brimming with ornately decorated pottery and earthenware.

The colonies were equally grateful for Tyoga's negotiating skills with
the tribes of the tidewater that had enabled mutually beneficial trade and
commerce between the two nations.

The New England colonies, mid-Atlantic estates, and southern plantations rewarded him with gifts of the finest furnishings, linens, glass,
and silverware money could buy. Trinity's closets overflowed with the
latest colonial fashions. Tapestries from the Far East, ivory from Africa,
spices from the Orient, silks and porcelain from China and Zanzibar
were delivered to Twin Oaks from benefactors unknown.

Twin Oaks had become so large and prosperous that Tyoga divided the acreage into five sectors. An overseer assigned to each sector was given the responsibility of supervising the labor of the families homesteading on their section of land. Each family was allowed to keep what they produced on their twenty acres, and shared in a percentage of the profits from the crops they tended for the estate on the rest of their sector's land.

Field hands tended to the crops; shepherds watched over herds of sheep, goats, and cows. Carpenters maintained barns and corrals while constructing new outbuildings for stores and supplies.

In five short years, the Weathersby's estate had expanded into a small community of fifteen cottages that lined a cobbled lane about two hundred yards from the main house where workers with specific trade skills lived with their families. Carpenters, a blacksmith, a wheelwright, and a tanner occupied some of the modest homes. Other cottages housed the families of those who served in the main house.

The residents of the "Lane," as the cobbled road was called, were given a large communal plot of land to tend in which they grew the crops necessary to feed the Weathersbys and themselves.

The representative of the British government, Lord Governor Nott, proved to be an equally powerful ally of the young couple over the years since their meeting at Middle Plantation, now called Williamsburg.

Even though nothing had come of the scheme to rid the continent of the French and secure the riches of the New World for the British Crown, Governor Nott never forgot Tyoga's ingenious plan that had gained such favor with his King. By his invitation, Tyoga and Trinity had become frequent guests of the aristocracy in Willimasburg, Newport News, Yorktown, and Philadelphia.

The link that the charismatic couple provided between the profiteers in the fur, lumber, and mineral trades and the Native Americans with whom the more scrupulous felt obliged to deal proved invaluable. The esteem in which Tyoga was held throughout the Indian Nations provided immediate credibility for the Europeans' cause. Yet, the trust placed in him by his Native American brothers proved a wise investment because of his unwavering defense of their rights to the resources of their lands.

Tyoga and Trinity Jane had become statesmen, negotiators, interpreters of the laws of nature and man, and, in the end, king makers or dream breakers in the wild and open land.

The home that they had established in a glade on the banks of the Mattaponi River four and a half years ago had grown from a tiny survival shelter into one of the largest estates in Virginia.

Tyoga had become a very wealthy man. Life had been good for the Weathersby family until that cold, starry, winter night when the quiet was shattered by the unmistakable howl of Wahaya-Wacon.

Chapter 55

Return of Wahaya

The dowlful cry descended from the midnight shadows and blanketed the east slopes of the Appalachian Ridge across the Mattaponi River from Twin Oaks with an eerie prescience. Tyoga opened his eyes first, unsure of what he had just heard.

The second cry was not closer, but louder and less temperate in its missive.

Throwing off the heavy buffalo robes with a casual wave of his powerful arm, Tyoga placed his bare feet on the pine wood floor and scurried, bent at the waist, to peer out of the chiseled glass adorning their front door.

Sitting up in bed, Trinity anxiously asked, "Tyoga, what is it? What is wrong?"

"Shhh. Nothin'," he replied. "Listen."

As the third cry drifted down the mountainside to fill the glade, Tyoga turned to her and said with a grin so broad that it nearly stifled the words, "It's him. It's him. He's come back!"

Throwing open the door latch so forcefully that it nearly ripped from its mooring, he stepped barefoot onto the freezing granite stoop of the cabin's entranceway. Stopping, he cocked his head to listen. Jumping over the steps, he stood on the cold frost covered earth and peered off into the distance.

It was a clear night and the full moon lit the slopes of the Appalachians from Turner's Pass to Luther's Gap. Tyoga could see across the reeds and open plain that carpeted the foothills on the far side of the Mattaponi River all the way to the base of the mountain the Indians called Akwesasne.

He cupped his hands over his mouth to shout as loudly as he could. "Wahaya! Wahaya-Wacon! Itse ta eho la eh alo!"

Dropping his hands to his sides, he gazed off into the distance.

With a furrowed brow, he swiveled his head from side to side straining to hear the wolf's reply floating across the river and filling the glade with the news of his return. Just as he brought his hands to his mouth to call out again, he noticed a speck of gray bobbing above the tall grasses of the plain. Like a seagall floating on the surface of the Chesapeake before a storm, the gray speck bobbed along a course headed straight for Twin Oaks.

When Tyoga saw the flash of Wahaya's bushy tail rise above the savanna grass, he knew that his spirit guide had returned.

Tyoga ran to the fire pit in the front yard of the cabin and stoked the dying embers into roaring flames to welcome the wolf home after nearly a five-year separation. As the flames rose to bathe the treeline in its warming glow, Tyoga called out again, "Wahaya! Itse ta eho!"

He turned to see Trinity standing in the doorway of the cabin wrapped in the red blanket. "T.J., it's Wahaya. He's come back to me." He turned back to face the distant mountains.

Trinity had heard the true story about Tyoga's encounter with the Runion wolf pack. She learned first hand that the stories told around campfires about the battle had been so embellished that they had become no more than a fuzzy reflection of the truth.

What had really taken place on that night so long ago was far more powerful than any story could ever recount.

Tyoga had told her the story about losing himself in the dark chasm of the wolf's endless eyes with a reverence and respect that bordered on a religious-like worship of the mighty beast. Words failed him whenever he tried to explain how the magnificence of the wolf filled him with the call of the wild that infused his heart and ignited his soul.

The bond between man and beast was inexplicable and powerful beyond measure.

She also had heard Tyoga tell the tale of releasing Sunlei to love another man if that was fate's call, and how he had sent Wahaya to protect and defend her from harm. The wolf's return could only mean that Sunlei was settled and happy and safe, or that she was dead.

He would not leave her unless she were dead, Trinity thought to herself.

She felt her heart skip a beat as the new life growing within her nudged its awareness of her fright. *Can he be smart enough to know that she is in danger beyond his means to help her, and that he has returned to take Tyoga away from me?* She placed her hand over her not yet burgeoning abdomen and rubbed gently. "Don't worry, Little One," she said out loud. "He will not leave us."

Hearing Wahaya's splash as he cast himself into the river to swim to be by his side sent Tyoga running toward the shore. When he got beyond the light of the fire, he thought better about surprising the wolf in the dark with his unexpected presence and slowly backed into the firelight. He heard Wahaya pause on the near bank to shake himself dry, and finally saw the brilliant, beautiful orbs of his glowing amber eyes emerge from the night as he walked slowly toward the fire.

Tyoga heard but did not respond to Trinity's gasp at the sight of his long lost friend.

While she had heard Tyoga tell the tales, she had never witnessed the magnificence of Wahaya-Wacon. Trinity found him terrifyingly large and unimaginably muscular. His chest was heaving from the strenuous run across the marsh and his tongue was dripping a viscous fluid onto the ground. He was much taller than any wolf she had ever seen. If he were standing next to her, she could have rested her elbows on the top of his head. His eyes were mesmerizing. She watched them burn through the blackness as they fixed upon his soul mate. She wanted to look away, but she could not. She brought her tiny hand to her mouth, wrapped her other around her waist and remained frozen to the cabin door.

Tyoga's first impulse was to run toward his old friend and greet him like he would a lost pet. Instead he held himself in check. This was the apex predator, Wahaya-Wacon.

It was the right thing to do.

Wahaya did not approach like a pet reunited with his owner. With hesitance, he stepped into the glow of the firelight and sat.

Tyoga knelt down onto one knee so that Wahaya's head was just slightly above his own.

At first, he appeared unchanged. A little thinner than Tyoga remembered, but still a magnificent animal. When he stood to once again shake the water from his coat, Tyoga noticed a linear patch of missing fur that ran nearly the length of his left haunch. His right shoulder bore the scar of a large puncture wound. Wahaya had fought hard – and often. It was clear to Tyoga that these were wounds inflicted by hatchet, spear and arrow. Still proud, strong, and resolute in his knowing, Wahaya reflected the acceptance of the battle scars without judgement or animosity. The affirmation had sustained his kind for time immemorial.

His eyes gave no hint about why he had returned. He broke the lock of their stare and flicked his eyes toward Trinity standing in the cabin door. He licked his lips and Tyoga could tell that he was hungry.

"Jayo si has, Wahaya?" Tyoga asked.

Standing up slowly, he walked casually, but confidently, over to the smokehouse and returned with the haunch of a recently butchered deer. With equal confidence, he came toward the wolf to lay it at his feet. At Tyoga's approach, the wolf stood up and cautiously backed away.

"Okay. Okay." Tyoga set the haunch down and stepped back toward the fire. When he had created enough space between himself and the meat, the wolf came forward, picked it up in his jaws and trotted off into the darkness.

"Well, what do you think of that, Trinity Jane?" Tyoga asked while watching the wolf disappear into the night. "Wahaya has returned."

He turned toward the door of the cabin with a big contented smile beaming from his face.

The doorway was empty.

Chapter 56

She's Alive

The next morning Tyoga was up before sunrise. He and Trinity Jane had been living as wealthy white colonists ever since Twin Oaks took its place on the frontier as a successful business concern.

As such, they had dressed the part every morning. Trinity's dresses had gone from linen to taffeta, while Tyoga's waistcoats were tailor-made of satin and lace.

Today, Tyoga opened his dresser drawer and pulled out his doeskin britches and fringed buckskin tunic. After pulling on his elk moccasins, he grabbed his long rifle and powder horn, and headed for the door. He was reaching for the latch, when he heard Trinity's voice call from their bedroom.

Putting on her silken robe, she rushed down the hall. "Tyoga, wait! Where are you going so early in the morning?"

He turned around to face her. "Trinity, Wahaya is back. You saw him last night."

"I did."

"Don't you want to know why he has returned? Aren't you curious about what this means?

"I am only curious about what you think it means, Tyoga?"

When he did not answer, she said, "The reason that the wolf has returned to you means nothing to me. Nor should it matter to you. How many times have you told me that the "why" of things makes no difference at all? How many times have you told me that events unfold exactly as they should and to think that we are capable of changing outcomes is like thinking that throwing a pebble in the Mattaponi is going to change its course? Sunlei is dead, or she is alive. She is happy in her life, or she is sad. She has forgotten you, or she has not. None of these things can you change."

"No, Trinity!" Tyoga said more passionately than he meant to. "I'm sorry," he apologized right away when he saw the startled expression on her face. "I didn't mean to shout, but this is important, Trinity. This matters. Wahaya has returned for a reason. There is sense to be made of this in the ways of the promise. The return is more than the wolf coming back. It means something that I don't yet understand. All I know is that I have to try to figure it out."

He turned and walked toward the door, just as he heard the pitter patter of little feet and a tiny voice ask, "Why is Papa shouting, Mama? What's the matter?"

Trinity stooped down to pick up Joshia. She clutched him to her bosom while he threw his legs around her waist and locked his ankles in the small of her back. "That's what your papa is trying to figure out, kanunu (little frog)." She peered over the top of his head.

Tyoga opened the front door. He hesitated for just a moment before closing it softly behind him. He jogged down the stone steps two at a time.

Wide-eyed with excitement, Brister, Twin Oaks' foreman and Tyoga's right hand man, met him at the bottom of the porch steps. "Massa Ty," he nearly shouted while marching after him with that awkward hitch in his stride. "Massa Ty," he continued trying to get him to stop to listen.

Tyoga slowed down his pace. "Yes, Brister, what is it?"

"I tink me see a wolf, Massa Ty. I never seen da wolf—Wahaya-Wacon—but las' night late, late, me tink I seen him sho' enough."

Tyoga stopped and waited for Brister to catch up. He was so anxious that someone share his excitement at the return of his old friend that he placed both hands on his shoulders and said with a big smile on his face, "You did. You did see Wahaya-Wacon last night, Brister. Isn't it wonderful? He's returned to me after all of this time."

"Yes, Massa," Brister said. "Me tink dis very good ting. But, Massa, what he come back mean, Massa Ty? What tink it mean he come back?"

Tyoga released his grip on Brister's shoulders and looked off toward the woods to the east. "I don't know, Brister. I just don't know," he said. "But I aim to find out. Come on."

With that the men hurried along the cobblestone way that had become Cottage Lane, and cut through an alleyway between the Cooper's workshop and the tannery. The tiny village of Twin Oaks was just waking up and the sounds filling the Lane were those of the tradesmen preparing for the day.

The blacksmith, a huge Nigerian with arms that dwarfed even Tyoga's, waved a blackened, calloused hand toward the two men as they hurried along their way.

"Monin' Massa Ty," he called out with a thin reedy voice that did not match his three-hundred pound frame.

"Good morning, Sabu." Tyoga waved with a smile.

"Makin' dos tongs for Ginny today," he said.

"Good, good, Sabu. We mustn't vex Ginny."

"No-sa! No-sa, we keep her 'appy, long she keep makin' dat conebread like she do," Sabu said with a wide toothy grin.

Tyoga stuck his hand high in the air as a gesture of absolute agreement.

Ginny, the four-foot-two 'matron de cuisine' who oversaw food preparations at Twin Oaks, made the best cornbread in all of Virginia.

It was about three-hundred yards from Cottage Lane to the edge of the woods. Along the way, they scared up a huge flock of wild turkeys. When about thirty of the beautiful birds took to the air all at once, the sound of their massive wings beating against the heavy morning air created a tumultuous sound as they passed overhead. Turkeys don't fly far, but they fly really hard. Before they reached the forest, a flock of deer, fifty strong, stood their ground to watch impassively as the two walked by.

Just before they entered the underbrush that edged the mighty pines and elm trees, Tyoga stopped suddenly in his tracks.

"Wus da matta, Massa?" Brister asked. "You hear somthin'?"

Holding his hand out in a gesture to quiet Brister, Tyoga closed his eyes and said softly, "No. Not hear, but feel. I feel him. He's close by. Stay here."

Without answering, Brister stood stone still. He watched Tyoga disappear into the woods. Uneasy about not being able to watch over him, Brister took ten more steps toward the brush line to stand on tiptoe and peer over the bushes and scrub pines to look for his friend. Unable to see him, he sat on the ground to wait.

After a ten minute hike into the woods, Tyoga stopped at a granite boulder at the base of an ancient pine tree. He climbed to the top of the rock and sat in the silence of the deep primal forest.

Closing his eyes, he emptied his mind and basked in the silence that spoke to him in time and depth and texture. Smiling, he heard the messages carried in the silence. He did not understand how it happened. He only knew that he understood.

When he felt him near, he opened his eyes.

Standing in a clearing twenty feet away was the magnificent Wahaya-Wacon. He was even more startling in the light of day.

Now that he could see him more clearly, Tyoga was astonished that the wolf appeared as if he had not aged a single day since they were last together at the entrance to the cave. The battles he had fought had taken a toll in flesh and hide, but if anything, Wahaya-Wacon looked stronger and more powerful than could possibly be explained by any measure understood in terms of the passage of time.

His fur was thick and lustrous save those spots where it had been lost to wound and scar. The light danced off of his coat's silver tips like the blinding sparkle from the surface of a mountain lake in the noonday sun. His haunches were more muscular and his chest muscles seemed to have doubled in size. He stood taller, and the girth of his neck left little demarcation between his head and back.

His eyes sizzled with an intensity that Tyoga could not decipher.

He dropped his head a bit, which was a sign of welcome and submission; and took four sharp steps toward him. Tyoga jumped down from his perch, but did not venture toward the wolf.

Looking up into Tyoga's face, Wahaya stepped up to brush his head against his upper thigh in a gesture of affection and trust that he had never allowed before.

Overcome with Wahaya's show of affection, Tyoga reached down and cradled the wolf's head in his hands. The wolf pushed against his hands with an equal pressure that conveyed a message that no words could speak. He rubbed the length of his body against Tyoga's upper leg, which nearly pushed him over with his spirited re-bonding.

It hit Tyoga like a cold winter wind on his bare arms. He furrowed his brow, knelt before the beast, and asked, "Wahaya, what is it? Why have you returned?"

The wolf circled Tyoga twice before sitting down at his feet, facing the northwest. Pivoting on his knee so that he was facing the same direction, Tyoga put his arm around the wolf's neck and looked through the pines. He looked into Wahaya's eyes. The wolf licked his lips and sighed a haunting moan.

His eyes gave Tyoga no clue.

"Why did you leave Sunlei, Wahaya? Is she—is she alive?" he asked without looking at the wolf.

The tension in the wolf's body while he continued to stare intently toward the northwest conveyed the answer that he had hoped for.

She was still alive.

"Okay. Okay, Wahaya." Tyoga patted the wolf's back. "I reckon you'll let me know in your own good time."

The wolf stood and took several steps toward the edge of the woods.

"Let's go home," Tyoga said.

The two walked toward the cabin side-by-side.

Chapter 57

Wild Restlessness

The harvest had been the best in years. The corn cribs overflowed with the bounty. Twin Oaks coffers were filled with pounds in payment for the food stuffs and fodder that the estate had supplied to farms, plantations, and towns dotting the tidewater and lining the Atlantic coast. From the Carolinas to New York, flour from Twin Oaks' grist mill, hay and straw for livestock, and produce for winter larder traveled by pack mule, wagons, and barges to Chatham Hill, Pointer's Landing, Canterbury and Whitehall. Game was so plentiful that an addition had to be built onto the smokehouse to cure all of the meat the families living on Twin Oaks gave to Tyoga and Trinity Jane. Knowing that they could come and get whatever meat they needed to feed their families throughout the winter, the Indians' hunting parties dropped game off at the smokehouse.

A generous man, Tyoga helped those in need no matter their race, color, creed, or tribe. He denied no man food and shelter, and was willing to pay an honest wage for an honest day's work. He was held in high regard, lavished with gifts of tribute and thanks, and protected by an unspoken allegiance with the Native Americans that shielded his estate from speculators, squatters, and raids from distant tribes. His kindness had been repaid many times.

Forever wild, Wahaya remained on the outskirts of the Twin Oaks compound and spent most of his time on the eastern slopes of the mountain on the far side of the Mattaponi. He was covetous of the time he and Tyoga spent together, and reluctantly tolerated intrusions by others. He had grown to know the children and recognized them as members of his human pack. Joshia was five years old and their daughter, Rebecca Jane, was two. Sometimes, he would hide in the tall grasses on the banks of the Mattaponi to keep a protective eye upon them when they were in the yard.

He had come to tolerate Brister, but shunned the company of others almost completely.

When Tyoga traveled through the backwoods with others at his side, the wolf followed behind at a great distance. Tyoga's traveling companions knew that he was always lurking in the shadows, but they made no effort to catch a glimpse of him. When Tyoga visited villages and towns to conduct business, Wahaya would hide in the omnipresent divide that separates the tame from the wild in the underbrush.

On a cool, late autumn evening in November, Tyoga and Brister were sitting in an ornate gazebo along the banks of the Mattaponi. One of his favorite spots, Tyoga would sit for hours staring into the distant mountains, and feeling the promise song fill his heart.

The plaintive wail of the wolf descending to the water's edge, spurred Brister to ask, "Massa-Ty, you notice sumpin different 'bout da wuf?" His English had improved over the years, but he still had a strong accent and difficulty with tense and gender.

"I have, Brister," Tyoga replied. "Yes, I have."

"What wrong you tink?"

"I don't know for sure, but he has been awfully restless. I hear him calling from as far away as Lasiter's Ridge. That has to be about seven miles northwest of here."

"'N da other evnin late, by da big house, he jes keep lookin' to da west. His head no move. Jes' look west. ."

"I don't want you to say anything to 'Missy Jane,' but I'm thinkin' he wants me to go back over the mountains with him." Tyoga paused, stood, and walked over to the railing of the gazebo. "Someone may need me," he whispered to the wind.

Since his arrival in the land of the Mattaponi, Tyoga had only spoken about Sunlei to Trinity Jane. Others had learned of his past through the legend that had grown around him. The loss of Sunlei and the brutal attack upon Seven Arrows that caused her to be sent away had morphed through time and interpretation into a story that reflected little of the truth. Some stories had Tyoga slitting Seven Arrows's throat, while others told of his demise by the fangs of Wahaya-Wacon.

The truth was quite different from the wild tales. Tyoga never let anyone know that he knew who had slit Seven Arrows's throat.

Although his old life at South Henge and Tuckareegee seemed a lifetime ago, he thought about home, and her, more frequently than he wished to admit.

Tyoga didn't share with Brister that he had noticed a great deal more about Wahaya's behavior than simply staring to the West. Signs of his restlessness and his vocal imploring for Tyoga to follow him over the mountains were far from subtle cues.

Something was amiss. He felt it in the breeze and smelled it pouring over the whispering pines.

The reason for Wahaya-Wacon's restlessness would become apparent very soon.

Chapter 58

Dreams of a Different Life

It was nearly a perfect early-winter's day in the later part of November. The golden maple and crimson oak leaves left clinging to the trees twisted in the breeze like tiny flags celebrating a life, well lived, but destined nonetheless to the ravages of decay.

Tyoga spent the day hiking to a favorite campsite on the shores of a beaver dam about seven miles from Twin Oaks. He left the well-worn routes traveled by land speculators with their mules and clanking metal pots and pans to venture along dark, canopied game trails as old as the mountains themselves.

With all of the land and wealth he had accumulated, he would give it all away in an instant to recapture the joys of his unfettered youth. He missed the old days when he and Tes Qua used to roam the Appalachians as wild as the eagles circling overhead and as care free as the frolicking squirrels. Even though he had a wonderful life—filled with the riches others worked a lifetime to possess: land, money, position, fame, and a wonderful companion who had given him two beautiful children—he would part with it all for just one more day running naked and free through the village of Tuckareegee with Sunlei and Tes Qua by his side.

He walked on, lost in his private thoughts.

Arriving at the beaver dam campsite in the evening, he started a fire, ate his venison jerky, turkey, squash, and corn, and lay back on the soft red blanket that had been his constant traveling companion for so many years. It was the red blanket that Prairie Day had given to Sunlei to pack for him when they crossed the mountains to attend the Shawnee council all those years ago. It was the same red blanket that he had covered Sunlei with when he carried her to his hideaway after rescuing her from the Shawnee braves searching for her after Seven Arrows's throat had been cut. It was the same red blanket that Trinity Jane had around her shoulders when she stood in the doorway of Twin Oaks on the cold moonlit night when Wahaya returned.

He turned on his side and brought the corner of the blanket to his nose and inhaled deeply. He wasn't sure if he was searching for a reminder of Sunlei or Trinity Jane.

Tyoga struggled to understand why circumstance had sentenced him to a life not of his choosing.

How different my life might have been if the wolf had never come into it. What would my life have been like with Sunlei by my side? How gifted and beautiful would our children have been? What doors would her beauty and command of the English language have opened for me? What would it have been like to open my eyes in the morning and see the dawn kissing her beautiful face?

"In all things, there are but two outcomes." Tyoga shook his head as he looked over at Wahaya who was pacing nervously just beyond the firelight.

Tyoga lay on the red blanket and stared up into the heavens above. The gentle swaying of the pine boughs and the chirping of the tree frogs calmed his spirit and soothed his soul.

He remembered his awakening as a young boy of six while standing next to his papa on Carter's Rock. He understood better than most that there was never any guarantee that life would unfold as one may wish. Indeed, the lesson of the promise was exactly the opposite. Therein lay the wisdom of knowing. The lesson of the promise was to accept the realities of the life one is given, and to passionately embrace the gifts bestowed for they are fleeting and fragile.

His faint smile revealed the awareness that he had caught himself questioning the natural order of things and the ways that unfold simply because they must. Chuckling, he whispered out loud, "The answer makes no difference at all."

Wahaya had been restless the entire time that they were hiking through the mountains. He would bolt ahead on the trail, turn around, and beckon Tyoga to follow him with a whining bark that was impossible to misinterpret. When Tyoga did not increase his pace, the wolf would skamper back, circle in front of him, and race ahead while imploring him to follow.

Restless now, he would not sit still. A nearly imperceptible high-pitched whine emanated from his throat, and would stop only when he needed to listen intently.

"What is it, Wahaya? What do you hear?" Tyoga sat up and lay his flintlock across his lap.

When the wolf's whine changed into an aggressive growl, Tyoga got to his knees and cocked the lock on his weapon. With a single fluid leap, Wahaya poured silently into the underbrush. Tyoga was right behind.

When he was clear of the light from his fire, he pressed his body against the trunk of an enormous hickory tree, and listened intently for any sound that might give a predator—or person—away.

The tree frogs and crickets were still blanketing the night with their incessant buzz. Whatever had spooked Wahaya was pretty far away. Tyoga heard Wahaya thunder over the ridge to the west. He ran back to the campsite, grabbed his powder horn and shot bag, and disappeared into the darkness of the Appalachian night.

Chapter 59

Reunion

It was a clear, moonless night. Had the transformation not already begun, Tyoga would have had a difficult time finding his way. As the muscles in his arms, chest, and thighs hardened with the blood that engorged them with readiness, his amber glowing eyes pierced the darkness like a flaming arrow showing him the way. His senses were alive with the rhythm of the night.

Running along a ledge that was higher up on the slope of the mountainside, Wahaya was a hundred yards ahead of him. The wolf silently sliced through the underbrush like an eel in the mudflats.

Tyoga caught up to him on a rocky ledge overlooking a fifty-foot drop straight down into a boulder strewn canyon.

His ears were piqued, Wahaya was staring intently down through the treetops to the canyon floor below. His concentration was broken for only a moment when Tyoga scurried onto the ledge and lay on his belly beside him.

Tyoga heard them, too.

Voices were bouncing along the dark granite canyon walls. Snippets of conversation escaped through the trees in an undecipherable fluid drone. The speakers were too far away for their words to be understood, but Tyoga could hear enough to know that they were not speaking English.

He slithered on his belly so that his head hung over the ledge and cocked his head in the direction from which the voices seemed to be coming. He knew this canyon well. It was in the shape of a crescent moon and the curvature of the canyon walls made it difficult to see very far in either direction. Before he pushed himself back from the precipice, he felt the wolf leap over his back and charge along the ridge in the direction of the voices.

He stopped himself from crying out, "Stop, Wahaya! Wait!" He had not yet descended into the depths of feral behavior responsible for his murderous rampage against the Shawnee braves nearly six years ago. Tyoga wanted to give some rational thought to what may await him in the gorge before releasing himself to the animal instincts that kept him alive.

Before he had time to think, he was barreling along the ridge at top speed while following behind the thundering paws of Wahaya-Wacon. Together, they descended toward the canyon floor.

He caught up to the wolf at a spot along the ridge that was directly above the campsite of the Indian party. There was no way to see down into the canyon from this vantage point, as there was a slight rise separating them from the wall of the gorge.

The wolf was sitting on his haunches with his head cocked so that he could listen more intently to the voices coming from below. His body was relaxed, his posture made him appear more dog than wolf.

Tyoga knelt at his side and peered up at the rise that was separating them from a clear view into the campsite.

The voices were clearer.

They were speaking Cherokee.

To get to the canyon floor, they would have to continue past the point above the Cherokee campsite, and follow the ridge's descent to the west.

Recognizing the Cherokee, Tyoga's mind was racing. He was anxious to get into the canyon to discover who these people were.

The wolf did not race off in front of Tyoga this time, but waited for him.

They hiked along the ridge until they rounded some large boulders and entered the narrow granite corridor. Once in the canyon, there would be no escape. There was one way in, and one way out.

Concealing himself behind rockslides, Tyoga approached the campsite with caution until he could get near enough to the Cherokee to determine their origin and intent.

The voices grew louder as he crept forward. Slipping from one hiding place to the next, he zig-zagged across the canyon. He looked behind him to see if the wolf was still close, but he was nowhere to be seen.

He worked his away along the canyon walls until he was about fifty feet from the band of Cherokee. The curvature of the canyon kept them out of view, but he could hear the voices clearly now. To his amazement, they were speaking Tsalagi and using the dialect of the Ani-Unwiya.

"Te ya wi-stan ge to *(How much farther)*?" Tyoga heard a familiar female voice ask.

"Gay-de ye. Tah leh ya d'sge pem-i-can *(Pass me some more pemican)*," he heard another voice say.

"Da gi o wiga, Mattaponi, su-na-lei *(Will we reach Mattaponi, tomorrow)*?"

When Tyoga heard the English reply, "I reckon," his hands went numb and his head swirled.

His eyes filled with tears and the swelling in his throat made it impossible for him to utter a sound. He raised his trembling hands to his face, and buried his head to muffle his sobs of joy. Listening to the familiar voices around the corner, he allowed the tears to freely stream down his face. Filled with an indescribable joy, he dared not move for fear that the moment would die. After finding the strength to stand, he stepped around the bend in the canyon wall into the light of their campfire.

He could not speak a single word.

The first to see him standing in shadows of the firelight was Walking Bird. When she dropped the pouch of Pemican she was handing to Night Bear, all the braves instinctively reached for their weapons. They did not know what to make of the expression on her face, until they heard her breathlessly whisper, "Tyoga."

Tes Qua was sitting with his back to him. He looked up into Walking Bird's face and saw the tears welling up in her eyes. Remaining seated, he slowly turned to face his life-long friend and savior, Tyoga Weathersby, glowing in the flickering shadows of their campfire.

Tyoga could not move.

Rising slowly to his feet, Tes Qua stepped over the log upon which he had been seated and began walking toward Tyoga. As he approached, a figure appeared overhead and to his left. On a rocky outcropping about twenty feet above the canyon floor, Wahaya-Wacon's silver mane sparkled in the fire's rising glow. Tes Qua peered up at the wolf for only a second before continuing his slow march toward Tyoga.

"O-si yu, U-do." Tes Qua said as he placed his hand upon Tyoga's shoulder.

"O-si yu. U-do, Tes Qua Ta Wa," replied Tyoga while looking into his brother's tearing brown eyes.

As the two embraced in the manly bear-hug that, by force and impact, permits an otherwise unacceptable display of intimate contact and emotional exposure, Tes Qua whispered in Tyoga's ear, "So, he picks this night to show himself to me."

"Don't question him, my friend," Tyoga said. "There is a reason for all things."

Chapter 60

The Hot Embers Land

Tyoga stayed with his friends in their canyon camp to talk through the night.

He learned that Tes Qua and Walking Bird were married in the spring of 1701, and they had two strong boys, Two Clouds and White Bull. His cousin, Walks Alone, who had taken Sunlei to the Chickamawgua, married Morning Sky and they moved to Tuckareegee last year.

Tes Qua told Tyoga about the death of his father, Nine Moons, and how devastated he was that his precious daughter, Sunlei, was not with him when he passed. Their mother, Wind Song, had moved in with her brother, White Feather, and was doing well.

Tes Qua paused when he added that Prairie Day had become the bride of Talking Crow, the son of the chief of the Black Water Cherokee, the northern most member of the five-tribe confederation. They were the buffer clan between the mid-Atlantic Cherokee nation and the Iroquois.

Tyoga looked up at the sliver of sky that could be seen from the depths of the gorge.

Tes Qua guessed that something had happened between Prairie Day and Tyoga. He was even suspicious when it took Tyoga so long to return from Green Rock Cove the day that they were summoned to Chief Silver Cloud's lodge, but he never asked. He gave Tyoga a few minutes to come to terms with Prairie Day's marriage, before adding, "Tyoga. There is something else that I must tell you."

Tyoga veered his gaze from the sky to him, and asked, "What is it, my brother?"

"Do you remember that night on the overlook when you told me and Prairie Day that you would leave the mountain?" Tes Qua asked.

Tyoga nodded.

"Do you remember what Prairie Day told you about Seven Arrows?" Tes Qua continued.

"She said that he was not dead. She told us that his spirit lived," Tyoga recalled.

"She was right," Tes Qua said matter of factly.

"I know, Tes Qua," Tyoga replied. "Seven Arrows is now the Chief of the South Fork Shawnee. I have known this for a long time, my brother. And still I do not understand how it is that he survived such an attack. I heard his men screaming that his throat was cut and that he was dead. How is it that he is still alive?"

"I don't know the answer to that, my brother. All that I can tell you is that when his body was placed at the feet of his Father, Chief Yellow Robe, the breath had not yet left his body. It is said that his hatred for you and Wahaya-Wacon is so great—he will not die until you and Wahaya-Wacon are punished for the death of his brothers. His revenge was to be his coupling with Sunlei. That did not come to pass. The debt that he now demands ..." Tes Qua paused, "is the head of Wahaya-Wacon."

"Why? Why kill the wolf?" Tyoga demanded. "Why doesn't he come after me?"

"Because, my brother," Tes Qua replied, "to kill the wolf is to destroy your soul. And you know as well as I that it is impossible for a band of Shawnee dog soldiers to get within a day's hard march of Twin Oaks. You and your family are protected by all of the Algonquin in the tidewater."

Tyoga nodded his head and said, "I know, Tes Qua. Seven Arrows has tried many times to get to me and my family. He has lost many braves in the attempt." They sat silently staring into the flames of the oak wood fire.

As the night wore on, the Ani-Unwiya listened politely while Tyoga recounted his harrowing travels across the Appalachians, and how Trinity Jane and his friends, the Mattaponi, had saved his life.

He told them about his two children, Joshia Thomas and Rebecca Jane, with an enthusiasm tempered by the history he shared with his audience. It was not that Tyoga was ashamed of his children, but their existence was tangible proof of betrayal of the love they all knew he held in his heart for Sunlei.

There was no need for shame, and they did not hold his being a man with needs and desires that required attention against him. It was the natural course of a relationship between a man and a woman. Even casual dalliances often ended with like results.

All that mattered was that he had a family, and that he was a good father and provider.

It was not necessary for Tyoga to boast of his success. That word had crossed the mountains with a solitary trapper or a band of Algonquin braves passing through Tuckareegee.

They were proud of his accomplishments and pleased with his success. They envied him not at all.

Tyoga knew that his Cherokee friends had not traveled across the mountains risking the winter cold and threat of storms simply for a reunion and to share good news. As is the Indian way, good manners demanded a cheerful exchange at their reuniting. Even though Tyoga was anxious to hear the true reason for their journey, he adhered to Native American custom and spent four hours exchanging happy news before pressing the point.

"The news that you bring to me makes my heart glad, my brother," Tyoga said to Tes Qua. "But surely you have not traveled all this way just to speak of these matters. Tell me. Is there any news of Sunlei?"

"There is, my brother," Tes 'A replied. "We know where she is. She is in great danger."

At this news, Tyoga felt his spine stiffen and his energy surge. He needed to know more. There was no need for him to ask.

Tes Qua continued, "She is living in the land of the Iroquois in the village of Kaniataro along the banks of the St. Lawrence River—very close to Lake Champlain."

Tes Qua paused to give Tyoga time to process what he was saying, and to allow him to brace himself for the news that he was certain he wanted to know.

Tes Qua looked at the ground. "She has been taken by the Chief of the Iroquois nation." He stopped and bowed his head.

Tyoga gazed off toward the canyon wall and whispered, "Quisquis?"

When Tes Qua did not answer, Tyoga shut his eyes in sorrow and disbelief.

Quisquis was a fierce and mighty Iroquois warrior whose cruelty in battle and barbaric treatment of prisoners was known and feared by Indians and settlers alike. He had many wives and children. He had been known to dispatch female offspring by bashing their heads against a boulder or tree trunk when the balance of male to female children was not to his liking. His wives who consistently gave birth to baby girls often met the same fate.

Both men stared silently into the fire for a long time. Tyoga finally broke the silence. "I should have tried to find her, Tes A. I should have tried."

"No, my brother," Tes Qua replied. "There was nothing that you—or the men of Tuckareegee—could have done."

"What do you mean, Tes?" Tyoga asked with a look of incredulity in his eyes.

Tes Qua paused for a moment, and replied, "When I could stand not knowing what had become of her any longer, I assembled a hunting party in defiance of Silver Cloud's wishes, and set out to find her. We traveled first to see Lone Bear in the village of Chickamaugua. We learned that Sunlei forced the People to allow her and Wahaya to leave the village. Lone Bear told us that she did it to protect the lives of his family and the Chickamaugua People. The Shawnee discovered that Sunlei was with the Chickamaugua, and a war party did arrive at the village to take her. When they learned that she had escaped, the Shawnee set Lone Bear's lodge on fire. Still, no one would tell them that Lone Bear's son, Kicking Elk, had but two days earlier taken Sunlei under the cover of darkness toward the northwest and the land of the Delaware."

"But, Tes A, that's toward the Iroquois," Tyoga said in disbelief.

"Exactly, Ty. Lone Bear was sure that the Shawnee would never follow them into the land of the Iroquois. It was risky for us as well. Yet, we were determined to find her, so we began our trek to the Ohio valley. We followed the Kanawha Trail and were very near to Chillicothe when we came upon a Cherokee hunting party camped south of the Scioto River. They told us that Sunlei and Kicking Elk were captured by a band of Cuyahoga Iroquois months before our arrival. The Braves told us that Kicking Elk's rotting, burned remains were found nailed to a tree. There was no sign of Sunlei."

Tes Qua stopped while Tyoga closed his eyes to grimace at the thought of Lone Bear sacrificing his son to secure Sunlei's safety. It must have been a horrible death. Sunlei must have witnessed it with her own eyes.

Tes Qua said, "We were determined to carry on our search for my sister. We left the Kanawha Trail and headed north along the banks of the Ohio River. We had not traveled a full day when we came upon many French marching to the south. We jumped from the trail and hid in the bushes until they passed us by. We journeyed on to where the Hockhocking River branches to the north from the Ohio, and found a French encampment of several hundred men. Iroquois walked among the French soldiers as if they were part of their army. We were too few, and were surrounded everywhere by the French and Iroquois. We waited until darkness, and ran from Ohio as quickly as our feet would carry us. We did the best we could." He searched Tyoga's eyes for reassurance that the tiny band of Cherokee Braves had made the right decision. "At least, we tried."

Tyoga put his hand on Tes Qua's shoulder and said, "I know you did, Tes. You made the right decision."

In the quiet of the canyon, they listened to the crackle of the dried pine as it burned to white hot ash.

Tes Qua continued, "A year ago, Prairie Day's husband, Talking Crow, ventured north into the land of the Iroquois to trade with the Seneca. He brought word back that Sunlei had been living among them along the northern shore of Cayuga Lake for about three years. They treated her well and she was content. But when Quisquis found out that she was with the Seneca, he made them give her to the Kanetairo

Iroquois under threat of war. He took her away, and she has been with him ever since.

Wahaya remained on the rocky outcropping overhead. He was illuminated by the light of fire only when a flare of pine pitch launched glowing ash toward the sky.

He was in plain sight, but neither man took notice. They were lost in their own thoughts.

Tes Qua was summoning the courage to tell Tyoga the rest of the story. He finally broke the silence. "There is more, my brother. The French have signed treaties with the Iroquois. They have given them many guns and much whiskey in exchange for their word to fight with them against the British. Chief Quisquis and all the braves in the village will leave Kaniataro to go south to their winter hunting grounds. The village will be left unprotected except for a small group of French soldiers. While it is the Indian way to allow an unprotected village to remain in peace while the braves are away on the winter hunt, the English are not bound by our ways. The British have assembled many soldiers. They are on their way to take the Iroquois land of Kaniataro Wanenneh."

Tes Qua paused once again to give Tyoga another moment to understand his words.

"Tyoga," Tes Qua continued. "We have to get Sunlei out of Kaniataro. The British soldiers are already assembling in Albany. We hear that they will begin the march north very soon. They will be in the land of the Iriquois when the braves have left the village unprotected. The orders from their great father are to kill everyone, the French soldiers protecting the village, old men, women, and all of the children in the Kaniataro. They will burn the entire village to the ground and leave nothing remaining for Quisquis to rule."

The news Tes Qua shared made Tyoga's blood run cold.

The plan that he had proposed to Governor Nott had the British taking over Kaniataro without firing a shot. It was to be a bloodless coup. The order to kill everyone left in the village while the warriors were away was little more than a plan for a massacre. It had taken all those years to plan the attack, assemble the soldiers and resources, and recruit the guides and interpreters.

By God, the British had done it.

But the plan Tyoga had outlined for the British to wrest control of Iroquois land from the French, and secure a quicker trans-Atlantic voyage for shipping the riches of the New World to Europe never included the murder of innocent women and children.

I had sent Sunlei away to keep her safe, but instead devised the very plan that has condemned her to death. What did I miss? Why didn't I anticipate something like this happening? If the lesson of the promise is that in all things there are but two outcomes, and that decisions made are always right because the end result is exactly as it was meant to be, how is it the right thing to do if my plan for securing the Mattaponi lands ends up killing the woman I love?

He knew better than to question why, but it would be inhuman to do otherwise.

He shook his head and looked up toward the stars shining in the early morning sky. High on a ledge of the valley's south wall, he saw the steady amber-orange balls glowing silently in the night. The faint gutteral growl locked their eyes in a union that had not occurred since that night on the escarpment.

Tyoga felt himself dissolve into the liquid fire of Wahaya's eyes, and the hazel drain from his own.

The sight and sound of Wahaya-Wacon clarified his course.

He felt his body begin to grow. His mind jettisoned the unforgiving errors of emotion and deliberation. He was infused with confidence and decisiveness. His choices had always been right. They would be right now. Lava-like rivers filled with the wild coursed through his veins to fuel instincts that were more animal than man. This was a time for instinctive response and primal decisiveness.

He would know what to do.

"Tes 'A," he said in a voice that was still his own but devoid of emotion or concern. "I am heading back to Twin Oaks. We are only about eight miles away. Let the others sleep. You get some rest as well. I will be waiting for you. There is much to do."

Uneasy with Tyoga's demeanor and tone, Tes Qua could not help but ask, "Ty, what are we going to do?"

"We are going to do what needs to be done. We're going to get Sunlei."

"Tyoga," Tes Qua continued, "there is one other that you will need to save."

Tyoga looked inquisitively at his friend but did not speak.

"She has a son. She named him Wahaya Utsti *(Little Wolf)*. He is five-years old."

Chapter 61

To Fill An Empty Heart

W hen Trinity saw Tyoga coming toward the house, she could tell from his determined stride and swollen chest that something was amiss.

Tyoga's steps were hard and deliberate, and she had seen that stare before. He walked right past Brister, who was peppering him with questions to which he would not respond. When they got closer to the house, she heard Brister asking, "Massa Ty, ya got to tell me wat's happ'n. Come on 'n let me carry your things into the house, Massa Ty. What you doin' home so soon anyway? Missy 'n me wasn't expecting you home til night. Massa Ty—Massa Ty—"

Tyoga left Brister at the foot of the steps, opened the front door, and walked inside. Brister looked at the door before turning and walking away.

"Papa, Papa," Joshia and Rebecca squealed in delight as they ran and hugged him around the legs.

Tyoga dropped his camping truck and picked them both up in his arms. Trinity, who was seated at the table, smiled.

"Hey there, Little Ones," Tyoga said in his friendliest father voice, "have you two been good while I was away?"

"'Yeswhatdidyoubringme," they responded in a one word sentence.

"Joshia, for you I brought the biggest acorn top I have ever seen in my life. I'll show you how to use it as a signal whistle later on." Whispering in his son's ear he added in Tsalagie, "Eetsa tel-a yeh a eh a ho *(It will drive your mother crazy)*!" They both giggled at the impish secret they shared.

"And for you, Becky Jane, I brought some sasafrass root so your mother can show you how to make some tea. How does that sound?"

"Yeah!" was all she said as her father set her feet back on the ground.

"Children, go outside and help Sissy in the garden," Trinity said. "Papa and I need to talk." As soon as the children closed the front door behind them, she asked, "Tyoga, what is it?"

"Trinity, Tes Qua and Walking Bird and five of my closest friends from Tuckareegee are camped beyond the Beaver Dam. I was up all night talking with them. They will arrive here this afternoon."

The news lit up her face while bringing tears to her eyes. She had longed to meet Tyoga's Ani-Unwiya family. There was still so much that she wanted to learn about Tyoga. She was sure that Tes Qua would be generous in conversation. She had heard so much about him over the years that she felt as though she already knew him.

It was a dream come true for Trinity Jane. She did not have a moment to lose. Springing up from her chair, she ran to the front door on her tip toes. She stepped out onto the steps and called, "Sissy, Rose Marie, Johnnnie-boy, Isum, Letty, come quick. Guests are coming. There is much work to do."

She ran to Tyoga and jumped up into his arms. "This good news is wonderful. I am so anxious to meet your friends."

As soon as she was in his arms and felt the swell of his granite hard biceps, her joy withered away. She dropped her bare feet to the floor. The smile left her face. She searched his eyes for answers. "What else, Ty. What has happened?"

He looked down at the troubled face that seconds before had been so alive with joy. "They have found Sunlei."

Turning away from him, Trinity walked slowly toward the front window. She placed the palm of her hand on the cool pane of glass, and gazed out at the garden where their children were helping to pull out the remnants of the tomato vines and placing them in the compost pile.

The front door opened.

Jessey carried an armful of seasoned oak and apple wood over to the giant hearth and placed the firewood in the caddy. He stoked the fire into roaring flames and went back out the front door without saying a word.

Laughing in anticipation of the fun they would have preparing for their visitors, the workers that Trinity had summoned were coming toward the house.

Still looking out the window, she said, "We'll talk about that later ..." Giving up on speaking English as she often did when anxious or angry, she continued in Tsalagie, "Ut eh ya ota itsh-tay oh. Ye si-ya to hey to eh alo. Nitch ti."

Tyoga turned toward the bedroom and disappeared behind the door.

Tes Qua, Walking Bird, and the others arrived in the early afternoon. Tyoga met them at the base of the stone steps that led up to the portico and the massive hickory door.

"Tsi-lu-gi, Twin Oaks," Tyoga said with just a bit more fanfare than necessary.

Tes Qua and the others looked in wide-eyed amazement at the village that Tyoga had built. They stood at the foot of the steps and turned around to take it all in. A cool breeze floated down the slopes of the Appalachians to the west to rattle the hollow reeds that lined the banks of the Mattaponi River. To the north, the sounds of construction and industry poured from the cottage lined cobbled lane while the cooper, black smith, and tanner tended to their chores. From the south the scent of smoking meats, fresh baked breads, and pies emanated from the kitchens and brick ovens while the neatly clad ladies scurried from building to cooking hearth in their white aprons and caps.

Tes Qua turned and placed his hand on Tyoga's shoulder. Grinning widely, he said, "You have done well, my brother. You do your people proud."

"Come," Tyoga replied. "Come into the house and meet my Trinity Jane. She is anxious to greet all of you."

Turning toward the house he opened his arms and guided his visitors up the steps. He passed them when they got to the portico, stepped in front, and swung open the heavy front door.

His guests entered the house to see Trinity Jane, dressed in her most ornate doeskin tunic, and fox fur boots. A long auburn braid fell in front of her right shoulder. Her thick lustrous brown locks on the right side cascaded over her face to hide her scar. Large silver and gold hoops adorned her ears and she wore a beautiful necklace of precious stones and puka shells.

Expecting her to be dressed in her finest colonial taffeta dress to meet their guests, Tyoga's eyes opened wide at the sight.

Trinity had made the wise calculation that that would have been a mistake.

"Eh-ya-to, mi yaga *(Welcome to our home)*," she said in Tsaligi. "Da gwa do a, Acohi Yutsa *(My name is Acohi Yutsa)*."

The Cherokee seemed unsure about this unexpected entrance. They knew that Tyoga had made a home with a white woman, and they fully expected to meet someone who would have set themselves apart by dressing differently and certainly not speaking in their native tongue.

An awkward pause caused Trinity to look down at the floor.

Tes Qua stepped forward rather formally, extended his hand and said in his most perfect English, "Hello, Trinity. I am Tes Qua."

Smiling, Trinity reached out to take his hand. He grasped it firmly before picking her up in a joyful bear hug that welcomed her into the Ani-Unwiya clan. She threw her arms around his neck and hugged him tightly. At this, the others stepped forward and threw their arms around the both of them. Walking Bird held tightly to her tiny hand and would not let go. Overjoyed to be with their boyhood hero once again, Coyote and Paints His Shirt Red greeted Trinity Jane just as enthusiastically.

Dancing Mouse and Morning Sky were awestruck by the grandeur of Twin Oaks. While they too were happy to see their old friend, they were mesmerized by the household goods the couple had come to possess. Furniture, iron skillets and knives, glass windows, spinning wheels, linens and down filled pillows left them speechless—and wanting.

They spent the afternoon talking and laughing and eating. They feasted on lamb, venison and duck. They tasted fruit from far away lands, and drank bottles of Bordeaux wines and Spanish Madeira. After their bellies were full, the laughter died down as the sleep inducing effect of the wine took its toll. Some of the guests retired to their quarters to rest while others stretched out on bear skin rugs in front of the hearth.

Trinity Jane, Tyoga, and Tes Qua stepped into the parlor to speak in private.

Tes Qua could tell from the look on Trinity's face that Tyoga had told her about his discovery of Sunlei's whereabouts. He recounted his attempt to find and rescue Sunlei, and explained in a way that his brother Tyoga would not have been able to do, the life or death situation she was in as the result of Tyoga's scheme to save the Mattaponi village of Passaunkack.

Understanding, Trinity Jane knew exactly what it meant. "So, Ty, when will you leave?"

"The day after tomorrow," he replied.

"I am going with you this time," Tes Qua demanded.

"Yes, Tes Qua, you will go with me to save your sister," he said. "But we will separate at Tuckareegee. I will go into Kaniataro alone to get her. You will follow after me to help with our escape. We will work it out along the way."

"Ah-ho," Tes Qua replied.

"Will the rest of our friends stay here with T.J. and the children?" Tyoga asked "We'll be gone for several weeks, and I will be obliged if Paints His Shirt Red and Coyote stay here at Twin Oaks until I return."

"They will stay," Tes Qua said. "All of them will stay." Leaving Trinity and Tyoga alone, Tes Qua excused himself from the parlor to retire to the guest quarters for the night.

Quickly getting up from her chair, Trinity crossed the room to where Tyoga was sitting. She knelt down in front of his chair and placed her tiny trembling hands on his knee. Her eyes welled with tears as she began speaking. "Tyoga, I know that you must go to rescue Sunlei. Your heart tells you that this must be done, but I do not think that you understand why. Ditlihi, the why is what is important. If you go to find her to protect her and her child from harm and to return her to her people, then the reason is good and just and the right thing to do. But if you go to find her thinking that your heart will once again be whole, then you are mistaken."

She paused to look around the room. Taking him by the hand, she stood him up and led him to the magnificent fireplace that lit the room with its warming glow. Stepping to the side of the hearth, they gazed out the window together at the land and the river and the mountains beyond.

"Tyoga, we have built a life here together that I cherish above all things. Because of who, and what we are, we bridge the white world from which we have both come to an Indian culture that burns within our hearts and ignites our very souls. The day may come when you must choose between the two. You have told me many times that in all things there are but two outcomes. And the one that is chosen is the right one because it will lead to the end that was meant to be. If that day should come, what will you choose? Will you choose the white world we have created on the edge of the frontier here, with me and our children, or will you return to the life that you led as a member of the Ani-Unwiya?"

Turning away from the window, she peered up into his face.

He continued to stare out the window.

"Tyoga, there really is no choice at all. This is your home. And this—" she added taking his hand and placing it over the new life swelling her abdomen. "This is what makes your heart whole."

He looked down into her face aglow in the light of the roaring fire, and then gazed out the window to the mountains gently glazed in the supple moonlight.

The call came from far away. Maybe all the way from Keyser's Ridge. Carried by the chilly autumn breeze, the haunting moan sailed down the jagged mountain slopes and through the hidden caverns and undiscovered valleys. The wail grew in pitch and intensity until it came in unending waves that penetrated the night with an urgency recognized by the wild things and those in whom the promise lives.

Trinity Jane looked up into Tyoga's face and recognized the vacancy of his eyes and the slight smile that tugged his lips.

He was already gone.

Epilogue

The Search Begins

It had taken Tyoga, Tes Qua, and Brister, a week to cross the Appalachians to the Ani-Unwiya village of Tuckareegee.

Tyoga stood alone on Carter's Rock.

He could see in the distance that the early morning mist was shrouding the jagged edges of Craggy Gap in a cloak of gossamer grey. Standing alone on the rise, he raised a knowing hand to shield his eyes from the piercing rays of the rising sun.

As he had done since he was a child, he bowed his head and looked away at the moment of sunrise. His Ani-Unwiya brothers had taught him that to intrude upon the privacy of the dying dawn was an act of which no man was worthy, but to revel in the splendor of the morning's birth was a covenant of being.

Through eyes squinted to razor edge amber slits he watched the dawn bow to the caress of the blazing orange ball. The morning emerged from the glistening folds of the jagged gap, and flooded the new day with currents of prisomed newness. Brilliant colors of every texture and hue poured over the dawn's pastel shadows to reveal the splendors hidden by the blackness of the night.

Far beyond were the rolling foothills of the Smokey Mountains. A step away and thousands of years below were the deep valleys and secretive hollows he had once called home.

He struggled to stand tall and to keep his feet. His papa would want him to stand tall. It was from this very spot that the awakening had occurred all those years ago.

On this day, the hallowed ground held no promise.

His senses were alive with the pulse of the wild, a second nature urgency that without taking notice was uncontested and free. He listened to the whispering breeze annoy the pines that surrounded him into a chorus of sensuous sighs. He could feel the musty loam beneath his feet quiver with promise, and the unforgiving certainty of its timeless age.

The kiss of the predawn air, moist and gentle upon his face, was as intoxicating as a lover's lips inviting him to enter while warning him to stay away.

He had never been so alone. He had never been so filled with dread.

He dropped to a knee and clutched the earth with his strong, calloused hand. For a long while, he knelt while his fingers burrowed into the dirt.

The pine needles pricked his fingers and the sensation awakened memories of those cold gray December afternoons when the family would venture into the woods around South Henge in search of the perfect Christmas tree. It was always he who would lie on the freezing snow covered ground while awkwardly wrestling the saw blade and tree trunk to a chorus of giddy squeals imploring him to hurry with the murderous deed.

He heard their voices now. As he raised the handful of dirt to his face, its loamy underbelly triggered the memory of plowing the fields with his papa in early spring and late fall. He remembered stumbling behind the mules and falling more times than he could count. His father's strong hand would reach down to grasp him by the waist band of his britches just before the forward motion of the rig would drag him face first through the newly lacerated earth.

Bringing the clutch of earth to his face, his powerful grip released the pungent scent born of birth and decay. He closed his eyes and deeply inhaled its life giving essence. He held the dirt away from his face, gazed at it for a long moment, and dropped his hand to his side.

A cold mountain breeze carrying the taste of winter stung his face. His eyes began to tear.

The promise speaks to those who listen, but oftentimes, the message is muddled and conveyed in phrases and subtleties rather than in sentences and absolutes. He thought it odd that he should recall the joys of Christmasses past and the strength of his father's hand and the voices of his family.

Completely absent from the promise's call were the faces and sounds of Trinity Jane and his children.

There was but one face seared into his mind's eye, and a solitary voice that called out to him. He did not question the rightness of the visions and sounds. They simply were.

The why mattered not at all.

From the escarpment, he could see for miles through the rising mist. When the sun peaked through Thompson's Gap, he was able to distinguish the silhouette of the Blue Ridge. Macy's Peak, Cormak's Pass, Clingman's Dome, Rocky Top, Potowa Trail, peaks and passes he had scampered along as a child, hiked as a young man—alone and with friends—for as long as he could remember. Of these times, the hours hiking alone were the ones he most cherished, and the ones he most terribly missed.

He loved the morning hours, the newness of dawn enveloping all that is with the promise of the day. The land encased in a diamond shroud of hoarfrost and dew would whisper to him when he alone shared the solitude with the dawn—and listened for the promise.

It was different when others were there. The secrets weren't shared. Often, the whispered promise lost in idle chatter went unrevealed, unshared, and unkept.

But the message was never silenced by the serenity of the awakening woods. Alone, he could listen. In the silence, he heard. In solitude, he understood.

It was silent now. And he knew.

To keep her alive—he had let her go.

His life was full, but he was empty without her.

He turned to face the great oak.

And took the first step to find her.

The End

Book II:

The Search for Sunlei

H.L. Grandin

Author Bio

H.L. Grandin grew up in Virginia and along the way developed a deep appreciation and respect for nature as well as a yearning to know the heritage of the land and of those who walked it so long ago. Educated in Virginia and France, H.L. has spent his career in healthcare, with a stint as proprietor/owner of a coffee and blues bar. He is a self-taught musician and was drummer for several bands throughout high school and college. He currently entertains his wife and dog with his 12 string guitar. For the last twenty five years, H.L. has lived on a small farm in western Maryland where he and his wife raised three daughters and a passel of critters.

A natural storyteller and prolific writer, H.L. has been quietly composing a cast of characters and their adventures for at least ten years. About three years ago he seriously put pen to paper and The Legend of Tyoga Weathersby was born. This is H.L.'s first novel. To learn more about this and future books please visit tyogaweathersby.com.